MY FIRST MISTAKE

"Mr. Allen," the detective said, "perhaps we can have your attention? We'll try not to keep you longer than necessary."

I sat, eager to show what a cooperative citizen I could be.

"Mr. Allen," the detective asked, "can you explain why your microphone cord was around the victim's neck?"

"My microphone cord?"

"Be very careful, Mr. Allen. The microphone, alone with its cord, will be examined by the forensic lab. Do you suppose we'll find your fingerprints on it?"

"Dennis changed my microphone twice," I told him. "Of course, I have no idea if the mike was one of mine or not. If it was, then of course it will have my prints on it."

"Thank you, Mr. Allen. We'll compare everyone's statements with what the lab has to tell us, and then we'll probably get back to you for more questions."

"That's an unpleasant way to die, being strangled," I said.

"Strangled?" the detective echoed. "Who said he was strangled? The microphone cord was a bit of window dressing designed to throw us off. Death came about in a different way."

I could tell from the detective's smug expression that he was not going to tell me anything more. It was at that moment that I vowed I would discover the killer myself.

What I should have done was to collect Jayne and take the first commercial jetliner back to California.

STEVE ALLEN

Wake Up To Murder

Kensington Books
Kensington Publishing Corp.

http://www.kensingtonbooks.com

To Gianni "Gaboa,"
a special boy.

KENSINGTON BOOKS are published by

Kensington Publishing Corp.
850 Third Avenue
New York, NY 10022

Kensington and the K logo Reg. U.S. Pat. & TM Off.

First Kensington Hardcover Printing: November, 1996
First Kensington Paperback Printing: December, 1997
10 9 8 7 6 5 4 3 2 1

Printed in the United States of America

Chapter 1

The earthquake hit at a few minutes past noon. Twelve-oh-nine, to be precise, on a gray, damp Friday in January, as I was walking into our kitchen.

"Three point four," I said immediately to Jayne, who was following me. "I'd say 4.2," she replied.

The fact that she was walking behind me had no connection with her having been born in China, one of many cultures in which men are expected to lead the way, nor did it represent a throwing overboard of her staunch feminist sentiments. She just happened to be walking behind me, probably for the reason that I was walking in front of her. But be that as it may—and I doubt that it was—my wife promptly differed with my assessment, as she has been known to do.

"By the way the chandelier swayed over the dining room table, I would say it was a 4.2," she said, "Maybe even a 4.3."

"What's your bet, Cass?" I asked.

"Three point nine," he said with confidence. Jimmy Cassidy is our resident leprechaun, a chauffeur/handyman extraordinaire and longtime friend. Our Man Monday, as he likes to call himself. Years ago he came to Hollywood from a ranch in Wyoming with the ambition to be a cowboy actor in the movies. But his timing was off—Westerns had just gone out of fashion—so he came to work for me instead.

To that point he had made no more progress than getting some sort of an audition reading, through a friend of a friend, for a three-line role in a TV "oater" as the showbiz trade paper *Variety* would put it, only to discover that he had one little problem—he couldn't act.

I realize that there are some major stars of whom the same could be said, but they represent the exceptions. It's true, of course, that requirements for acting in Westerns are generally rudimentary, but it was still no dice for Cass. When I at one point brought up the question, as gently as possible, and suggested that I would even be glad to arrange a few acting lessons for him at one of the local establishments set up for the purpose of either preying upon or productively instructing would-be thespians, he surprised me by the perceptiveness of his response. "No, thanks," he said. "I'd rather learn on the job."

"That works well in lots of trades," I said, "but should it apply to acting?"

"Hey," he said, "it worked pretty well for John Wayne and Clint Eastwood."

Actually, he was right. If you've ever seen either John's or Clint's early movies, you'll note that their careers started before they had any knowledge of their craft whatsoever. But little by little they had truly mastered the trick, so that in their later years both men were among the most believable actors in films and deserved their superstar ranking.

Cass helped himself to a cup of instant coffee while the debate about the power of one of Mother Nature's nastier little surprises continued.

"Let's review the bidding," I said, "and write down our guesses, so there will be no doubt later as to who said what."

I'm a compulsive note-taker, largely for the reason that I have no confidence at all in the human memory, which has always seemed to me a tragic joke played on us by the process of evolution. "We have a 3.4, a 4.2, and a 3.9. Anybody want to change his bet?"

"I'll stay," said Cass, ever the cowboy poker player.

"I'll change to four even," Jayne said cagily. This way she would win anything four and above.

"Usual rules?" Cass asked.

"You bet," I said. "Lunch at the Enchanted Broccoli Garden. Winner is treated by the other two."

"*If* the Enchanted Broccoli Garden is still standing," Jayne said.

"Earthquakes never destroy cute health food restaurants," I assured her. "Particularly when we have a mere 3.4 on the Richter scale. Hardly enough to stir a martini."

"Let's not bicker, gang," Cass said wisely. "Time to turn on the news and settle this."

I suppose that to people who live outside of California, the fact that Cass, Jayne, and I place wagers on the size of earthquakes sounds cavalier. But when you live in Los Angeles, either you develop a sense of humor about these things or you'd better move to Iowa. Between earthquakes, riots, mud slides, and fires, life in the Golden State isn't always easy these days.

"I just got an idea," I said. "Come on in to the piano, and I'll show you."

We trooped back into the living room, to the Steinway standing in the corner near our front door. Two days earlier I had written into a song lyric I was working on a reference to the docks in the Redondo Beach area that had collapsed after being assaulted by the Pacific Ocean in yet another bit of evidence consistent with the theory of the Last Days.

"Aftershocks" I shouted. "That's the rhyme I was looking for." Making a quick pencil notation on the lyric sheet in front of me I played and sang the song now completed lyric of the song I had titled "Livin' in L.A." The ungrammatical style is deliberate, given that the category is rock.

> We got floods,
> We got fire,
> We got mud slides,
> With muck and mire.
>
> We got earthquakes
> And a million aftershocks.
> And, when the tide comes in,
> Those old collapsing docks.
>
> We got riots,
> People sleepin' on the streets.
> We've got drive-by gunplay
> And USC defeats,
>
> But hey—
> We can be forgiven
> 'Cause we're livin'—in L.A.
> And I think I see
> some locusts on the way.
>
> We got talk shows
> Where the guests are freaks.
> We got strip joints
> Where you can meet a lotta geeks.
> We got cave-ins
> And folks who want to close up schools,
> And a lot of goofy cults
> Takin' money from a lot of fools.
>
> We once had a city
> That was really kinda' pretty

And the skies were always blue.
Life was smooth as butter,
Now we're livin' in Calcutta
And that's a kinda dumbo thing to do.

We got poor folks,
Some livin' in their cars.
We got an awful lot of bimbos;
We call 'em movie stars.

But hey—
We can be forgiven
'Cause we're livin'—in L.A.
And I think I see
some locusts on the way.

"I like it," said Cass.

"That's cute, dear," Jayne said.

"Thank you, dear," I said, "and so are you."

As we repaired again to the kitchen, Cass used the remote
to flick on the television. The good news was that the TV
actually came on; you know you're in big trouble when TV
stations have been knocked off the air. The screen showed a
map of Southern California with an area circled in the desert
near Bakersfield.

". . . initial reports from the seismic center in Pasadena say
the shaker was 3.2 on the Richter scale. The epicenter was in
a remote area fifty miles southeast of Bakersfield on a previously
unknown fault line. There are no reports of injuries or damage
at this point, but . . ."

"I win!" I said cheerfully. "You guys gotta buy me lunch!
I think I'll have the lobster and champagne!"

"They don't *have* lobster at the Enchanted Broccoli Garden," Jayne said sourly. "Nor champagne, Steve." My wife
actually uses words like *nor*.

"Then I'm going to have the biggest bunch of broccoli in the house, and a giant mango-banana smoothie, and an entire carrot cake for dessert."

Cass could not repress a sigh. I knew he would have preferred a cheeseburger with a pickle and a side of fries for lunch, but the last few years Jayne and I have been working to overhaul his diet. Now he ate more wisely, but the shadow of regret sometimes clouded his eyes.

"Well, let's get it over with," he said unhappily.

"Last time you said you *liked* the Broccoli Garden," Jayne reminded him.

"Sure," he agreed. "No fat. No sugar. Herbal tea. Swell."

He was about to turn off the TV when something on the screen got my attention.

"Hold on a second, Cass. I want to see this."

In Los Angeles, an earthquake of 3.2 on the Richter scale is nothing. Hardly worth mentioning for us battle-scarred veterans of paradise. The local station had returned to its usual programming at this time, "News At Noon." What caught my eye was a young woman Jayne and I used to know, little Cathy Lawrence, the daughter of our good friend Ed Lawrence. Only she wasn't little Cathy anymore—today the world knew her as Cat Lawrence. A few months earlier she had become the highly successful co-anchor of "Good Morning, U.S.A.," the two-hour network news show broadcast live five mornings a week from New York. It's always a surprise when a kid you used to see on a bicycle with bruised knees and pigtails grows up to become a huge success.

For obvious reasons that sort of thing is more common in the world's film capitol. Janet Leigh and Tony Curtis's daughter, Jamie Lee Curtis, used to come to parties at our house when she was a teenager since she knew our sons Steve and Brian, and the same was true of Sally Fields and Cindy Williams.

It's wonderful, of course, but it makes you feel a little old. I had read recently in the *Hollywood Reporter* that our little

Cathy had just signed a three-year contract with the network, for several million dollars. She could buy a lot of bicycles with that. The one time I caught her morning show, I was impressed how cool and beautiful she appeared interviewing former president Jimmy Carter. Little Cathy Lawrence had become a highly intelligent and sophisticated woman. But from "News At Noon" I learned that today she had had a lousy morning.

"Viewers were shocked this morning to witness a near-tragic accident on the set of the highly rated UBS network news broadcast, 'Good Morning, U.S.A.,'" said a newsman. "A klieg light came loose from the studio rafters and crashed onto a desk below, narrowly missing veteran newscaster Peter McDavis and co-anchor Cat Lawrence. . . ."

As the broadcaster continued, Jayne, Cass, and I watched a replay of the incident, a shocker. Peter McDavis and Cat were seated behind a desk on the set of a cozy, faux living room, each with a cup of coffee in front of them. Cat was leading into a commercial break, telling the audience about a rock star who was going to appear later in the program. One moment Peter and Cat looked as calm, unruffled, and urbane as it's possible to be on live television. And then the next moment it seemed as if the sky fell in on them. A huge metal object crashed thunderously onto the desk with a shattering of glass. Both Cat and Peter screamed and instinctively raised their hands to protect their faces and heads. The camera caught the horror and confusion for hardly more than a second, and then the picture was replaced by a "stand-by" message as Studio B in New York City went briefly off the air.

A moment later "Good Morning, U.S.A." producer Zeke Roth issued a statement that the two co-anchors, Peter McDavis and Cat Lawrence, had miraculously escaped injury. "Meanwhile, the network has launched an investigation into how an overhead light managed to break loose from its mounting. Initial reports suggest a bolt holding the klieg light to a metal bar came loose. . . ."

"How awful!" Jayne said, frowning. "Poor Cathy must have been terrified."

As TV veterans ourselves, it was easy to imagine what a nightmare the incident must have been. There is a large part of show business the audience never sees—thick electric cables, heavy lights, cameras, sound booms, and the like, all of which are potentially dangerous. A performer does his or her job assuming the equipment will not come down on his head. But occasionally—very rarely, considering the technical complexity of films and television—something goes awfully wrong, and people are hurt or killed.

Cass turned off the television after we saw a repeat of the incident in slow motion. There was the briefest moment when you could see the look of horror in the eyes of the two co-anchors as the thought flashed like lightning across their minds that they were going to die. Sometimes I wonder if it's proper for television to capture and replay endlessly these true-life disasters, the Kennedy killing, the deadly race-car crashes, and all the rest.

Jayne, Cass, and I drove to lunch at the Enchanted Broccoli Garden. But after watching the near encounter with death, none of us had much of an appetite.

It has always, of course, been nonsensical to refer to the more dramatic ravages of nature as *acts of God* now, unless we assume that the Almighty is the most purposely vengeful and destructive monster of all history. But there sometimes does seem something almost consciously malign about the connection between natural disasters and the neighborhoods in which they occur. Much of the earthquake damage of the world seems to wreak its most violent destruction in poor neighborhoods. Even in the case of the Southern California quakes I don't recall hearing much about serious damage in Beverly Hills or Bel Air. And tornadoes, too, seem to have a way of locating trailer parks, which are largely occupied by lower-income folks.

Chapter 2

Cathy Lawrence. When I close my eyes, I visualize a scrawny blond ten-year-old kid with a dirty face in cutoff jeans who always seemed to be shouting hello at me from up in a tree or hidden in a bush. She had huge blue-green eyes, a pixie smile, and was not the sort of little girl who was shy around grown-ups. Sometimes she would put her fingers in the corners of her mouth and let loose with a whistle you could hear a block away, an ability I've always envied because, though I tried and tried, I could never get so much as a peep out of the combination of my fingers, lips, teeth, tongue, and respiratory system.

Her father Ed Lawrence, the producer of the hit TV cop show, "Chicago P.D.," lived with his family in a rambling two-story white clapboard house across the street from our house in the Royal Oaks section of Encino. Why such houses are referred to as rambling has always been a bit unclear to me, though—come to think of it—a friend of mine had a house that did ramble—albeit only about six feet—during a recent quake. Ed and I became friends after his dog ate my *L.A. Times* one morning. Lawrence was a big man with a crew cut who looked more like a high school football coach than a successful television producer. We were never close friends, but enjoyed each other's company two or three times a year at various backyard barbecues or benefit dinners. He often said he wanted to produce a TV series with Jayne and me, but somehow, like a lot of things in Hollywood, it never happened.

Ed's wife, Susan, was fresh, pretty, and blond, his high school sweetheart. All together, the Lawrence family had a kind of all-American good-egg quality about them. They weren't exactly Ozzie and Harriet—even Ozzie and Harriet weren't—but close. They radiated good health, prosperity, and fun. At the height of our friendship, some twenty-odd years back, we once took a two-family trip over Christmas to Oahu and checked into the Royal Hawaiian Hotel on Waikiki Beach. The trip was a mistake. Ed got drunk one night on mai tais and made a fool of himself. That same night Susan made a pass at me and hinted at a midnight rendezvous behind a break-water on the beach. It was terribly awkward. I told Susan as politely as I was able that I thought that my marriage vows precluded the swingers' lifestyle. We never referred to it again, but by the time we were back in California the bloom was off the friendship. Jayne and I still saw Ed and Susan, but less often than before and only at large gatherings.

Then unfortunate things started to happen for Ed. Halfway through the fifth season of his show, he was abruptly fired. There were rumors about town that he had done something disgraceful, though I do my best not to listen to gossip so I never knew exactly what it was. A few months later, I heard that Susan ran off with a young actor. I ran into Ed not long after that at Chasen's. He was having dinner with a brassy blonde, and they were both so drunk the *maître d'* had to go to their booth and ask them to behave themselves. By the summer of that year, there was a FOR SALE sign on the lawn outside the white two-story house, and by the fall a doctor and his wife had moved in.

I read in the *Hollywood Reporter* a year later that Ed Lawrence had died from a self-inflicted gunshot wound. A friend
in the business told me he was broke at the time and living in
a small apartment south of Santa Monica Boulevard in an area
known for prostitutes and drugs. It was hard to square this
with my previous image of a golden, all-American family. But
Hollywood is funny in that way. You meet seemingly wonderful
people who don't quite have the strength for the game. They
may enjoy a brief season of success—a hit show, a big house
with a pool, friends crowding around. And then they seem to
self-destruct. The big house gets sold, the friends disappear,
and you don't see them again. It's a high-wire act, a Hollywood
career, and you need to keep a sense of balance amid all the
pressure and money and fame. Most of all you need to remember
who you really are, as opposed to what your publicist is saying
about you, and to find your inner strength, if any, and not get
carried away by the applause. Jayne and I love the business,
but it's not for everyone.

I forgot about the Lawrence family for the next several
years. Then one summer I put an ad in the paper for a typist/
receptionist for my L.A. office. Generally my head secretary
does the hiring for this sort of position, but in this instance she
poked her head into my office door and asked if I would like
to meet the new girl.

"Says she's an old friend of yours, Steve."

"Really? Then show her in, by all means."

The young woman ushered into my private office that morning was in no way familiar to me. She was tall with thick blond
hair and an elegant oval face. She had classic features, the sort
of face you might find on a statue or in a painting. Not what
I think of as a California blonde, but more a Renaissance,
Botticelli beauty. I couldn't imagine why she said we were old
friends. I was certain I'd remember such a young woman.

Then she grinned at me. It was a conspiratorial grin, full of

mischief. Not entirely an appropriate grin for a new typist/
receptionist to flash at her potential boss.

"You don't remember me, do you?"

"I'm trying."

What she did next startled me so much I nearly fell out of
my chair. This elegant young woman, my would-be employee,
put two fingers into the corners of her mouth and let loose a
piercing whistle that most likely was heard halfway to Beverly
Hills. It was a whistle that had been aimed at me before from
treetops and shrubbery. It was only then that I saw something
familiar in her huge blue-green eyes.

"Cathy?" I said hesitantly.

"Right. Only now you have to call me Cat . . . Cat Lawrence.
I decided Cathy was a little nebbishy."

"But you've . . . you've grown up!" I said in astonishment.

"It happens," she assured me.

"What have you been doing with yourself all these years?"

It was good to see her. I told one of the office staff to hold
all phone calls for the next half hour and Cat settled into the
armchair across from my desk and gave me a rundown of what
had happened to her after her family had self-destructed. It
hadn't been an easy childhood. For a year she had gone back
and forth between Ed and Susan, until her father's death, and
then she spent all her time with her mother. Susan eventually
married again, a cinematographer who had a house in Malibu.
But he drank and had a bad habit of hitting people, particularly
his wife and stepdaughter. After two years of this, Susan
divorced the jerk and married a man who owned a restaurant
in San Francisco. This seemed a happy conclusion to Susan's
restless life, but not so wonderful for Cat. The restaurateur, who
had five children from a previous marriage, was not inclined to
open his heart to a new daughter. Cat, who thought him a
boorish oaf, was miserable until she went away to college—
south once again, to UCLA.

And this brought her up to the present. She had completed

two years as an undergraduate in Westwood, and now she had momentarily run out of money with which to continue her education. Which led to reading the employment ads and applying for a job at Meadowlane Enterprises, my production company. Her plan was to work like a maniac for a year or so, save money, and return to college in the fall.

"Can't your mom help you out with school?" I asked.

"Mom doesn't have a penny. And if she did, she'd spend it on clothes and hairdressers."

"What about your stepfather, with the restaurant?"

"He doesn't believe that girls need an education. Be a waitress, he says. Smile pretty and maybe a rich man will marry you. I told him, no thank you."

"Well, good for you, Cat."

And so began phase two of my relationship with Cat Lawrence, neé Cathy, no longer a scrawny little girl but a beautiful young woman. Jayne and I did our best to help her. I even raised her salary after a month to quite a bit more than the going wage. We had her over to the house for dinner twice because we felt vaguely responsible for her, like proxy parents. Jayne tried to play Cupid a few times and fix her up with eligible young men—all of whom were smitten and, in time, finally hurt.

It took us some time to learn that poor Cat Lawrence with her huge blue-green eyes was trouble. Big-league trouble.

Chapter 3

I should have caught on earlier, I suppose, but I kept making excuses for Cat. When our new typist/receptionist began showing up late for work, I told the others, she had an old car that wasn't reliable and we just had to be patient. Within a week after Cat joined my staff, she started appearing in torn jeans and tank top T-shirts that showed more than enough of bare stomach. I run an informal office, but this was going too far. Still, I told myself, the girl has no wardrobe, she's saving her money for college, and perhaps I needed to relax our standards and accept that she was part of a new unwashed generation.

I made every allowance for Cat's difficult childhood. Jayne took her shopping for clothes one afternoon at a trendy store in Westwood. I asked Cass to fix her car, an ancient VW bug that seemed to be running on youthful optimism. We all tried to help her in every way we could; as a result, she took us for suckers.

Late one night, about two months after Cat came to work at Meadowlane, Jayne and I were awakened by our ringing telephone. The caller was a sergeant from the Beverly Hills

Police Department, who said they had in their custody a certain Cat Lawrence who had given my name. Cat had been picked up with a young man speeding along Sunset Boulevard at nearly 70 mph in a Corvette. Beverly Hills frowns on such activity at the best of times, but the scenario got even worse. When the officer radioed the license plate number to his dispatcher, he discovered that the Corvette had been stolen. Cat and the young man were handcuffed and hauled down to the station. After a body search, the man was found to possess nearly two ounces of high-grade marijuana.

Cat's position in all this was open to interpretation. She claimed she had only met the young man an hour earlier at The Troubadour, a music club on Santa Monica Boulevard at the edge of Beverly Hills. They danced for a while and then he suggested they go to a party he knew about in Coldwater Canyon, where a few famous musicians were supposed to be jamming. Cat said she had simply accepted a ride, claiming she had no idea the Corvette was stolen, or that her new friend was carrying drugs. She cheerfully supplied my name as someone who could give assurance to her sterling character.

I told the desk sergeant I had known Cat Lawrence since she was a child and that it was highly unlikely she would knowingly ride in a stolen automobile or use illegal drugs. She was just an innocent girl, I said, and it had to be an error in judgment that she had accepted a lift to a party with a young man who was not her equal in character. I said all this and more, and even believed part of it—though not all. The sergeant was moved by my eloquence. He said they would not press charges and I could come down to the station immediately and take the naive, virtuous girl home.

It was nearly two in the morning by the time I arrived at the Beverly Hills police station—it was the old station, before Beverly Hills got so fancy—located in the basement of City Hall. Due to the hour I was grouchy. In fact I was sore as hell. I drove Cat back to The Troubadour parking lot, where she had left her VW bug, and we sat in my car for more than forty-five minutes while I gave her my best four-star lecture.

"But Steve," she said, "I just wanted to go dancing. It all seemed so . . . innocent."

"*Never* get in a car with a man you don't know" I warned her. "You're lucky to be alive, kiddo. I want you to promise me you're never going to do anything so foolish again."

Naturally Cat promised on her virginal word of honor to avoid in the future all Corvettes, rock clubs, and young men who had not been thoroughly vetted by someone older and wiser. She looked me in the eye and said she had learned her lesson. She apologized with touching sincerity for disturbing my sleep and hauling me down to the Beverly Hills police station in the middle of the night. She looked at me with those big blue-green eyes of hers, and to tell the truth, it was hard not to forgive her.

After that night, Cat behaved herself—for about a week. She arrived at work on time each morning, dressed more conservatively, and acted like a thoroughly repentant young woman who was indeed saving her money to return to college. Then, imperceptibly, her wardrobe began to morph, as we say in the movie business. We saw once again her torn jeans and T-shirts, and she was apt to arrive in the morning closer to ten o'clock than nine.

One afternoon a few weeks later my secretary stepped into my private office and closed the door behind her.

"Steve, I need to talk to you about your young friend."

"She's not doing her work properly?"

"Worse than that. She's been stealing from petty cash."

"I don't believe it! There's got to be a mistake!"

"I don't think so. Money's been disappearing for the last month. At first just ten or twenty dollars I couldn't account for. I thought perhaps I was making mistakes, so for the last two weeks I've been keeping track of every purchase—stamps, sodas, groceries, envelopes, absolutely everything. I'm afraid there's no possible way I can be wrong about this, Steve. I estimate she's lifted more than three hundred dollars the past few months."

"You're sure it's her? You're absolutely *certain?*"

She raised an eyebrow at me. "Unless you think it's me."

I sighed. My head secretary had been with me forever and knew my business better than I did myself; if *she* was stealing, I might as well close down the office. Still, I couldn't accept Cat's guilt without a small test. In those days we kept a few hundred dollars in a cookie tin in a file cabinet—it was a Christmas tin, I remember, with a little Santa Claus on the top. I trusted my staff completely to make whatever small purchases they needed for odds and ends to keep the office up and going. It was a fairly casual arrangement, but Meadowlane, Inc., has always been more like a family than a workplace. While my head secretary watched, I took four crisp twenty-dollar bills from my wallet and marked each one with a small T—T for Thief—with a red pen in the upper-left hand corner. Then I gave the money to her.

"Put these in the Santa Claus tin," I told her. "Make sure you check every morning and evening if they're still there— it'll be interesting to see where they end up."

Two days later, toward the end of the afternoon, my head secretary once again came into my office. "They're gone," she said.

"All four bills?"

"The whole eighty."

One of the reasons I like the woman is that she properly uses the word *as* instead of *like,* as most young people presently do. I have also never heard her say *the bottom line, the whole nine yards* or *give me a break,* and the one time I did hear her say "I couldn't care less" at least the word "couldn't" was correct, as contrasted with the increasingly more common "I could care less," which makes no sense whatever.

"And they were in the cookie tin this morning?"

"Yes, I've handled it exactly as you told me. I checked the tin during the time Cat went out for her lunch break as well, and the money was still there. So she must have only just snitched it."

"Then she'll still have it on her," I said unhappily. It gave me no joy to catch little Cathy Lawrence stealing from me. It had not been a great amount of money, but the act of theft itself was unpleasant, and it left me with a hollow feeling. I couldn't let such a thing go unchallenged in my office. So I told my assistant to give Cat an extra typing job that would keep her late while I telephoned a friend of mine from the LAPD, Sergeant W. B. Walker, who owed me a few favors. I explained the situation to the sergeant, told him what I had in mind, and he agreed to hurry over in a squad car with the sirens and emergency lights going full blast for effect.

It was a nasty business. At first Cat was indignant. How dare we accuse her of stealing money! She insisted she had not touched a penny of petty cash. When Sergeant Walker began to search her handbag, she made a bigger fuss still and insisted he had no right to do this without a warrant. The sergeant played his part perfectly. He flashed a sadistic smile and told her that normal procedure did not apply in this instance, not when someone had ripped off his pal Steve Allen.

The four twenty-dollar bills, alas, were indeed in Cat's purse. Now she lied again and insisted that this was her money, not from petty cash. When I showed her the small "T's" in red ink on each bill, she broke down in tears and begged for forgiveness.

But I wasn't having any more of it. Sergeant Walker put her in handcuffs, hauled her off to the county jail, and threw her into a crowded holding cell with a group of prostitutes, junkies, and at least one murderer. What we did next wasn't strictly legal, but it was effective. Basically we arranged simply to forget about Cat Lawrence for a week. Seven long days and even longer nights in the county jail, a small eternity of hours to ponder her life and decide if this was truly the direction she wished to take. I heard later that one tough old prostitute beat her up and that the cell was so crowded she had to sleep on the concrete floor.

It was strong medicine, but at the end of a week, Cat had seen the light. I felt bad for her but I wasn't planning to take her back into our office. It was Jayne who convinced me to give Cat another chance—and Jayne's instincts turned out to be right. I don't know precisely what Cat thought about during her week in county lockup, but she emerged a more serious young woman who was determined to make something of her life. From that moment on, she was never late for work, she appeared each morning in demure clothing, and petty cash never experienced another shortage. Offhand I would say Cat Lawrence was one of the most dedicated receptionist/typists Meadowlane, Inc., ever had, though quite a few good people have passed through that job over the years.

Cat was nineteen years old at the time of the petty cash episode. A year later, Jayne and I helped her arrange a student loan so that, along with what she had saved, she could return to UCLA. We never had to worry about her again. She majored in political science and graduated near the top of her class. She did so well, in fact, that Columbia School of Journalism gave her a scholarship when she applied for graduate work there. After two years at Columbia, she landed a job as a reporter for the *International Herald-Tribune* in Paris. Three years in France and then she got a better job with a big raise in salary as the bureau chief for *The New York Times* in San Francisco. Jayne and I saw her only rarely, but every Christmas we received a card with a long newsy letter. Perhaps Christmas reminded her of the Santa Claus tin that had nearly destroyed her life. One Thanksgiving, when Jayne and I were on the road in the play *Love Letters,* we shared a turkey with Cat and her live-in boyfriend at her Sausalito home. She seemed happy but perhaps too concentrated with her career. From a Christmas card the following year, we learned that she and her boyfriend had separated. As she put it, she was too occupied with her work to have a serious "relationship."

I believe she worked for the *Times* in San Francisco nearly four years before she made the leap from print journalism to television. The ABC affiliate in San Francisco hired her to be a co-anchor on its local evening news broadcast. From her first night on the air, Cat was a hit. She was a natural for the TV news form—beautiful, intelligent, calm, well-spoken, and extremely competent. After five years of local television, her big chance appeared: the UBS network had become increasingly unhappy with Nancy Vandenberg, the co-anchor of their coast-to-coast morning broadcast, "Good Morning, U.S.A.," and had set about to search the local stations for a replacement. As I heard it, the chairman of UBS, Mr. Stephen Kinley the Second—the big shot himself—happened to be overnight in San Francisco at the Fairmont Hotel, having just flown in from Tokyo on his way back to New York. As fate would have it, he flipped on the local news and saw Cat doing a story about a gangland slaying in Chinatown. The Great Man experienced what passes among network executives for a religious moment. He couldn't take his eyes off her. And what's more, he couldn't imagine *anyone* else taking his or her eyes off her either. She had that magic quality that made you want to look at her and never change the channel. As everyone knows, Stephen Kinley the Second *always* gets what he wants, and within a week, Cat Lawrence was packing her bags for New York City.

And so life seemed to turn out well after all for little Cathy, the scrawny kid who used to whistle at me from the treetops. Jayne and I, of course, felt just a little proud of her success. There had been that time in my office when it appeared she might end up in the penitentiary rather than a penthouse, but successful people often have complex stories. I wouldn't be surprised if quite a few of our national heroes experienced some desperate moments in their youth, arriving at a crossroads where failure was every bit as possible as fame and fortune.

Such was our long friendship with Cat Lawrence, the reason Jayne and I reacted with particular alarm when we turned on our TV and saw her nearly killed by a falling klieg light on the set of her morning show. It would have been a particular tragedy for Cat to come so far in life only to meet such a tragic end.

Jayne, Cass, and I talked about her all through lunch at the Enchanted Broccoli Garden. I was still thinking about her later in the afternoon when the phone rang. Somehow I was not surprised that it was Cat. She was crying so hard it took me some time to get her calmed down and coherent. She was older now, in her mid-thirties, wealthy, a household name throughout America. But for me, she was still a little girl. And she needed my help more than she had ever needed help before.

Chapter 4

"Calm down, Cathy," I said into the transcontinental receiver, hardly realizing I had called her by her childhood name. "Cat," I corrected, "you had a near miss, but it's over now, you're all right, and it's a million to one a spotlight will ever fall anywhere close to you again."

"Oh, Steve," she sobbed. "I wish I'd stayed in San Francisco!"

"Honey, your nerves are shot from the accident. So have yourself a relaxing weekend—go skiing or something. Monday you'll be ready for live television once again."

"I only wish it were that simple."

"What's so complicated about it?"

I heard her take a deep breath. "Because," she said, "because it *wasn't* an accident."

"You're saying the light was deliberately set to fall on your head?"

"Either on my head or my co-anchor's—Peter McDavis. I know it sounds crazy, but I just *know* it was deliberate. Everything's been so damned crazy ever since I got to New York.

I've never been on a show like this, where everybody seems to hate everybody else. I mean, the weatherman threatened to kill the producer last week—I hope he was kidding—the producer has it in for the director, the stage manager actually *slapped* the makeup woman on Monday . . . and then there's this cuckoo astrology person who keeps telling everybody they're going to die in horrible ways! Honestly, Steve, it would take me all day to tell you about the crazy things that have been going on here. The damned light this morning was only the latest installment. Peter says he's not going to stand for it anymore. This afternoon he announced he's taking a two-week vacation to his house in Santa Fe, whether the network likes it or not, and by the time he gets back there had better be safe working conditions on the set or he's going to sue for a bundle. That's why I'm calling, actually. About Peter McDavis leaving the show for two weeks.''

"It could be a good experience for you to do the show on your own, Cat,'' I told her. "It'll build your confidence.''

Cat wasn't crying anymore. Her voice was suddenly remarkably calm and businesslike. "It's not in the cards. The producer, Zeke Roth, has a certain image of the show's format—he wants to see a casual conversation between two people, a man and a woman . . .''

"No,'' I said.

"But you haven't even heard my proposition.''

"Cat, you should save your propositions for younger men.''

"Honestly, when's the last time you and Jayne were in New York? The opera, the theater, the restaurants! Not to mention the Met, which I happen to know is one of your favorite museums. . . .''

"No, no, no,'' I told her.

"Steve, listen to me a moment. All I'm asking is that you take over Peter's anchor chair on 'Good Morning, U.S.A.' for two weeks—we're talking about ten measly mornings! And you'll make oodles of money.''

"I don't need oodles of money."

"Then think of the satisfaction. Do you know how many millions of people watch 'Good Morning, U.S.A.' every day? All those people out there laughing at your jokes! You could write your own commentaries. You could even talk about some of your favorite causes, you know, like the Dumbth problem."

Cat was referring to a problem indeed, that of the constantly declining level of intelligence in our country during, say, the last fifty years. A few years earlier I had written a book titled *Dumbth—And 81 Ways To Make Americans Smarter* which, like the "Meeting of Minds" television series that preceded it, was an attempt to encourage rational thinking and civilized discourse.

I shook my head.

"You could play the piano," she tempted. "I've cleared it with the old man.

"With Stephen, of course."

"You are referring to Stephen Kinley the Second?"

"Naturally. I couldn't be offering you this job without his approval. Actually, he's going to phone you later in the afternoon to make the offer official. He's really an awfully dear man. I told him we were old friends, of course, and asked if I could talk to you first, since I had a feeling you might be reluctant."

"Your feeling was accurate, Cat."

"But why, Steve? All kidding aside, this would be a great career move. Think of the visibility. Steve Allen returns to network television!"

"Sweetheart, I've already made all the great career moves I care to make in one lifetime. And as for visibility, low is what I have in mind for the immediate future. I'm flattered you thought of me, but for the next few weeks I'm looking forward to a nice roaring fire, a few good books to read, and maybe a new tune or two on the piano. However, I can probably suggest some names to help you out the next several weeks until Peter comes back from Santa Fe . . ."

"No good. To be perfectly honest, there's another reason I thought of you for the job. Besides your comedy, and your sophisticated piano playing, and your ability to put guests at ease, I *need* you!"

"Cat, it's been many years since you've needed me or Jayne."

"Not true," she said. "But you have a certain talent I need very much at this particular moment. A talent no other co-anchor is likely to possess."

"Which is?"

"Your success the past few years in solving crimes." I was quiet, so she went on: "Look, if you're here the next few weeks, I can't tell you how much safer I'll feel. I just know you'll be able to figure out who's trying to kill me, or Peter— or what the hell is going on."

"You're convinced the light thing was no accident? Do you have any proof?"

"No, but I feel it in my bones. And I'm terrified."

"Then perhaps you should do what Peter McDavis is doing. Go to Santa Fe for two weeks. Or the refuge of your choice."

"I can't. Peter's established himself in television and can call the shots—me, I'm just starting out. If *I* go, I won't have a job to come back to. Look, you've already helped me so much—won't you help me this one time more?"

I sighed. I shook my head. Ground my teeth. I really didn't feel in the mood for a two-week television stint. But I *did* worry about Cat. Ever since I had seen the replay of the heavy light falling from the ceiling earlier in the afternoon, I had been wondering myself exactly how such a thing could have happened. It seemed a very strange accident—if indeed it was an accident.

"I tell you what," I said. "Have Stephen Kinley give me a

call. I'll talk to him at least and see if we can work something out."

Cat started crying again.

"What's wrong now?" I asked.

"Nothing. It's just I'm so relieved. Oh, get here quickly, Steve, I'm scared to death!"

Chapter 5

"What an adorable airplane!" Jayne said. "Considering what they cost," I said, "it had better be."

It was Sunday morning and we were at the Burbank airport inspecting the network's Learjet Stephen Kinley had sent for us. Cat had not misled me. The chairman of the board telephoned within fifteen minutes after she hung up the phone, offering the temporary co-anchor assignment on "Good Morning, U.S.A." He was very pleasant on the phone, and the salary he offered was more than adequate. He threw in a few perks as well to sweeten the deal—use of the network duplex on Fifth Avenue during our two-week stay, complete with maid and butler, a limousine at our disposal in New York, and a private jet to whisk us back and forth from California. On Saturday a written agreement was faxed back and forth to my agent, Irvin Arthur, and on Sunday morning Cass drove Jayne and me to the airport. The plan was for him to close up the Los Angeles house and join us in Manhattan later in the week.

Jayne and I were in a great mood, ready for a new adventure. To mark the occasion, Jayne wore a red dress to match her

flaming red hair—she does not believe in being inconspicuous—and she had packed four suitcases so she'd have a change
of clothes in New York. Along with my two bags, the crew
had a bit of lifting and hauling to do before we got off the
ground.

"Darling, I think *we* should have our own jet one day,"
Jayne said dreamily.

"The answer is no. There's enough overhead to keeping an
automobile these days. Insurance, tax, gasoline."

The Learjet *was* adorable, I must admit. A flying living room
with leather armchairs, a coffee table of polished wood, a
sharply focused TV set, a small shelf full of books. Very homey.
The crew consisted of Fritz the pilot, Ernie the copilot, and a
fashionable young woman named Brittany, who was the stewardess. They all wore welcoming smiles and dark blue uniforms
with the network logo on their right sleeves.

Jayne and I settled into adjoining armchairs and fastened our
seat belts as the jet taxied toward the runway.

"A glass of champagne?" Brittany offered. "Perhaps a
mimosa?"

"How about a virgin mimosa?" I asked.

"Me, too." said Jayne.

"Two glasses of freshly squeezed orange juice coming right
up," Brittany said with her best smile. But she returned a
moment later with a forlorn expression. "Oh, dear, the squeez-
er's broken. I can't imagine what's wrong with it. Can I get
you something else? Coffee? Tea?"

"Tea," we said.

"Earl Grey, Irish Breakfast, orange pekoe, peppermint, Red
Zinger, camomile, or Blackberry Delight?"

"Blackberry Delight," we said in what sounded like harmony.

But once again she was back in a few minutes with an even
more forlorn expression than before.

"No tea?" I guessed.

"Oh, we have plenty of tea," she said. "But for some reason the microwave isn't working. Can't make hot water without the microwave, I'm afraid."

"We'll just have two glasses of cold water," Jayne told her.

And so Jayne and I sat with two glasses of water—very tasty water, too—as the jet made a final turn, gunned its two engines, and taxied off the edge of the earth into the insubstantial air. In a moment, flying high above the brown smoggy haze of the San Fernando Valley, we made a right turn and headed east.

"You can see now why you don't want to own a jet," I told my wife. "Lots of expensive maintenance and things going wrong."

Climbing higher into the ultraviolet sky, the engines purred contentedly as we made our way across the continent. By the time we had passed over Las Vegas there were many choices of things to do. We could read, watch television—or see a movie from a supply of tapes, use the telephone to call our friends, or the fax machine to bombard the earth below with messages beamed from the heavens. In the end, we selected Mozart's clarinet concerto in A-flat, which I had had to learn to finger when I did *The Benny Goodman Story* film. Civilized indeed. Somewhere over Kansas I fell asleep with the sun streaming in the window, the poems of T. S. Eliot open in my lap, and violins sweetly singing in my ears. The only way to fly.

I'm glad I enjoyed it while I was able.

I woke up in free fall. My stomach got left behind at thirty thousand feet. It took me a moment to comprehend fully that our lovely flying living room had taken a near nosedive and we were plummeting like a falling egg from the sky toward the earth below.

Chapter 6

Well, *that* was exciting," I said to Jayne, after we had leveled off at five thousand feet and it appeared, for the moment at least, that we were not going to die. During our free-fall dive, Jayne and I had instinctively found each other's hands. We were still clasping one another tightly.

"Perhaps commercial air travel is best after all," Jayne said.

Ernie, the copilot, came back into the cabin from the cockpit; his face was ashen. He conferred a moment with Brittany, the stewardess, who fortunately had been strapped into her chair, and then he came toward us.

"Everyone all right?" he asked with a forced smile.

"What happened?" I demanded.

"Nothing major. Just a temporary loss of power. Fortunately, we still have one engine."

"*One* engine?" Jayne said.

"Yes. Number two seems temporarily on the blink. Can't figure it out, really. We did a complete maintenance check on the entire plane last week after we nearly crashed in Philadelphia."

"You, er, nearly, er . . ."

"Yep. Small fire in the cockpit. Nothing to be concerned about. Though it *was* touch-and-go for a few minutes. Fritz and I put it down to The Jinx."

"The Jinx," I repeated dully.

"Haven't you heard? Strange accidents. Things seem to be going wrong with the entire network. Three weeks ago an electrical short blew UBS off the air for nearly eight minutes, a blackout from New York to Cincinnati. Then that actor—what's his name, from that cop show?—he fell off a stepladder and broke his leg. A few days after that the weather-girl at WBLX in Buffalo ran her car into a tree in an ice storm. Then we had our little cockpit fire over Philadelphia. And, of course, you've heard about what happened Friday—the light that nearly clobbered Peter McDavis and Cat Lawrence. People who work for UBS are starting to call it The Jinx."

"Funny. No one mentioned this when I took the job," I said unhappily.

"Let's get back to the matter of our one remaining engine," Jayne persisted. Occasionally she dazzles me with her practicality. "Just how dangerous is our situation?"

"Oh, no danger at all!" insisted Ernie. "Two engines are a sort of built-in redundancy. One is more than enough for a plane this size!"

"As long as it doesn't conk out, too." I said.

Ernie laughed. "We'll keep our fingers crossed," he said with a wink.

"Then you intend to make it all the way to New York?" Jayne asked.

"Oh, absolutely. Just a little over an hour to La Guardia. A piece of cake!"

"Cake's not on my diet," I muttered.

Brittany meanwhile had been fiddling in the galley and now came our way with a bright smile. "You'll never guess what's happened!" she cried.

"I shudder to think," I said.

"The microwave's working again. Somehow it must have fixed itself during the dive!"

"Isn't that marvelous?" said the copilot. "Now we can all have a hot lunch."

"I'll pass," I said. "Somehow I don't have much of an appetite."

"I'll wait to have lunch in New York," Jayne said.

"Well, we'll just keep our fingers crossed we'll make it!" said Ernie with an inappropriate horselaugh. Then he left us for the terrors of the cockpit.

I've experienced worse landings in my years of flying, though offhand I can't recall any. Jayne and I held hands. I told her I loved her and that whatever happened we had certainly had a great time over the years. She asked my forgiveness for her shopping sprees and all the times she ran her credit card over the limit. At last we came down through the clouds and saw the towers of Manhattan in a gray sky in the distance. An optimist by nature, I tried to look on the bright side of the situation. If we were going to crash, it was nice to see New York one last time.

The good part of having one engine out was that we were given immediate clearance to land and didn't have to circle the airport endlessly. I must say, Fritz and Ernie handled the plane admirably. We came down on solid earth in a graceful glide. A small bounce and we were safely on the runway. Outside our window I noticed a fire engine and an ambulance with their red and blue lights flashing racing our way.

"Welcome to New York, Mr. and Mrs. Allen," said our pilot over the intercom. "Please wait until we have come to a complete stop, and then you may leave by your nearest emergency exit."

"Why the *emergency* exit?" Jayne wondered.

We found out soon enough. The regular exit had jammed shut, for some reason. Brittany thought it might have something to do with the microwave, which made no sense to me. Or perhaps it was only The Jinx. Frankly, Jayne and I didn't care how we got out of the plane, as long as we got out fast. We crawled out the emergency exit and slipped down a collapsible slide.

"Whee!" I said, without much enthusiasm as I slid into the grip of a waiting fireman. It was a hell of a way to arrive in New York, but at least we were there.

Chapter 7

Inside the terminal, I noticed a woman in a black coat, a black floppy hat with a wide brim which partly concealed her face, and huge dark glasses, altogether a portrait of studied anonymity. The dark lady seemed to be peering in our direction, though that was only a guess. Hardly more than the tip of her nose was visible, but there was something familiar in it.

"Cat? Is that you?" I asked.

"Oh, Steve! Jayne! Thank God you two are all right! I've been terrified ever since I heard you had engine trouble. I don't know how the bastards did it, but no one's safe around here anymore, no one!"

Cat gave us each a quick hug and then looked about the terminal nervously—for what? Spies, perhaps, or roving assassins?

"We'd better get out of here," she said, "before anything else happens."

"The stewardess said she'd see that our bags were unloaded from the plane into the limo the network was sending for us," Jayne said.

"I canceled the limo. I brought my car instead," Cat told her.

"It's the safest bet to avoid anything connected with the network," she whispered. *"Anything."*

It was apparently National Paranoia week.

She peered over her dark glasses and for a moment I saw her huge blue-green eyes. It was Cat, all right, underneath the celebrity disguise.

"You think it was paranoia that made that light nearly fall on my head?" she asked dramatically, having correctly interpreted my raised eyebrows. "Or perhaps it was paranoia that made one of the engines go out on your flight from California?"

"Cat! You're scaring me to death," Jayne said. "Perhaps Steve and I should have stayed home."

"Don't worry, I'm not going to let anything happen to you guys. We just have to be careful, that's all." Impulsively, she gave us each another hug. "Oh, thank you both for coming! I've never been so happy to see anybody in my life!"

Cat went off to see about our bags, leaving us with strict instructions not to talk with any strangers who looked—well, strange.

"So what do you think?" Jayne asked when we were alone.

"Either she's ready for the loony bin, or we are, for getting involved in this."

"Perhaps it's only her nerves from her near miss with that falling light," Jayne wondered.

"Listen, *my* nerves are doing cartwheels from *our* near miss falling from the sky. But do *I* seem paranoid?"

It was a rhetorical question. Fortunately Jayne did not have a chance to answer. Cat was hurrying back our way from across the waiting area.

"It's all arranged," she said. "Let's get out of here before something else happens."

Paranoia is contagious, like a case of the giggles or seeing someone yawn. I found myself peering about nervously for suspicious strangers or the ceiling falling in. Cat led the way out through the terminal to the sidewalk, where a policeman was guiding a tow truck to a two-seater Mercedes-Benz convertible.

"Stop!" Cat cried. "That's my car!"

"Sorry, lady, you're in a no-parking zone," said one of New York's Finest.

"But I'm leaving right away!"

"Too late, ma'am. We're impounding your vehicle."

"No, you can't! Look at me—I'm a lady in distress. You wouldn't do this to a lady in distress, would you? You, a blue knight."

"Lady . . ."

She removed her dark glasses and huge hat. "Perhaps you recognize me from television?"

The long and short of it was that Cat got her way. The cop called off the tow truck and Cat even gave him her autograph. Meanwhile Brittany and the copilot from the plane had appeared with our baggage on a metal cart, and now we were left to deal with a slight problem of physics—how to get our bags into a sports car. The bulk of the question, so to speak, was solved when Brittany offered to transport our luggage in a taxi to the Fifth Avenue duplex. Now it was only a matter of Jayne, Cat, and me squeezing into the front seat. Cat put the top down so we could load more easily. Jayne sat on my lap, which is always a pleasure—though our canceled limousine might have been a greater pleasure still. At last, Cat closed the top, put the little car in gear, and we joined the crush of traffic headed toward Manhattan.

Despite the strangeness of our arrival, it was exciting to be in the big city again. Coming from California, you're always struck by the hustle, the raw energy of the city. It was late afternoon, almost dusk. We drove toward the unmistakable profile of Manhattan in the distance, the tall buildings framed against a steel-gray wintry sky.

A beam of orange sunset pierced the clouds just as the sun

went down over distant New Jersey. Then the lights of the tall buildings twinkled forth as in a fairy tale. It looked like an enchanted metropolis, the American city of Oz. A hard town, certainly, in which one could find great success, or stunning failure. Both extremes seemed possible here—life at the top. Or anonymous death on the sidewalks below.

Chapter 8

The network's duplex was on the ninth and tenth floors of a modern building on Fifth Avenue and Eighty-second Street, across from the Metropolitan Museum and the snowy trees and fields of Central Park. The living room was enormous, two stories tall with huge tinted windows looking out onto the museum and park. The walls, white and cheerful, were hung with modern art. There was a kitchen, den, bathroom, and dining room downstairs. To get to the three bedrooms above, you could either take a small elevator from the foyer, or climb the freestanding circular staircase at the north end of the living room.

"How lovely!" Jayne cooed as she, Cat, and I explored room to room. The final touch of luxury was Anna the maid and Benson the butler, who hovered about decorously to see if they could be of service. Just so they wouldn't feel useless, I asked if they would serve tea and hors d'oeuvres in the living room. After exploring our new quarters, the three of us sat on fluffy white sofas with delicate blue-white cups filled with Earl Grey, and small slivers of bread with smoked salmon on top.

From the living room there was an incredible view across Central Park to the buildings on the other side, Central Park West, where the windows sparkled warm with light.

"Cat, you're looking more beautiful than ever," Jayne remarked.

"Thanks, but I don't feel beautiful. I've been totally stressed-out since Friday morning."

"I understand, dear. But now you must relax," Jayne said in her most soothing manner. There's nothing Jayne likes better than playing mother hen to lost chickens, and Cat Lawrence at the moment was looking like a very lost chicken indeed. As soon as we had arrived in the duplex, she had removed her disguise, the dark glasses and floppy hat. It was nice actually to get a look at her. Over the years, Cat's natural prettiness had matured and evolved. The years in Paris and San Francisco had added an aura of grace and elegance. She was one of those women who look more striking in their mid-thirties than in their twenties. Nevertheless, I could see a touch of anxiety in her eyes.

"Well, Cat, I think it's time to tell us what's been going on," I prompted.

"It's quite a story, Steve. I told you on the phone how I got the job. It seemed at first like a fairy tale come true. I've always been ambitious, of course. Probably it comes from my father being such a failure. When I was a little girl and we had to move from that nice house across the street from you, I swore that one day I was going to succeed in television, no matter what. So when Stephen—Mr. Kinley—offered me the co-anchor spot I was just about dancing on the ceiling. When I arrived in New York in August I was so pleased with myself it took a few weeks for me to notice all the friction and backstabbing. Have you ever walked into a room where people have been fighting? You come in with a silly grin on your face, but no one smiles back. Then the vibes hit you that something is wrong, but you don't know exactly what, because no one will tell you anything, or even look you in the eye. It's like that with 'Good Morning, U.S.A.' To tell the truth, I *still* don't know entirely what's going on, though I have a pretty good fix on who hates whom—all the different factions that are set up against each other. You'll see what I mean when you come on the set tomorrow morning. There are undercurrents like crazy. But no one talks about what's really on his mind.''

"But you've been there a few months now, Cat," I said. "Surely you can hazard a guess or two about what's happening?"

"Part of it has to do with Nancy Vandenberg, the woman I replaced. There are some people at UBS who are still pretty upset that she was fired."

"I've watched her a few times," Jayne said. "She was very pretty—and young."

"Maybe *too* pretty and young. I think Peter McDavis and Bob Hutchinson, the weatherman, were both in love with her."

"Peter's married, isn't he?" I asked.

"You bet. And so is Bob. My theory is that Bob had an affair with Nancy a few years back, and then Peter stole her for himself. There's certainly some bad blood between those two."

"Why do you suppose Nancy got the ax?"

"That was Stephen Kinley's decision. From what I understand, the ratings were down and he decided Nancy was too much of a glamour type. The idea is that with a morning show, women don't want to look at someone they unconsciously think might steal their husband. Men aren't entirely awake yet themselves at that hour and would rather see a wifey sort of woman than a sexpot; that's the theory anyway. So that's me, you see—pretty, but not threatening. A little older, sophisticated. A career woman other women can relate to. Someone the men can lust over a little, but not too much."

"Aren't you selling yourself short?" Jayne asked.

"No. I have a pretty good idea of where I stand on the

beauty scale, and I don't have any complaints. But on television, everything—and everybody—becomes a kind of commodity. As you know, Steve, there's some very subtle psychology involved in what sells and what doesn't. My theory about Nancy Vandenberg was that being pretty was not the thing that got her fired—but that she looked—well, *available.* She could have gotten away with that on nighttime TV—in fact, it would have been an asset. But not at seven o'clock in the morning. So I do my best to look pretty but *not* available. You'll see tomorrow, Steve. I dress for the part in clothes that are attractive, but just a touch businesslike.''

"I see.''

"Anyway, back to Nancy. . . . Beyond Peter and Bob fighting for her favors, the crew seems fairly evenly divided between a pro-Nancy faction, and a group who broke open the champagne when she got fired. The people who liked Nancy did not exactly welcome me with open arms.''

"How about Peter McDavis?'' I asked.

"For the first two months, he was friendly enough on-camera, but the moment the red eye was off, he acted like I had a contagious disease.''

"He was hostile?''

"Oh no; he pretended I didn't exist. He didn't look at me. He didn't talk to me unless it was absolutely necessary. I can tell you, it wasn't easy to work with a co-anchor who treats you like you're invisible. But recently he's eased up a bit. Occasionally he's even friendly, in a cautious sort of way.''

"For example?''

"A week ago, after we finished the show, he offered to buy me brunch. I turned him down in as friendly a way as I could manage. I'm glad he's not treating me like I'm invisible any-more, but I don't want to encourage him into thinking I might become a replaceable bedmate for Nancy. Peter's wife stays mostly at their retreat in Santa Fe—she hates New York, from what I hear. So he has a lot of time to fantasize about other women.''

''It sounds like you've landed in a viper's nest,'' Jayne said.

''It's terrible! There are all sorts of other undercurrents as well. Zeke Roth, the producer, and Bob the weatherman own a restaurant together on Third Avenue, and I gather there have been some problems concerning their partnership. Frankly, I've done my best to stay clear of all the intrigues and just do my job. I thought I was doing fairly well, actually, until that damned light fell out of the rafters Friday morning!''

''And yet, perhaps that *was* an accident, after all,'' Jayne said.

Cat shook her head violently. ''It wasn't. Someone planned it—I just know it. I can't explain *how* I know it, but I do! You'll see I'm right, Steve, when you come on the set tomorrow. It's something you can just sense in the air.''

I smiled what I hoped was a comforting smile. Cat was understandably upset, and I was inclined to believe she was letting her imagination run away with her. I decided I'd reserve judgment and keep my mind and eyes open. The fact was, if the klieg light incident was *not* an accident, I might have to watch my own head.

Chapter 9

The alarm clock rang at four in the morning, a very uncivilized hour for rising from bed. The bedroom was dark and it took a moment to remember where I was and the reason for the ringing alarm clock. Jayne stirred briefly on her side of the bed.

"Break a leg, darling," she murmured. And then she returned happily to the sweet embrace of sleep. Lucky Jayne. Early in my TV career, as some of you may remember, I was host of the original "Tonight Show." The hours had been a snap. Or at least so they seemed now in retrospect as I rose grumpily two hours before dawn to make my date with early morning television.

I lingered in the shower, allowing the hot water to massage my neck, and then shaved. I found in the closet a nice gray, pinstriped suit I thought would look good on television. A light blue shirt with French cuffs. A burgundy tie with a swirling pattern that was perhaps a little loud. I had just finished dressing when the intercom rang from the lobby downstairs. It was the doorman saying the limousine was waiting to take me to the studio. One final yawn, a last look in the mirror, to little avail, and I was on my way to the elevator.

Cat, Jayne, and I had gone out to dinner to a restaurant the night before and had stayed up too late talking about Cat's mother and father and the old days when she had lived across the street. It was fun to reminisce—and I was glad to get Cat's mind off falling objects. But I vowed to get to bed earlier in the future.

The studio was on Tenth Avenue and Forty-eighth Street, a modern eight-story building that did not fit in with the rest of the neighborhood. This was a rough part of town—warehouses, little shops and run-down tenement buildings. The limo delivered me to the front door at a few minutes past five. I signed in with a sleepy-looking security guard who sat in front of a console of closed-circuit TV monitors. He let go of his mug of coffee long enough to pick up a telephone and announce my arrival to someone on the other end.

In a moment, a remarkably energetic young woman came rushing at me from out of an opening door. "Mr. Allen!" she cried, "How wonderful to meet you! I'm Debbie Driscoll, one of the talent coordinators."

"Good," I said. "My talent could stand a little coordinating."

On the young woman's humor-perception mechanism the line registered a zero.

"Our producer, Zeke Roth, asked me to show you around. He'll be here about six, for a meeting with you and our director, Ken Byrnes. Meanwhile, let me show you to your dressing room. If you want coffee, orange juice, *anything* at all, just let me know."

She pumped my hand so vigorously I felt minor discomfort in my arm socket. Ms. Driscoll was in her early twenties, tall with dark hair and a kind of long, horsey, but friendly face. She wore bib overalls that seemed more appropriate for work on a farm than at a television studio, but it's best not to question the sartorial habits of the young. Her voice was loud enough to carry to the street outside.

"How was your flight yesterday?"

"Well, actually . . ."

"Terrific! I bet it's nice and warm in California. We're supposed to have a huge snowstorm here in New York tonight. I have a cousin in Redondo Beach, but I haven't been out there for years. . . ."

Talking a mile a minute, Debbie led me down a maze of corridors to a door that had my name on it, opened it with a cliché, "Tada!" and led the way into a small suite: a sitting room complete with sofas, an armchair, small refrigerator, and makeup table and mirror surrounded by lights. There was also a bedroom that wasn't much more than space for a single bed and reading lamp, a bathroom with shower, and a walk-in closet. As dressing rooms go, it was better than most. Comfortable, cheerfully decorated, but not a place you'd want to spend your leisure time in. The biggest drawback was the lack of windows, for we were deep inside the studio.

"Lovely, isn't it?" Debbie cried.

"Breathtaking," I said.

"Zeke left some background information for you on today's guests. Let's see," she said, separating several sheaves of paper from her clipboard. "There's an author. An actor pushing his newest movie. And Maya Rusanovsky—"

"Who?"

"—That gorgeous Russian model who just married what's-his-name, the rock star. Zeke also left a bottle of champagne in the refrigerator for you, and he says if there's anything you want, *any*thing at all . . ."

"I'll let you know. I *would* like some fresh orange juice and a few raisin-bran muffins if that's possible."

"Right away!" The girl was exhausting. She flew to the telephone to bark out orders for my requests, then took me down the hall to makeup, where I sat in a barber's chair while

Nadia Wolfe, the makeup specialist, applied a bit of pancake, then dusted and patted my face with powder. Nadia was a large blond woman in her mid-fifties with a motherly face and twinkly blue eyes.

She talked—mostly to herself—as she worked, in a kind of rhythmic singsong. "Just a little dab here . . . a pat on the nose . . . and here, too . . . and no, no, we can't forget the ears!"

"Have you worked on the show a long time, Nadia?"

"Oh, years and years. I do everybody. Even that poor Nancy Vandenberg. Such a pity she was fired! She took a long time in makeup, of course, sometimes a whole hour. But oh, what a beautiful girl! And now her life . . . it's down the drain, I think. Kaput."

"Surely she'll find a new show, perhaps on another network?"

"Who knows? Such an insecure life, television. And you know why she lost her job, don't you? It's all on account of that . . ."

Nadia was clearly a great gossip, and I was interested in what she was about to say. But at that moment we heard a bloodcurdling scream from outside in the hall.

"My God! What's going on?" I cried, jumping up from the chair and rushing into the hall. A man dressed in a silver jogging suit and tennis shoes was hopping up and down on one foot. He was not a young man—in his late fifties I would guess—and he had a round face and a nearly bald head with a fringe of curly dark hair around his ears. He was cursing wildly, using certain words I will not repeat.

"Goddamn beepity-beep television show!" he shouted. "I'll kill the son of a bitch who did this!"

"What's the matter?" I asked.

"I stepped on a beeping tack, *that's* what's the matter! Just look at this mother-beeping floor!"

The floor was strewn with dozens of brass upholstery tacks. It looked as if someone had simply dumped a box of them along the corridor. They certainly had not been there when I had walked from my dressing room to the makeup room, or I would have been hopping on one foot, too. Still swearing oaths of revenge, the man put a hand on my shoulder and hopped into the makeup room.

"A nasty accident," I said.

"Accident?" he scoffed. "This goddamn bleeping TV show's going to kill me! I'm Zeke Roth, by the way—I was just coming to see you. Wait 'til I find out who was responsible for spilling those tacks in the hall!"

I knew Roth by reputation—he had been producing successful television shows for years, both on the West Coast and in New York. But our paths had never crossed until this moment. I got him to sit in a chair and helped remove his damaged left sneaker. One upholstery tack had pierced the rubber sole and gone about a quarter of an inch into the fleshy part of his heel. It was a painful jolt, but more of a shock than a medical emergency. Nadia used the telephone to ask a maintenance person to come over immediately with a broom.

"Is this part of the famous jinx people have been telling me about?" I asked.

"Jinx!" he sighed. "I don't know *what's* going wrong with this show, but I'm about ready to have a nervous breakdown. My ulcer doesn't need the aggravation, I can tell you!" Zeke made a heroic effort to calm down. "Anyway, Mr. Allen— may I call you Steve?"

"It's better than Bob or Charlie," I said.

"Well, we're all awfully glad you've agreed to sub for Peter for a while. Welcome aboard—it's not always like this, I promise you. Meanwhile, did you get the list of today's guests? Basically, for the first couple of days, I thought we'd let you handle the interviews and give Cat pretty much everything else. Just until you get the format down. Actually, for someone with your talk show experience, this whole thing should be a piece of cake."

"Are you really all right?" Nadia asked him. "Perhaps I should send for a doctor."

"No, no, I'm okay—it hurt like hell, but the show must go on. Even this one!"

I returned to the makeup chair, and Nadia finished dabbing and patting at my face. Zeke sat massaging his foot while he explained the show's format. When my makeup was finished, he took me down the hall to meet the director—keeping a careful eye peeled, I thought, for upholstery tacks and other terrors. Ken Byrnes, the director, was in his mid-thirties. A thin, slight, soft-spoken individual wearing corduroy pants and a plaid shirt, he gave me more details as to my part of the show. "Good Morning, U.S.A." would be carried live on the East Coast, then shown in a taped delay to the subsequent time zones going west, so that from California to New York each station would begin the program at 7:00 A.M. Reading a Tele-PrompTer and interviewing guests is a lot easier than many people think. It certainly doesn't require talent. The tricky part of any television broadcast—and live television in particular—is the timing, cutting in and out of commercials, getting the various segments in their proper place, and avoiding that worst of all TV sins—dead air.

Zeke and Ken sat at a conference table with me for nearly half an hour going over the day's format on a computer printout that accounted for how every second of time would be spent from 7:00 A.M. until 9:00. A commercial break at 7:10:30. Go to Bob Hutchinson, the weatherman, at 7:21:25. Break to the newsroom, Carol Ardman and Dan De Vries, at 7:29:45. And so on, all the way to the end of the broadcast. None of this caused me much anxiety. I would have a copy of the rundown to refer to on my desk during the show, as well as a flesh-colored earpiece hidden in one ear to receive Ken's verbal prompts. To make things even easier, I would simply follow Cat's lead for the first few days. And if all else failed, I had learned over the long years how to ad-lib.

I've always thought the ability to speak extemporaneously is a somewhat overrated gift. We've been ad-libbing all of our lives, have we not? I mean, were you given the script for last Thursday when you got out of bed?

Since my sleep requirements are greatly in excess of the norm—I'm groggy all day if I get less than ten hours—I did not look forward with pleasure to the early-to-bed requirement I had just incurred. I remember years ago discussing the problem with my friend Dave Garroway, who was at the time hosting NBC's "Today Show." "Isn't it awful," I said, "having to get up in the middle of the night day after day?"

"Yes, it is," he said, "but only for the first few minutes. Once I get into the hot shower, the coffee, the orange juice— I'm okay."

In both our cases we were well paid for putting up with a few minutes of torture each workday morning.

At a quarter to seven, Cat came into the conference room and kissed me on the cheek—a careful kiss so as not to muss her hair and makeup.

"Ready for morning television?" she asked with a smile.

"If I can survive the hours, I'll be OK," I told her.

Cat looked older and more dignified in her TV makeup and conservative beige dress than she had the night before. It was part of her conscious attempt that no one should mistake her for a bimbo.

American culture has now come to such a depraved pass, incidentally, that I'm not certain Cat's concern about her image was reasonably grounded. Not too many years ago the state of bimbo-ness was looked down upon, I have little doubt, even by the poor souls who so designated themselves. They were usually young women with nothing much to offer the world but a cheaply sexual surface quality, frequently enhanced by the wearing of unnecessarily tight and low-cut dresses, flamboyantly colored hair, extra heavy makeup, and whatever additional accoutrements might further contribute to a hookerlike impression. But since, roughly speaking, 1990, such an image was no longer seen as something to avoid by very young actresses with any hope for a serious career in the theater or films.

There aren't many hipper "alternative" magazines than *Spy*. But in its issue of August 1995, it carried a long feature the essential point of which was that bimbos had basically taken over so far as motion pictures were concerned and that a good many top stars, far from trying to pass as Audrey Hepburn or Meryl Streep types, as they would have in earlier years, were deliberately descending to the level of tramp, to use a word that Joan Rivers had earlier brought back to popularity. Cat Lawrence, by way of contrast, had evidently decided to downplay her natural sexiness.

I followed Cat out to the studio floor, and we sat in our places behind a desk in a fake living room while Dennis, the audioman, attached small microphones to our lapels.

The studio was one large room with various corners that would be used for the different segments of the show. There was a blue chroma-key screen for the weather report off to one side, two armchairs for cozy interviews in a different part of the room, and the main living room where Cat and I were now situated. The three cameras were set in the middle of the studio and could be swiveled or rolled in any direction, depending on where the action was. Beyond that, there were cables and monitors and a bright flood of lights. I resisted the temptation to look upward at the heavy lights in the studio rafters above the desk.

"You know, this is a dream come true for me," Cat said quietly as we sat together waiting for the hands of the clock to move to seven. "When I was a little girl, I used to watch you do 'The Steve Allen Show,' and I promised myself that when I grew up I'd be on television with you."

"And here I'm on *your* show," I said with a smile.

"I had a crush on you, Steve. I still do, if you want to know the truth. You're the reason I got into this business."

I laughed politely, though her tone worried me.

"Jayne and I have always been very fond of you, Cat," I said.

Her eyes glittered humorously in my direction. "Maybe I arranged all this, the light falling, everything—just to get you here by my side."

I laughed again, though her tone seemed odd. But it was too late to run. Don, the floor manager, was counting down the seconds. "Ten, nine, eight, seven, six, five—"

The last five digits he did silently on his fingers.

We were live on the air.

Chapter 10

"Good Morning, U.S.A.," Cat said brightly into the lens of camera number one, "and welcome to our Monday, January 13 show, coming to you live from New York City. I'm Cat Lawrence. Sitting in for Peter McDavis this morning I'm pleased to welcome a very special friend, Steve Allen . . . Good morning, Steve! It's great to have you."

"It's great to be had," I said as the red light of the number two camera blinked on, and a somewhat too tight close-up of my face filled the monitor.

"I have to tell our audience that Steve and I go way back. . . ."

Cat and I made small talk for a few moments, explaining how she used to be a scrawny tomboy climbing trees, living across the street from us in California.

"Steve, talk louder. We're having trouble with your microphone," came a voice in my ear. It was the director, Ken Byrnes, speaking from the control booth through the flesh-colored earpiece in my left ear. I was telling an anecdote about Cat setting up a lemonade stand on the sidewalk when she was ten or eleven years old, and how Jayne and I used to buy Dixie cups of her wares on hot summer days.

I spoke more loudly.

". . . then one day, I remember the price went up from a dime to fifty cents. I bought a cup anyway, took one sip and had the surprise of my life. The lemonade was spiked. . . ."

"With bourbon," Cat admitted with a mischievous smile. "From my father's liquor cabinet. Sales were down, and I thought it would jump-start my business."

"It certainly jump-started *me*. . . ."

"Louder," hissed the voice in my ear. "The damned microphone!"

Fortunately our two minutes allotted to chitchat were coming to an end, and Cat took over, reading from the TelePrompTer about the day's guests and what treats we had in store for our viewers that morning. When I first began in television, lines were written on cue cards which were held up near the cameras. Today, the TelePrompTer is a square screen of some nifty transparent material fitted directly over the lens of the camera. The result is that because you can look directly into the camera you don't seem to be reading. Like all good television performers, Cat changed a word now and then from what was flashing by on the TelePrompTer.

"And now we're going to Carol Ardman and Dan De Vries in the newsroom for our first look at the national and international headlines. Carol and Dan, good morning. . . ."

The monitor switched to Carol and Dan, who were broadcasting from a different part of the building, and Cat and I were off the air.

From the schedule on the desk, I read that after the news, we would take a break for commercials. Cat and I had exactly five minutes and forty-five seconds to relax until the red eyes of the cameras once again blinked our way.

Up to this moment, I had not seen much indication of the various hostilities and undercurrents Cat had told me about.

But the moment we went temporarily off the air, the studio filled with a number of people I had not met before, and I received a crash course in ugly behavior.

A large man with a babyish face and protruding stomach ambled our way, followed by a makeup assistant with powder puff in hand.

"The nose is a little shiny," she whispered, at which I stood and moved to one side. In the meantime the man, whom I recognized as the usually genial Bob Hutchinson, one of the nation's friendlier weathermen, although they all seem to be chosen from the cheerful category, said, "Well if it isn't Mata Hari. How is our woman of mystery this morning?" Even with my glasses off, to make it easier for the makeup woman to de-shine me, I had the impression that Cat's smile had something bitter about it.

"Steve," she said "you know Bob Hutchinson. If you were watching the show yesterday, you'd recall that he said the sun was going to be shining brightly this morning—which is why I brought my umbrella to the studio."

Bob let rip one of his famous booming laughs. "Funeee," he said. Then, lowering his voice, he stepped around to the other side of me, out of Cat's hearing, and whispered "You'd better watch yourself at all times, Steve-o."

"I thought that's what the monitors were for," I said, hoping to deflect his negativity with a laugh, albeit modest.

"I'm not kidding," he muttered. "She may be a friend of yours, but she made sure Nancy Vandenberg got the ax, and now with Peter gone as well, I'd watch my back if I were you."

Although I don't believe Cat could hear what Hutchinson was saying, she seemed to assume that it was something critical.

"You look like your weight's up again, Bob," she said.

Hutchinson flashed a false smile, and said to me, "How to make friends and influence people, eh?"

This was getting nasty. I was glad to see Ken Byrnes and

Dennis, our audioman, coming our way across the studio floor. Dennis was a pleasant-looking young man in jeans and sweatshirt. His longish blond hair was tied behind in a ponytail, and there was a baseball cap on his head. "I'm going to give you a new mike, Mr. Allen," he said. "We've been getting you so far, but only by turning up the volume so high there's some distortion."

"Let's hope *this* one works," Ken fumed. "I can't believe the schlocky equipment they give us around here! I started in television working in a little station in Nebraska that had better equipment than we do. Welcome to the big time!"

In the background I saw Zeke Roth approaching.

"And here's the big man himself," Bob said, listening in to our conversation. "Mr. Tightwad in person."

Roth walked toward us accompanied by a short young woman I did not know.

"What are you complaining about now, Bob?" Zeke asked.

"Why don't you spend some money to buy decent equipment?" Bob said. "Look at this junky microphone!"

"I don't *buy* microphones," Zeke replied, rather too loudly. "We get all our stuff from the network."

"Then why don't you make certain we get equipment that works?" Bob asked.

"Hey, boys and girls," I said, "what is this, 'Romper Room'?"

Bob, Zeke, and Ken were not amused, and I realized I had unwittingly entered the nastiness. Dennis meanwhile was fitting me with a new microphone, threading the wire through my suit jacket and pinning the miniature electronic device to my lapel.

"Mornings like this, I think I should have been a teacher instead," he said. "That's what I wanted to do."

"Why didn't you?"

"I thought this would be more glamorous," he said with a dry laugh.

"We're coming back, Dennis. Get the damned mike hooked up!" Ken told him.

I was starting to wonder if I was going to survive two weeks of this when the short woman who had come onto the set with Zeke walked my way with a big smile. It's difficult to express what a joy it was to see at least one happy face on the set of "Good Morning, U.S.A." Not an especially pretty woman— she had a kind of funny face with semi-buck teeth—but in the gloom of the moment her smile was like a beam of sunlight.

"Hi! What a pleasure to meet you, Mr. Allen! I'm Sherry Gold. May I call you Steve?"

"It's better than Bob or Charlie," I said.

"Now don't tell me, I bet you're a Libra. There's a sense of balance about you. A yearning for justice. What sign *were* you born under?"

"Furnished rooms for rent, I believe it was."

"Thirty seconds, everybody!" called Don, the floor manager.

"We'll talk later," Sherry said, waving goodbye. "I'll predict your future."

"Fat chance," I said, but to myself, not aloud. No one can predict the future, and if anyone could, just a few days spent on Wall Street or, for that matter, at Santa Anita, would make them fabulously wealthy.

I was reminded of the time when I happened to be a guest on Mike Douglas's talk show along with Jeanne Dixon, whose erroneous predictions have been repeatedly exposed by *Free Inquiry, The Skeptical Inquirer, The Skeptic,* and other rationalist periodicals.

At the time, some years ago, I was conducting a search for a half brother I had never met and concerning whose existence I knew nothing until my mother died, leaving behind certain evidence that she had had a child about fifteen years before I was born. Ms. Dixon told me she had a very strong feeling that the gentleman was no longer alive. Fortunately she was mistaken, and I later got to meet my long-lost relative, a Southern attorney named Young Smith. Her prediction, of course, was based on the fact that as of the moment we spoke Smith would have been seventy-three years old and most seventy-three-year-old people are dead.

The set cleared, and Cat and I sat next to each other behind the desk, waiting for our return to the living rooms of America.

"Who was *that?*" I asked in an undertone.

"Sherry Gold. Look on the schedule, page three. She does the astrology report."

"Astrology?" I said. "Swell. You know, one of the most fascinating sciences of them all is astronomy. There is literally nothing more exciting, more marvelous, but Americans, in general, don't give a damn about it. You give people a choice between fantasy and reality, and most of the time they head right for the unreal."

"You're right," Cat said. "We're a pretty goofy lot. Everybody I run into is complaining about taxes, and yet at this very moment there are millions of people heading off to the nearest gambling joint for the privilege of *throwing* their money away. At least when you pay a dollar in taxes you know it's going to go to some practical purpose like paying for highways, policemen's salaries, helping the poor—whatever."

"I agree," I said, "but astrology—I was surprised when Ken mentioned that earlier. It doesn't seem to make sense on a show that disseminates news."

"Go figure," she said. "But Sherry also does garden hints and stuff like that. Her predictions are about as accurate as Bob's weather forecasts."

The floor manager did a countdown and we were back on the air, as smiling and cheerful a group as you'd ever want to see. Cat once again spoke glowingly about our guests, who would appear later in the program. But first it was time for a look at the weather around the nation with jolly Bob Hutchinson. Cat introduced Bob as though they were the closest of friends, and from the way Bob beamed back you would have thought they were brother and sister.

It's fascinating to watch a weatherman do his stuff in front of a blank blue screen—all the storms and clouds, the maps and animations are added off-camera by the computerized magic of the control room. Bob was good at the showbiz side of his profession. He gave away an official Bob Hutchinson thermometer to a woman in Cedar Rapids, Iowa, and then launched into the nation's weather, gesturing with great accuracy to particular spots on the empty screen behind him, while keeping an eye on the off-camera monitor that had the computer animation filled in.

"Locally, you New Yorkers will be glad to know the snowstorm that was heading our way yesterday has now shifted direction and will pass well to the north of us," Bob said. "Residents of Vermont and upper New York State can expect as much as two feet of snow. But here in Manhattan, we can look forward to a sunny afternoon, blue skies, and springlike temperatures. . . ."

"Oh-oh!" Cat whispered in my ear with a mischievous smile. "Hope you brought a good pair of snow boots, Steve!"

Chapter 11

My part of the show was a breeze. At 7:22:30 I did a four-and-a-half minute interview with Maya Rusanovsky, the internationally famous model and ballerina who had recently married a rock star whose face I have seen on the supermarket tabloids, but whose music I have managed to avoid.

I had first heard of him a few years earlier when he was with the group called Night Soil, in which he worked with the former drummer and bass player of Underarm Deodorant—these people have a lot of class—then he had worked with Sick City and was now on his own. Note that I did not refer to him as a rock singer for the purely practical reason that what he did for a living was not, strictly speaking, singing but screaming. Screaming is not a legal offense, but it is nevertheless what the majority of rock vocalists do. There are probably two reasons for this in that most white rock singers basically try to sing like blacks, for whom the guttural, raspy kind of articulation is at least more authentic. This has nothing whatever to do with race. Joe Williams and Ray Charles are singers, James Brown is a screamer.

The problem with most white screamers is that only a small percentage of the messages they are presumably attempting to communicate can actually be interpreted.

Maya was pencil-thin and flat-chested, but she had huge expressive eyes that made her quite pretty. Like the majority of models, she was not as impressive in the flesh as on-camera. Maya was eighteen years old, not particularly brilliant, and I had to work a little to keep a conversation going. The most interesting fact about her, as far as I was concerned, was that she was Russian. So I got her talking about her childhood in St. Petersburg and what life was like there as a fashion model since the fall of communism. Maya's main complaint about the post-communist era in Russia was the continued lack of rock concerts by Western stars, and no haute couture—but she had satisfied her thirst for such things first in Paris and now in New York.

"Your interest in rock, and perhaps roll as well, would strike most people as odd," I said, "given the gentility, the sensitivity, the beauty of its truly classical music, the ballet is culturally a million miles away from the culture of rock, if I may use the word *culture*."

"What?" she said.

"What, indeed," I said. "The question I was perhaps ineptly attempting to raise was: Doesn't it strike you as odd that a ballerina would have any interest at all in a rock singer?"

"Oh, I see what you mean," she said, smiling fetchingly.

Unfortunately, she did not subsequently fetch anything.

I heard Cat Lawrence giggle far off-mike. Then, to my surprise Maya said "People think he is a bad boy because he sang for two years with Organized Crime."

Now it was my turn to say, "What? He was connected with the Mafia?"

"Oh, no," she said. "That was the name of his group. His own name, at the time, was Tommy Trash."

"Was Trash his family name," I said, "or are we talking about—well, white trash?"

"I do not know," she said.

I made a mental note to hold a future public discussion on what Thomas Aquinas used to call invincible ignorance but elected not to follow up on the thought at the moment.

"Tell me," I said, "what would be your opinion, culturally speaking, of a singer like, say, Frank Sinatra?"

"Who?" she said, and then added, "I'm sorry; I'm only eighteen."

"I wish I were," I said.

Her face was so sweet, so Audrey Hepburn-like, that I was moved to continue my attempts to communicate, about anything.

"Onstage," I said, "your husband is in the habit of not only smashing his guitars but smashing them over the heads of other musicians and, in one instance, over the head of an unlucky fan who wandered onstage. How do you personally feel about that?"

"He can afford to buy a new guitar," she said.

"He can afford," I said, "to buy new guitars for the entire population of Latvia. I didn't plan to bring this up," I said to the sweet-faced Maya, "but last year your new husband was arrested not only for raping one of his admirers but also molesting her nine-year-old daughter."

"He was not my husband at the time," she said.

"I never assumed he was," I responded, "but I seem to be beating around a remarkably leafless bush here. What I've been trying to find out is how you—perceived by the world as an exquisitely ladylike young creature would—"

"I am not a creature," she said.

"I didn't mean as in Creature-from-the-Black-Lagoon," I said, "but rather in the sense that we are all creatures, are we not? If I may return to my task—do you find anything objectionable about Mr. Trash's conduct?"

"Yes," she said, "I don't."

"The state has no further questions, your honor," I said, looking directly into camera two.

I did a better interview at 8:10:15 with a woman who had just written a low-fat cookbook. We talked for three minutes about cream sauces made with nonfat yogurt and buttermilk, and such ideas as sautéing a boneless, skinless chicken breast with a squeeze of lemon juice rather than butter or oil. She had interesting ideas on how to use a great deal of fruit in cooking. I simply let her talk. You can't go too far wrong with the TV public when you're discussing how to eat gourmet meals and still stay thin.

The most important interview of the day came toward the end of the show, at a few seconds past 8:36. Terry Torrent, the young actor who had made such a huge hit on a TV soap opera, came on the show to push his first movie, a romantic thriller called *Tough Love*. Mr. Torrent, as every woman in America knows, has wavy black hair and moist brown eyes and the most classical profile since Tyrone Power. We watched a thirty-second clip from his film, a dramatic moment in which the writers had contrived to have him, bare-chested and glistening, rescue a beautiful young woman from a burning house. When that was finished we talked for four minutes and forty seconds about his life and aspirations. He was a pleasant young man, all in all, serious and soft-spoken, whose ambition it was to one day find Ms. Right and do Shakespeare on the legitimate stage. "Why Shakespeare?" I asked. "I dig that old language," he confessed. "And it would be a blast to dress up in those outfits they used to wear—you know, the tights and all—and have sword fights and everything."

"Wonderful," I said. "Would you rather play in *Hamlet* or *King Lear?*"

"*Camelot,*" he answered.

"I see," I said.

I had a good time on the show in general and would have

been happy except for the unpleasant atmosphere among the cast and crew that made itself felt in the odd moments when we weren't on the air. It was difficult not to get involved in it. Halfway through the show, Dennis the audioman needed to give me yet another microphone.

"Get it right this time! Or don't bother coming to work tomorrow!" Zeke Roth barked at him.

"I can only work with the materials you supply, Mr. Roth," Dennis said quietly.

"Yeah," Bob Hutchinson encouraged, standing off to one side, speaking sotto voce. "Cheap microphones, cheap show. Old Zeke will sure as hell never get another job in television after the way he's botched this one!"

"What did you say?" Roth challenged, turning red in the face.

"Just kidding, man. Relax."

A few minutes later it was Bob's turn to get hot under the collar during the next weather report. The computer graphics messed up. Bob was talking about a high pressure area over Colorado, plenty of sunshine, while the screen showed low pressure and snow. At one point, all the temperatures on the map went crazy. Los Angeles went from 110 degrees to minus 5 before the figures came up right, a modest 62. Boston showed a tropical typhoon. When Bob called forth the latest satellite images of North America, the blue screen on the monitor presented us, for some unexplained reason, with a tranquil color picture of tulips in Holland. Bob handled all these surprises with unflappable good humor as long as we were on the air. But the moment we broke for a commercial he started screaming.

"Goddamn it, Zeke! That was deliberate sabotage!"

"Calm down, *man,*" Zeke replied with vicious sarcasm. "It was only an unfortunate screwup, that's all. Anyway, it's Ken's job to push all the buttons and levers. You know I never touch a thing in the control booth."

"So you say! But I *know* you were responsible for that idiocy, and if I ever find out how you did it, you're dead meat!"

In my time, I've been on a few TV shows where there was tension, but never anything as bad as this. It was remarkable how everyone managed to switch gears and put on a smiling face when the cameras were active. The last segment of the morning came at 8:47—Sherry Gold's astrology report. We got a rundown on the zodiac, from Pisces: "You're going to have a good morning, Pisces, but look out for something fishy to happen this afternoon. If you're offered an unbelievable business opportunity—someone is trying to con you." To Aquarius: "Your natural love of harmony is going to be sorely tested this evening, Aquarius. Be on guard for family quarrels."

After Sherry, we went to Carol Ardman and Dan De Vries in the newsroom one last time with a final check-in on the day's events. At last Cat read a small tease on the TelePrompTer about the following day's guests. Then we both said a final good morning to the nation and were off the air. I yawned and stretched. Though the work is easy, two hours of live television is a long time.

"You did fine, Steve," Cat said, impulsively kissing me on the cheek. "You see how nasty things are on this show. I can't tell you how thankful I am to have you here by my side!"

"Thanks," I said with a smile. "Anyway, what's a little animosity among seasoned pros? At least no one's been murdered yet."

But I spoke too soon.

I was sitting by myself five minutes later at the desk on the set, jotting down some notes that had come into my mind for the next show. The hot studio lights had been turned off and the various technicians were milling about, putting covers over equipment and shutting down for the day. The set belonged to them now, and probably they would have been happier if I had gone to my dressing room. But I've learned to make notes when I think of them, rather than wait; a good idea can be lost forever if you don't trap it. I was just finishing dictating a few thoughts into my pocket-size tape recorder when I heard a horrendous scream from behind the thin walls of the fake living room set. I rushed from my chair to see what was wrong. It was Cat who had called out. Her face had drained of color and she was standing in the half-darkness at the rear of the set, among electric cables and two-by-fours that were holding the insubstantial walls in place. At her feet was a crumpled form.

It was Dennis, the audioman. A cord from one of the miniature microphones was wrapped around his neck. He was as dead as it's possible to be.

Chapter 12

There were a good deal more staff and crew members responsible for getting "Good Morning, U.S.A." on the air than the ones I've mentioned so far. When we were all gathered on chairs on the set, I estimated there were about thirty-five of us who had been present in Studio B at the time Dennis the audioman had been murdered. The group included stagehands, makeup people, cameramen, electricians, lighting technicians, production assistants, computer experts, two assistants to the director, a TelePrompTer operator, people who pulled levers and played with dials and did all the mysterious wizardry that enables a television production to go on the air. We made a glum group, all in all. Several uniformed policemen guarded the two exits to Studio B; none of us had been allowed to leave the scene of the crime. But the police had not arrived for at least fifteen minutes after Cat had screamed, and the killer could have gotten far away.

Cat sat next to me saying little, resting her chin on her hands.

The police were interviewing us individually, leaving the rest of the group to wait their turn. No one was happy to be detained. I heard one electrician say to a coworker that he hoped they were still on the clock. Only Bob Hutchinson seemed his normal jolly self. Across the room, he was telling off-color jokes to a small group of men gathered around him.

"Why don't you just shut up, Bob," Ken Byrnes told him finally. "Have some respect for the dead."

"Hey, I'm sorry the guy was offed," Bob said defensively. "But we were weren't exactly friends. It would be hypocritical for me to pretend my heart was broken about some guy I barely knew."

"What a sensitive human being you are, Bob!" Zeke said sarcastically.

"At least I'm not a hypocrite," Hutchinson said. "And I'm not a killer either."

"You're saying *I* am?" Zeke demanded.

"I'm not saying anything," Bob replied sullenly. "At least not to you."

"Can you believe this group?" Cat asked me in an undertone. "These people can't even mourn without getting into an argument. Peter McDavis sure found an opportune moment to be on vacation in Santa Fe!"

"Very opportune indeed," I agreed. "Incidentally, Cat— what were you doing back there behind the set where Dennis was killed?"

Cat gave me a searching look. "It's a shortcut to my dressing room—there's a side door to the hall. I go that way nearly all the time."

"Let me get this right. You had left Studio B already, hadn't you?"

"Yes. I got to my dressing room, then realized I had forgotten my briefcase. I was coming back to the set when I came across Dennis—it was horrible, Steve, to see him lying there!"

"And the first time you left the set—did you go by that back way?"

"No. The first time I left by the main door. I saw Ken Byrnes there, and I needed to have a word with him. Why?"

"No reason. I'm just trying to get it straight in my mind."

Cat was about to say something when one of the uniformed cops called out my name.

"Mr. Allen, please."

"My turn," I said, rising to my feet and giving Cat a reassuring smile.

"Steve, I hope you don't hate me for getting you involved in this horror show," she said unhappily.

"Not at all, dear. Relax."

I followed the officer out of Studio B and down a long corridor. We went past my dressing room, turned a corner, and came to a door that was marked simply Production Office. Inside two plainclothes detectives were seated at a large desk with a window behind them. I had been inside the windowless television studio for so long now that it was good to see a small slice of the outside world—the Hudson River and a brooding steel-gray sky over New Jersey. It appeared as if Bob Hutchinson's weather prediction of sun and springlike conditions was not going to come true.

"Mr. Allen, perhaps we can have your attention?" one of the detectives said.

"Oh, sorry. Just looking at the sky." I returned with some reluctance to matters closer at hand. The two detectives were as different from one another in size and shape as it is possible to be. One of the men was tall and lanky with a mournful, elongated face and a head that was nearly bald. The other was short and squat with a round face, round body, and a mop of unruly brown hair hiding his ears. They were a real Mutt and Jeff combination. The tall, thin detective wore a dark gray suit that seemed too large for him, while the short one was dressed in a light brown suit that appeared one size too small.

It was Mr. Short who had spoken, and indeed he proceeded to do nearly all the talking—while Mr. Tall looked on in a mournful manner, sighing from time to time and taking notes.

"I'm Detective Sergeant Max Morgenfield," said Mr. Short. "And this is my assistant, Detective Frank Marcotti. Please have a seat, Mr. Allen. We'll try not to keep you longer than necessary."

I sat, eager to show what a fine, cooperative citizen I could be.

Morgenfield consulted his notes and shook his head dramatically. "I can tell you right away, Mr. Allen, this doesn't look good. Does this look good to you, Frank?"

Mr. Tall shook his head in agreement, and stared at me with two of the saddest eyes I have ever seen this side of a basset hound.

"What doesn't look good?" I asked.

Narrowing his eyes at me, Morgenfield spent another few moments reading his notes. I could recognize a psychological ploy when I saw one. Finally he looked up as though he had come to an important decision. "Mr. Allen," he said, "can you explain why your microphone cord was around the victim's neck?"

"My microphone cord?"

"Be very careful, Mr. Allen. The microphone, of course, along with its cord, will be examined by our forensic lab. Do you suppose we'll find your fingerprints on it?"

"On the mike? Well, it's possible, I suppose."

"It's *possible,"* Mr. Short said in a sarcastic aside to his taller partner. Mr. Tall shook his head again, as if now he had heard everything.

"Dennis changed my microphone twice," I told the policeman. "Of course, I have no idea if the mike that was found around his neck was one of mine or not. If it was, then of course it will have my prints on it."

The short detective leaned forward and smiled coldly. "I see you call him by his first name. How well did you know the victim, Mr. Allen?"

"I never met him in my life until this morning," I said heatedly. "As for calling him 'Dennis,' that's the way he was introduced to me—it's his *last* name I don't know."

Mr. Tall affected great astonishment. "No kidding!" he said. I was surprised he could actually speak. His voice, when it came, was low and hoarse, with a New Jersey accent.

"Wait a second," I cried. "This is ridiculous. And I'm not certain that *was* my microphone, anyway. All those small mikes look the same. Besides, I just arrived from California yesterday. I never met Dennis before, or anybody connected with 'Good Morning, U.S.A.,' for that matter. With the single exception of Cat Lawrence, of course."

Detective Morgenfield raised a speculative eyebrow.

"I knew Cat when she was a little girl," I said immediately. "We called her Cathy then. She lived across the street from Jayne and me in California. Her parents were friends of ours. Later she worked in my office for about a year while she was saving money to return to college."

"I see," said the detective. "She's a very beautiful young woman, isn't she?"

I did not compliment his innuendo with a reply, but simply stared at him.

He smiled, at last, the thinnest possible smile, and felt I had won a point in some obscure game we were playing where I did not know all the rules.

"Well, Mr. Allen, perhaps you will do us the favor of describing your morning. We're particularly interested, as you'll understand, with who was where, and exactly when."

I spent the next half hour detailing my movements from 4:00 a.m., when my alarm clock went off, to a few minutes past nine, when I heard Cat scream. Probably it was good thing I was on network television for a portion of that time, and there were plenty of witnesses to corroborate my story. Detective Morgenfield was naturally interested in the trouble with my microphone, but there was not much I could tell him about that. While I was speaking, Mr. Tall continued to take copious notes.

At last, Mr. Short stood up from behind the desk to indicate the interview was at an end. "Thank you for your time, Mr. Allen. You understand we are taking a brief statement from everybody who was in or near Studio B at the time of Dennis Lovelace's death. We're trying to get the overall picture at the moment. We'll compare everyone's statement with what the forensic lab has to tell us, and then we'll probably get back to you for more questions."

"I'm glad to help in any way I can," I said. "Am I free to leave the studio now? My wife is probably worrying about me."

"You're free to go, sir."

I shook hands with Mr. Short, and Mr. Tall as well.

"That's an unpleasant way to die, being strangled," I said.

Detective Morgenfield seemed amused. "Strangled? Who said Dennis Lovelace was strangled, Mr. Allen?"

"Well, the microphone cord. I assumed . . ."

"You assumed wrong, Mr. Allen."

"Then the cord?"

"Probably a bit of window dressing designed to throw us off. The death came about in a different way."

Detective Sergeant Max Morgenfield seemed vastly pleased with himself. I was naturally curious to know how the audioman had died, but I could tell from the detective's smug expression that he was not going to tell me anything more.

"We'll be seeing more of each other, Mr. Allen," he said.

It was at that moment, I think, that I vowed I would beat Mr. Short and Mr. Tall to the punch and discover the killer myself. It's always a mistake, of course, to go into competition with the police. What I should have done was to collect Jayne and take the first commercial jetliner back to California.

Chapter 13

Later in the afternoon I was lying almost asleep in the huge Jacuzzi in a swirl of bubbles on the second floor of our Fifth Avenue duplex when the phone rang, after which it kept ringing on and off all day.

"Poor baby," Jayne sympathized. "You have a dead body on your first day of work, and now people won't even let you soak in a hot bath in peace!"

"It was a worse day for Dennis Lovelace," I said.

Jayne shuddered. "Horrible! Do you think there's any connection with that light nearly falling on Cat's and Peter's heads last week?"

"I don't know what to think," I told her. "But I'm sure as hell going to find out what this is all about."

Jayne fielded the calls for me, at first answering in a flat Midwestern twang, pretending to be a secretary. It's fun to be married to an actress. I was not available to the *Daily News,* the *New York Post,* and two television stations that wished to tape an interview. But I did speak to Cat when she called, talking on the Jacuzzi phone, turning off the jets so I could hear better.

"God, Steve, I've been sitting here wondering if I should call Stephen Kinley and quit the show," Cat said. "I mean, is it worth it, putting up with these horrible people—you saw them today!—and now a murder? I just got off the phone with a friend in San Francisco, who said I could probably have my old job back on the local news there. But I keep coming back to the fact that 'Good Morning, U.S.A.' is my main chance for national exposure. And chances like this generally aren't offered a second time!"

"Cat, if I were you, I wouldn't do anything rash. Just hold tight for the time being until we find out what's going on. But *be careful.* Watch where you go and who you see, for the time being."

"You *are* going to help me, aren't you?"

"I'm going to try. But I need your help. First off, tell me everything you know about Dennis Lovelace."

"Dennis? I didn't know him very well, but he seemed like a real sweetheart. Sort of quiet and shy. I only saw him at work, of course, but he was one of the few people on the set who was even slightly bearable."

"Was he part of one of the different feuding factions?"

"Not at all. As far as I know, he managed to avoid the fighting. He did his job and kept to himself. I'm sorry, but that's about all I know of him."

"Did he ever say anything about his personal life? Was he married? Have a girlfriend?"

"He never said."

"He probably never mentioned where he lived?"

"No . . . oh, wait a second! He *did.* We were talking about Indian restaurants, and he mentioned that there were some wonderful and inexpensive places on East Sixth Street near St. Mark's Place. He said he lived near them in Alphabet City."

"Alphabet *what?*" I asked.

"That's the area between Avenue A and Avenue D. The East Village."

"I see. In the old days we just called it the Lower East Side."

"It's fancier now, at least in certain sections. Some of the old tenements have been gentrified. It's almost fashionable these days—the East Village."

"Do you know anyone who might know Dennis's address?"

"The personnel office would have it. I know one of the women who works there. Would you like me to call her?"

"I'd appreciate that. I'm not sure if I'll discover anything about why he was killed, but his home seems a logical place to start."

"I'll call you back," Cat promised, hanging up.

Zeke Roth called fifteen minutes later. I was still relaxing in the bubbles, but I turned off the Jacuzzi jets a second time when Jayne told me who it was. I was interested in what Zeke had to say.

"Just called to see how you were doing," he told me. "Look, I'm awfully sorry about today. What a hell of a way to start work on the show!"

"It wasn't your fault, Zeke," I told him. "Unless, of course, you were the one who killed Dennis."

He laughed, but not merrily. "I certainly got the third degree from Laurel and Hardy! That Morgenfield and Marcotti—what a comedy act, huh? What about you, Steve? Did you have fun with them?"

"About the same as you," I admitted. "Look, Zeke, I assume you know your cast and crew fairly well. You must have some idea why Dennis was killed."

"I don't have a clue," he told me. "Not even a suspicion. Dennis was a nice guy, really. Can't imagine why anyone would want him out of the way."

"A very quiet person, I understand."

"*Quiet!*" he cried. "Who told you that? Dennis was the life

of the party. Used to keep us all entertained with his wisecracks
and stories. A real lady's man, too. You wouldn't know it by
looking at him, but the women ate him up.''

"Interesting," I murmured, contrasting this in my mind with
the very different picture Cat had given me of the man. "How
long had he worked for 'Good Morning, U.S.A.'?"

"About five years."

"Did you know him away from the job?"

"Not at all. But he'll be a loss to the show. And what a
gruesome way to die!"

"I understand he wasn't strangled."

"Right, Abbott and Costello aren't saying anything about
it, but I just got a call from Dan De Vries in the newsroom.
We have one of our reporters down at Police Plaza with his
ears open, and he got the word. Take a guess, Steve."

"He was hit over the head with a blunt instrument?"

"Nope."

"Stabbed in the back with a dagger?"

"Try again."

"A slow-acting poison?"

"Listen to this—he was stabbed through the heart with something long and sharp and small—like a knitting needle or an
ice pick."

"No kidding!"

"The puncture wound was so small, that's the reason there
wasn't a lot of blood. The cord around his neck was put there
after he was dead. Why, I don't know."

I absorbed this in silence for a moment, considering the
ramifications. My first thought had been that it would have
taken a man to strangle Dennis with an electric cord. Even
when I learned that strangulation was not the cause of death, I
had still been thinking of the male gender. But a long, needlelike
instrument through the heart was a subtle maneuver. More
likely feminine.

"Zeke, you mentioned that Dennis was a lady's man. How do you know that?"

"Just rumors. Bob Hutchinson had gone out drinking with Dennis a few times, and he passed on some wild stories. But you know Bob—not exactly a pillar of accuracy. So maybe the stories of Dennis being a great one for the ladies is like the prediction for sun this afternoon."

"I see. So you don't know if Dennis was married or had a particular girlfriend?"

"No. Why are you interested?"

"Well," I said, "someone dies, and you wonder about them."

"Yeah, I guess so," he agreed. "Life, death . . ." Then his voice brightened. "Anyway, Steve, the reason I called was to make sure you're all right for tomorrow morning. The show must go on, you know."

"Naturally."

"You're a real vet. I appreciate it. I'm going to messenger over some background material on tomorrow's guests to help with your questions. I was going to give them to you this morning after the show, but with Dennis and all . . . hell, it just didn't seem right to talk business."

"I understand, Zeke."

I had earlier explained that I preferred not to be provided with the usual numbered list of questions that are commonly given to talk show hosts and interviewers. I had learned as far back as the original "Tonight Show" that interviews were more—well, organic if I just did a bit of homework about the guests and then let the conversation flow naturally.

Suddenly Roth giggled. "God, I'm a son of a bitch! I really *hate* myself," he said, but in an oddly playful tone.

"What have you done, Zeke?"

"It's not what I've done. It's what I'm *thinking.*"

"Yes?"

"I mean, I've been stressing out the past few weeks with

all the terrible things that have happened. It hasn't been easy, to be the producer of a show from hell. But it just occurred to me that what with that damned light falling from the rafters Friday, and now this thing with Dennis . . . man, our ratings are going to go sky-high!''

"That's for sure."

"The American people love a little blood and gore. Why do you think football is our national pastime rather than ballet? Call it a macabre curiosity, but I'm willing to bet that half of America is going to tune into 'Good Morning, U.S.A.' tomorrow. So you'd better get your beauty sleep tonight, man. We're a huge success!''

A few minutes later, Jayne found me standing in the bathroom with a towel around my waist and a thoughtful expression on my face.

"A dollar for your thoughts," she said, which seemed highly inflationary.

"I was just thinking," I told her, "that my idea of success is fundamentally different from Zeke Roth's."

Chapter 14

There were two more phone calls of interest that afternoon. The first was from Cat, who had come up with a home address for Dennis Lovelace—332 East Fourth Street, which was located between Avenue C and Avenue D in the East Village. The UBS network gave health benefits to unmarried partners, and according to Cat's friend in the personnel office, Dennis had given the name of Heather Dorn, at the same address, as his eligible significant other.

I thanked Cat for the information. "By the way," I said, "are you certain Dennis was the shy, quiet type?"

"Absolutely. At least he was around me. Why?"

"Just wondering. Anyway, I've got to dash. I'll see you tomorrow morning."

I had hardly put down the phone when it rang again. Jayne answered, as my all-purpose secretary—momentarily German. "*Ja?*" she said. "*Dis ist da Steve Allen residence . . . ja . . . Ja . . . ein moment, por favor.*"

She put her hand over the receiver. "It's Stephen Kinley's

secretary. He wants to take us for dinner at the Four Seasons tonight. Seven o'clock. Vat do you say, darlink?''

''I say, there goes my diet. And by the way—with *ein moment* and *por favor,* you have managed to combine approximately three European languages. Four, if we count English.''

Taking her hand from the speaker, she said *''Ja,* Herr Allen vill be delighted to make ze rendezvous *ce soir.* Heiress Allen also. Zeven o'clock, *ja. Ciao.''*

And so our plans for the evening were in place. I would make the journey to the East Village alone and meet Jayne afterward at the Four Seasons for dinner. Jayne, ever the adventurer, wanted to come with me. I had to gently persuade her that Alphabet City was not a good place for a flamboyant redhead in a mink coat. I dressed for dinner but put on one of my older hats and topcoats. We detectives are often called upon to be masters of disguise.

''I'll phone for the limousine,'' Jayne said as I was about to go.

''Sweetheart, you take the limo to the restaurant. I'll be fine with a cab.''

''You're sure?''

''Of course. As a musician, I've traveled to some funky places. And to go to Alphabet City, you gotta be able to talk the talk, and walk the walk. If you dig what I'm saying.''

''Yes, dear,'' said my most understanding wife. ''And you really *were* a hipster, Steve . . . about 1958.''

''Once a hipster,'' I assured her, ''always a hipster.''

Outside it was snowing hard, huge snowflakes drifting down. It was like being inside one of those old-fashioned crystal paperweights. Already several inches of snow had settled upon the cars and streets, covering the dirt and grime of the city. So much for Bob the weatherman. I hailed a taxi for Alphabet City.

Chapter 15

East Fourth Street between Avenues C and D was a block of classic brownstone tenements—narrow buildings squeezed tightly against one another with metal fire escapes hanging on to the outside facades. Each building had a stoop—concrete steps and top platform, to a non–New Yorker—leading from the sidewalk to the first floor. Number 332, however, turned out to be an old house of worship wedged between tenements. I could still make out the outline of HOLY WORD PENTECOSTAL CHURCH from where the letters had been removed at the top of the building. Before I left the taxi, I checked my notebook to make certain this was the correct address. It was. Real estate in Manhattan, being limited, is expensive, and there are people living in fairly odd situations—converted stores, churches, warehouses, factories.

I paid the taxi fare and received a dusting of snow as I stood by the front door of the church searching for some sort of doorbell. An early night had fallen and the wind whipping the snow against my face was bitter cold. The street was empty of people, all in all not a friendly landscape. It occurred to me

that I should perhaps tell the cab driver to wait, but when I
turned to call to him I saw his red taillights disappearing in
the slushy gloom.

I was relieved to find the buzzer and a small square of paper
on which was neatly printed Lovelace-Dorn. I pressed, hoping
for the best, but nothing happened in response. Meanwhile the
falling snow absorbed all sound and made everything seem
unearthly. With the old church, the empty street, and the storm,
I was starting to feel as if I had entered the Twilight Zone. I
buzzed a second time and was about to give up and go away
when a thin voice came through a small speaker near the doorbell.

"Yes?" It was a woman's voice, not inviting.

"This is Steve Allen. I'd like to speak to Heather Dorn."

"The police have already been here," said the voice in a
monotone.

"I'm not the police. This is Steve Allen," I repeated. "I
know this must be a bad time for you, but I was hoping I could
speak with you for just a few moments about your . . ."

Your *what?* I wondered. Boyfriend? Lover? Roommate?
Partner? Our English language does not adequately provide for
the social realities of today, when so many people live together
outside of marriage. I paused for an awkward moment.

". . . your friend," I decided.

"Steve Allen?" she questioned. We weren't getting anyplace
fast.

"You might have seen me on 'Good Morning, U.S.A.'
today?" I added hopefully.

"Oh. *That* Steve Allen. Well, all right, I guess," she said
without enthusiasm. I was glad she was willing to buzz me in
before I turned into a snowman. I went through a large double
door into an entranceway and did my best to shake off the
accumulation of snow from my hat and overcoat. When I passed
through a second double door I found myself at once in the
large open area where the church had once been, only now the

pews were gone and the space had been converted into a sculpture studio. The room was dimly lit with candles and I could vaguely make out huge pieces of metal and stone that seemed to fill every corner. Near where the altar originally must have stood I saw a winged angel, perhaps ten feet tall, made entirely from junk metal—what looked like old lawn mowers, typewriters, car axles, and similar odds and ends that had been cleverly welded together to form a graceful shape. The angel was holding a large lit candle in each of her outstretched arms.

"I'm up here," she said.

"Up where?"

"Seek and ye shall find," she told me. "Bring a glass from the kitchen, and you can share my vodka."

"That's okay," I told her. I had no idea where the "kitchen" might be in this strange household, and vodka has never been of interest. I did locate the young woman, however. She was upstairs in the rear of the church in an area that had once been the choir, now converted into a moderately exotic bedroom. I climbed a narrow flight of stairs and found her sitting, in a lotus position, on a mattress that was covered with an Indian bedspread. Dozens of candles had been set about on the floor in various holders.

She was in her early twenties, quite pretty, wearing jeans and a sweater several sizes too large for her. There was a bottle of vodka in one hand and a glass in the other. "I'm trying to get drunk," she said. "Funny thing, really. I don't drink. One glass of wine with dinner and I'm out of it for the rest of the evening. Anyway, here I'm finally trying to really tie one on, and I'm stone sober. What did you say your name was?"

"Steve Allen."

"Oh, yeah. I remember now."

"And you must be Heather Dorn."

"Yep. In person. . . . Do you think maybe this vodka *is* defective somehow? Could *that* be the problem?"

"What I think, Heather, is maybe you should go easy on the booze. The effect might sneak up on you."

"Yeah, sneak up on me. Like death," she said moodily, staring into the flame of a candle.

Since there were no chairs in sight, I sat down on the floor near the mattress, hoping my creaky joints would be able to rise again. The girl, very pale, had a delicate face and long, curly brown hair. I was at the age myself where I could too easily imagine she had parents somewhere who must be worrying about her because she lived the artistic, Bohemian life in the East Village. The moment I was seated, a black cat sprang into my lap from somewhere in the shadows.

"Whoops," I said. "I love cats, but I have an allergy to them."

"I'm sorry," she said, "but I don't know what I can do about that."

"You can't do a thing," I said, smiling. "But it does mean that I'll only be able to stay here for a short time. Otherwise, there will be a whole lot of sneezing going on. But more importantly I want to tell you how sorry I am about Dennis. I only met him this morning for the first time, but he seemed like a very nice young man."

"Nice," she repeated. "A real nice guy. My Prince Charming. But dead as a doornail. That's a strange expression, isn't it?"

"So it seemed to Charles Dickens," I said.

"Are you sure you don't want any vodka?"

"Positive. Maybe the cat does. How long were you and Dennis together?"

"Ages and ages and ages," she said. "A year and a half."

"Heather, I'm sure the police asked you this—but did Dennis have any enemies?"

"Enemies? How can you not love Prince Charming?"

"I take it, then, he wasn't feuding with anyone?"

"Nobody, nobody. Nice, nice guy. Only feuding with me."

"With *you?* You were having problems in your relationship?"

"No problems."

"Then . . ."

"I kept telling him he should quit that lousy job working for mind-rotting television."

"You wanted Dennis to be an artist?"

"A poet. That's what he really loved to do. Write poetry. I told him television would kill him. Make him a prawn of the industrial-military complex."

"A *pawn,*" I suggested gently.

"Exactly." She took a long swallow of vodka, directly from the bottle.

"Easy," I told her. "Wouldn't you like a nice cup of coffee?"

She shook her head, an exaggerated motion. "Coffee doesn't cut it."

"Now, Heather, was Dennis happy at work? Were there any particular problems he told you about recently with 'Good Morning, U.S.A.'?"

"Problems!" She sighed. "Well, he was afraid about all the accidents."

"Accidents?"

"You know. People tripping over electric cables. One of the electricians got a bad shock, had to go to the hospital. Two weeks ago, a scenery flat somehow got loose and fell over on one of the production assistants. Then there was that spotlight last week. Dennis was spooked."

"Did he have any idea why the accidents were happening?"

She shrugged. "He said it was an unlucky set. The whole crew was spooked. Told him to get out of there. Be a poet. Do what you love to do. But he didn't listen to me."

"Did he talk about people fighting?"

She shook her head. "Only accidents. A cameraman slipped

on some soapy water someone left on the floor—broke his leg. Did I mention that?''

''No. When did it happen?''

''The week before last, I think. Lots of bad things happened. Can't expect me to remember them all.''

Heather took another swig of vodka. It was tough going to get any information out of her, but I remained patient. This had been a bad day for her.

''Were there any friends Dennis had at the studio? People he talked about? Or saw after work?''

She shook her head. ''It was just a way to pay the bills. His heart wasn't in it.''

''Heather—would you describe Dennis as a quiet person, or was he outgoing? I'm trying to get a better picture of him.''

She considered this a moment. ''Sort of in between quiet and outgoing,'' she decided. ''I mean, sometimes he could be very quiet. For days at a time. But then he'd get excited— about ideas, books he had read, music he liked. Then you couldn't shut him up.''

''He sounds very nice,'' I said. I had been thinking of how to get my next question in without being offensive. I threw it out with a smile and in an offhand manner. ''Something of a lady's man, I bet.''

''Not really,'' she said. ''Actually, he was sort of awkward with women.''

I glanced at my watch and saw it was nearly six-thirty. With the snow outside, I was going to be late for dinner at the Four Seasons if I didn't leave soon.

''So you can't tell me anything, Heather—about why someone might want to murder him?''

She shook her head sadly.

''He seemed happy recently? Nothing was bothering him?''

''Sure. Except maybe for that one thing.''

''What one thing was that?''

''Didn't I tell you? This was about two weeks ago. One

evening he was depressed and real fidgety. He kept pacing around downstairs in the studio—it wasn't like him. So finally I asked what was bothering him.''

''And?''

''He said he heard something at work he didn't much like. And he didn't know what to do about it.''

''Heard something?'' I pressed. ''Heard *what,* Heather?''

''I don't know.''

''He didn't tell you?''

''No. He never talked about his job since he knew how I felt about television. He just said . . . I can't remember now.''

''Please, Heather, *think.* This could be important.''

She screwed up her face trying to think. And took another drink of vodka. ''He said . . . he said . . . I just can't remember. It was something about one of the people at work, but I've forgotten now.''

''I know this is painful for you, but please try.''

It seemed to me that one moment Heather was sitting cross-legged on her mattress trying to think, and the next she was crying hysterically. I'm sure the strain of the day had been building to this moment, and now she simply broke. Probably nothing in her young life had prepared her for the pain of such a loss.

I expressed all the sympathetic clichés I could summon forth, and meant them, too, but I knew they wouldn't do any good. Her heart was broken, and only time would heal it. Meanwhile there was no more information I could get from her. And at that point I began to sneeze.

Chapter 16

I couldn't leave Heather Dorn sobbing her heart out by herself in a converted church in the East Village with a bottle of vodka that was three-quarters empty on the evening of her boyfriend's murder.

Unlike Jayne, I am not predisposed to taking responsibility for stray kittens, though maidens in distress *do* pull on a rusty heartstring or two. It was a difficult situation since I was late for dinner with the chairman of the board. I asked Heather where her parents were, hoping they might be induced to fly to the rescue and take care of their daughter. "Somewhere in Saudi Arabia, I think," she answered between sobs. "Or maybe it's Cambodia this month." Apparently her father did something or other for the CIA and got around the globe at a steady clip, with Heather's mother in tow.

"Are there any friends I can telephone for you?" I asked. "Someone who might come over and stay with you?"

She had stopped crying for a moment, but now fell apart again. "I don't want to see them!" she wept, handing me a box of Kleenex for my allergy.

"But why not?"

"Because they're . . . they're Dennis's friends, too . . . and it'll just make me too sad!"

And so, the long and short of it is, I decided to take Heather along with me to the Four Seasons. It was a desperate move. I'm sure she was a young lady who had survived quite well before she met me. But in all conscience I couldn't leave her alone at the moment. She accepted my invitation eagerly enough, saying it would do her good to spend the evening with strangers. Unfortunately, she had gone a bit floppy on me. Since the Four Seasons happens to be one of the most expensive restaurants in the universe, I suggested she put on (and quickly, please) some good clothes. This however required basic motor coordination skills she did not at the moment seem to possess. When she asked me to help her out of her jeans, I decided quickly she was dressed just fine as she was.

Between sneezes I found an electric light switch, spent about ten minutes blowing out candles, and helped Heather into a coat. It was a nice coat, fortunately. Some sort of fake fur, since it is no longer *chic* to wear real fur. But it was elegantly cut and I had the bright idea that she could keep it on inside the restaurant to hide her jeans and oversize old sweater. Just before we left the church, I had to discourage her from bringing along the bottle.

"Heather," I said sternly, "the vodka is a no-no."

"But I'm stone sober," she insisted.

"Because they sell vodka at the Four Seasons, they discourage people from bringing their own supply."

Reminding myself of her grief, I got her out the front door and into the storm. Another three or four inches of snow had come down since I had entered the church, and the East Village looked like a winter wonderland. A few kids were throwing snowballs at each other, but otherwise the street was empty of traffic. Not a taxi in sight. We had to walk all the way to First Avenue before I even caught sight of a cab. But this was New

York, and though the taxi was empty, it passed us by. On Third Avenue we had better luck, but I was so cold I almost wished she had brought the vodka after all.

"You know, there is *something* Dennis told me," she said in the taxi riding uptown.

"About what?"

"About what you were asking me earlier. What he heard that bothered him at work."

"Yes? You remember now?"

"No. I forgot. Do you ever get that feeling, like there's something you can *almost* remember, but when you try to pin it down it sort of—."

"Keep trying," I urged. "It'll come to you. Try to visualize Dennis that day. What was he wearing?"

"His old blue jeans. The ones with the holes in the knees," she said. And then she burst into tears again from imagining him too clearly.

What had Dennis heard? I wondered. And did it have anything to do with getting him killed? Heather put her head against my shoulder and seemed to fall asleep for the last dozen blocks of the taxi ride. I let her be, hoping the sleep would do her good. I had a strong feeling that what Heather had forgotten was of crucial importance and there was no time to lose.

The Four Seasons is in the Seagram Building on Park Avenue, a glass-and-steel tower that was the latest word in modernity when it was built in the early sixties. Now there is a new generation of futuristic skyscrapers, but the Seagram Building still has a certain cold elegance that is unsurpassed, despite the fact that when it was first built I said on the TV comedy show I was doing at the time that I thought, given the building's name, it should be topped with an enormous cork.

Heather refused to wake up when we arrived. I shook her, gently at first, then harder.

"Heather, we're here . . . Heather, wake up, dear."

"Uh," she moaned. "Lemme alone."

"Not a chance. Upsy-daisy. Miles to go before you sleep."

A sprinkling of snow in her face did the trick where mere words failed. The flakes came from a clump on my overcoat which had not melted in the taxi. Heather clung to my arm as I led the way through the atrium up a few stairs to the restaurant.

"Maybe this isn't such a good idea," she muttered. "Who did you say we're meeting for dinner?"

"My wife, Jayne. You'll like her. And the chairman of the board of the network, who happens to be one of the richest and most powerful men in the country. But don't let that worry you, my dear. He's just a brainy, ruthless guy who got lucky."

"I'm feeling a little sick."

"Food will make you feel better."

The Four Seasons is a cavernous room, darkly lit, with huge floor-to-ceiling windows that must be at least thirty feet tall. The windows are draped with shimmering translucent material that keeps people on the street from seeing in. Despite the awesome proportions of the restaurant, the tables sit in warm individual pools of light, and there is a feeling of quiet intimacy.

A hat-check girl took my overcoat and fedora. Before I could stop her Heather shed her coat as well. Before I could get her covered up again I saw the maître d' coming our way with the ruthlessly polite smile of his profession.

"Mr. Allen," he said. "How nice to see you again. But I'm afraid we can't allow the young lady in the restaurant dressed in jeans."

I took the man aside and whispered urgently in his ear. "Good Lord, man, do you know who she *is?*"

He glanced at Heather, then back to me.

"I'm afraid I don't quite recognize her. . . ."

"This is Heather Dorn, probably the biggest name in television. She's *huge.*"

"Oh, right. She's the actress in that new show . . . what's it called?"

"That's the one! And you know how these young actresses

are inclined to dress casually. She's from California, of course—lucky she didn't come in a swimsuit! But Stephen Kinley is expecting us at his table, and I know he'd be awfully upset . . ."

"Say no more. We'll make an exception for such an important star. But perhaps in the future . . ."

"Absolutely. These young people just need to be housebroken," I assured him.

And so we made it past the podium. The maître d' led us through the expensively muted restaurant, over a soft carpet toward a table by a marble pool in the center of the room. We passed a few people I knew, a producer, Norman Lear, and writer Leonard Stern, who gave me a searching look to see me with a pretty young woman a third my age dressed in ratty blue jeans and a loose sweater. I braved it out, smiling as though it were the most natural thing in the world to come into the Four Seasons in such circumstances. I had never met Stephen Kinley, but I hoped he was a progressive, broad-minded sort of chairman of the board.

Chapter 17

Alas, he was nothing of the sort. Oh, well. This was not the first time I had offended the rich and powerful.

Physically, Stephen Kinley the Second was a tall, elegant fellow in his early sixties with carefully combed gray hair and mild blue-gray eyes. He was dressed in a conservative dark blue suit that had a white handkerchief protruding just the prescribed amount from his breast pocket, and a pink face that had a look of being well satisfied with itself. And why not? Stephen Kinley the Second had inherited his wealth and position about fifteen years earlier from his father, Stephen Kinley the First—an irascible but brilliant tyrant who had been the real force in creating the UBS network.

Sitting next to the present Stephen Kinley was a stout, gray-haired matron who I soon learned was Mrs. Edith Kinley, formerly of the Rhode Island Daphneys—a family even wealthier than the Kinleys. Sitting next to Mrs. Kinley, moving around the table in a counterclockwise direction, I was glad to find Mrs. Allen, my own significant other. Jayne was lovely as usual in a velvet, burgundy-colored gown, her red hair up in a simple bun to show her neck. Jayne flashed me a wry smile and rolled her eyes upward, at which I sensed she was finding it heavy-going making conversation with Mr. and Mrs. Kinley and was glad I had arrived.

Mr. Kinley rose when I came to the table, but his polite smile froze when he grasped that the young woman in the jeans and old sweater was not only with me but planning to sit down for dinner.

"Sorry I'm late," I said with a smile. Shaking his hand energetically, and then his wife's, I leaned forward and said quietly: "I'm sorry to add an unexpected guest to our party, but I asked Heather Dorn to join us. She's the girlfriend of Dennis Lovelace, the audioman who was killed this morning. She's awfully upset, and, frankly I couldn't leave her on her own tonight."

Mr. and Mrs. Kinley stared at Heather in astonishment. I sensed that if Dennis had been a star, Heather might have received a more rousing welcome. But the girlfriend of an audio technician! *Really!* their expressions seemed to say. There was nothing for me to do but bumble ahead with the introductions. "Heather, this is Mr. Kinley ... Mrs. Kinley ... and this is my wife, Jayne."

"So pleased to meet you, dear," said Jayne, making up in warmth for the Kinleys' cool. "I was awfully sorry to hear about Dennis. You must be devastated, poor thing ... Oh, waiter, please bring us another chair. We've expanded to five."

"We started our appetizers without you, I'm afraid," said Mr. Kinley sternly. "You're half an hour late."

"I got caught up in the East Village," I admitted.

"The East Village!" Mrs. Kinley cried with a twitter. "My goodness!"

"We've already ordered," her husband said grumpily after we sat down. "I'm having the New York steak. I recommend it highly. It's what I always have when I eat out, don't I, Edith? I don't go in for all this fancy California *nouvelle* business."

"Stephen owns a large cattle ranch in Texas," Edith confided. "He gets awfully annoyed at people who say red meat isn't good for you."

"I've eaten red meat all my life, and look at me!" Mr. Kinley huffed. "Strong as an ox. My father ate red meat before me, and his father before that. None of us were ever sick a day in our lives!"

"I'm a vegetarian," Heather said to the hovering waiter.

"I could bring you a nice pasta primavera, Madame."

"How about a vodka and tonic?" she wondered. *"That's* vegetarian."

"Heather, why don't you have the pasta," I suggested.

"I'm trying to get drunk," she pouted.

"And she's sober as a judge," I assured the Kinleys. Then to the waiter, "My young friend will have the pasta and a mineral water. For myself, I'd like a nice piece of fish grilled with lemon and a drop of olive oil."

"We have some very fresh swordfish tonight, sir."

"Fine. And just some steamed vegetables on the side."

One thing about really good restaurants, the kitchen will make up anything you want, however simple or elaborate. Tonight I was in the mood for simple.

The chairman of the board made a conscious attempt to be friendly, since Jayne and I were his guests, but I could see it was an effort—particularly after I ordered fish rather than a nice slab of red meat.

"Well, Steve, Edith and I just wanted to welcome you to New York and thank you for filling in for Peter McDavis on such short notice."

"Glad I could do it. Is Peter all right, by the way? It *does* seem a bit peculiar taking off so suddenly from the show."

"Oh, Peter was ready for a vacation, even before that incident with the light," Mr. Kinley said. "He and his wife have a lovely hacienda in Santa Fe, and he hardly ever has a chance to get out there and see it."

"His wife *refuses* to come to New York," Mrs. Kinley confided. "She insists on staying in New Mexico. I may be old-fashioned, but personally I think a wife's place is with her husband."

"Well, dear, Santa Fe is supposed to be very charming," Mr. Kinley said.

"I was in New Mexico two years ago," Edith said. "My sister lives there—she married an art dealer. Personally, I think Santa Fe is overrated. It *isn't* Palm Beach, you know? A lot of very *nouveau* people. And that Spanish food is so spicy."

"Mexican," Kinley corrected.

"I know," his wife said.

"I'll take Jackson Hole," Kinley remarked. "They have great steaks in Wyoming."

Making conversation with the Kinleys was a slightly uphill task. While Stephen, Edith, and I discussed the best places to get a steak, Jayne and Heather were having a more interesting conversation about Heather's sculpture. Jayne, who is endlessly curious, has a great knack for getting people to talk about themselves. Frankly, I wished I was involved in Jayne and Heather's conversation rather than slugging away at tedious small talk with the Kinleys.

"I understand there have been quite a series of accidents lately in Studio B," I said to Kinley, steering the conversation away from red meat.

"It's Zeke Roth's fault," the chairman replied sourly. "After all, *he's* the producer—*he's* the one who's supposed to make sure everything runs like a well-oiled machine! I had a good long talk with him Friday afternoon—so let's hope everything is shipshape from now on. Frankly, I told the man he'd be looking for other work soon if these accidents don't stop. You can understand my position, I'm sure. I can't expose the network to a possible lawsuit from some stagehand who's tripped on a slippery floor and broken his neck!"

"What about the heavy light on Friday morning? Have you figured out what happened?"

"We've had a whole team of experts on it. It seems there's a bolt that broke in half—probably the metal itself was defective. A freak accident."

"There was no sign that the bolt had been tampered with?"

"I beg your pardon?"

"I'm wondering about a possible human factor in the accident. With the death of Dennis Lovelace this morning, we have to face the possibility that the light breaking loose was a deliberate act of sabotage. Possibly even an attempt to murder Cat Lawrence or Peter McDavis—or both, as far as that goes."

Stephen Kinley turned red in the face. "Nonsense! It's just a run of annoying accidents, that's all. As I said, Zeke Roth has been running a loose ship, but that should stop now that I've put the fear of God into him. And as for that audio person," he said, lowering his voice and giving Heather Dorn a sideways look, "as a large corporation unfortunately we hire all sorts of people from different walks of life. Who knows what kind of shenanigans this individual was up to. The man lived in the East Village! I shouldn't be surprised if he was taking drugs!"

"Perhaps the autopsy will have something to say about that. Meanwhile, there seems to be an awful lot of tension on the set," I said. "People fighting. Bad feelings that might have exploded into violence."

Kinley narrowed his eyes at me. "I don't have much interest in the personal lives of my employees, Steve," he said coldly. "They can fight among themselves all they want, for all I care, as long as they do their jobs properly. Television is not an easy life, as you well know. It demands personal sacrifice. The tension can lead to broken marriages, people fighting, ulcers, all sorts of unpleasantness. But there are big rewards for those who can tough it out."

"Television," said Heather, joining our conversation, "sucks your brain right out of your head."

"I *beg* your pardon?"

"Might as well get a lobotomy and be done with it," Heather told him. "Did you know that the average American watches five, maybe six hours of TV a day? No wonder this country is in such bad shape!"

The chairman of the board was not happy. "I know *exactly* how many hours a day the average American watches television, young lady," he said. "And believe me, because of television, the modern American knows a good deal more about the world than his grandparents did. Television is a chance to travel, to get the news from distant places, to learn all kinds of fascinating things. Don't you agree, Steve?" he asked, turning his pink face back in my direction.

"There are certainly some very worthwhile shows on TV," I agreed. "And also a good deal of junk."

"It's nothing but a drug," Heather insisted. "Even with the good shows—it's totally passive to watch hour after hour. Turns people into couch potatoes. Like I said, sucks your brain right out of your head."

Jayne's eyes twinkled in my direction, and I smiled back. As someone who has spent the majority of his life working in television, I obviously do not believe the medium is entirely without value. But it was fun to watch Heather have a go at the chairman of the board.

"Of course, even reading a book can be a passive activity," I reminded Heather. "Like a lot of things, television can be a wonderful tool, or it can be a mindless escape. It takes intelligence on the part of the individual viewer to know the difference."

Heather shook her head. "Before television, families used to play musical instruments, or parlor games at night. They used to talk to each other. They read books aloud to their children. Now we have a society of mindless zombies. Personally I think everybody should throw their TV sets out the window."

Fortunately our food arrived at this moment and the sight of a thick New York steak put the chairman of the board in a better mood.

"Yuck!" said Heather, glancing at his slab of rare meat.

He glared at her. I guided the conversation back to matters I found of greater interest.

"I couldn't help but notice this morning that Bob the weatherman and Zeke Roth don't seem particularly fond of one other."

"Oh, that!" Kinley said with a dismissive gesture. "Bob and Zeke are partners, actually. They own a restaurant together over on Third Avenue. I went to their grand opening last year. Not a bad place, really. But it seems they've had some sort of falling out."

"Really? Do you have any idea what about?"

"As I said, I make it a point to stay out of these personal matters. But in this case, I *do* know a little about it. Apparently, they've been arguing about food. Bob wants to keep the restaurant more traditional—steaks, hamburgers, fish and chips. It's a pub, actually, and I think Bob's on the right track here. Zeke, on the other hand, believes they should be doing chichi pastas, and all that."

"This is a cause for argument?" Jayne asked, astonished.

"Well, there's money involved, of course. A different vision of what will be successful."

"I'm surprised they became partners in the first place. What's the name of the restaurant?" Jayne asked.

" 'As You Like It.' A little play on Shakespeare. The decor is like an old English tavern. Lots of atmospheric wood and a bar where they serve a variety of English ales on tap. There's even a dartboard. Of course, there's a number of Brit exiles in Manhattan who love that sort of thing, not to mention the Anglophiles, so it's been successful enough."

"Not precisely our kind of place," Mrs. Kinley added, her nose held high.

"Now, dear, not everyone can afford to eat at the Four Seasons," her husband said with a tolerant smile.

"I got it!" Heather announced suddenly, quite out of nowhere. We all looked at her. She had eaten most of her pasta and seemed almost sober.

"Got what?" I asked.

"I remember what Dennis told me now. About what he heard at work."

"He heard something?" the chairman inquired, interested in Heather for the first time.

"Yes. Steve was asking me about this earlier. A few weeks ago, Dennis came back from the studio awfully upset. When I asked him what was wrong, he said he had heard something that bothered him—he didn't say what though."

"How interesting," the chairman said with a smug smile, implying it was not. "Please go on."

"Well, I just remembered—I didn't pay much attention at the time because I was working on a piece of sculpture. But he said he made a tape."

"A tape of whatever it was he heard?" I asked.

"I guess so. He didn't explain."

"Did you see this tape?"

"No. He didn't tell me where he put it either. But it must be back on East Fourth Street with his other stuff."

It seemed to me that Stephen Kinley the Second, despite a have-it-all pose, was suddenly nervous. I knew where Jayne, Heather, and I were headed after dinner.

Chapter 18

Outside on the streets it was snowing harder than before. New York was in the grip of a major winter storm. We used the limo the network had put at our disposal to ride down to the East Village. There was not much moving about in this weather, and what traffic there was moved slowly.

"I think I've passed from being sober to a huge hangover, without ever being drunk!" Heather complained. She was sitting between me and Jayne, looking miserable. "I'm never going to drink again."

"It doesn't help solve your problems, my dear," Jayne told her gently.

The girl sighed. "It seemed the traditional thing to do, I guess. I'm not sure how good I'm going to be coping with Dennis's death. Right now I'm starting to get really angry about it. Dennis was such a sweet and gentle person! It just seems so unfair that anyone would kill him!" she said. "Why would anyone do that?"

"That's exactly what we hope to find out," I assured her. "With your help."

"Did you notice that anxious look in Stephen Kinley's eye when Heather mentioned the tape?" Jayne asked. "I wonder what he has to hide?"

I put a warning finger to my lips and gestured to the chauffeur at the front of the limo, a middle-aged man named Ron. From where we sat, all we could see was his cap, the back of his head, and two protruding ears. I wouldn't be surprised if he later reported our conversations to someone at the network. Jayne got my point and nodded sagely.

"What?" Heather asked. The girl saw what passed between Jayne and me, but she did not have a suspicious nature.

"I was just thinking what a lovely dinner it was," I told her pleasantly.

"I thought it was all so uptight. God, did you see the way the maître d' looked at me just because I was wearing jeans?" Heather asked. Not only did she not have a suspicious nature, the girl apparently had no innate respect for money. "I've eaten better in little ethnic dives on First Avenue. Anyway, it seems immoral to spend so much money when a lot of Americans are going hungry. I bet an average middle-class family could live for a week on what our bill was tonight."

I smiled. Youth and idealism are an attractive combination.

"Are you selling any of your sculptures?" I asked.

She shrugged. "A bit. There's a gallery in SoHo that has a few of my pieces. But I'm not sure how I feel about the whole gallery game either. Most artists I know in New York care too much about money—I think that spoils the purity of your work."

"Even an artist has to eat," Jayne said.

"Oh, I eat most of the time. Some months better than others, of course. This month I'm doing great because Cat Lawrence bought one of my big pieces for ten thousand dollars."

"Cat bought one of your sculptures?" I asked with considerable surprise. "You *are* talking about my co-anchor on 'Good Morning, U.S.A.'?"

"Sure. Don't you think I'm good enough that someone might buy one of my pieces?"

"It's not that at all, Heather. I just didn't know that you and Cat knew one another. Did she buy your piece from a gallery or from you directly?"

"From me. Dennis brought her down to the church one afternoon and she bought one of my angels that I weld together from all sorts of junk metal and odds and ends. Maybe you saw the angel I have down at the church now—it's the companion piece, nearly identical."

"Yes, I was very impressed by it," I told her. "I was amazed you could take old typewriters and things and put them together into something as beautiful as an angel."

"That's what Cat liked about it. She said . . . well, maybe I shouldn't tell you this."

"No, please tell us. It could be important," I said.

"Well, she said it reminded her of herself. That she was put together like that. A lot of junky old parts, rust and steel that somehow gave the illusion of beauty."

"She said that, did she?" I was seeing my old friend Cat in a new light.

"She bought the one I call *Midnight Angel.* The one I still have at the church is *Angel of the Dawn.*"

"Did Cat know Dennis well?"

"Look, Steve, I know what you're thinking, but you're wrong. Dennis wasn't like that. We were absolutely honest with each other. He and Cat were only casual friends. In fact he told her about me just to make certain she didn't get the idea that he was single and free. I guess he went on a bit, describing the work I do welding junk together into all sorts of shapes and she became interested. That's why she came down to East Fourth Street, to see all the sculpture Dennis had been describing to her. And as I say, she fell in love with Midnight Angel."

"Because it reminded her of herself?" Jayne mused.

"Was that the only time you met Cat?" I asked.

"There was one other time. I saw her a week later when I delivered the sculpture to her brownstone across town. She lives in the West Village, on Bank Street. I hired a truck and two guys to help me move the piece, and she took us all out to lunch afterward at a sushi bar near Washington Square."

"Do you know if Dennis ever saw her outside of work besides that one time when he brought her to Fourth Street."

"I don't think so. Of course, if he just had coffee with her or something after the show, he might have forgotten to tell me. I mean, no big deal. We each have . . . had our separate friends."

Heather had given me a good deal of food for thought. I sensed waves of complications concerning the murder of Dennis Lovelace. For the first time in many years I remembered the incident in Cat's youth when she stole money from petty cash. *Midnight Angel,* indeed. I wondered if there were still some rusty parts rattling about in the undergrowth of Cat's psyche.

I was thinking about these things when the limousine turned off First Avenue eastward onto Fourth Street.

"Look, the sky's lit up," Jayne noticed.

She was right. Peering through the snow I could see an orange glow to the east of us, and it grew brighter as we crossed Avenue A and Avenue B. By the time we reached Avenue C, I was getting a bad feeling. The street was blocked off by a police car with its emergency lights flashing patterns in the snow. Beyond the police car I could make out three fire engines and men rushing about with hoses and equipment.

"Oh, no!" Heather cried.

We emptied out of the limousine, but a policeman stopped us from walking down Fourth Street.

"I live on this block!" Heather cried to the cop.

"What number?" he asked.

"Three thirty-two."

"The old church? That's the building that's on fire, I'm afraid."

"Oh, my God!" she said. Her mouth opened in disbelief. The poor girl—it was simply too much to absorb that her boyfriend might be murdered and her house burn down on the same long day.

The cop was sympathetic. "Come on, I'll take you to the fire captain," he said.

We followed him past the police barricade through the deepening snow halfway down the block. The scene was a nightmare. Dozens of men were shouting and rushing about in apparent disorder. Some of them were using hoses to drench the old church and the buildings on each side with hard streams of water. The situation did not appear promising. Tongues of orange flame and plumes of black smoke were pouring out of the church windows and from the roof. Neighbors were standing about and staring from open windows from across the street. The heavy snowfall gave everything a dreamlike quality, a strange softness. The revolving emergency lights from the fire engines were weirdly beautiful against the falling white flakes, a spectacular show of fractured light.

The policeman who had led us from the corner spoke to one of the firemen, who turned and came our way. He was dressed in a yellow rubber suit and his face was grim.

"You live here, Miss?"

"Yes. In the church. It's my studio. I have to get inside."

He shook his head. "I'm sorry."

"But everything I own is in there! My work. My entire life!"

The captain only continued to shake his head. "I wish I could give you better news, Miss. But we're going to lose the entire structure. At this point we're concentrating on trying to save the buildings on either side. You must have some combustible materials in there. This is a very intense fire."

"I have welding equipment, propane tanks, paint, things like that . . . I'm an artist."

"Well, possibly that explains it then," he said. "I'm afraid there's not going to be much left."

Heather collapsed onto her knees in the snow. "Oh, God, I already lost everything I care about today! How can I lose anything more?" she cried.

Jayne got down onto the snow next to Heather. She took the young woman gently by the arm. "I think you should come with us now, dear," she said. "Fortunately we have a huge apartment with bedrooms we don't even use. You'll stay with Steve and me until you get on your feet again . . . it's going to be all right. You're young and you'll be able to start all over again. . . ."

Heather buried her face in Jayne's coat collar and allowed herself to become encompassed by my wife's compassion. I stood next to the fire captain, feeling angry and helpless.

"You know, after all these years of watching fires, it still breaks my heart to see a young woman like that crying," the captain said.

"Me too," I told him. "Me too."

Chapter 19

"Good morning, I'm Cat Lawrence," Cat said into the lens of camera two. "And in the chair next to me this morning is Steve Allen sitting in for vacationing Peter McDavis. How are you doing, Steve? I bet with all the snow we had overnight, you're wishing you'd stayed home in California."

"Actually, we Californians find snow a real treat," I told her amiably. "When I drove through the streets of Manhattan to the studio this morning, I was struck at how beautiful everything looked. Of course, I was able to get here only because the network sent a four-wheel drive Jeep to my apartment to pick me up."

"Well, let's hope all the people who need to get to their jobs this morning have four-wheel drive as well. What do you have in store for us today, Bob?" Cat asked. And then added, cattily: "Yesterday morning you were predicting sunshine. What went wrong?"

On the monitor, I saw that we had gone to Bob Hutchinson. Despite his size and pudgy face, Bob was able to put on a kind of little-boy charm. He smiled ruefully. "Occasionally Mother

Nature likes to make us weathermen look ridiculous. What happened, Cat, is the jet stream moved quite a bit farther south than I anticipated. In fact, today's storm dumped snow south all the way to West Virginia. In New York City we had fifteen inches overnight, and it's still snowing quite heavily. But the front will start to move out to sea later this afternoon, and we'll be seeing plenty of blue skies. Incidentally, Steve, back in Los Angeles, they're having a near-record heat wave for this time of year. You would be sitting around your swimming pool if you were home today."

"And miss all the fun here?" I mock-protested. "Never!"

"We'll be back with Bob Hutchinson's full weather forecast, a Steve Allen interview with rock star Tony Testosterone, and much, much more in just a moment," Cat told a few million Americans, smiling at each and every one of them with her sunny, good-morning cheer and special intimacy.

The moment the red light on camera number two blinked off, a mighty yawn escaped my lips. By the time Jayne and I had got Heather back to our Fifth Avenue duplex, I managed less than three hours sleep before the inexorable ring of my alarm clock at 4:00 A.M. This wouldn't have been laughs for anybody, but it was particularly rough in my case because my sleep requirements are greatly in excess of the norm. Much to my displeasure I need about ten or eleven hours a night to be in my right mind the following day. I was too old, I told myself, to survive on so little sleep. But I only had to make it through two short hours of live television and then I could spend the rest of the day in glorious bed.

I yawned again.

"Stop it, Steve," Cat said, joining me in a yawn. "It's contagious."

"Maybe we should just call the show, 'Good Night, U.S.A.' and put everyone to sleep with a lullaby," I suggested. "What were you up to last night, Cat?"

"I stayed home and planned to get an early night. But I

didn't sleep well. I kept thinking of that poor man, Dennis Lovelace.''

Cat and I were sitting behind our desk on the set of our fake living room while commercials flashed by on the monitors. I tried to gather my sleepy brain into some semblance of focus.

"Cat, you misled me yesterday," I chided smilingly. "You said you didn't know where Dennis lived and needed to check with the personnel office to give me his address. But actually you had been to his house, that converted church on East Fourth Street, to buy a piece of sculpture from his girlfriend, Heather."

Cat's green eyes looked up directly into mine. I could almost see her brain ticking. I was willing to bet she would come up with something convincing, but, before she could speak, Bob Hutchinson came storming over from his position at the far side of the stage in front of the blank blue screen. The chummy, on-camera smile was definitely gone from his face.

"Listen, bitch, don't ever do that to me again," he hissed at Cat. "When I make a mistake with a weather prediction, I don't want to be reminded of it the next day."

"Don't call me a bitch, you fat slob," Cat shot back. "I was doing you a favor, making a joke of it."

"Just don't do it again. Ever, you hear me? The American public has a collective memory of about two and a half minutes. If you hadn't mentioned my prediction yesterday, no one would have remembered it. You made me look like a fool."

"Oh, dear me!" Cat told him with mock-contriteness. "I would never want to make *you* look like a fool, Bob."

He turned red in the face. "You just watch your step, kid. Or you just might find yourself out of a job."

"Fifteen seconds!" called the floor manager. Bob hurried back across the stage to his weather station. With this much venom in the air, it wasn't so easy to turn on instantaneous smiles the moment the cameras recommenced their live broadcast. But these were professionals. From watching the show that morning, the television public might easily believe that Cat and Bob were the very best of friends.

We got through the next section. Cat and I chatted a bit, we cut to Carol and Dan in the newsroom, chatted a little more, and then went to Bob for a full national weather report. New York, he insisted, was going to be bathed in sunshine by midafternoon, and this lovely springlike weather would last until the weekend, when we might expect some light rain. I wasn't fooled. I knew enough by now to be prepared for a typhoon, a blizzard, or anything in between.

I wondered how a weatherman who so rarely managed an accurate prediction got to keep his job. Then came yet another mystery concerning "Good Morning, U.S.A." While Bob hammed it up with the weather, I noticed a young man with a shaved head, an unshaved chin, and a gold ring through his left nostril being seated in the interview corner, the two armchairs across the stage. I presumed this must be Tony Testosterone, the international rock star whom I had never heard of until that morning. A new audioman—a young man who until yesterday had been Dennis Lovelace's assistant—was feeding a microphone wire up through the inside of Mr. Testosterone's T-shirt, which had PARTY NAKED written in large letters across the front. I was glad, despite such a motto, that my guest had consented to dress for his network appearance. Along with the T-shirt, he was wearing jeans with holes in the knees and ratty old sneakers without socks.

"Good luck!" Cat murmured, following my gaze.

"Why," I asked her, "did Roth schedule two interviews about rock musicians so close together?"

"The philosophy around here is to go for the young audience," she explained.

I returned my attention to Cat herself. "You were saying, my dear."

"About not knowing where Dennis lived? But I *didn't* know, Steve."

"But you went there, Cat. I don't understand."

"Look, it's simple. I didn't want to say anything yesterday, but there was just this little spark between Dennis and me."

"Spark?"

"A minor flirtation. Nothing earthshaking. You know, he was kind of cute, and I saw him every morning, five days a week. And it was slightly intimate sometimes when he would hook me up with a microphone, threading the wire though my jacket or blouse. A few times our eyes met while he was getting me wired, and I knew we were both thinking the same thing. Actually, I've been too career-oriented the last few years to have much of a private life, and I guess I was feeling a little lonely."

"Go on," I said.

"There's nothing more to it. Just a few looks back and forth. As I told you yesterday, he was quiet and shy, and he certainly didn't come on to me in an aggressive way. We talked now and then about the city and restaurants and impersonal things. When he said he lived in the East Village, I asked about the art scene down there—I'm curious about things like that—and he told me he had a woman friend who did wonderful sculpture out of scrap metal and junk, welding unlikely objects together into beautiful shapes. When he described the two angels she had done, they really sounded marvelous to me, and I asked if he would set up an appointment so I could see them."

"Wait a second, Cat. You said yesterday you didn't actually *know* that Dennis lived in the East Village, but you assumed it from talking about Indian restaurants in the neighborhood."

"What is this, Steve? The third degree? Yes, it was something like that. We were talking about the Indian restaurants on East Sixth Street near St. Mark's Place—you should try them sometime, by the way. Wonderful food, and inexpensive."

"Cat."

"I'm not evading your question. Frankly, I forget exactly how I knew he lived in the East Village. Maybe he mentioned it. Maybe I just assumed it from what he said. But the point is, I didn't know that Dennis actually lived at the converted old church on East Fourth Street. He didn't tell me that. I assumed Heather Dorn was his girlfriend—though he didn't tell me that either. He was leaving the door open just a little, you see, that something might happen between him and me.''

''You didn't see his clothes there at the church? Any of his belongings?''

''Goodness, Steve, you're serious about this, aren't you? You think I'm lying to you?''

''No, it's not that at all, Cat. But a murder has been committed and it's essential to sort out all these small details.''

''Are you saying I'm a suspect? Good God, I was sitting by your side on-camera when the murder took place!''

''Well not exactly, Cat. We were off the air, and you had been gone about five or six minutes, if you recall. Now, of course, you're *not* a suspect, at least not in *my* mind. But inconsistencies bother me, and I'm trying to get the entire picture straight. So about Dennis's belongings . . .''

''I only went into the downstairs part of the church, Heather's studio. I didn't see *anyone's* clothes or belongings, only sculpture. I fell in love with the piece she calls *Midnight Angel* and decided I must own it, though ordinarily I'm not a big collector of art.''

''Heather said you identified with it.''

Cat laughed. ''You bet *Midnight Angel!* That's me!''

''Thirty seconds!'' cried the floor manager. Cat and I had whispered our way through Bob's weather report and a string of commercials. Now I had to make a quick dash over to the interview corner and my guest.

Cat held my hand for a moment while I was standing up from our desk.

''Look, Steve, years ago when I stole that money from your office . . .''

"Cat, you were just a kid back then. I've forgotten all about that."

"No, you haven't. And I don't blame you either. It's why you're suspicious of me now, isn't it? But I swear to you, I'm telling the truth."

"Of course you are," I said with a reassuring smile.

"Mr. Allen, please!" urged the floor manager.

It was time to rock and roll. I dashed across the stage to say hello to my guest before we actually went on the air. But in my mind, the image of Cat Lawrence would not quite fade. So beautiful, cool, and elegant. But could you really trust a midnight angel?

Chapter 20

"A year ago he was playing in a bar band in Seattle. Six months later he was signed by Rush Records. Today he has the number one selling album in the country. I'd like to welcome an American success story, Tony Testosterone . . . good morning, Tony. Thank you for braving the blizzard and making it to the studio today."

"A pleasure to be here, Mr. Allen," he replied in a raspy voice.

"I hope you don't mind if I ask you this, but I have to inquire about your name. I understand from your bio that your real name is John Percival and that originally you wanted to be a high school math teacher. I'm wondering how a nice young man named John Percival, a future teacher, turns into Tony Testosterone and sells millions of records."

"Well, like I'd been playing music ever since the seventh grade, but I just wasn't getting anywhere with the name John Percival on the posters outside of clubs," he informed me. "I was kind of nerdy, to tell the truth. Wore nice slacks and clean shirts and a conservative haircut. Looked more like an honor student, which I was, than a rock 'n' roller. I thought I'd need a real job to support myself, so I was studying to be a math teacher. But music was always my first love.''

"And then . . .''

"A friend of mine convinced me to change my image. Shave my head, find a new name. Frankly I thought it was a lot of BLEEP because for me music was the thing, not the haircut. But I said to myself, what the BLEEP, might as well give it a try. Anything was better than teaching BLEEPing math to BLEEPing children who are probably all too stoned anyway to listen to a thing I tell them.''

By this time I suppose America had become accustomed to hearing foul-mouthed language on television. The network was actually partially protected against it by a two-second tape delay with the result that the offensive terms were replaced by the familiar high-pitched tone. Testosterone himself, however, assumed that his ugly message was getting through.

"So you became Tony Testosterone?''

"Right. The music's the same, though. I haven't changed a note of the songs I used to play as John Percival. It's not my fault the country's full of BLEEPing idiots who only care about merchandising. I figure the joke's on them.''

Tony Testosterone, *née* John Percival, was not a pleasant individual, nor did he seem particularly thrilled at being a rock star. Say what you like about the rebellious kids of the sixties and seventies—at least they had some fire in them. The new crop of rebellious youth, the so-called Generation X, often seem more dead than alive. There are more zombies among them.

I was asking Tony what he planned to do with all his money—"Oh, I don't know. Not much, really. Maybe get a gun and shoot myself. Ha! Ha!''—when I noticed the diminutive figure of Sherry Gold, our show's astrologer, standing next to camera three. She was gesturing to me, trying to get my attention, frantically pointing up into the studio rafters.

"I understand the name of your album is *Might As Well*

Blow Your Brains Out," I said to Tony as I glanced discreetly upward. "Do you think that is a good message to give to the nation's young?"

"Why not?" Tony said, following my glance. "What do the kids have to look forward to, anyway? Crime, unemployment, AIDS, pollution, a declining standard of living. Probably another world war. Might as well get it over with, man."

Apparently Tony was not about to join the Optimists Club any time in the near future. What we both saw in the rafters filled me also with an impending sense of doom. One end of a metal bar that held half a dozen lights had come completely loose over our heads. The situation overhead seemed stable but precarious. At any moment the heavy lights might slide off the dangling piece of metal and fall to where we sat below.

"Tony," I said, "I think this might be a good time to run your new video."

He nodded dumbly, unable to speak.

"The video's not on-line yet," Ken Byrnes, the director, hissed through my earpiece.

I smiled somewhat insanely into camera three. "We'll be back with Tony Testosterone's new video, the number one hit in the nation," I said forcefully, "after these messages from our friendly sponsors. . . ."

"What the hell?" Ken exploded into my ear.

But I continued to smile into the camera until he was forced to cut away into an unplanned break.

"I think we had better stand up very quietly and tiptoe out of here," I said to Tony when we were off the air.

"I'm too scared to move!" he gasped.

"I thought that with crime, AIDS, and unemployment, we might as well just blow our brains out?" I wondered.

"I thought so, too," he managed. "Until I looked up and saw death hanging over my head!"

"Come on, we'll move on the count of three," I told him. "One . . . two . . . THREE."

We stood and walked briskly away. When we were out of danger, well away from the interview corner, I looked around for Sherry Gold to thank her for spotting the hazard overhead. But she was nowhere to be seen.

Ken Byrnes and Zeke Roth were storming our way from the control booth.

"Are you guys trying to kill me?" Tony screamed. Now that he was safe, he had gone hysterical thinking of his near bout with death. "I'm going to sue this network for every cent you got! You're going to wish you hadn't put *me* in the hot seat. You bastards! You miserable sons of bitches!"

I'm afraid Tony's testosterone failed him utterly in this his moment of need. He collapsed weeping near camera three. "I almost *died* there!" he moaned. "My nerves are shot. God knows if I'll ever be able to sing again!"

While Tony carried on, Zeke and Ken stared gloomily upward at the broken light bar.

"This is the last straw," Ken said. "I'm going to cancel today's show. We'll air an old movie instead."

"Hell, we will!" said Zeke. "Not when *my* ass is on the line with Stephen Kinley! Steve, you and Cat can improvise, can't you? Talk about the blizzard for five minutes . . . people never get tired of hearing about the weather. We'll use up some time that way, and then do your last interview on the main set. Meanwhile, let's put some chairs up or something to barricade the unsafe area. We'll take care of the broken light bar after the show. . . . By the way, where the hell is Cat?"

"She must have gone to powder her nose," I suggested.

"Damn! She'd better hurry back! I'm going to have a heart attack one of these days over this show! Sometimes I ask myself, is anything worth all this aggravation? You see what I have to put up with, Steve!"

Zeke was talking a mile a minute, seeming close to a nervous breakdown, when someone on the set screamed. It was a blood-curdling, high-pitched cry of terror. At first I thought it was

Tony suffering a relapse of fright, but he was blubbering quietly a few feet away from where I was standing. Everyone peered about anxiously trying to locate the source of the new disaster.

Then came another scream, not so high-pitched or terrified. "Over here! In the same place as yesterday!" cried Debbie Driscoll, the production assistant.

Ken and Zeke and I ran around to the back of the set, and there in the shadows among the two-by-fours and cables was a crumpled body. I was feeling a disagreeable sense of déjà vu.

I knelt by the body. It was not a man this time, but a woman. My heart just about stopped beating when I saw who it was: Cat. I put a finger to the pulse on her neck.

"She's alive!" I said. "Someone call an ambulance quick!"

"Thirty seconds to airtime!" cried the frantic floor manager. "What the hell are we going to do?"

"Steve, take your place, please," Zeke pleaded. "We'll get an ambulance, we'll take care of Cat . . . but meanwhile the show must go on!"

"Not on your life," I told him. "This show is dangerous to a person's health."

At that moment, Cat stirred to consciousness. She looked about with a dazed expression and then sat up painfully, rubbing her head.

"What happened?" she asked.

"Thank God you're all right! Someone attacked you," I told her. "Did you see who it was?"

She shook her head. "No."

"What were you doing back here, Cat?"

"I don't remember . . . I heard something, I think."

"Well, don't worry about it now. There's an ambulance on the way."

"Steve! You gotta finish the show!" Zeke cried as the seconds ticked down to airtime. "I beg you. I'm a ruined man if you don't pull through for me!"

"I'm okay, Steve. Do it," Cat told me.

Still I hesitated. I could tell that Cat was in pain despite her assurances that she was all right.

I shrugged. Finishing the show was about the last thing I felt like doing, but since Cat seemed out of danger, I thought it best to carry on.

"All right," I said to Zeke. I made it back in front of the cameras with half a second to spare.

Chapter 21

Cat Lawrence was taken to the emergency room at the Doctor's Hospital. I finished the show by myself somehow, ad-libbing like crazy, filling in for Cat's absence with an expanded report on the effects of the winter storm on the East Coast. During a commercial break I asked if there was a piano available and Zeke had one rolled in from the next set, which made it possible for me to deliver a little ad-lib essay on the comparisons between the popular music of today and that of the Golden Age, a roughly thirty-year period covering the 1920s, 30s and 40s. That was the time, I explained, in which composers still acknowledged as the greatest of the century, had given us their best work. I was, of course, referring to Jerome Kern, Cole Porter, Hoagy Carmichael, Duke Ellington, Irving Berlin, Harold Arlen, George Gershwin, Jimmy VanHeusen and a few others. I also expounded upon the distinction between what lyricists such as Ira Gershwin, Johnny Mercer, and Mitchell Parish did for a living and what was now passing for coherent material in the popular market. This segued into taking a few phone calls from viewers, some of whom wanted to know why the program was so different this morning and others who had sensed that there was something definitely wrong and wanted to know why the details were not being shared. Meanwhile no one went anywhere near the dangling light bar with its ton of death waiting to fall. When nine o'clock came and we went off the air, I can't ever remember being so relieved a show was finished.

"Any word on Cat?" I asked Zeke.

"She's okay. It turned out to be only a small concussion. A blow on the head. Thank heaven for that, at least. I don't mind telling you, Steve—if one more thing goes wrong on this show, I'm about ready to commit hari-kari."

Zeke's hair was messed up, his eyes were bulging, and he certainly seemed close to a nervous breakdown. "So take good care of yourself, Steve," he said wildly. "If anything should happen to you, I just couldn't handle the stress."

"Easy, Zeke," I told him. "Cat's the one in the hospital at the moment, not you."

"She's okay, I tell you. Sherry called the hospital to see how she was doing. Apparently they took an X-ray and sent her home. That chick has a hard head!"

"Zeke, I'd like to phone Sherry later to thank her for spotting that broken light bar. Do you have her number?"

"Stop by my office on your way out. My secretary will give it to you. Her name is Candy."

As I left Studio B, Zeke was anxiously watching a crew of workmen who were attempting to bring down the heavy light bar with cables and pulleys without destroying the set underneath. I went to my dressing room, changed into my street clothes, and then stopped in the production office before leaving the building. Zeke's secretary, Candy, who I found in an outer room sitting behind a computer screen, was blond, young and shapely, wearing a tight pink sweater, the sort of secretary people make tasteless jokes about. She was almost painfully perky.

"Oh, Mr. Allen! I enjoyed the show today!"

"You're the only one who did, I'm afraid. Mr. Roth said if I stopped by the office, you would give me Sherry Gold's home number."

Candy punched a few buttons and brought up Sherry's number and address on her computer screen. When she pushed another button the printer next to the screen whirled into motion and gave me what I wanted.

"Can I use your phone?" I asked.

"Sure, why don't you use the phone in Mr. Roth's office."

I didn't suppose Sherry would be home yet, but I wanted to give Cat a call to see how she was feeling. I passed through an inner door into Zeke's office. It was what you would expect for an important TV executive. The room was spacious with a large desk near the tinted floor-to-ceiling windows. At the far side of the room there was the standard arrangement of couch, two matching armchairs, and a glass coffee table. A bookshelf crammed with scripts and books, a few paintings on the wall, a photograph on the desk of an attractive thirtysome-thing woman and two small children.

Conscious that I was in someone else's space, I sat down behind Zeke's desk and used the phone to call Cat. She answered on the second ring.

"How's your head?" I asked.

"Sore!" she said with a rueful laugh. "I'm going to have a bump on the back of my head for a few days, but otherwise I'm okay. Frankly, I was more worried about you, Steve. How did you finish the show without me?"

"The world will little note nor long remember," I said. "Tell me what happened."

"I wish I could. One moment I was walking along, the next moment I was lying on the floor, coming back to consciousness with you standing above me and my head hurting like crazy. Someone must have hit me from behind, but I don't really know. It's a complete blank."

"What were you doing back there behind the set, Cat?"

"I don't even remember that, Steve. It's the weirdest thing. The doctor in the emergency room told me that memory can get a little screwy with a knock on the head, though probably everything will come back to me in a day or so."

"Right after you woke up, you told me you thought you had heard something back there behind the set, and that you went to investigate—do you remember telling me that?"

"No, I don't. I guess I still have a few bolts loose. I'm sorry not to be more helpful, Steve. The police asked me the same questions of course—those detectives Morgenfield and Marcotti characters. But I couldn't help them either."

"Well, you just get some rest, my dear, and I'm sure it will come back to you."

"I'll let you know as soon as I remember anything."

I let Cat go after promising I'd call later in the evening to see how she was doing. Then I tried Sherry Gold's number. I expected to get her answering machine, but she answered in person and recognized my voice immediately.

"Steve! How nice of you to call!"

"I wanted to thank you for spotting that broken light fixture above my head and letting me know about it. How in the world did you ever happen to look up there, Sherry?"

"I can't quite explain it, Steve. I just had a feeling something was wrong. I'm psychic, you know."

"Ah," I said politely, given that I am skeptical by nature.

She laughed. "You say that like an unbeliever—don't deny it! I read your book *Dumbth*. I don't mind. Most people don't believe in psychic phenomena. Doesn't faze me a bit. Nevertheless, I trust my own instincts in these matters. I had a strange sense of danger. It was like something—or rather *someone*— led me to walk around the set and look up in time to see that broken light bar. You're probably going to say I'm crazy, but I'm convinced it was Dennis who led me there."

"Dennis? You mean . . ."

"Dennis Lovelace. Yes, I know he's dead, but I had a good long talk with him last night."

The last thing I was in the mood for was a fuzzy-minded New Age clairvoyant, but a detective must persevere. "When you spoke to Dennis last night, what did he tell you?"

She lowered her voice dramatically. "I can't tell you over the phone, Steve! Why don't you come to my apartment this afternoon, and we'll have a long talk."

"Well, all right," I said, trying to summon the energy. "Look, Sherry, I'm exhausted—I had about three hours of sleep last night. What I'd like to do is go back to my apartment for a nap and maybe catch you late in the afternoon."

"Come for tea," she offered. "At four o'clock. I live on West Eighty-sixth Street just off West End Avenue."

"Look forward to it," I lied.

I put down the phone. I was so exhausted I felt like a zombie. I was tempted to put my head on Zeke Roth's desk and simply fall asleep. Yet as I sat there a flicker of curiosity got the better of me. I don't ordinarily rifle though people's desks, but a murder had been committed and several more deaths had nearly occurred as well—including my own if that light bar had chanced to fall at an inopportune moment. A detective, I told myself, is *supposed* to be nosy. And Zeke Roth, frankly, was as good a suspect as any.

I opened the top center drawer and found stamps, rubber bands, paper clips, pencils, and erasers. But with the next drawer I opened—the top left—I came upon something a lot more interesting. A huge pistol, a Colt .45 that looked like something Wyatt Earp might have used. It was sitting next to a box of bullets. Was this a normal office item, I wondered, for a TV executive? Perhaps. We live in an age where paranoia has run amuck, and some people simply love guns.

I lifted the revolver and found a piece of paper underneath. The paper was a bill from Gene Ptak, Private Investigations, and it was itemized as follows:

Surveillance	
Two operatives,	
37 hours @$150 per hour	$5550.
Incidental expenses	1000.
(payoffs)	
Total due:	$6550.

A .45 revolver, surveillance, and payoffs! Suddenly I was no longer even slightly sleepy. I wrote down the Sheridan Square address of Gene Ptak, Private Investigations, and then I got out of Zeke Roth's office before he could return and catch me going through his personal effects.

Chapter 22

Snow was still coming down lightly but in great volume upon the streets of Manhattan, and the mechanics of getting around town had become increasingly difficult. From listening to Carol and Dan reading the headlines this morning, I knew that airports were closed, subways were running erratically, trains had stopped completely, and the mayor had asked everyone to stay home and off the streets, except for emergencies. To put it succinctly, New York was paralyzed.

Only four-wheel drive vehicles, a few cars with tire chains, and snowplows were moving about the city streets. Unfortunately the network's Jeep was in much demand—it would pick me up tomorrow morning so I could make it on time to work, but it was not available at the moment. This left me with an unexpected dilemma. I stood outside the studio with the snow swirling down around me, pondering my options. I watched enviously as one of the crew members from ''Good Morning, U.S.A.'' left the building, strapped on a pair of cross-country skis, and skied happily away down Forty-eighth Street.

''Mr. Allen!'' I heard someone shout. I peered up and down

the snowy street to see who had called my name. "Mr. Allen! Over here!"

Across the street I saw a taxi driver waving at me. He was a huge fellow with a beard and a broad, round face, sitting in the most decrepit, beat-up yellow taxi I had ever seen. There were dents in the doors and the fender, and the windshield was cracked, held together in one place by silver tape.

"Mr. Allen! I recognize you from ze boob tube. You want ride?"

"Well . . ."

Without waiting for my answer, the huge bear of a man did a U-turn and brought his wreck of a taxi to where I was standing by the curb.

He had a thick Slavic accent. "Come on, I take you vere you vant to go."

"I was hoping to go to Sheridan Square," I said with some hesitation. "Do you think your cab will actually make it there in this weather?"

His booming laugh made the taxi shake. "Vere I used to live in Russia, ve vould not even call this a snowstorm! This only a little piddle-paddle passing cloud!"

I still hesitated, being somewhat fond of my skin.

"Mr. Allen, I big fan. I take you safely vere you vant to go."

It was the best offer at hand. The only offer, as a matter of fact. So the ex-Russian untied the passenger door—yes, it was held shut by a piece of clothesline—and soon we were off on our merry way through the blizzard, sloshing through the snowdrifts in a manner more like a speedboat than a car. I have survived a Learjet plunging toward earth, I told myself. I hadn't even been killed that morning when a light bar broke loose over my head. Surely I could survive a mere taxi ride to Greenwich Village.

There was a silver samovar next to the driver in the front seat. "You vant *chai* . . . nice cup of tea?"

"No, thank you." I glanced anxiously to his taxi license on the dashboard to make certain he *had* a license, and saw that his name was Boris Vladinovsky.

"Where did you live in Russia, Boris?"

"St. Pete," he said. "Ve used to call her Leningrad, of course."

"You drove a taxi there?"

Again the booming laugh. The entire cab bounced up and down on ancient shock absorbers and for a moment I thought we were going to bounce clear off the road.

"I vas nuclear physicist. Now I start all over again in America, drive taxi. Not so bad. Life goes on."

There are some interesting people driving New York cabs. Boris certainly knew how to drive through deep snow. He executed a thrilling skid while making a right turn onto Seventh Avenue that made me feel like I was in the Winter Olympics. Yet somehow we stayed on the road, and I had faith that he knew what he was doing.

"Boris," I said, "If we actually get to Sheridan Square in one piece, how would you like to stay with me for the rest of the day? I need to get around a few places this afternoon, and I think only a Russian or an Eskimo can handle Manhattan on a day like this. I'll make it worth your while, of course."

"Delighted!" he boomed. "And you pay me vatever you vish."

And so I had found myself an unlikely chauffeur. Seventh Avenue was nearly empty of traffic, and New York appeared an exotic white and unfamiliar land. It took me some time to realize that the soft, snowy mounds lining each side of the street were in fact parked cars that had been completely buried in the blizzard and by the few snow plows operating. The address I had in Sheridan Square was for a musty old building above a restaurant. From the outside, not even the fresh snow could disguise the shabbiness of the place.

"You sure you vant go in a place like that, Mr. Allen?" Boris asked, eyeing the building through his cracked windshield.

"If I don't come out in a half hour, send for the cavalry," I told him.

"Cavalry?" Boris puzzled. "This is ze place Christ died?"

"That's another cavalry," I assured him. "Never mind. I'm going to be okay."

I left Boris in his taxi and entered a dim hallway. There was a row of mailboxes with buzzers underneath. I was able to make out a buzzer with Gene Ptak, P.I., written on a small card. I rang, far from certain I would get a response. On a day like this, many people were probably not in their offices. I was about to give up and return to Boris in the cab when a loud answering buzz opened the door to the inside hallway. I walked in. There was no elevator, and the narrow stairs were dark and old.

"Up here! Top floor!" a man's voice shouted from the top of the stairwell.

I trudged up four flights of stairs, taking a short rest on landing number three. The walls were painted an ugly avocado green, and nothing seemed entirely clean. From a closed doorway I heard piano music coming from someone's stereo. I knew the album—it was Vladimir Horowitz's final concert in Moscow—and the familiar music gave me the energy to climb the last flight. A bare lightbulb shone in the hallway at the top of the stairwell but I didn't see any sign of the man who had called down to me. There were four closed doors off the top landing, and I read each of them before I found a small, faded card that said Gene Ptak, P.I.

The door was unlatched and it opened with a creaky whine of rusty hinges under the pressure of my knock. I found myself in an office that was so old-fashioned I felt I had entered a time warp. There was a rolltop desk piled high with papers, a swivel chair, a huge manual typewriter. The air smelled of stale cigarette smoke and the window to the street was nearly opaque with yellow dust. The mood was 1940s film noir. All it needed was for Humphrey Bogart to step through a door. But there was no one in sight.

"Mr. Ptak?" I called.

I stepped into the office. There was an open door leading into a bedroom, and on the bedside table I saw a cigarette burning unattended in an ashtray.

"Mr. Ptak!" I called again. I stepped into the bedroom and I felt something hard and cold pressed into my back.

"Don't move, buster," a voice whispered hoarsely in my ear. "Or you'll find yourself with a second belly button!"

I smiled, despite the danger. I think I had been waiting all my life for someone to say a line like that to me.

Chapter 23

We did not get off to an auspicious start.

"Actually, that line about the second belly button would be more appropriate," I told him, "if you were holding the gun on me from the front. If you're going to use a cliché, use it correctly, I always say."

"Wise guy!" he hissed. "Put your hands on your head and turn around real slow. Try any funny business, and I'll blow you away."

"Actually," I said, "I do funny business for a living, but I—"

"Shut the hell up!" he snapped.

I did as he instructed and turned to see a man who was in his late forties with dark, short-cropped hair. He was overweight with a pale, babyish sort of face and piercing brown eyes. He was badly shaved and there was a haggard, unhealthy look to him. He was dressed in a wrinkled, dark brown double-breasted suit with a bow tie. The gun was in his left hand and it seemed huge.

"Gene Ptak, I presume?"

"I'll ask the questions."

"Fine. Meanwhile I suggest you stub out the cigarette burning in your ashtray. It's bad enough to destroy your health—
you shouldn't create a fire hazard as well."

"I'm trying to quit," he said mournfully. "But why worry
about lung cancer when there's a bunch of guys trying to kill
you?"

"Who's trying to kill you?"

He gave me a long look. "Not you, I guess." He stuffed
his huge pistol into a leather shoulder holster beneath his brown
jacket and then walked to the bedside table to put out his
cigarette.

"So you're that Steve Allen guy," he told me.

"Yes."

"You look older in person."

"How old is your set? Now we can stand here and act
tough, or we can talk about why Zeke Roth hired you to put
a surveillance on somebody and make a thousand dollars' worth
of payoffs."

"Let's talk in the office," he suggested, walking from the
bedroom toward his cluttered desk. He gestured me to a chair
facing him. "We gotta get one thing straight. Mr. Roth is my
client, and anything that has transpired between him and me
is confidential. I betray a client for nobody, certainly not for a
dude who breezes in here out of a snowstorm. You got that?
It's like the relationship between a priest and the guy in the
confession booth. A sacred trust."

"I can pay," I told him. "How much would it take to break
that sacred trust?"

He held up the palms of hands toward me, shocked. "I do
not take bribes," he said in a wounded tone. "However, you
may hire me. Then *you* will be my sacred client."

"You mean, if I hire you, then you'll tell me what I want
to know about Zeke Roth?"

"Put it this way," he said carefully. "I'll investigate the

matter. And my clients rarely go away without what they came for.''

"And how much would it cost me to become your client?''

"A five-hundred-dollar retainer will cover a little over six hours of my time at seventy-five dollars an hour.''

"But I don't need six hours of your time!" I complained. "Probably about half an hour will do.''

"Take it or leave it,'' he told me.

"All right,'' I agreed. "But I don't have that much cash on me. You'll have to take a check.''

"No checks. But I do accept credit cards.''

I looked on with some amazement as he took out a high-tech credit card processing machine from his ancient wooden desk. It was the sort of device that could get electronic approval over the telephone. I watched as he processed my American Express card for five hundred bucks.

"Now,'' I said, "tell me. I presume you were doing a surveillance on Zeke's partner in his restaurant venture, Bob Hutchinson?''

"No.''

I was surprised.

"It wasn't Bob I was paid to watch. It was Carol.''

"Carol Ardman? The lady who reads news with Dan De Vries?''

"That's the one.''

"But why her?''

"I was supposed to get any dirt on her that I could come up with. I put hours on it, even hired another operative to help out. Your Mr. Roth owes me a whole lot of money, as a matter of fact, which he has not as yet paid.''

"What did you find out about Carol Ardman?''

"Nothing special. She's having an affair with Dan De Vries, who is married. Big deal. Beyond that, she has a number of outstanding parking tickets, and she flunked a college course at Barnard eight years ago because the professor thought she cheated on her final exam. I could write the book on the lady. I can tell you what she has for dinner, how much she pays for her apartment on East Seventy-third Street, give you a list of her last five boyfriends. But none of it is very interesting. It wasn't what Roth was hoping for anyway.''

''What about the thousand dollars of payoff money you listed in the bill you gave him?''

''Some of that went to the doorman who let me into her apartment when she was at work. Some more to a cop I know who checked her record. But most of it went to a shrink she was seeing in college—he gave me a Xerox of her patient file.''

''That's terrible! You're telling me her psychiatrist sold her out?''

The detective shrugged. ''A bad apple, I guess. Anyway, her file was nothing earthshaking. She hates her mother and secretly loves her father. Most of the men she's been involved with remind her of her old man in some way—I guess De Vries fits into that mold because he's quite a bit older than she is. But that relationship came after her analysis, of course, so there's nothing in the file about it. Beyond that—anxiety, guilt, a feeling that she can only survive in the world by fooling people. My own feeling is that she has a defective id and needs to get more in touch with her superego . . .''

''All right, all right. But you still haven't told me *why* Roth was interested in Carol Ardman?''

''Didn't I tell you that? Because she's blackmailing him, that's why.''

''Blackmail! Are you sure?''

''Yeah. I even delivered one of the monthly checks for five thousand dollars. It's killing him, poor guy. Draining all the moolah he's put aside for his kids' education. It's the reason he's trying to get his investment money back from As You Like It—that restaurant he owns with Bob Hutchinson. But old Bob isn't being very helpful. So Mr. Roth's getting desperate. The guy's really strapped. Which is the reason, I suppose, he's ignoring *my* bill.''

''But what does Carol have on him?''

Eugene looked at me for a moment without answering. His eyes became very sleepy.

''I can't answer that question.''

''What do you mean? I just paid you five hundred bucks to be my personal private eye!''

''I didn't say I *won't* answer. I said, I can't. I don't know for certain what Mr. Roth has to hide. He hasn't told me.''

''But surely you have some ideas?''

''Ideas are not facts, Mr. Allen. And I won't besmirch a man's reputation unless I know something for certain. However, I am willing to investigate the matter for you—now that you are my client. I still owe you about six hours of my time. Would you like me to use that time finding out the pertinent details of what Carol Ardman has on Roth that's worth five grand a month?''

''You couldn't just tell me now, I suppose?''

''It wouldn't be ethical.''

Gene Ptak, P.I., had decidedly odd scruples, but there was not much I could do about it.

''All right,'' I agreed. I gave him the phone number at the Fifth Avenue duplex. ''Call me as soon as you know anything. Lives are at stake—mine, for instance. Very unpleasant things are happening in Studio B.''

''Truth cannot be rushed,'' he told me with inscrutable wisdom.

''Make an exception just this once,'' I urged. ''Rush it just a little.''

''No can do,'' he insisted.

I was about to leave when I remembered something he said.

''You told me that guys were trying to kill you,'' I questioned. ''What guys?''

He shrugged. ''Someone took a few shots at me as I was

coming home from eating dinner at a restaurant around the corner last night. I don't know who did it, but I do know why. My problem, Mr. Allen, is that, as they used to say in the old movies, I know too much. When you're a seeker of truth, you gotta accept that some people would like to see you dead. It's happened to newspaper guys, cops. Hey, it could happen to you.''

Chapter 24

I went home and took a nap for two glorious hours. Since I wanted to take no chances on losing Boris, my intrepid Russian taxi driver, I took him home with me and asked Jayne to give him lunch while I slept. When I woke at nearly three o'clock, Jayne told me she had taken Boris and Heather to the Russian Tea Room, a very expensive place near Carnegie Hall, which was not quite what I had in mind.

"What a fascinating man!" Jayne enthused as I was dressing after my nap. "Did you know that Boris was a brain surgeon in Moscow?"

"That's weird. He told me he'd been a nuclear physicist in St. Petersburg."

"Well, maybe he was a physicist *after* he was a brain surgeon. A change of career."

"Hmm!" I hummed.

"Anyway, I told him I would take him shopping at Saks tomorrow. I just *hate* to think of such a lovely, educated man going around New York in such old clothes. It breaks my heart to think what hardships a Russian exile must endure!"

"It breaks *my* heart to be taken in by fast-talking con men!" I growled.

"Does it really matter if Boris was a physicist or a brain surgeon? The fact remains, the poor man needs some good clothes."

"All right," I grumped, knowing that once Jayne has set her mind on helping one of her many lost kittens, there's no turning back. "But let's make it Macy's rather than Saks."

"Good idea. Macy's it is! That will leave enough money to get him a good shave and haircut!"

"How's Heather doing today?" I asked.

"Better, but not great. This morning she took the subway down to East Fourth Street, but everything she owned was destroyed in the fire. I think I should take her shopping tomorrow as well—don't you agree? It'll perk her up."

"Naturally," I sighed.

It was time to brave the blizzard again for the trip across the Park to Sherry Gold on the West Side. Boris was in a very good mood, as well he might be, driving us careening merrily through the Park on a street where a snowmobile might ordinarily fear to tread. Sherry's apartment on West Eighty-sixth Street was one of those huge old places that make many New Yorkers prefer the West Side. A young boy, nine or ten years old, answered the door. He was a good-looking lad, but he had the most serious eyes I think I have ever seen on a child. They were an odd color, almost violet, and he stared at me as though I were a visitor from outer space.

"Well, hello! Who are you?" I asked.

"My mother is expecting you," he answered. "Follow me, please."

The boy led me down a long hallway that had a seemingly endless number of bedrooms off it, into a large, high-ceilinged living room with windows overlooking West End Avenue and a sliver of the Hudson River beyond. The room was overheated and fussy, by my standards, crammed full of knickknacks and furniture, books and paintings. For all such Jayne uses the Chinese word *dungshis*, meaning dust collectors. Sherry stood up from a couch and shook my hand.

"Glad you managed to make it here through the snow, Steve. I see you've met Crystal Rainbow."

"A handsome boy," I said. I looked about, but the child had disappeared without a word.

"He's gone back on-line. The Internet, you know. He spends hours every day at his computer talking with friends in Europe, Asia—all over the world."

"How interesting for him."

"Personally, I wish he would get out and play more with other youngsters. Of course, it's a constant challenge to raise a child in the city," she admitted. "I'm a single mother—my ex-husband left us high and dry when Crystal was hardly more than a baby. I wept for about six months and felt sorry for myself, but it's what made me strong. In the end, I had to get ambitious and figure out a way to make a living to support the two of us."

I have not yet described Sherry in detail and must take a moment now, for she was an unusual woman. She was in her early forties, I would guess, hardly more than five feet tall, with a head that seemed too large for her body. Her nose was long and her mouth was large and prominent, showing a lot of teeth when she smiled—and she smiled constantly. Part of the reason her head seemed too large for her body was that she had Big Hair—brunette swirls and curls rising several inches above her forehead then falling about her cheeks in a rarity of elaborate ways. In the midst of all this extravagance, her eyes seemed small—they were an icy blue; they became slits when she smiled.

"Scorpio!" she exclaimed.

"I'm sorry?"

"You're Scorpio, aren't you? Full of secret passions."

"Well, we're all that, but actually I'm . . ."

"Don't tell me! I'll guess eventually! To be honest, astrology isn't really my area of expertise. I'm more into the Tarot cards, and, of course, the crystal ball. But astrology is what most people prefer on television, so that's what I do for the show."

"I'm surprised the network went for an astrology section on what is basically a morning news program," I told her.

She smiled so broadly that every one of her teeth showed and her eyes became the thinnest possible slits. "As it happens, our chairman of the board never makes an important decision without consulting an astrologer or the cards. You know, like the Ronnie Reagans, and that financial wizard out in Orange County."

I find it truly depressing that in an age when just about all of the dazzling achievements of the last several centuries of scientific feats are readily available, and when we have television, radio, magazines, newspapers, textbooks, audio cassettes, CDs, computer print-outs, video tapes, and motion picture films at our fingertips, so many people seem supremely uninterested in what has been scientifically, firmly established and instead heed myth, legend, superstition and various other forms of nonsense.

"Oh, yes," I said. "The man who threw a good part of Southern California into bankruptcy.

"But Stephen Kinley? I wouldn't have thought it," I said. "He seems so stuffy and conservative."

"So are the Reagans and the Orange County guy." Sherry said. "But Mr. Kinley's a Taurus, a very bull-headed person, but a mystic nonetheless. Most people are superstitious when it gets right down to it. Don't you think it's astonishing that there is not a single skyscraper in New York that has a thirteenth floor?"

"I know," I said. "So it was Stephen Kinley's idea to do an astrology bit on 'Good Morning, U.S.A.'?"

"Yep. Not only is he a believer himself, but he's always looking for ways to boost the ratings. Most people only *half* believe their horoscope—but they will listen to it intently. I mean, have you ever gone to a Chinese restaurant without reading your fortune cookie? Beneath the rational surface of modern man, there's something older in our psyches—deep down inside, people still believe in omens and signs.''

''Well, I'm interested in omens and signs,'' I told her agreeably. ''Particularly if they can help figure out why Dennis Lovelace was killed. And why Cat was attacked this morning, and why the rash of accidents in Studio B.''

Again that smile, the slit eyes and sharp gleaming teeth. ''Let's have a cup of tea, Steve, shall we? And then I'll let you talk with Dennis directly. He's very close by, you know. The recently murdered linger in a special limbo. They *want* to tell us the secrets of their deaths so they might be avenged.''

We had a nice hot cup of Earl Grey. And then we went to talk with the dead. Was I speaking to a phony or a mental case, I wondered.

Chapter 25

For the séance, Sherry led me to a small room off her long hallway. The room had a single window which was covered with heavy dark red velvet drapes that allowed no light inside. I felt as if I were entering a tomb.

I sat cross-legged on a cushion on the floor across from Sherry at a low table. Two small candles cast a dim, flickering light on Sherry's face. There was a faint scent of incense in the air. In the center of the low table there was a crystal ball, perfectly smooth and hard and round—quite beautiful, really—that caught and magnified the candlelight in a mysterious way. It was all very eerie. The rest of the room was so dark, I couldn't even see the walls from where I was sitting. In the intense darkness, the walls seemed to disappear, and I had the illusion of being in a huge cavern, or a deep forest.

"You're not a believer, Steve. I know that," Sherry said pleasantly. "So all I'm going to ask you is to keep an open mind. Allow yourself to be neutral. Don't fight what's about to happen, or your hostile energy will drive Dennis away."

I made a mental note to take out a one-year subscription to

the *Skeptical Inquirer,* an excellent magazine published by the Committee for the Scientific Investigation of Claims of the Paranormal.

"Good. Now I'm going to ring a small silver bell, a very old and special bell whose vibrations will cleanse the air."

I wanted to stare into the woman's face and say, "On what grounds, on the basis of what actual evidence, do you believe that the sound of a ringing bell—whether old and special or not, could possibly cleanse the air? It is possible to make out a list of objects that will indeed cleanse air and almost all of them are commercially available. But bells, ringing or not, are not on the list."

She continued. "Then we're just going to sit here without saying a word. It might take a long time, or we might make contact in a few minutes. You can never tell in advance. I'm going to do all the channeling, so you don't have any work to do at all. You can meditate if you want, or think about what you're going to eat for dinner. Whatever. Just don't go to sleep on me, okay?"

"Okay," I agreed, gritting my teeth.

"All set then?"

"All set."

We were quiet for a moment. Then Sherry picked up a small bell from the table and struck it dramatically with a metal rod three times. The sound of the bell was very pure and silvery. As Sherry struck each time, she allowed the sound to vibrate fully in the room and then slowly dissipate before she struck again. I told myself this was nothing, just a piece of theater, but despite such fine rationalizing, I felt a strange surge of depression.

I'm not sure how long we sat there. It seemed like an eternity, but it may have only been five minutes. The room in which we sat must have been in the rear of the building with thick walls and heavy curtains keeping out all sounds of the city. After the ringing of the third bell faded slowly away, there was an absolute, uncanny silence. Even my heartbeat seemed to be absorbed in the thick darkness. I didn't think about dinner, I didn't meditate. Nothing was happening, and yet I sat as if I was at a suspense movie during the climactic part, breathlessly waiting to see how everything worked out.

Then something happened. A cold breath of air entered the room. It made me sit up straight, all my senses straining to see and hear. *Ha!* I told myself. *Very clever piece of special effects! Probably she has her air-conditioning set on a timer to go on at just this moment.* Yet, despite the tongue of cool air, I found my forehead moist.

Soon I heard a low moaning sound. I didn't know at first where it was coming from. The voice was deep and quite terrifying. As it grew louder I saw it was coming from Sherry. Her eyes and lips were closed. The moan seemed to come from somewhere deep inside her body. At last she opened her mouth and spoke. But the voice that emerged was not her own. It was deep and distinctly male, a terrible voice. It is, of course, quite a simple matter for a woman to speak in a voice that sounds like a man or vice versa.

"I am here!" the voice cried. "I have come from a great distance! What do you seek from me?"

Was it Dennis's voice? I couldn't be sure, since I had known Lovelace only such a brief time. But it sounded a bit like him, I had to admit.

"What do you seek from me, Mr. Allen?" the voice repeated. "I don't have all day."

The "Mr. Allen" gave me the cue to speak. I like polite spirits.

"That you, Dennis?"

"It is I," the voice rumbled.

"Glad you could make it," I said, feeling silly. "Dennis, I was hoping to ask you a few questions."

"Yes?"

"For example—I don't suppose you could tell me who killed you?"

My question was greeted with silence.

"You still there?"

"Yes. There is a cloud on my memory. The moment of death is very traumatic. Even the dead like to forget."

"I can imagine."

"You can *not* imagine," the voice said with scorn.

"So you don't know who killed you?"

There was another silence.

"A woman!" the voice hissed at last. "I can't quite make her out."

"Was she tall? Short? Can you describe anything about her?"

"Good-looking," he said.

"That's nice," I told him.

"I was walking in the darkness behind the set. Suddenly a woman appeared. She stabbed me with something. A long needle, I think. Or an ice pick. I felt a great pain in my chest, and deep sorrow."

"This woman," I prodded. "You say she was attractive. Cat Lawrence?"

"No ... I don't think so."

I was struck with an interesting possibility. "How about your girlfriend, Heather Dorn?"

"No, no ... Heather wasn't anywhere near Studio B at the time of my death."

"What about the production assistant—what's her name?"

"Debbie Driscoll? Mr. Allen, *really*—I don't like 'em that young."

"Sorry. What about—"

"Carol!" he screamed suddenly in a fearful voice that made me levitate briefly a few inches off my cushion.

"Carol Ardman?" I asked.

"Carol!" he screamed again. "Don't do it! Don't kill me, Carol!"

"Okay, calm down, Dennis. It's all done with now—you can't die a second time. Now take a deep breath and tell me—why do you think Carol had it in for you?"

"I *can't* take a deep breath, Mr. Allen," he sobbed.

"Well, you know what I mean. Think. What motive might Carol Ardman have for sticking an ice pick or needle in your heart?"

"It hurt," he complained.

"I'm sure it did. But *think*, Dennis. Carol is probably going to get away with your murder unless we can come up with a motive."

"I'll testify in court," he said.

"Dennis," I said, "I'm sure you're familiar with the old expression, 'fat chance.' How could you possibly testify in court?"

There was no answer.

"I don't know why she did it. I always thought she was a nice person."

"You mean, she just jumped out of the dark and stabbed you for no reason?"

The spirit sighed. "That's the riff, Biff," he agreed.

"Look, Dennis, you told your girlfriend that you *heard* something and that you made a tape recording. Can you tell me anything about that?"

"A tape?" he wondered. "Yes . . . a *tape!* I remember that now. I picked up voices on a microphone that no one thought was on."

"Who was talking?"

"Carol . . . Carol and someone else."

"Carol and Zeke Roth?"

"Perhaps . . . it was a man, I think. I don't remember."

"But what were they saying?"

"Something about . . . about . . . Carol is not who she claims to be. She is . . ."

Without warning, Sherry—or the voice of Dennis Lovelace—let loose a terrible scream.

"What's the matter?" I asked.

"Gotta go, Moe," he told me.

"About the tape," I insisted. "Where is it now, Dennis?"

". . . ask Stephen Kinley," he said, but his voice was fading.

"Why Stephen Kinley? Don't go yet, Dennis."

"He has the tape . . . that's the story, Dorie. I'm like out of here."

"Dennis, what do you mean Kinley has the tape? Why would *he* have the tape? . . . Dennis, come back. . . ."

But Dennis, real or fake, was gone. With a small, strangled cry, Sherry fell forward headfirst against the table. I stood up from my cushion and went to her side.

"Sherry, are you okay?"

I raised her head from the table. I blew out the candles and helped her back into the living room. Then I found a wet towel for her head.

"I'm all right, Steve," she insisted. But her voice was weak. "Did you get what you wanted?"

"I don't know. It was all confusing, really."

"If you don't mind, I think I'll go lie down now," she told me. "It's extremely draining work to be a channel with the dead."

I left her to recover from her ordeal. I could not accept that her clairvoyant show had been legitimate, but it certainly had given me some food for thought.

Chapter 26

We have an English friend, Lady Joanne Eustace, who was throwing a party tonight at her New York apartment, just around the corner from us on Park Avenue and Eighty-fourth Street. It would be a small bash to celebrate the blizzard, Lady Eustace told Jayne on the phone. Anyone who was feeling housebound and could walk, ski, or snowshoe over was invited to attend.

I surprised Jayne by saying, "Let's go. Just for a while, at least. We can always duck out early."

Frankly, I was tired of thinking about murder and blackmail and a television show gone amuck. I was ready for a bit of R and R, maybe even a few drops of B & B. Lady Eustace's parties were generally fun, both at her Mayfair house in London and in New York. I would see some old friends there, and Jayne and I would certainly not have to worry about dinner— her canapés were generally plenteous and rich.

Having decided to walk we left our Fifth Avenue digs about seven and made our way single file along a narrow path that had been shoveled in the snow the few blocks over to Park Avenue. The snow had stopped falling for the moment, the air was crisp and cold, and I could see a few stars in a break in the clouds. We had invited Heather to come along, but she said she was in no mood for a party and remained back at the duplex. I was just as glad. After all the commotion, it was nice to take a walk alone with my wife. We did not once mention "Good Morning, U.S.A."

Almost fifty people had managed to brave the weather to arrive at Lady Eustace's impromptu soiree. Some were in ski clothes, others in gowns and dinner jackets. It was a mixed group of movie people, the theater crowd, British aristocrats temporarily based in New York, a few high-powered Wall Street types, and, fortunately, a few friends, namely producer-writer Jim Lipton and his beautiful Eurasian wife Kedikai, and Ron Clark, the playwright and his charming Sheila. The apartment was large enough to hold such a group without seeming crowded. Lady Eustace's taste in furniture was very nineteenth century: lots of plush velvet, severe love seats that were not particularly comfortable, huge paintings of people on horseback on the walls, a roaring fire in the hearth.

Our hostess greeted us as we came in. Lady Eustace was one of those fashionably ageless women who might have been anywhere from forty-nine to a hundred and forty-nine years old. She was wearing a cream-colored silky pantsuit and diamonds dangling from her ears, around her neck, on several fingers, and around her wrist. We all kissed on the cheek and spent a few minutes catching up on our movements since the parties at which we had seen each other last. I'm not certain I have ever seen Lady Eustace in a group of under a hundred people, and yet we consider ourselves to be great friends. She was exhausted with the "season," as she put it, the unrelenting social whirl, and planned to escape to her "cottage" in Palm Beach (a mansion of thirty rooms) at the end of the month.

After the period of obligatory chitchat, Lady Eustace took Jayne off to meet a Bulgarian poet she said was a genius, and I escaped across the living room to visit with Alan Alda who had just finished a film in Europe. A cocktail party, even the most exalted, is a bit like a square dance. You do-si-do and change partners and dance through the room. In seamless fashion, I passed from my Alan and his darling wife Arlene to the brilliant director Martin Scorcese, and thence to a pretty young fashion model, an aging tycoon, a British art collector, the Earl of Something, and finally to where I was headed all the time— the baby grand piano that was nestled in a cozy corner beneath a few Degas prints.

Perhaps I should explain that I not only enjoy playing the piano, I am, in a sense, literally addicted to the art. Whether I am unusual among other professional pianists in that regard I honestly do not know. I was never conscious of the phenomenon until my middle-teen years when I became aware that if I went more than four or five days without being able to get at one of the instruments, I began to feel a vague unease that could be satisfied only by a vigorous keyboard workout lasting at least an hour. If I was in strange territory I would literally haunt the area looking for an instrument, like a wolf in the forest loping along keeping his eye out for prey. In the sense that a hungry person becomes exquisitely sensitive to the sight and smell of food, or those who are addicted to heroin, alcohol, or tobacco often become finely-tuned seekers after their particular form of pleasure, I sometimes simply *must* play the piano. The mysterious urge, oddly enough, has nothing whatever to do with a wish to perform for others. At such times it does not matter to me whether I have an audience or not, and in the great majority of cases I am entirely alone. One element of my appetite is the thirst for beautiful music of the sorts so richly provided to us all during America's true Golden Age of popular music—the 1920s, 30s and 40s—by George Gershwin, Hoagy Carmichael, Richard Rodgers, Jerome Kern, and the other giants of their day.

It is during such mysterious periods, too, that my unexplainable gift for the composition of melody often takes over and directs my psyche to construct combinations of notes and harmonics never before heard. Ordinarily, I would not have detained the reader with this digression were it not that just as I had gotten into Irving Berlin's undeservedly obscure "Maybe It's Because I Love You Too Much," a woman who had been recently much on my mind sat down on a chair next to me.

To my surprise, it was Carol Ardman—blackmailer, if I was to believe the stories about her, and possible murderer as well.

"You don't mind if I join you?" she asked sweetly. "We've never been properly introduced. I've only seen you from afar."

"Yes, on the monitor screen. How do you do, Carol? Actually I was going to make a point of stopping by the newsroom tomorrow morning and speaking with you."

"Were you?"

This was the first time we had met in the flesh. She was a redhead, in her late twenties, prettier and more vibrant than she appeared on morning television reading the news. Her complexion was like a young, dewy rose. Her eyes were hazel and at the moment they were regarding me with an odd expression.

"Let me guess. I bet people have been telling stories about me."

"Well, as a matter of fact, Carol—yes, they have. How did you know?"

She laughed, a flirtatious little trill. "There's no shortage of gossip on 'Good Morning, U.S.A.' I'll bet you—oh, five bucks I can even tell you what they're saying about me."

"You're on," I told her.

"Okay. Someone has certainly told you I got my job because I'm sleeping with Dan De Vries. The underlying prejudice is that a pretty young redhead couldn't *possibly* get into the newsroom otherwise. Right?"

"I've heard about you and Dan," I agreed.

"All right. That's number one. Now try this—not only am

I having an affair with a married man, I'm blackmailing Zeke Roth. . . . I see I've surprised you," she said, watching the expression on my face.

"That's not just gossip," I said, taking advantage of her frankness. "You *are* blackmailing Zeke Roth," I told her. "I spoke to a gentleman this afternoon who delivered one of the monthly payments."

"Who *claims* he delivered one of the payments," she corrected.

"Fair enough."

"Let's leave that alone for the moment and get on with accusation number three," she said with a mischievous smile. I felt Carol was actually enjoying the moment. "Knowing the envy and malice of my coworkers, I wouldn't be at all surprised if at least one individual whispered in your ear that I was the one who murdered Dennis Lovelace."

I reached for my wallet and gave her five dollars.

"Whispered in my ear is not quite the way I would describe it. But basically you score a triple bull's-eye. Are any of the accusations true?"

She laughed. "The first one is, certainly. The second is, sort of. But the third is definitely wrong."

"May we discuss this at greater length?"

"Not here," she replied, smiling dangerously. "There's a bar one block over on Madison—The Fallen Angel. It's a very discreet and intimate place. Why don't we meet there in twenty minutes and become better acquainted?"

She leaned forward and kissed me softly on the cheek, oddly close to my lips, her breath girlish and minty. "You know, you're kinda cute," she said. Then she stood up and wiggled provocatively away, a slow dance for my benefit across the crowded room. Left alone at the piano, I sighed, and shook my head at the folly of youth and age, love and sex. Then I fetched my coat so as not be late for the rendezvous. Locating Jayne in animated conversation with Marty Scorcese—they were joking about the briefness of our cameo scene in his film *Casino*—I told her I suddenly had to follow up a hot lead and would be back in less than an hour.

Oh, the things I have done in the name of crime!

Chapter 27

The Fallen Angel was a dark and discreet cellar of urban sin, just as Carol described it. The walls were of old red brick, the tables covered with red-and-white checkered tablecloths, isolated from one another in the separate glow of individual candles. To my pleasant surprise Andy Williams was heard on the public address system—thank God, at low volume—singing an old song of mine called "Tonight."

The bar was not crowded, probably due to the storm. Only a few couples sat at different tables, their voices low, their heads close together in earnest conversation. The Fallen Angel seemed to be a place for lovers who were breaking up, getting together, or merely pondering their future over a few cocktails.

Carol was sitting at a table near a small green-and-gold Tiffany lamp. She was looking cool and quite lovely. There was a drink in her hand, and she regarded me with feline concentration.

"I wasn't certain you would come," she teased. "Does Jayne let you off the leash very often?"

"Jayne shares my curiousity about what's happening on 'Good Morning, U.S.A.' "

"Is that really the only reason you came, Steve?"

Oddly, my primary emotional reaction to her question was an instant depression. In both my capacities as a human being and an amateur philosopher, I have long been dismayed at the haphazard quality-control work apparently done at whatever factory it is that produces human beings, as regards the related but distinct issues of love and sex. When we are young, and therefore naive, we tend to think that the world is fairly evenly divided between good people and bad people. Eventually we come to learn that while there are indeed a few remarkably evil individuals and an even smaller number of those who are inspiringly virtuous, the great bulk of the human race is both good and bad. And nowhere is our peculiar predicament more dramatically and painfully clear than as regards sexual function. Among relatively normal, healthy individuals there is something simple and animalistic that may take place when we meet someone who has every qualification for being sexually attractive. Perhaps if human beings were reproduced in the way that watermelon or zucchini are—delivered by storks and left under cabbage-patches—it would not matter so much that we can be sexually, romantically attracted to quite a long list of those we encounter. But, the rules of the humanity game that are operational in almost all known societies, simply do not permit us to act on the basis of those natural-enough casual attractions. At the moment I looked at Carol's pretty face, all of this, as I say, saddened me.

Although Carol Ardman might not have fully realized it, she was speaking, at the moment, to two quite separate me's. One, which I hope would remain dominant, was the cool, analytical sleuth, allbeit amateur. The other was a healthy, red-blooded male and I confess that in the latter capacity I was having a bit of trouble keeping things in focus. For one thing, I was only approximately, not fully, certain that she meant her question to be taken flirtatiously. A moment later she resolved all doubt.

"In case you're wondering," she said, still very pleasantly, "I am not 'coming on to you'—I hate that expression."

"I'm relieved to hear that," I said.

"Are you really?" she asked. "Or are you just trying to talk yourself into behaving virtuously?"

"Ms. Ardman," I said, "I am very favorably impressed by your intelligence and powers of observation. Knowing what I do about human nature—and I have a few years advantage over you in that regard—I suspect that neither of us is fully conscious of all our motives at the moment. I suppose you want to know if I'm also impressed by your youth, your beauty and your charm. The answer is of course I am. Probably every man you've ever met would say the same. But we both know there are other considerations. And," I added "given my age, if you do indeed find me attractive it's probably because I remind you of your father."

She laughed, although there was something a little sad in her laughter.

"Maybe," I suggested, "the same could be said of Dan Devries."

"You're probably right," she said. "The poor guy says he's in love with me and for the past year he's been trying to get up enough nerve to leave his wife."

"And three children," I added.

She frowned even more deeply. "I know," she said, "I'm that terrible creature, The Other Woman, breaking up a happy home. Well, for whatever the point is worth, that home was unhappy long before I showed up."

"Have you ever thought," I asked, "of just telling Dan thanks and goodbye and good luck and all that?"

"I think of it everyday," she confessed. "And it isn't just considerations of virtue that make me say that. I think maybe I'm ready for new adventures."

"The problem with looking for new adventures," I said, "is that they can resemble your old adventures in no time at all."

At that moment, I pointedly looked at my watch, holding it up to the Tiffany lamp to make sure I was reading it correctly.

"Carol," I said, "I don't have much time. You're adorable but at the moment I'm involved with something I think you'll admit is a bit more important—a murder investigation. Why are you blackmailing Zeke Roth?"

The waitress came over right at that moment to see what I wanted to drink. She was a pretty young woman in a black leotard and black tights, a fallen angel if ever I saw one. I really didn't want anything except for her to go away, but to pay my rent on the table I ordered a light beer.

"I don't know about this, Steve," Carol said after the waitress had left. "If I tell you about Zeke, I'll lose my leverage over him. What do I have to gain by telling you anything?"

"How about your freedom?

Maybe even your sanity? Blackmail is a crime, in case you're forgetting. And as for murder, New York has recently reinstated the death penalty. So I would advise you to stop playing games, Carol, and tell me what's going on. There are some nasty things afoot, and I may be the only friend you've got."

"Oooh!" she exclaimed. "I like it when men take charge!"

I stood up from the table. "I'm going back to the party," I told her.

"Sit down. I promise to behave. Cross my heart," she said.

"All right. I'm all ears," I told her.

"It's not what you think. Six months ago I loaned Zeke some money. He simply needed some motivation to pay me back. I can be generous, Steve, but I don't like to be taken advantage of."

"Who does? How much did you lend him?"

"Fifty thousand dollars."

I arched a questioning eyebrow.

"Does that sound like a lot of money?" she asked. "Well,

I suppose it is. I don't advertise the fact, but I'm well-off. I inherited a great deal of money from my grandfather when I was twenty-one. I don't work as a TV journalist because I need the job, Steve."

"Why do you do it then?"

She shrugged. "I was bored doing nothing. I thought television would be fun."

"Fair enough. Now let's get back to Zeke. Why did you agree to lend him fifty grand? Were you . . ."

"Were we lovers?" she asked with a harsh laugh. *"Please,* I have better taste than that!"

"Then why?" I repeated. "No matter how rich you are, fifty thousand dollars is a good deal of money."

"Perhaps it is if you've worked for it. But not particularly for me. To be honest, I inherited nearly forty mil. It all seems like confetti after a while. But I *did* have my motivations, of course. I'm ambitious in my own way—I'd like to work my way up the TV ladder, maybe become a sort of Barbara Walters one day. I thought it wouldn't hurt to have an important producer like Zeke Roth in my debt."

"Did he tell you why he wanted the money?"

"Oh, he made up a dumb story about a balloon payment due on his house in Westport. He said he had all his money tied up in the restaurant he owns with Bob Hutchinson, and that the investment had been a real mistake."

"Why was it dumb?"

She laughed. "You may think of me as the pretty girl who reads the headlines on the half hour. But I'm not a bimbo, I'm trained as a journalist, and I have my ways of finding things out."

"Tell me what you found out about Zeke?"

"I'll make you a deal. I'll tell you . . . for a kiss."

"Stop it, Carol! You may have gotten into television because you were a rich girl who was bored, but this has gone way beyond playing games. Someone's been murdered, and you may be next, for all you know. If you want to survive morning television, I suggest you level with me and do it quick.

"Okay! I know perfectly well why Zeke needed the money. He's been . . . let's be kind and say he's been *borrowing* money from the payroll. Fifty thousand dollars' worth. He needed to pay it back before there was an audit."

"You're telling me he's an embezzler?"

"You used that word, not I. I'm inclined to be less judgmental. Still, I expected to be paid back—our agreement was that he would give me five thousand dollars every month until the entire sum was repaid over a period of ten months. I thought I was very nice about it—I didn't even charge him any interest. Unfortunately the first month passed and I got nothing but excuses. The second month it was the same thing. As I said earlier, I'm generous with my money, but I greatly resent it when people take advantage of me. When the third month came and went with no check for five grand in the mail, I told Zeke that he'd better mend his ways. Or else."

"Or else what?"

"I'd go to Stephen Kinley, our beloved honcho, and tell him about the embezzlement. Result—I have received my monthly five thousand dollars for the past two months. So that's what I meant when I said it was *sort of* blackmail. I've used a bit of pressure, I admit, but the fact of the matter is the money is mine."

I absorbed all this information without great joy. Murder, embezzlement, blackmail—even "sort of" blackmail . . . the picture I was getting of "Good Morning, U.S.A." just kept getting darker and darker.

"Do you know a private investigator named Gene Ptak?" I asked.

"Creepy little guy who tries to act like he's Humphrey Bogart? Yes, I know him. I suspect Zeke hired him to get some blackmail leverage on *me*. But it won't do him any good, of course."

"You're saying you don't have any deep, dark secrets, Carol?"

"Not particularly. Oh, I've been a bad girl—I won't deny that. I'm sure there are things in my past many people would find shocking. But I don't particularly care who knows about them. That's what makes me a poor prospect for blackmail. If the worst comes to the worst, I have enough money that I'll simply quit television and go to live in Paris or Kathmandu."

I took a sip of my beer. I wasn't certain how much of Carol's tale I should believe, but she seemed convincing. I thought of a final question.

"You seem to have ways of finding out things, Carol. You keep your ear close to the ground. So tell me this—who do you think killed Dennis Lovelace?"

She smiled. "No, I really won't speculate on that," she said. "But I'll tell you someone you should ask."

"Who's that?"

"Your old friend, Cat Lawrence."

"What would Cat know about it?" I asked.

Carol laughed. "You like her, don't you?"

"Only as an old friend," I said. "And I'm sure if she knew anything about Dennis's murder, she would have told me."

"Oh, yes? Then she's told you, I imagine, that she and Dennis were having a wild affair? . . . Don't look so shocked, Steve. Cat's always liked those tough working-class guys. A taste for the rough trade."

"I don't believe it!" I scoffed.

Carol looked at me with mocking eyes. "You think maybe she's pure and innocent?" she laughed. "You men really are such fools!"

The thought of Cat lying to me—if it was true—left a bad taste in my mouth. I took out my wallet and threw down some money for our drinks.

Chapter 28

Wednesday's show went without a hitch, which was a relief. No equipment dropped from the sky, no bodies were discovered behind the scenery, and everyone pretended to adore everybody else—at least while the cameras were on. I interviewed yet another author with a new book he was pushing, and yet another actor with a new film. I even had a chance to play the piano. Cat had promised, of course, that I would be able to do a bit of music when she had first telephoned me in California. But it had taken a few days to get a good quality grand set up in Studio B. Music is the great distraction, and I partially forgot all about blackmail and murder while I played.

Gradually I was learning the names of the various cameramen and crew milling about on the set. There was Chris, a big fellow who looked like a football linebacker, on camera one. Antonio, a smooth Italian, on camera two. Richard, a soft-spoken African-American, on camera three. The new audioman was Carlos, and he had an assistant, Emily, a young woman who was working hard to enter what was still mostly a male profession. Then there were Dan and Bill, who were electricians, Christine, who was in charge of props, and Danny Ferraro and Lucky Mendoza, two hefty stagehands who moved the Steinway grand piano onto Studio B and seemed to perform any of the odd jobs on the set that required brute strength. I've already mentioned Debbie Driscoll, the production assistant. There were two other P.A.s as well, young people learning the business—Skip and Darcy.

There were still a number of crew members I did not know, particularly those who worked in the control booth and in the newsroom down the hall, places I normally had no reason to venture. But the blur of strangers I had encountered Monday morning were starting to take a more distinct form in my mind by Wednesday. Generally I find the off-camera technicians quite interesting people, and over the years, working onstage and screen and television, I have made an effort to know all my colleagues, not just the stars. But in this instance, I had a particular reason to keep my eyes open. It seemed to me obvious that the strange accidents and near-accidents that had happened on the set of "Good Morning, U.S.A." could only have occurred with the participation of someone in the crew. Maybe he or she was working on his own and had some personal reason to cause mayhem. Or perhaps that person was in the pay of one of the on-screen stars. I didn't have a clue, but I was determined to watch everything and everybody connected to the show with more than usual concentration.

"You seem very quiet today, Steve," Cat mentioned during one of the commercial breaks.

"Do you blame me? This is a dangerous group of people you've got me involved with, Cat."

She looked very pretty this morning, in a light blue dress and her blond hair done in a new style—short and feathery. There was a small strand of pearls around her neck that suggested just the right amount of understated elegance. She was a veritable princess, cool and perfectly arranged. Yet I wondered if I really knew her at all.

"Cat, I think we need to talk," I suggested. "How about lunch today?"

"I'm busy for lunch. Why don't you drop into my dressing room after the show?"

It was a relief that the show went off smoothly, but I was not looking forward to my talk with Cat. At about nine-thirty, after stopping in my own dressing room to change clothes and wash my face clean of makeup, I walked three doors down the hall to Cat's dressing room. It pained me that this girl I had known for such a long time, since she was a child, had lied to me. I wanted to think the best of Cat, to give her the benefit of the doubt—but Carol Ardman had spoken convincingly last night, and it was impossible to discount her story.

Cat opened the door dressed in an old kimono, her hair wet from the shower. Without her makeup, she looked ten years younger, hardly more than the teenage girl who had once worked in my office. Her dressing room was a lot more homey than mine—she was here on a permanent basis, of course, and it was worth her while to make the place attractive. There were bookshelves and paintings on the wall and a CD player with an old Kenny Rankin album on softly. I was surprised to see a black-and-white photograph of her father on her dressing-room table.

"Yeah, I still miss him," she said, following my gaze. "It's funny for me to think that he's been dead now more than half of my lifetime. It seems like yesterday he was pitching softballs to me in our backyard."

"Your father was a likable man," I said.

"Yeah. It's a shame he wasn't stronger and wiser as well. I have this weird feeling about my childhood, Steve. It's like everything was perfect until I was twelve years old. I had the happiest childhood I can ever imagine. And then, out of nowhere, my whole family seemed to self-destruct and I was left with nothing. I still can't quite get over it."

"Perhaps it wasn't so sudden, after all," I told her. "Your

father was drinking even when everything seemed to be going so well. You were just too young to see the signs.''

''Maybe,'' she agreed, sitting down on one of the sofas in her dressing room. She put her bare feet up on the dressing table in a less-than-elegant gesture her TV viewing public would not have recognized.

I sat down at her crowded makeup table and turned to face her.

''Cat,'' I said, ''You've not been honest with me.''

''What do you mean?''

''I mean Dennis Lovelace. Don't bother to deny it—you and Dennis were having an affair.''

''Damn!'' she uttered. ''Who told you that? . . . No, don't tell me. It really doesn't matter, I guess. I've never been around such a bunch of old gossips in my life!''

''Then it's true?''

''Well . . . kind of,'' she admitted grudgingly.

This was getting tiresome. Last night I had a ''sort of'' blackmail. Now I had a ''kind of'' affair.

''Look, Steve, I feel terrible about this,'' she said. ''I didn't mean to lie to you.''

''People lie when they're trapped.''

She sighed and buried her head in her hands. ''It's just that after I stole that money from you when I was young, I've always wanted you to think the best of me. I didn't want to tell you I was involved in something shabby, like sleeping with a guy I knew had a steady girlfriend. I knew it wasn't a very attractive thing for me to do, but I couldn't help myself.''

''Cat, you still should have told me! Don't you see—by your lying about your relationship with Dennis, the police may even come to suspect you of his murder!''

Cat wouldn't look at me. ''I told the police. It was only you I couldn't tell, Steve. You and Jayne.''

I sighed. ''All right, go on,'' I said. ''Tell me about you and Dennis.''

"There's not much to tell. I was lonely and here was this young, good-looking guy touching my blouse every morning, threading the microphone up through my clothing. He was a little rough around the edges, but I like guys like that. So we got to talking one morning about music, and I told him I had a new Bruce Springsteen album in my dressing room he really should hear. I told him to drop by after the show and when he arrived, I was just out of the shower and not wearing too many clothes. And, well . . . It wasn't exactly a love affair though. It was just sex."

"Did it happen more than once?"

"Yeah."

"You met outside of work?"

"Only once. Frankly, we always met here in the dressing room. . . . I'm sorry to shock you, Steve."

"Cat, I'm old enough to have had some exposure to the world."

"Well, maybe I shocked myself. A couple of times Zeke or Ken came by about something, and I would hide Dennis in the shower until after they'd gone. So one afternoon I arranged to get a hotel room nearby. I thought it would be nice to have some time with Dennis without worrying about someone knocking on the door. But that afternoon was probably what ended the whole thing."

"What do you mean?"

"I think that's where we both saw this *was* turning into a real affair. Dennis had begun to feel awfully guilty about Heather, and he said he wanted to break it off between him and me. He was in love with Heather, you see."

"Heather never knew?"

"No. Dennis lied to her. I don't think it bothered him too much at first, but day after day it began to weigh on him that he was leading a double life. By this time, I had come to like Dennis quite a lot. When I saw he was unhappy, I let him go without a struggle. I'm not a monster, Steve."

"I know you're not, Cat. But why in the world did you arrange to go down to Heather's studio and buy that piece of sculpture?"

She smiled ruefully. "That was about a week after the hotel afternoon when Dennis and I agreed to stop seeing each other. I guess I was curious about what kind of girlfriend he threw me over for. He had talked about her work a few times, and I knew she was supposed to be very talented. So I told Dennis I wanted to meet her and maybe buy something expensive to help her out. He was very reluctant, of course, to take me to her studio, but I convinced him that I would behave myself and she would never suspect the truth. I kept my word, too, and I'm glad I went down there."

"Why? I don't understand what good could come of it," I told her.

"A lot of good, as a matter of fact. Heather became real to me, not just a name for a rival. I liked her. And somehow that made it easier to give Dennis up. And I fell in love with her sculpture, too. Frankly, I had come there prepared to buy something expensive, but it was just guilt money, I suppose. But as soon as I saw *Midnight Angel,* I knew I had to have it, guilt or not. I was pleased to write out a big check to her, and I ended up feeling a sort of a sisterly glow toward Heather and Dennis both. It was a kind way to make the fling with Dennis not quite so shabby in my memory."

"And that's all that happened?"

"I swear. So do you think I'm an awful person now?"

"Cat, I don't think anything of the sort," I protested. "I just feel sorry that you're so lonely, a pretty young woman like yourself, with so much intelligence and talent—what I don't understand is why you don't have a nice guy of your own."

For the first time during our conversation her face reflected a great sadness.

"I don't either," she surprised me by saying.

"Maybe," I suggested, "you've bought the incredibly stupid

idea so excessively promoted by our culture that love—yes, even true love—is somehow old-fashioned and square whereas sex is hip and with-it. The weird thing is that although guys talk a lot about sex—because they think of it—there's some little part of wisdom, tucked way back in their brains, that makes them look for a woman of substance and common sense as a life-long companion and mother of their children, rather than the town pushover. An even funnier—or perhaps I should say sadder—thing is that even if they do marry somebody who's been available to dozens of men, her swinging days are supposed to be over, period, once they rope and tie her.''

"I can't argue with you," she said, "but there's something so—I don't know—sweet, so tempting about the early days of a new relationship.''

"Tell me about it," I said, although I hate to employ such clichés. "It's mother nature's way of propagating the species, and she appears to have been just as mindless as regards mating arrangements for humans as for those of bed-bugs, salmon and baboons. The tragic thing is that it works well for all the lesser creatures but leads to endless heartbreak for humans. You see, to me, the guys that are *really* sexy—to use that tiresome word—are those able to maintain a sweet, romantic, passionate attachment to one woman. Hell, anybody who really wants to, and has a few bucks in his kick, can have an endless parade of women, just as any half-way attractive woman can have a different man every night, if that's what she really wants. You show me two groups of men—Group A consists of guys who have been married five, six, or seven times, which really means that they have failed, they've struck out in the great ball game of life four, five, or six times. Group B consists of guys who have stayed with one woman over the long haul. It's the men in Group B we should emulate. They also raise a much superior brand of children.''

Something about her expression suggested she might be getting tired of my lecture. "Oh, it's easy for you to say all that.''

"No," I said, "it isn't. I learned all this the hard way. Both Jayne and I were married before. And in our first marriages we were failures. One thing we've learned is that even a reasonably good marriage is never perfect. Nothing in human experience ever is. When I was young, and consequently stupid, I used to envy the guys who had an endless procession of chicks. I'm ashamed to confess that I must have been about 45 before I realized that all the fellas on that list were the unhappiest sons of bitches I knew, though I admired some of them as actors, singers, trombone players, or what-have-you. But now," I said, "let's get back to our case.

"Dennis told Heather that he heard something and actually made a tape of whatever it was that disturbed him. Did he ever mention this to you?"

She shook her head.

"Have you remembered anything more about who attacked you yesterday?" I asked.

"Not a thing. It's still a complete blank. I don't even remember much of the show yesterday, to tell the truth. I'm sorry. I keep having this feeling I'm a real disappointment to you."

"Cat, it doesn't matter about me—I just don't want you to be a disappointment to yourself."

I gave her a hug and then I returned to my dressing room for my briefcase and overcoat. You worry about people you've known since they were children in a special way, and I was worrying so intensely about Cat Lawrence as I walked down the hall that I did not fully absorb how odd it was that my dressing-room door was unlocked.

As soon as I was inside the door, I had an odd feeling. Then in the makeup mirror I saw a shadow move behind my left shoulder. I cried out and began to spin around to face it, but I wasn't fast enough.

There was a piercing blow on my skull. I saw stars flashing in the sudden darkness. And then I saw nothing at all.

Chapter 29

Cold fizzy water dribbled down my face. I must be sitting in a lovely mountain waterfall, I thought. Then I woke up enough to understand that it was not a waterfall but a bottle of San Pellegrino water from my dressing-room refrigerator that was being poured over my head.

"Wake up, you son of a bitch!" someone said angrily.

Though I was lying on the floor, momentarily I could not remember how I got there. When I sat up my headache got even worse. I groaned, massaged the back of my head with my hand, and opened my eyes.

"That's right, open your eyes! Look at me, you bastard!" the voice said.

My glasses had fallen somewhere onto the floor and the image in front of me was blurred. The man was hovering in my vision, holding something in his hands that looked like a stick.

"Look at me," he said. "I want you to be looking into my eyes when I kill you!"

"Who the hell are you?"

"You know perfectly well who I am, you creep! You Hollywood scumbag Romeo! Thought you were pretty clever, didn't you?"

The voice was familiar but I could not make out who was about to kill me, or why.

"Look, are you sure you got the right dressing room?" I asked reasonably. "I don't know who you are or what we're talking about."

"Oh ho-ho!" he cried. "The man's a comedian. God, do I hate slick Hollywood sons of bitches like you! You'd better start praying, slick. You've got exactly five seconds left to enjoy planet Earth! One . . . two . . ."

"Whoa! Hold on a minute! Let's talk this over."

"Three . . . four . . ."

"I can't see a thing without my glasses," I told him hastily. When the count of five went by and I was still alive, I realized I was on the right track. "You want me to know who you are, don't you, before I die? Well, you'd better give me my glasses then."

"You really can't see me, huh?"

"You're just a blur to me, I'm afraid."

"All right," he agreed sullenly. "They're on the floor by your left hand. Put 'em on and we'll start our countdown again from the beginning."

"Swell!" I felt about on the floor and found my glasses, but I hesitated before putting them on. I was torn between my curiosity to know who was about to kill me, and a reluctance to start the sequence that would leave me with five seconds to live. In the end, my curiosity got the better of me. I slipped the glasses over my ears and the world came into focus. I was astonished to see Dan De Vries, Carol Ardman's older lover and co-anchor of the news. The man was disheveled, his tie was loose, his hair was a mess, and the stick in his hand turned out to be an automatic assault rifle whose barrel was only a few inches from my nose.''

"One . . . two . . .''

"Hold on, Dan! If you're going to kill me, you might as well have the decency to explain why.''

"You know why, you bastard! Three . . . four . . .''

"Idon'tknowwhy,'' I managed, probably the fastest phrase ever shot from my mouth.

"AndIreallythinkyouowemeanexplanation,'' I added in double time.

"Five!'' he said. But he didn't pull the trigger. "You really don't know, huh?''

"We've never actually met before, remember? So how can I know why you want to kill me or anybody else, for that matter. Naturally I've listened to you read the news on the half hour, and I've always been a fan. But I'd be much obliged if you'll stop and satisfy my curiosity. It's really bugging me—why for instance did you kill Dennis Lovelace.''

"Kill *Dennis?* What the hell are you talking about?''

"You killed him, of course. And I presume that's why you're about to murder me. Maybe you think I'm hot on your trail. Is that it? You're afraid my investigation is getting too close to the mark?''

"You're crazy,'' he said.

"*I'm* crazy?'' I huffed. "I'm beginning to think *I'm* the only sane person on this damn show!''

"You can't bluff me—I *saw* you last night trying to steal my girl! You son of a bitch—you even took her to The Fallen Angel, which is *our* place! I looked in the window and there you were at *our* table, your heads all close together, so lovey-dovey!''

"Oh, *that's* what this is about!'' I cried.

"You got it, buster. And now here's your final countdown. One . . . two . . . three . . .''

"Dan, hold on! You've got it all wrong. I'm investigating

the murder of Dennis Lovelace—I thought Carol might have some information.''

''. . . four . . .''

''That'stheonlyreasonIsawher,honest,dammit!''

Dan paused on the final digit. His face was red, his forehead glistened with sweat. The guy was really out on a limb, emotionally speaking. I thought I was a goner. I could even see the headline in tomorrow's headline: BERSERK NEWSCASTER SHOOTS COMEDIAN WHO FANCIED HIMSELF A DETECTIVE.

Time slows down at crucial moments. I saw at least a few fragments of my life pass in front of my eyes. I wondered how Jayne was going to manage without me. But Dan De Vries did not pull the trigger. Instead he burst into tears, awful sobs that seemed to come from deep inside of him. He collapsed onto the chair by my makeup table, dropped the assault rifle onto the floor, and buried his face in his hands.

I picked up the weapon, an AK-47 with a banana clip. I wondered what a mild-mannered newscaster was doing with such a heavy piece of machinery. In fact, I wondered a lot of things.

''There, there,'' I told him. ''I think the moment is ripe, Dan, for you and me to have a good talk.''

Chapter 30

Dan De Vries had been a TV journalist for a long, long time. He had covered three wars, a dozen assassinations, two cult mass suicides, countless murders, fires, earthquakes, floods, celebrity scandals, scientific breakthroughs, five Presidential elections, and nearly thirty years of the American circus that some people call politics. No wonder he was a little crazy.

Physically, De Vries was in his early sixties. He had a round face with lined skin, short curly brown hair that was starting to gray, and a kind of old-fashioned intellectual look to him. Normally he was quite an attractive man—not a glamor-type, certainly, but the sort of older, slightly wizened gentleman you tend to trust when you watch the news. This morning, however, his face was red and puffy, and he was a mess. He sobbed for nearly ten minutes before I got the first coherent word out of him.

"Don't ever fall in love with a girl who's young enough to be your granddaughter, Steve!"

"I won't," I assured him.

"I can't tell you how I've suffered. I've betrayed my wife,

my family, everything—all for Carol. And now she doesn't
want me anymore. You don't know what it's like when I see
her talking to another man! I go a little off the deep end, I
guess. When I saw you with her last night, at our place, at our
table—something snapped in me. All I could think about was
killing you."

"But what in the world were you doing lurking outside in
the snow last night on Madison Avenue?"

"Following her, of course. Hoping to see if she would betray
me. I do that every night, stupid schmuck that I am. I wait
outside her brownstone on East Seventy-ninth Street to see
what she's doing and who she's with."

"Dan, this is a very bad business," I told him. "You need
to get a grip on yourself, man. Where the devil did you get
hold of an AK-47?"

"Nicaragua, 1988. A souvenir. I was down there covering
the Contra operation."

"Well, I think I'd better hang on to this rifle for a while,
Dan. Just until you're in a better frame of mind."

"Who cares," he told me. "Back in my apartment I have
a grenade launcher, three machine pistols, an Uzi, a shotgun
and three revolvers . . . all souvenirs from various assignments.
I'm ready for the worst."

"But *why?*"

He shrugged. "When you read the news headlines year after
year, I guess you get a negative image of the world."

"You should take a long vacation," I advised. "A nice sea
cruise to someplace where there's no TV. And take your family
along."

"That's what Peter advised when I had dinner with him on
Monday night," he agreed. "Maybe you guys are right. I should
get away from all the pain and misery."

"For a while, at least. You're no good to yourself this way,
Dan."

I had passed from being the guy Dan De Vries wanted to

murder, to his bosom buddy. But I had a lurking suspicion that I had missed something important. My brain at present was not all it might be. I had taken three ibuprofen pills, but I still had a splitting headache from being whacked unconscious.

"Wait a second," I said. "What did you say about Monday? You had dinner with Peter? Peter *McDavis?* The guy I'm filling in for?"

"Sure. Peter and I are old buddies. We really tied one on, at the bar at the Sherry Netherland. I don't know if it did me much good, but at least that was the only night the past few weeks I wasn't out in front of Carol's apartment."

My brain came out of a cloud and suddenly I saw what was wrong with the story Dan was telling me. "Are you sure you have the right night? Monday?"

"Of course. Why?"

"Because Peter McDavis was supposed to be in Santa Fe then. That's the reason I'm here in New York subbing for him!"

"Whoops!" he said. "I guess I let it out of the bag."

"Let *what* out of the bag, Dan?"

"This is supposed to be a secret from the network. Peter didn't actually go to New Mexico. He decided to hang around New York to take care of some business."

"What sort of business? Did he say?"

"You won't tell anyone about this, will you? Peter and I go way back and I promised to keep quiet. I wouldn't even think of telling you, but hell, I tried to whack you out . . . and I guess with a guy you try to kill, there's a kind of bond."

"Right, we're blood brothers, though I'd feel better about that if it hadn't been my blood. But I can be discreet, Dan, when the occasion demands it."

"Right. Well, the deal is this—Peter's negotiating with another network for a chance to be anchor on their evening news." Dan named the network and the present anchor who was apparently about to get the ax—one of the biggest names in television. "It would be a huge step up for him, as you can imagine. Of course Stephen Kinley can't hear a word of this yet."

My foggy brain not only cleared, but now it did a quantum leap. The mysterious happenings on the set of "Good Morning, U.S.A." suddenly began to make a terrible sense.

"Tell me this, Dan—I bet Peter has a fairly tight contract with UBS to continue 'Good Morning, U.S.A.'?"

"You bet it's tight. Stephen Kinley has Peter tied up for another eighteen months. It's going to be a bitch for Peter to get free."

I smiled happily for the first time in several days.

"Dan," I said, "I think you have just helped me solve Dennis Lovelace's murder. I need to see Peter McDavis right away. What's his New York address?"

With our new bond, being blood brothers and all, Dan quickly gave me Peter's address—a penthouse on Park Avenue quite near the party I had attended last night at Lady Eustace's.

"But I don't know if you'll find him there, Steve. I think he said he was flying out to New Mexico today or tomorrow."

"I'd better get right on it," I told him. "Look, Dan. You're a mess, pal. Why don't you wash your face and comb your hair, and lock my dressing-room door on your way out. We'll have brunch tomorrow after the show—okay?

He shook my hand. "Thanks, pardner. You've been a real pal."

"Don't mention it," I told him. "What's a skull fracture among friends?"

I opened the door to make a quick exit and walked right into the arms of Detective Sergeant Max Morgenfield and Detective Frank Marcotti, my Laurel and Hardy friends from the NYPD.

"Mr. Allen," said Detective Morgenfield. "Just the man we've been looking for. You will come with us, please, to the station for a little chat."

"Sorry, gentlemen, maybe another time. Right now I'm in a big hurry."

"Frank, put the cuffs on him," Detective Morgenfield directed. "If he resists arrest, you have my permission to use force."

"What?" I cried. "This is preposterous! What are you charging me with?"

"Accessory to murder. Material witness. Jaywalking—what does it matter? Believe me, sir, we'll come up with something creative by the time we get you downtown."

Chapter 31

Detectives Morgenfield and Marcotti whisked me in an unmarked car to a small interrogation room at One Police Plaza downtown. I was glad the room had a window, at least; it was my only cause for optimism. Besides the window, there was a metal desk, three straight-backed metal chairs, two lines of fluorescent lights overhead, and a Police Athletic League calendar on the otherwise bare walls. I had a lot of time to get acquainted with these simple objects because when we arrived at police headquarters, Morgenfield and Marcotti abandoned me in the small room for more than forty-five minutes in solitary without any explanation.

It was psychological warfare, I assumed, and I rose to the occasion. I suspected someone was watching me through a hidden camera for signs of guilt and stress, so I sat with my right leg crossed over my left knee trying to look as casual and guilt-free as I was. After twenty minutes or so, I began to whistle some Cole Porter standards. At thirty minutes I removed my sport coat, stood up, and began to do some stretching exercises—neck rolls, waist bends, toe touches. I thought *that*

would show them how a relaxed, confident person behaves in
an interrogation room. My head still hurt just a little from where
Dan De Vries had hit me, but my ego was flying high. I had
solved the case. At least the broad outline thereof. I was certain
the odd nagging details would soon be resolved by the brilliance
of my deductive powers.

Morgenfield and Marcotti filed back into the room, making no
apology for their long absence. Without a word, the overweight
Detective Morgenfield seated himself behind the metal desk
while the thin and mournful Marcotti stood and stared at me.

"Hi, fellas," I said cheerfully. "I thought maybe you had
forgotten about me."

Detective Morgenfield opened a folder and began to examine
a sheet of written notes in silence while Marcotti breathed
heavily. This took about three minutes.

Suddenly I recalled a partially-written song lyric that had
been in my inner jacket pocket for the last few days. Taking
it out, I opened the paper on my knee and began to hum the
melody for which the words intended.

Morgenfield looked up at me sleepily as if he had forgotten
I was there. At seeing that I was smiling he said, "Do you
think this is a joke, Mr. Allen?"

"No, not a joke," I told him. "I think the correct word to
describe your efforts to intimidate me is farce."

He smiled unpleasantly and then consulted his notes once
again. "Well, let's see if this is a farce, Mr. Allen. On Monday
evening, only a few hours after the murder of Dennis Lovelace,
you were seen by a neighbor entering the residence of the
victim's girlfriend, Heather Dorn, on East Fourth Street. What
is your relationship, sir, with Miss Dorn?"

"I met her for the first time that night. There were some
questions I wanted to ask her."

"I see. Would you describe Ms. Dorn as an attractive young
woman, Mr. Allen?"

"Certainly."

"Now you remained with Ms. Dorn alone in her residence for approximately forty-five minutes, and then you took her to dinner at the Four Seasons, one of the most expensive restaurants in New York. Did you open a few bottles of champagne, Mr. Allen? Were you perhaps celebrating the death of Dennis Lovelace?"

"Ridiculous!" I snorted. "What are you insinuating?"

"I am suggesting, Mr. Allen, that now the boyfriend was out of the way, there were no further obstacles to keep you and Heather apart. You've already admitted that you were deeply attracted to her."

"I admitted no such thing! I simply agreed she was an attractive young woman. Besides, this intimate dinner you're describing at the Four Seasons was actually a fivesome—the chairman of the network was there, Stephen Kinley, as well as Mrs. Kinley and my wife Jayne Meadows."

Morgenfield shook his head and turned to Marcotti. "He says his wife was there! Can you imagine that?"

"I sure wish *my* wife was so liberal a guy could bring his tootsie along and she won't object!" Marcotti said in a hoarse whisper.

Despite Marcotti's attitude at the moment, I had a certain respect for him for what may sound the odd reason that he was: a. Italian and b. working on the right side of the law. The monsters of the Mafia, despite the fact that some of them have been warmly welcomed in the homes and offices of a number of my Beverly Hills entertainment-world friends over the years, have perpetrated so much evil that their depredations have besmirched the good name of the great majority of law-abiding Italian-Americans. To this day successful Italian politicians and businessmen, no matter how honest, are haunted by the suspicion that at some point their own gears might be meshed with those of the Mafia. Consequently, as I say, I have a special respect for lawmen with Italian surnames who devote their lives to putting organized crime people behind bars.

"Hollywood people, they live by a different set of rules," Morgenfield confided to his partner.

"You guys are going to be so embarrassed when all this gets straightened out."

"That sometimes happens. But now let's try this on for size—later in the evening, Ms. Dorn's residence happens to catch on fire, and who do you think shows up on Fourth Street? Mr. Steve Allen!"

"Of course. Jayne and I were dropping her off after dinner," I explained.

"Yeah. And the old church just *happened* to be on fire? An arson fire, by the way. That's what the fire department is calling it. Maybe you left a small incendiary device when you were there earlier in the evening? Or are you trying to tell me it's just coincidental that everywhere you go, Mr. Allen, there's bound to be a crime."

"Of *course,* it's coincidental! Why in the world would I want to burn down Heather's studio?"

Morgenfield turned sadly to Marcotti. "He calls her Heather! Pretty chummy for a guy who says he only met the young lady a few hours earlier."

"Detective, this is the last decade of the twentieth century. People get on a first-name base fairly quickly these days."

"Well, I'd say you got on a first name basis with Heather Dorn *very* quickly. First you have an intimate rendezvous with her alone at her place. Then you take her to an expensive dinner. And the next thing that happens, you're watching a fire together."

"Some people think watching a fire together is pretty sexy," Marcotti added.

"The arsonist almost always returns to the scene of the crime to watch his handiwork," Morgenfield said with a weary sigh.

I laughed, though my mouth was dry. It's no fun to be harassed by cops. "This really *is* a farce," I told them. "And I suspect your investigation isn't going too well if you're spending all this time hounding me. Why don't you ask Heather Dorn what happened Monday night?''

"Oh, we will!'' Detective Morgenfield assured me. There was a new twinkle in his eye. "And where exactly is Ms. Dorn now, Mr. Allen? Perhaps you will be so good as to tell me.''

"Well, she's at my apartment, actually.''

"Your apartment! How very cozy.''

"My apartment and Jayne's,'' I explained quickly. "It's a huge duplex on Fifth Avenue that the network gave us while I'm doing the show. When Heather had no place to go after the fire, it seemed reasonable to offer her one of the bedrooms.''

"A Fifth Avenue duplex!'' said Morgenfield, as though this certified a life of sin. "And his wife is there as well.''

"Sounds like one of them menagerie things,'' Marcotti whispered.

"No, it's called simple decency—giving a person a place to live after they've lost everything. Now, gentlemen, this is certainly a fun way to spend the day, but I'm going to have to ask you to either charge me with a crime or let me go.''

They let me go. They had nothing. They were simply fishing in the bluntest possible manner, trampling the grass, muddying the stream, hoping to bully their way clear to some information—probably *any* information at all. As a practitioner of a more subtle form of the detective arts, I found this approach an aesthetic insult. Normally I am not a vindictive guy, but after spending a few wasted hours with Morgenfield and Marcotti, I was going to enjoy solving the Lovelace murder and lording it over them a little. In my mind, I had the case all wrapped up.

Chapter 32

I left One Police Plaza and found a cab to take me uptown to Peter McDavis's apartment on Park Avenue. The streets of New York were a slushy mess, but other than that life and traffic were almost back to normal after the winter storm. My driver screamed at other cars, almost ran down several slow-footed pedestrians, and talked nonstop of how the city was going to hell—in other words, a typical New York taxi ride.

Peter McDavis lived in an ornate, pre–World War I building that exuded a dignity now all too rare. The lobby was dominated by a huge old crystal chandelier and mirrors with gilt frames. I was stopped by an ancient doorman in dark blue uniform and cap. He was a gray-complexioned, elflike man who looked as though he had been at his post since the building opened.

"Good afternoon, Mr. Allen," he greeted. I was surprised he knew my name, though I'm sure the average Park Avenue doorman knows a good deal more than we assume.

"I was just dropping by on the odd chance that I might catch Mr. McDavis at home," I told him. "Would you please call up for me and say it's rather urgent I see him."

"Oh, Mr. Allen, I'm afraid there's no one home. Mr. McDavis is out of town and the apartment is empty."

"Out of town?" I prodded delicately. "I know he was planning to go to his home in Santa Fe, but I hoped I might catch him before he left."

"He left for New Mexico last Friday afternoon, sir."

"*Friday* afternoon?" I repeated. "Are you certain? A friend of mine mentioned he saw Peter in New York this Monday."

"Yes, I'm quite certain, Mr. Allen. Friday afternoon. I remember it distinctly because Mr. McDavis was in a bit of a tizzy that day, sir, when he asked me to keep his mail for him. He was fairly upset at the accident at work Friday morning— that light dropping on him, nearly killing him like that. He said to me, 'Andy, I'm going to stay in New Mexico until the network makes it safe for a person to work there." I told him in return, I says, 'Yes, you do that, Mr. McDavis. No job worth that kind of danger and aggravation.' "

"I imagine you and Mr. McDavis talk quite freely," I said.

"Oh, yes, Mr. Allen. I've been working in this building for forty-two years, I have, sir. And I'm proud to say many of the tenants treat me like family."

"And you're sure it was Friday that he left for New Mexico?" I repeated.

"Oh, absolutely, Mr. Allen. Your friend who said he saw Mr. McDavis in New York on Monday was mistaken, sir."

"And no one's been in the apartment at all?"

"Not a soul, sir, since Friday. Locked up tight as a drum."

I would have loved to get my hands on a passkey to look about Peter's apartment, but I knew it was pointless to even hint at such a thing to Andy. A Park Avenue doorman might talk a bit too loosely, but he would certainly not allow a nonresident like me to gain access to a tenant's apartment.

I left Peter's building and walked the half dozen blocks back to the duplex on Fifth Avenue. Jayne smiled as I came in the door.

"You're late, dear," she said.

"Morgenfield and Marcotti decided to impress me with the strong arm of the law. They dragged me down to One Police Plaza for a contest of wills—theirs against mine."

"And who won?"

"At the moment, my darling, it appears to be a draw. But I am about to pull into the lead and solve this case."

"You know who the killer is?"

"I suspect it's Peter McDavis. At least, he seems to be behind it all. He must have one or more accomplices, probably crew members in his employ who have been loosening klieg lights and generally sabotaging things on the set."

"But why? It doesn't make any sense!"

"Oh, yes it does," I told Jayne. "Peter's trying to break his contract."

Jayne and I sat in the living room overlooking Central Park while I told her about how Peter had been offered a job as anchor for the evening news on a different network. It was a big step upward in his career—but first he must somehow free himself of the binding contract he had with Stephen Kinley the Second. If he could prove negligence and unsafe conditions on the set of "Good Morning, U.S.A.," he would be free to take up his new job.

"But why kill Dennis Lovelace?" Jayne asked.

"Because Dennis apparently got wind of what was going on. He overheard a conversation of some sort and actually had a tape machine record it. I presume Peter's accomplice, whoever that is, did the actual deed—stabbed poor Dennis in the heart with some sort of needle. But Peter is the one with the motive."

"I don't know, Steve," Jayne said, shaking her pretty head at me. "All this mayhem to go from a morning show on one network to the evening news on another? I've heard of ambition, but—"

"It's more than a job, Jayne, or even an increase in salary. Peter McDavis is hoping to be the next Dan Rather or Walter

Cronkite, hobnobbing with presidents and prime ministers. These evening news anchors are some of the most powerful people on the planet. It must be extraordinarily frustrating to be held back from such glory just because of a previous signature on a piece of paper.''

"But the accident last Friday—Steve, the klieg light nearly killed both Cat *and* Peter. Surely Peter would not arrange an incident where he might easily die.''

"Yes, but in fact the light did miss by several feet. I'm not sure, Jayne, but it seems to me such a thing might be arranged by measuring exactly where the klieg light was in relationship to the desk below.''

"It still sounds awfully dangerous!'' Jayne objected.

"Perhaps. But for Peter the stakes were high. He was willing to take a few chances. I bet if we look at a replay of Friday morning, we'll see that Peter was sitting as far back from the desk as he could manage.''

"But why hit Cat on the head?'' Jayne asked, as I was making a note to myself to get hold of a videotape of last Friday's show.

"I'm not entirely certain about that, I admit. But the more dangerous Peter makes that show appear, the more likely a judge is going to release him from his contract.''

I was sure I was on the right track. At the moment I had two possible avenues of attack. The first was to track down Peter McDavis, question him, and make him confess. And the second was to get at him through whoever was his accomplice—singular or plural—at the network.

I had my work cut out for me. Among the dangling mysteries was the question of why Dan De Vries should tell me he had gone drinking with Peter on Monday night when Peter's doorman had assured me that Peter had left New York three days earlier? Had Dan lied to me, or the doorman? Or did Peter have another New York hideout, someplace he went when he didn't wish the world to find him at his Park Avenue address?

I left Jayne and disappeared into the study to make a series of phone calls. The first was to Dan De Vries, hoping to clear up the mystery of Monday night. But Dan was not home, and I cleared up nothing. Next I tried to phone Peter's Park Avenue number on the off chance some message as to where Peter might be reached had been left on his answering machine. But the phone rang and rang to an empty apartment, and if Peter had an answering machine, he had turned it off. I decided to try him in Santa Fe, but the New Mexico operator soon informed me that his number was unlisted. This meant more wasted time calling Zeke Roth's office where I struck out once again; first Zeke's secretary and finally Zeke himself refused to give me the number on the grounds that it would be worth their jobs to do so. Peter McDavis, they said, had fled town to his idyllic New Mexico retreat with instructions that absolutely no one was to call him there.

"Having fun, dear?" Jayne asked, bringing a sandwich to me in the study.

"Oodles," I said glumly. "Peter is proving a hard man to reach. I can't even get his Santa Fe number."

"Try Cat," Jayne suggested. "Surely as Peter's coanchor, she must know how to reach him in an emergency."

It does help that Jayne's I.Q. is higher than my own. I phoned Cat, and she did indeed have the New Mexico number.

"But please, Steve, *don't* tell him you got it from me," she pleaded. "He goes to Santa Fe to do the recluse bit, and he'd be furious at me if he—"

"You know, it's very odd," I told her. "I spoke with Dan De Vries this morning, and he insists he had drinks with Peter here in New York on Monday night."

"That doesn't sound at all likely to me," Cat said. "You know, Dan's been drinking more than he should lately—I gather he and Carol are having some problems. He might have gotten his nights mixed up."

"Maybe," I said. I hung up the connection with Cat and dialed the number in New Mexico.

A woman with a melodious voice answered the phone. She said, simply, "Yes?"

"Hello, this is Steve Allen calling from New York. May I speak with Peter McDavis, please."

There was a decided pause on the Santa Fe end.

"How did you get this number?" she said.

"I'm awfully sorry to bother you, but it's really extremely urgent that I reach him," I told her, sidestepping her question. "Is this Mrs. McDavis?"

"Yes, this is Angela McDavis." Her voice was guarded.

"Look, I know your husband is anxious to be on vacation and avoid the problems we're having in New York. But I'm sitting in for him on the show for two weeks and there really are a few things I need to talk with him about."

"Of course, I know who you are, Mr. Allen," she said. Then she added, "You don't remember me, do you?"

"Angela McDavis?" I pondered. I couldn't recall ever meeting the lady.

"My unmarried name was Angela Brier."

"Angela *Brier!*" I cried. "Good Lord, I haven't seen you for what—fifteen years?"

"More like twenty."

I had known Angela Brier in Los Angeles when she had been a very pretty young singer who had seemed on the edge of a big career. We met when she recorded two songs I had written for her first album. I liked her interpretation of my material, and I had expected great things from her. But then, like a lot of talented young people in Hollywood, she disappeared from the business without a trace. I presumed she had settled into a more secure profession, or had gotten married. I hadn't even heard her name for years.

"So you're married to Peter and you live in Santa Fe now," I said. "I believe someone told me you're an artist?"

"A potter," she explained. "I make plates and cups and bowls that I glaze and paint with Southwestern designs. Actually, I do quite well at it. My work is in all the stores around here—even in some of the art galleries. It's not quite the splash I had intended to make in the world, though."

"Well, it sounds like an enviable life to me," I assured her. "To live in New Mexico and do something clever and creative. I can understand why you don't come to New York very often. How long have you and Peter been married?"

"Twelve years now, Steve. And the reason I stay in Santa Fe isn't because I'm too much of an arty recluse for the big city. It's because I'm . . . I'm in a wheelchair. I lost the use of the lower part of my body ten years ago. Ten years and three weeks, to be exact."

"I'm awfully sorry to hear that, Angela." There was a bitter tone in her voice that had not been present when I knew her as a young singer on the verge of a big career. "How did it happen?" I asked.

"Christmas Eve in Connecticut. We were living in Westport in those days. Peter was driving us home after a party. He skidded off the road into a tree. He walked away from the accident without a scratch. I never walked again."

"Lord, how terrible!" I sighed. "He hit a patch of ice, I imagine."

She laughed unpleasantly. "What he was hitting in those days, Steve, was the bottle. He was drunk as a skunk."

"I never knew Peter had a problem with drinking," I said.

"Oh, he doesn't now. He never touched a drop again after that Christmas Eve. Isn't guilt a splendid thing? I can't tell you how happy it makes me that I lost the use of my legs for such a gratifying reason—so Peter could finally get his act together!"

She did not sound gratified and I feared it was not a happy marriage—Peter McDavis tied by guilt to a crippled, unforgiving wife.

"Well, Angela, I hope to see you again sometime," I said

uncomfortably, not quite knowing what to say. "Meanwhile, I really would like to speak with Peter if he's around."

"You think the great Peter McDavis would waste his time in Santa Fe with a wife in a wheelchair?"

"He's not in New Mexico?"

"He flew into Santa Fe last Friday night. Saturday morning he left to go skiing in Taos. I haven't seen him since. Of course, I offered to go skiing with him, but I doubt if I would be much fun at the slopes."

"Do you have his number in Taos, Angela? Is he at a hotel?"

"He has a small ski chalet in the mountains. But there's no phone. It's Peter's way of getting absolutely away from things."

"And he hasn't called since he left Saturday morning?"

"I haven't heard a whisper from him. But what else is new?"

I sighed. The spitefulness of Angela's tone when she talked about her husband was understandable but depressing. I wanted to tell her that a lot of handicapped people have interesting and fulfilling lives and that it was doing her no good to be consumed with bitterness for a terrible mistake that occurred ten years ago. But I didn't know Angela well enough for such a conversation. In the end, I saved the lecture for a better time and simply asked her to tell Peter I was trying to reach him if he did call.

"Take care of yourself, Angela," I said as I hung up the phone.

Jayne found me five minutes later staring out the window at the clouds that were gathering over Central Park. This morning the sun had been shining, but now it looked as if it could snow again.

"You look glum, dear. What's the matter?"

"Just thinking of the waste of ruined lives."

"How pleasant for you. By the way, I forgot to tell you, we've been invited to a premiere of a movie tonight. It's the big budget extravaganza of the season and there's a party afterward at the Plaza, so I hope your tuxedo is pressed. Also, Cass called from California. He's closed up the house and is flying into New York tomorrow."

"Cass," I repeated in a numb stupor, still staring at the gray, wintry sky.

"Yes, Cass. You *do* remember your good buddy and Man Monday?"

"Cass!" I exclaimed, coming awake. "Why didn't I think of him before?"

"I'm not sure," Jayne muttered, regarding me for signs of a mental breakdown.

I phoned the California house and got Cass on the line.

"Cass!" I sang into the wire. "When's the last time you went skiing, pardner? . . . Thirty years ago? Well, never mind— they say it's like riding a bicycle. Once you learn how, you never forget. On your way east tomorrow, I'd like you to make a small detour to New Mexico."

Chapter 33

The movie premiere was at Radio City Music Hall and it was the biggest opening to hit New York since *Pocahontas* played on a huge screen in Central Park. The mayor was present and just about anyone else who had managed to dig out from the snow and slush. I saw a whole galaxy of stars, gossip columnists, studio executives, international celebrities, and even had a glimpse of Princess Di. It was one of those glittering evenings where even the people who weren't ''anyone'' managed to bedeck themselves and look as if they were.

Jayne and I made it to our seats through a throng of friends and acquaintances, asking politely about kids and careers and receiving the kind of superficial answers you expect at such public occasions. Jayne was in a lovely rose-colored gown and I was in my spiffiest tux. The pre-movie glamor was marred only briefly when a famous actress who was wearing a floor-length mink coat was attacked by another famous actress, an animal rights activist who screamed a few choice obscenities. But America is a culture divided against itself, and the contentious issues will follow a person even to a glamorous movie opening.

The movie itself was almost an anticlimax. It was one of the most expensive movies ever made. It had everything for everybody, dazzling special effects, brilliant photography, a thrill a minute—everything in fact that a person could ask for in a movie except a coherent script and realistic acting.

"Perhaps we should skip the party afterward?" Jayne whispered in the dark, after the third explosive car crash.

I agreed. There are few things more embarrassing than making pleasantries to the actors and producers of a movie you've just seen and disliked. I once had the misfortune to run into studio mogul Jack Warner at a public function and, feeling that I had to make some sort of pertinent observation, I said, "Jack, you've done it again." Jayne and I were escaping through the lobby after the film was finished when I felt someone tug at my sleeve.

"Steve, I need to talk to you," the someone said.

I turned and, to my surprise, saw Edith Kinley, the wife of the chairman of the board, whom I hadn't seen since dinner at the Four Seasons. Mrs. Kinley was dressed with dowager dignity in a conservative dark dress that might have been fashionable in 1959. She was wearing expensive jewelry, but her eyes were frantic and full of fear. Even her frosted silver hair seemed somewhat mussed.

"What *is* it?" I asked in alarm.

"It's . . . oh, here comes my husband. I can't talk now. You're going to the party at the Plaza, of course—I'll find you there."

"Well, actually, Jayne and I were thinking of an early night. . . ."

"It's a matter of life and death!" she hissed.

"We'll be there, Edith," said my obliging Jayne.

We all tried to smile pleasantly when Stephen Kinley arrived, but I'm sure we had the guilty look of conspirators.

"Ah, *here* you are, Edith," Stephen Kinley said, eyeing his wife suspiciously. "Thought I lost you, my dear."

"I saw Steve and Jayne, and I just had to dash over to say hello," she lied brightly. "We'll have to do dinner again soon, won't we, Stephen?"

"Certainly," the chairman said, though a bit gruffly. "Though perhaps next time we might leave out that young person in blue jeans who doesn't like television. What was her name?"

"Heather," I told him. "She's an artist."

"Humph!" he said. "Probably one of those artists who expects money from the government! Why can't artists decently starve in an unheated garret as they used to in the old days? These young people today want to be mollycoddled."

Edith twittered with embarrassment. "I *like* young people myself," she said bravely. "Particularly artists."

Stephen Kinley the Second was a man used to having the last word, and he had it now, taking his wife off with him through the crowd. Edith Kinley managed to turn and flash me a pleading look as she was led away.

"What a horrible, arrogant man," Jayne declared. "I wonder what poor Edith wants to tell you?"

"I suppose we'll have to go to the Plaza and find out," I said with a small sigh. In my mind I could visualize the warm bed that was waiting back at the duplex.

"We'll only stay long enough to hear what Edith has to say," said Jayne, leading the way from the theater to the waiting limousine. The party was a noisy affair held in a large ballroom on the second floor of the Plaza Hotel. There were large round tables gathered about a dance floor, and a rock band playing on the bandstand.

Several years ago I wrote a book called "Dumbth," about the collapse of almost everything in our society. A perfect example, and one that is all too common, of *dumbth* is booking groups of rock musicians to provide the music at social gatherings where it is certain that the attendees will actually be interested in conversing with each other.

The music itself is one thing and naturally a hundred individuals will have almost as many reactions to it, ranging from adoration to loathing. But the *volume* at which such music is customarily amplified is quite another matter. At a rock concert, the sky's the limit. And even if permanent damage is being done to the hearing of those in attendance it is as a result of their own choosing. But when intelligent adults are convened there is something truly stupid about providing allegedly background music that unfortunately does not remain in the background but obtrudes to such an extent if any conversation at all can take place it must be done by means of shouting.

Waiters circulated with bottles of champagne and an elegant though basically dreary hotel dinner was served to the five hundred invited guests—a choice of filet mignon with a *béarnaise* sauce, or grilled salmon with a congealed yellow substance on top that was theoretically *hollandaise*. Jayne and I had the salmon to be polite, but took one bite apiece and pushed our plates away. Photographers and TV news cameras were roaming in predatory fashion through the ballroom searching for celebrities.

All in all, it was a commercial event and the mood in the ballroom was about as intimate as Grand Central Station during the evening commute. Among the shrill crowd, I saw no sign of Edith Kinley.

"Who's that?" I asked Jayne. I had just caught sight of a huge fellow in a tuxedo with a bulldog face. He looked strangely familiar, but I couldn't place him. He had been staring at me, but he turned away quickly when I glanced back in his direction.

"Who's who?"

"That big guy over there. The one that looks like a football player. He's walking away now ... I *know* I've seen him somewhere."

"Maybe he *is* a football player, dear."

"I don't think so. I think . . ."

But before I could think any further, a waiter handed me a folded piece of paper. I opened the note and read a few lines of florid, overly feminine penmanship:

Steve,
   Would you mind too terribly much meeting me downstairs in the bar of the Oak Room?

Edith Kinley

Jayne read the note over my shoulder. "I'm coming with you," she said.

"Please do," I said.

"I'm curious what that poor woman is so eager to tell you."

Chapter 34

It was giddy freedom to escape the ballroom and the hysterical hype of studio executives who had just spent $60 million on a movie and knew deep in their glitz-lined souls that it was a lemon. My ears stopped ringing, the muscles around my eyes relaxed, a smile came spontaneously to my lips.

"How I love the absence of shrill noise," I said.

Jayne took my arm and we made our way across the grand court of the Plaza lobby toward the Oak Room bar. One of the joys of the Plaza Hotel is that there is a sense of history to the place, and you can easily fantasize yourself backward to an earlier age of the city. The Oak Room, with its high ceiling and ornate oak paneling, still a reminder of turn-of-the-century New York—the nineteenth century that is, that was bursting with energy and destiny, pushing itself headlong into modern times. Eloise, the little girl from the storybook, played here, and so did such diverse characters as Salvador Dali to John Kennedy. Jayne and I glided into the elegant old bar and looked about for Edith Kinley. Only about half the tables were occupied. There were businessmen talking in low voices over drinks, matrons from Connecticut in town to see a show with a glass of sherry in hand, and quite a few foreign tourists speaking a babel of languages. But no Mrs. Kinley.

"Strange, I don't see her," I said.

"Where, oh where can she be?"

"Oh, oh," I said. There was no Mrs. Kinley, but I *did* catch sight of a figure I recognized—a man in a rumpled suit, badly shaved, sitting by himself at a table with his back to the window overlooking Fifty-ninth Street. He had a glass of something amber in his hand and an unlit cigarette dangling at a corner of his mouth.

"Who is that disreputable-looking gentleman?" Jayne asked. "And why is he staring at us?"

"Come along. I better introduce you."

"Are you sure, Steve? What about finding Edith Kinley?"

"I have a feeling this is the person we've been summoned to meet. . . . Jayne, I would like you to meet Gene Ptak, Private Investigations, of Sheridan Square."

Gene rose upon his stubby legs, took Jayne's hand and—it is difficult to report this with a straight face—bowed in an absurd fashion and kissed her fingers. I took Jayne's hand myself immediately afterward to make certain her wedding ring was still there.

"Swell to meet you, Mrs. Allen," said Gene. "It's like, I'm *awestruck.*"

"How sweet of you to say so," said Jayne.

"All right, where's Mrs. Kinley. Did you eat her up, Ptak?"

"Let's just say I'm Mrs. Kinley's representative in a sensitive matter," he told me with a slight leer. "Sit down and have a glass of whiskey with me. It'll be worth your time."

"I doubt it," I told him. But we sat anyway and ordered a

pot of tea when the black-and-white-uniformed waiter hurried over. "Now what gives?" I asked. "Edith Kinley told us at the movie premiere to meet her at the Plaza later. Was that her idea or yours?"

"Mine. I told her to approach you that way at the movie theater in order to get you here. It was a setup. I knew you could never resist a damsel in distress."

"And you sent the note up to the ballroom?"

"It's her writing. She gave it to me earlier."

"And where is Mrs. Kinley now, if I may ask."

"Who cares? She's done her part, now it's my turn."

"But why all this trouble to get us here?" Jayne asked.

"I like to do things in style, lady," Gene said grandly. He turned to me. "You can't begrudge me my little games. Anyway, there's a particular reason I wanted to meet you at the Plaza. There's someone staying here you've been looking for."

"Go on," I told him.

"See that guy in the turban?"

An elegant East Indian gentleman with a white turban wrapped on his head was passing from the dining room through the bar on his way to the lobby. Jayne, Gene, and I stared at him as he made his passage.

"What about him?"

"You don't recognize him?"

"No. Is he some trendy new swami?"

The private eye sat back in his chair and took a sip of his whiskey.

"If you were a famous television person and you wanted to stay in New York without anyone knowing where you were, what do you think you would do about it?"

I blinked. "A disguise?" I asked. "You're saying that's Peter McDavis in *disguise?*"

He smiled. "You need to be more observant, Mr. Allen. A

little face paint and makeup, a turban round his head—but look at the features carefully and you'll see it's McDavis.''

I got up from the table to follow the man into the lobby and see for myself. But Gene grabbed hold of my arm.

''You can talk to him later. I got his room number—he's not going nowhere. Anyway, McDavis is just the icing on the cake. I got more important things to tell you.''

Reluctantly, I sat down again at the table. It was difficult not to chase after Peter McDavis when I had been looking for him all day. But the private eye had aroused my curiosity. He kept grinning at me, inordinately proud of himself.

''Okay,'' I said. ''Tell me your information. But make it quick please.''

His smile became broader. ''Aren't you interested in how I came to represent a classy dame like Mrs. Kinley? It's because I went to her with the goods.''

''The *goods?* Meaning what?''

''The info, man. The lowdown on everything that's been going on at the network.''

''You know who murdered Dennis Lovelace and why all the accidents have been happening?''

''You bet!'' Eugene was grinning in quite an unbearable manner.

''And you went to Mrs. Kinley—''

''With a proposition that she hire me to do a little digging around. She went for it, man. You're looking at a private detective with a very rich client, Mr. Allen. I'm movin' up in the world, pops.''

''Great.''

He laughed. ''Okay. You probably think it's all about Peter McDavis trying to break his contract with the network. But it isn't. The story is this—''

Gene Ptak never finished his sentence. He sat bolt upright in his chair, as though he had been hit by a bolt of lightning. His eyes opened wide with surprise.

"Mr. Ptak, what's wrong?" Jayne cried.

But the private detective was in no mood to reply. He remained upright for a moment and then slowly crumpled facefirst onto the table. What was wrong, I saw, was the small bullet hole in the window directly behind the back of his chair.

Chapter 35

In politely expensive places like the Plaza, people mind their own business. Which may explain why, as yet, there was no fuss or holler raised about the gentleman near the window who happened to have his head on a table. I noticed one of the aristocratic matrons at a nearby table glancing from the corner of her eye at the unfortunate man who appeared fast asleep at the table, but naturally she was too discreet to say anything. No one had noticed the small round hole in the window to the street, and not even Jayne or I had heard the actual shot, so noisy is Manhattan.

The Oak Room is raised just slightly above street level. I gazed out the window in question, but I saw no sign of a sniper, only a steady stream of traffic along Fifty-ninth Street. It seemed to me the shot must have been fired from the north side of the street that bordered Central Park; had the shot come from the sidewalk closest to the hotel, it would have needed to be fired at too great an angle upward. As I stood by the window studying the scene, I noticed the usual line of horse-drawn carriages by the curb alongside the Park. A group of the drivers were talking excitedly among themselves.

"Let's leave," I suggested to Jayne. "There isn't much we can do to help the late Mr. Ptak."

"Isn't there some law about leaving the scene of a crime?" Jayne worried.

"Probably. There's a law about nearly everything else these days. But at the moment, I'm more concerned with getting our hands on Peter McDavis. I think that we will do best to divide forces. I want to have a word with those horse people across the street."

Jayne and I made a few hasty plans and then she exited the bar in the direction of the lobby. I approached the bartender for a moment before I made my own exit. I paid the bill for our tea and Gene's whiskey, and then said: "By the by, the gentleman with his head on the table—I'm afraid he's in for a rather long sleep. You may want to call the police."

"The police? Sir, perhaps you should wait . . . Sir!"

I stepped quickly from the room and made a sharp left turn down the side exit to Fifty-ninth Street. The night outside was sharp and cold. The sky above was yellow, dense with imminent snow and reflected city lights. New York needed more snow about as badly as it needed another murder.

Before I describe my own escapade, I think it best at present to follow Jayne's progress. Though I was not there, she has recounted her adventures to me in some detail, and knowing Jayne as well as I do, I am fairly confident I can switch now to what we call in the movie business, her POV—point of view, that is.

Fortunately, Jayne had gotten a good look at the East Indian gentleman in the white turban as he had stepped through the bar on his way to the lobby. But unfortunately, she had no idea how she was going to track him down. To make matters worse, she was not exactly dressed for detective work. With her rose-colored, floor-length evening gown, her flaming red hair, and her best costume jewelry around her neck, wrists, and fingers—she was not an inconspicuous figure who could blend easily into a crowd.

Deciding to try the front desk first, she fluttered her eyes very prettily at a young man behind the desk who had a name tag on his blazer pocket that said, Thomas Melzer, Asst. Manager.

"Good evening, Miss Meadows," he said pleasantly. "And how are you tonight?"

Jayne took it as a good beginning that he recognized her. She enjoys her separate identities; for some occasions she is Miss Jayne Meadows, and at other times she is pleased to be Mrs. Allen. Tonight she was glad for the Miss rather than the Mrs.—and she used her natural charm shamelessly.

"I'm very well, Thomas. Actually, I just escaped an absolutely dreadful party in the ballroom upstairs. It was much too loud and full of people looking about for celebrities."

Thomas smiled. "You went to the premiere at Radio City? I heard the movie was awful."

"Awful is the word alright. But Thomas—Tom—the reason I stopped by—I was sitting in the bar just now, and I had a glimpse of a man I met in Bombay—an East Indian gentleman in a dark blue suit wearing a white turban. He must have walked through the lobby only a moment ago. He took my husband and me on a most wonderful tour of the countryside—and I'm horribly embarrassed but I can't for the life of me remember his name. I believe he's staying here at the hotel."

"Mr. Abawashi, perhaps?"

"That's it! Thank you, Thomas. Mr. Abawashi. Anyway, I thought I might send him a little gift—you couldn't tell me his room number, could you?"

Jayne fluttered her eyelashes and flashed her famous TV smile. But Thomas of the Plaza would not betray his profession. He suggested that Jayne leave the gift with him, and he would see that it arrived at its proper destination. Or, of course, she could use the house phone and call Mr. Abawashi directly.

Jayne chose the latter. She found a row of house phones near the elevators and asked the operator to be put through to Mr. Abawashi's room. He answered on the second ring.

"Hello? Is this Mr. Abawashi?" Jayne asked.

"Yes, yes!" he replied with just the right touch of an accent, and surprisingly friendly. "And you must be . . ."

"Jayne . . ."

"What a pretty name!" he said warmly.

"How nice of you to say so," said my wife. "And let me guess your first name—I bet it's . . . Peter!"

"Peter? Oh, no! Me Tarzan," he said playfully. "You Jayne!"

Jayne rolled her eyes. Peter was certainly in a merry mood. Jayne suspected he had been drinking.

"But you know, my darling, at the agency they told me the girl tonight would be called Andrea," he mentioned coyly. "I must tell you, I much prefer having a Jayne."

"The agency?"

"Aphrodite Escort Service, of course."

"Oh, yes!" Jayne agreed. Suddenly the situation was very clear to her. Dreadfully clear. "Well," she ad-libbed, "Andrea is tied up tonight, I'm afraid."

"Tied up?" he laughed with disgusting innuendo. "*Tied* up? Oh, dear me—how intriguing! Now I think you must fly up to my room, my angel. Room 1045."

Jayne put down the house phone distastefully. She had gotten the room number—a small victory—but now she wondered if this really could be Peter McDavis. She could imagine Peter staying at the Plaza under an assumed name and in disguise—and quite a clever disguise it was, pretending to be an East Indian. But with his career at such a crucial juncture, and two murders now in the works, it seemed unlikely to Jayne that Peter would be sending out for female companionship to the Aphrodite Escort Service.

What if Gene Ptak had been wrong and Mr. Abawashi were

nothing but what he seemed—a lonely businessman from India? It could be a sticky situation to go to his room. And *most* embarrassing, thought Jayne. And how was she to get away if he insisted she stay?

Jayne pondered these delicate questions for a few moments as she stood by the house phones. She debated waiting for me to return; then we could go together to Room 1045. But if I found some lead to the killer among the horse carriages, I might be gone a long time. And if Mr. Abawashi *was* indeed Peter McDavis, time might well be crucial. Jayne decided to chance an embarrassing situation and go to Room 1045 alone. If Mr. Abawashi got out of hand, she intended to whack him with her handbag—in Jayne's case, a formidable weapon.

Jayne rang for the elevator and rode with a group of Japanese tourists to the tenth floor. She made her way along the hallway to number 1045 and rang the buzzer. To her surprise, there was no answer, and in a moment she rang again.

"Yoo-hoo, Mr. Abawashi! Your Aphrodite has arrived!" she called. Finally she rapped on the door itself, thinking perhaps the buzzer was broken. The door swung open onto a darkened suite of rooms.

"Hello in there! Mr. Abawashi?"

Hearing no answer, Jayne walked cautiously into the sitting room. The door creaked shut behind her. She was about to turn around when she felt the cold barrel of a gun pressed into the back of her neck.

"I wouldn't turn around if I were you, Mrs. Allen," a voice told her quietly.

"Tarzan, I presume?" she asked tartly.

"Please just keep moving into the sitting room and don't speak unless I ask you a question."

The voice no longer had the slightest trace of an Indian accent or friendliness, but Jayne was not entirely certain it was Peter McDavis. She had seen Peter on television but had in fact never met him in person, so it was difficult to make a positive identification. There was something about the voice, however, that made her do exactly as she was told.

"Mrs. Allen, you have put me in a difficult position, I'm afraid. I need to make something of an escape, and your presence is awkward. What I'm going to do is let you decide between two options. Do you understand?"

"Yes."

"Good. Here's choice number one—I can shoot you right now in the back of your neck. Frankly, I don't think you'll feel it very much. It would be like a light switching off."

"I don't think I like option number one very much," Jayne managed, finding her mouth was very dry.

"Option two is this—you allow me to tie you securely to a chair and put a gag in your mouth. Furthermore, you agree to close your eyes this instant and keep them closed, and not make any attempt to see me. If you look at me, I'm afraid, then option one becomes automatic."

Jayne closed her eyes tightly. She was no fool. Between a bad choice and the worst choice of all, she knew very well which option to take.

Chapter 36

A few snowflakes were floating in the night sky as I crossed Fifty-ninth Street. I made my way to the half dozen drivers who were standing together near their horse carriages. I could hear their voices rising and falling and arguing among themselves as I approached.

"It was nothing, Edward, my lad—a car backfired, that's all."

"You're wrong, Douglas. I saw the man with a rifle just a dozen feet from where I'm standing now. He stood in that shadow there, raised the gun, aimed carefully, and fired one shot at the hotel."

"We should call the police," said a new voice.

"Never!" declared a fourth. "I am an anarchist, as you well know, and I am philosophically opposed to cooperating with the police under any circumstances. Anyway, I doubt if any harm was done—a single rifle isn't going to do much damage to such a proud edifice of capitalism as the Plaza Hotel!"

Drivers of horse-drawn carriages in New York City tend to be an eccentric lot. At least two of the men in the group had long, gray hair, unkempt whiskers, and might easily be mistaken for homeless street characters. But there was one middle-aged man in a dark suit who could have been a banker, and two of the drivers were in fact attractive young women. It did not appear an easy profession, yet there is a certain romance to it.

"Good evening," I said, approaching the group.

"Want a ride, sir? . . . Edward, here's a customer for you."

"What I'm looking for is information, not a ride," I said. "I was sitting in the hotel bar across the street when a bullet killed a man at my table. I was hoping you can give me a description of whoever fired the gun."

"Killed someone, did it?" muttered one of the drivers.

The circle seemed to break up instantaneously into amorphous bodies moving back toward their individual carriages. These drivers were outsiders, like gypsies—outside the regular structure of work, marriage, credit cards, and debt that most of us call home. They didn't want to get involved in a police affair.

"Wait a minute! Edward!" I called, walking after one of the gray-haired men. "I heard you say that you saw a man with a rifle."

"Must have been an audio-hallucination, sir," he said with his back to me, adjusting the feedbag on the mouth of his gray horse. "Yes, sir, a lot of people hallucinate in *this* city, hear all sorts of things!"

"Edward, I'm not a cop. I'm just someone who was having a cup of tea when the person next to me was shot to death. If you know anything, please tell me."

He turned to face me. Edward was dressed in an ancient tuxedo that had seen better days, a thick dark topcoat, and a stovepipe top hat that was bent comically, pointing south. His face had the rough look of someone who had spent many years outside on the New York streets. Yet he was quite handsome, distinguished in an odd way. He carried himself, and his costume, with more dignity than many of the people I had seen at the movie premiere and party afterward.

"You write music, don't you?" he asked unexpectedly, studying my face every bit as carefully as I was studying his.

"That's right. My name is Steve Allen. I'm an entertainer."

"Hmm," he said with disapproval. "That's all music is for most people, I suppose—entertainment."

"Well, that's a *part* of music, certainly," I said mildly. "Are you, er . . . a musician?"

"I taught composition for many years at Juilliard. Gave it up, of course. Figured if I was going to deal with a lot of horse manure, it might as well be the real thing rather than the spiritual and metaphorical variety . . . isn't that right, Wolfgang?" he said with affection, turning to his gray horse.

I was certain there must be quite a story here, how a professor of composition at Juilliard became the driver of a horse carriage. But I was in a hurry, and it was a story that would need to wait for another time.

"Well, music is a wonderful thing," I told him, "and so are horses, I'm sure. But at the moment, Edward, one human being has murdered another—a sleazy, funny little guy named Gene. The world won't miss him very much, but it still makes me very angry, and I would like to find the bastard who killed him."

Edward did not seem happy to cooperate, but at last he told me what I wanted to know.

"I saw the whole thing," he admitted finally. "The guy came out of the Fifty-ninth Street entrance from the Plaza and jaywalked across the middle of the street. Two cars almost hit him, but he seemed to be in a hurry. I noticed him because I thought he was coming to hire a carriage, and it was my turn to have the next customer."

"What did he look like."

"Tall, big shoulders—built like an athlete."

"Like a football player, perhaps?" Lights were flashing in my brain like the Fourth of July, an unexpected jackpot.

"I suppose so," Edward admitted. "I *hate* football! If people in America paid less attention to the Dallas Cowboys and more attention to who they elected as president, this country might stand half a chance!"

"But you were describing the man with the gun. How was he dressed?"

"Overcoat. Dinner jacket, black tie—just like you, as a matter of fact."

"What did he do after he crossed the street?"

"He studied the hotel very carefully, as though he were looking for something. Then he stepped into that shadow by the edge of the park."

Edward pointed to a park bench that was beneath the overhang of a bare tree. The tree did not create the shadow as much as the spacing of the streetlamps. It was about as discreet and invisible a spot as you might hope to find on a winter's evening in downtown Manhattan.

"Then what happened?"

"He stood up on the bench, to get more height, I suppose. I was watching the whole thing. He took out the gun from the lining of his overcoat. It was in three pieces—the barrel, the stock, and the middle. There was a telescopic sight on the thing as well. He screwed them all together to make a sort of rifle—then he aimed and fired. The gun wasn't very loud, really. Just a nasty pop. Then he jumped down from the bench, unscrewed the gun quickly, stuffed it back into the lining of his overcoat, and walked away fast."

"Which direction?"

"West. Toward Columbus Circle."

I thought of rushing off in pursuit, but nearly ten minutes had passed now since the shooting, and I knew the killer could have jumped into a taxi or a waiting car and be miles away by now.

"Edward!" I chided. "You saw all this happen! Why didn't you try to stop him?"

"I didn't realize he was going to fire the damn thing. It all happened so fast. And it's not my business," he said stubbornly. "Let the idiots kill each other, for all I care—Arabs, Jews, Catholics, Protestants . . . Muslims killing for the glory of Allah, everyone at each other's throats! All a lot of crap."

"Well, Edward, you'd better give me a phone number or address where I can reach you. You witnessed a murder and you're going to be needed eventually to testify in court."

"Hell with that!" he said. In one easy move, he bounded upward into the driver's seat and picked up the reins.

"Giddy-up, Wolfgang!" he cried. And then he, the carriage, and the gray horse took off with a clatter down Fifty-ninth Street.

"Edward!" I called after him. "You can't ride away from this! You have to take some responsibility!"

"Why!" he cried in return, his constant refrain. However, I knew it would not be difficult to find him. There could not be too many ex–Juilliard professors driving carriages powered by a gray horse named Wolfgang in New York.

I had learned enough to identify the killer should I ever see him again, and I was cold from standing on the sidewalk. So I turned my feet toward Fifth Avenue to use the crosswalk back to the hotel. I was walking along the line of horses and drivers when I chanced to see a woman sitting in one of the carriages. She was wrapped up in several thick blankets so that only her face was visible. Two huge frightened eyes glanced at me, then turned quickly away. I was so lost in thought that I walked on several paces before I realized that the frightened eyes peering out of the blankets were familiar.

I turned back to the carriage.

"Edith Kinley!" I called. "Whatever are you doing sitting in this carriage? You must be freezing!"

Indeed, her teeth were chattering.

"Oh, dear, I didn't expect to see you, Steve," she protested timidly. "You're supposed to be in the Oak Room right now."

"Yes, having a talk with *you!*"

"I'm awfully sorry . . . It's all a terrible mix-up, I'm afraid. Didn't that little man speak with you?"

"Gene Ptak? Edith, I am really surprised you even know someone like that."

"I *don't* really know him, of course. He came to me and seemed to have quite a lot of information. I thought it best to do as he told me."

"How strange!" I muttered. "Look, I think we need to have a good long chat, Edith. Why don't we go back to the Plaza?"

Just as I was offering my hand to help her down from the carriage, I heard police sirens converging on the Plaza from three separate directions. Edith Kinley stood on the sidewalk, looking very small and cold.

"Oh, dear, oh, dear!" she declared. "I hate the sound of sirens! It always makes it seem as if something terrible has happened!"

"It has," I assured her. But I thought it best for both of us to avoid the consequences of terrible events for just a while longer. When five police cars came screaming up to the Fifty-ninth Street entrance of the Plaza, I decided the Oak Room was no longer a quiet and cozy place to enjoy a drink. I guided Edith Kinley kitty-corner across Fifth Avenue to the Sherry Netherland instead.

Chapter 37

Mrs. Kinley wore a politically incorrect floor-length chinchilla coat. She was an old-fashioned woman whose sense of the world seemed to exist in a time capsule from the Eisenhower fifties. The chinchilla, nevertheless, had not managed to keep her warm. She was so cold from her long sit in the horse carriage that she continued to wear the coat in the Sherry Netherland bar, oblivious to disapproving glances from other tables. I ordered two snifters of cognac and after a few sips her teeth finally stopped chattering.

"Now, Edith," I said firmly, "I want you to tell me exactly what you were doing with Gene Ptak. You said he came to see you—when was that?"

"Yesterday evening when Stephen was out at his club. He phoned first, then came over to our apartment. He promised to help me if I did what he said. Oh, I know I've behaved like a fool, but I've been so desperately concerned about Stephen. Both Stephens, of course. I'm sure you understand."

I did not understand. *"Both* Stephens?"

"Didn't you know, Stephen Kinley the Second, is my husband, of course. And Stephen Kinley the Third . . . our son."

"I didn't know you had a son."

"Well, we did . . . we *had* . . . oh, it's a terrible story. I'm
really awfully embarrassed to even begin. Do you mind if I
have another cognac first?"

I called over the waiter and told him to bring the bottle. I
was anxious to get Edith talking before New York's Finest
managed to trace my movements from the dead body in the
Oak Room to where we sat across the street.

"Little Stevie was born in 1955—he was the sweetest, most
imaginative child, always drawing pictures and telling stories.
He used to put on puppet shows for us after dinner—a born
entertainer, his grandfather used to say. His grandfather, of
course, adored him."

"Stephen the First?" I asked, trying to keep this plethora
of Steves straight in my mind.

"That's right—Stephen the First, who built the network out
of nothing. My husband's father. I'm afraid Number One adored
Number Three, but he didn't like Number Two very much. My
husband was an unloved child."

"Where is your son now?" I asked. "You speak of him in
the past tense. Is he still alive?"

"That's what we don't know, you see. He disappeared nearly
twenty years ago."

"Disappeared?"

"I told you it was a terrible story. Stevie was just a perfect
child . . . up until the time he went to boarding school at the
age of fourteen. We sent him to Choate, which seemed a very
respectable place to go. But somehow he began getting strange
ideas . . . yes, I think Choate was the start of all our trouble
with him."

"What sort of strange ideas, Edith?"

"Well, he wanted to ban the bomb, you know. That sort of
thing. Now, his father and I were perfectly willing to let him

go through a period of adolescent idealism, but he actually went on a march to Washington and got himself arrested. Then, as if that wasn't bad enough, he began to see a girl . . . quite a nice girl, I suppose, but she was definitely *not* our kind. If you know what I mean.''

''No, I don't know what you mean. What was wrong with her?''

Edith Kinley took a sip of cognac and refused to answer for a moment.

''She was a Negro,'' she said at last. ''Her name was Ann. Now I am the *least* prejudiced person in the world, I swear to God! But Stevie actually brought her to dinner once at the apartment without warning us about her . . . race. Our building is restricted, of course, and in those days, well . . . colored people were expected to use the servants' elevator. Stevie had quite an embarrassing row with the doorman trying to get her up to the apartment in the front elevator. My husband was furious, naturally.''

''Furious with the doorman, I hope.''

''Well, no . . . with young Steve.''

At that same time, by odd coincidence—well, all coincidences are odd—I happened to be writing a book about black/white relations in the U.S., a project motivated by my dismay at the slowness of American progress up out of the three-centuries long atrocity of slavery and its depressing aftermath. But it would have been irrelevant to comment on the subject to an audience of one and I had other business to attend to at the moment.

Edith continued: ''Then over winter vacation that year, Stevie actually had the nerve to bring the girl to the annual Christmas party at the network. That's when Stephen—my husband, the Second, that is—decided to do something.''

''What did he do, Edith?''

''You see, Ann went to a boarding school near Choate— Rosemary Hall. She was a scholarship student, of course. I think the only Negro in the school. Stephen had her . . . well—expelled.''

"Expelled?" I cried. "How in the world could he manage that?"

"Stephen's sister went to Rosemary Hall years ago. The Kinley family endowed an athletic field there. Or maybe it was a new dormitory—I forget, but they had a lot of pull in those days, and it was easy enough to get Ann—er—thrown out. Stephen did it, of course, believing he had little Stevie's best interest in mind. He has nothing against Black people himself, you understand—we had an awfully sweet Negro maid once who was *almost* part of the family! But he knew Stevie would face such an uphill battle in society. My son was so pigheaded—he was even talking about marriage, taunting his father with the prospect of it, though he was only seventeen. And an interracial marriage, you know, would ruin his chances to get ahead in the world. So my husband had the girl thrown out of the school in order to separate them. He isn't a *vicious* man, Steve. . . . Unfortunately, the girl took it rather badly."

"How badly?"

"She went back to Alabama, or maybe it was Arkansas—one of those backward Southern states. And she—she committed suicide, poor thing."

"My God."

"I suppose she thought she'd never get ahead in the world without an education."

"And how did your son react to this?" I asked grimly.

"He was devastated. He never forgave his father, and nothing was ever the same afterward. All this happened in the spring term of his last year at Choate. He had been accepted at Yale and he could have had such a *good* life. But he was so angry . . . he ran away from Choate, he stole a car to go to Ann's funeral, and later he refused to go to Yale. He let his hair grow long and he grew a beard and he began to smoke marijuana."

"He no longer lived at home?"

"Oh, no! He moved to San Francisco and got a job cooking in a health food restaurant. It broke my heart. I asked my husband to go to him and try to make amends, but Stephen can be awfully stubborn. He was certain he had done the right thing so he refused to apologize. It was a matter of principle, he said. When Stevie began to live like a hippie, my husband simply washed his hands of him. I . . . I . . . never actually saw my son again after he moved West."

"How sad."

"Once a year at Christmas, my son wrote me a letter—he was never so angry at me as he was with his father. They were really quite beautiful letters, I thought. All about how he was trying to 'find' himself, you know. He lived in a commune in northern California for a few years, and then he went to India to become a disciple of some allegedly holy man. But he was restless and unhappy and nothing seemed to take. The last card I received from Stevie came from New Mexico. He was living in a tepee in the mountains, poor thing, like a savage. This was fifteen years ago. Then . . . then . . ."

Mrs. Kinley's face seemed to disintegrate. She burst into tears.

". . . then I never heard from my son again!" she sobbed.

She was in some ways a foolish, narrow-minded woman. But I felt truly sorry for her.

"Did you ever try to find him?" I asked, patting her hand as it rested on the table.

"Of course, I did! Five years after Stevie disappeared, I hired a detective to find him. But the detective had no luck. A year after that, I was so desperate I went to New Mexico myself, but I didn't even know where to begin to look. It was hopeless. Then ten years ago, my husband's father died—Stephen the First, that is—and this time my husband hired a private detective to try to find our son. But again, nothing. It's as if our little Stevie simply vanished into thin air without a trace! At this point, I would almost welcome the news that he was dead, just to know something definite. It's an agony to wonder and wonder about him, but never to know anything for sure!''

''As a father of four sons myself, I can imagine your sorrow,'' I told her. ''You mentioned your husband tried to find Stevie after *his* father's death. Was Number Three in Number One's will, by any chance?''

Edith dried her tears with a handkerchief and gave me a sneaky, sideways look. She was not good at concealing information. ''No-o,'' she said airily. ''I don't believe so. Not that I recall, at least.''

''Edith!'' I chided. ''Tell me the truth!''

''I promised my husband I would never tell a soul!'' she whispered.

''Then I think we had better go to the police and let them sort this out,'' I said, deliberately sounding heartless.

''Oh, no! You can't do that! I'll tell you, but you must promise to keep it to yourself. You've probably heard that my husband inherited all of his father's stock in the network?''

''I did hear that, yes. Your husband is the majority share-holder, isn't he?''

Edith sighed. ''Yes and no. He owns fifty-one percent of the stock. But the problem is, he doesn't really own them.''

''What do you mean?''

''I told you, Stephen the First adored his grandson. When the horrible thing happened with Ann, Number One took his grandson's side. He said my husband had acted like a bloody fool. He never really forgave my husband, or got over his grandson's disappearance. So when he died, he left everything, the stock in the network, the estate in Connecticut, the town house in New York—everything to my son. My husband didn't receive a penny.''

''But your son had disappeared by this time, hadn't he?''

''Yes, though Stevie has still never been declared legally dead. My husband is simply the trustee of all the Kinley holdings—holding everything in trust for our son, should he ever reappear.''

"Amazing! I never heard this before!''

"No one has. Number One very wisely put a secrecy clause into his will. He was enough of a businessman to know that my husband could not possibly be an effective head of the network if the news ever leaked out that he would lose his job, his house, everything—the moment Stevie came home.''

"*If* Stevie ever does come home,'' I said thoughtfully. Edith Kinley's story had certainly put a new twist on the story. I wasn't certain what her son's disappearance had to do with the current problems at the network, but I was willing to bet that it fit in somewhere.

"I feel quite faint,'' Edith told me. "I think I should go home and lie down.''

"We'll be finished here in a moment. First tell me about Gene Ptak. What did he contact you about? And why in the world did you agree to his little deception to get me to meet him in the Oak Room?''

"Mr. Ptak was the private detective we hired ten years ago to try to find our son.''

"I suspected as much. How long did he work for you then?''

"About a year. Then we never heard from him again. Until he phoned me yesterday. He said he had found Stevie.''

"Really?''

"I was terribly excited, as you can imagine. But Mr. Ptak refused to tell me any details. He wanted to meet with you first, he said.''

"But why? I don't understand?'' I asked.

"I don't either. He was very mysterious—a terrible little man, really! He said he wanted to see you in some 'posh place,' as he put it. I think he was having his little gloating game— he was quite full of himself! Then he told me exactly how I was supposed to approach you and lure you to the Oak Room.

I did what he told me, hoping to learn about my son. You *do* understand, don't you?"

"To some extent. Gene told you to wait in the horse carriage across the street?"

"He promised to come to me after he spoke with you. He said he would take me to Stevie."

At this moment I noticed two individuals I very much wished to avoid: Detectives Morgenfield and Marcotti had stepped inside the Sherry Netherland and were walking past the entrance of the bar toward the lobby. I didn't have much time left if I wished to escape them.

"Edith," I said quickly. "If your son *is* still alive, how old would he be today?"

"Forty-two years old, seven months, and three weeks."

"And how long did you say he spent in India with his guru?"

"Almost two years. Is that important?"

"I'm not certain. But meanwhile, you are about to have some unwelcome official company. I suggest you keep everything you've just told me *entre nous* for the time being. Is that understood?"

"I won't breathe a word," she promised.

"I'm going to leave you to pay our drink bill, I'm afraid. I'm in a bit of a hurry."

I slipped out of the bar and kept my head tucked as I moved through the lobby. I had a glimpse of Morgenfield and Marcotti with their backs to me, less than a dozen feet away speaking to the concierge. I kept moving out the door into the wintry night. I was one step behind disaster, and one step ahead of the law.

Chapter 38

Back in the Plaza lobby, I noticed a squad of cops—plain-clothed and in uniform—lurking by the entrance to the Oak Room. I removed my eyeglasses, hunched my shoulders and kept my head down. As a respectable citizen, I had no intention of avoiding New York's Finest forever. But at the moment I simply had too much to do to waste time chatting with Morgenfield and Marcotti.

I approached the assistant manager at the front desk. "Excuse me, but have you by chance noticed a flaming redhead in a rose-colored evening gown who is wearing enough jewelry to drive any husband into the poorhouse?"

"You must be referring to Jayne Meadows," said the assistant manager. It was, happily, the same Thomas Melzer that Jayne had spoken to earlier in the evening.

"Where might she be?" I wondered.

"She was trying to locate one of our guests—a Mr. Abawashi, Mr. Allen."

"Did you give her Abawashi's room number?"

"Oh, no, Mr. Allen! I could *never* give out a guest's room number. I suggested she call him on the house phone."

"Good idea. Think I'll do the same thing myself."

I was about to move off to the house phones but Thomas stopped me.

"One moment, Mr. Allen. Mr. Abawashi left this note for you when he checked out a few minutes ago." The assistant manager handed me a crisp white envelope.

"For *me?*" I said, astonished. "Let me get this straight. Abawashi checked out *after* my wife called him on the house phone?"

"Yes, about twenty minutes after she went up to his room."

"You notice everything, don't you, Thomas?"

"Thank you, sir, I do. I find it pays to be observant."

I was moving off to read the note when Thomas stopped me again.

"Er, Mr. Allen—there is a policeman looking for you. A Detective Sergeant Morgenfield, sir."

"Thank you, Thomas."

I stepped to one side and opened the envelope. The message inside was handwritten on Plaza stationery by someone who was either from India, or trying very hard to make it appear that he was:

Fondly Mr. Allen,

Pliz excuse hasty need to tie Missus Allen to chair and place unpleasant gag in her mouth. I feel most embarrassed not to offer traditional hospitality due to beeg hurry I am in. You find her in room 1045.

Veery dearly yours,
K. J. L. Abawashi

A flat key card was enclosed in the envelope. K. J. L Abawashi was a very polite gentleman, as gentleman go who gag your wife and tie her to a chair. I hurried to the elevator, rode to the tenth floor, and used the key card to open the door to Room 1045. Jayne was in the sitting room in the exact predicament Abawashi had described. I removed her gag first and then worked on the ropes.

"My God!" Jayne exhaled. "But what took you so long?"

"I thought I was rather prompt. Are you all right?"

"Yes, scared to death. But otherwise unharmed. For a mugger or whatever he is, Mr. Abawashi was very considerate."

"I was thinking the same thing myself. Did you get a good look at him?"

"No look at all. Not even a glimpse. He came upon me from behind and made certain I never saw his face."

"What about his voice? Did he have an accent?"

"Yes, but I'm not convinced it was real."

"And now the big question, my pet. Could Mr. Abawashi have been Peter McDavis in disguise?"

"Possibly. But I can't say for certain."

"Well, it was *someone* involved in this network business, that's for sure," I told her. "If not Peter, then it's Stephen Kinley the Third."

"The Third? Haven't you added an extra Roman numeral?"

"Not at all. Stephen the Third is—or was—the son of Stephen the Second and Edith Kinley. It's a wonder that family keeps all their Stephens straight! Steve is a wonderful name, of course."

"I didn't know the Kinleys have a son. Or is it, *had* a son? You speak about him as though he's no longer alive."

"I don't know. It's a new twist to the murder investigation, I'm afraid. And a very tragic tale as well."

Jayne rubbed her wrists and ankles to get her circulation going while I related the unhappy saga of Stephen the Third, whose parents had alienated the young man about as badly as parents might ever do, driving the girl he loved to suicide. I was particularly interested in the fact that Stephen Number One, the grandfather, had left all his stock in the network to the missing grandson. This made the present chairman of the board a very lame duck indeed. Stephen Number Two would lose everything if his son ever reappeared.

"So perhaps the murders and various accidents have to do with this old tragedy between father and son?" Jayne asked. "I don't see how it all quite fits together."

"Neither do I," I admitted. "But there are some evil possibilities here—people have murdered for considerably less than the television empire the young man will inherit if he's ever found."

"But why kill Dennis Lovelace? Or Gene Ptak, for that matter?" Jayne asked. "It doesn't make sense."

"No, it doesn't," I agreed moodily. I hate it when all the facts do not add up to a sensible picture. "So perhaps, after all, it all has to do with Peter McDavis trying to create enough mayhem on the set so he can get out of his contract. That would make *more* sense, I suppose. Or it might be something connected with Zeke Roth's embezzling funds from the show. Or even Cat—I don't believe I told you yet, but Cat apparently was having an affair with Dennis Lovelace."

"I'm sorry to hear that," Jayne said, frowning.

"So am I," I complained. "Among other things, it makes for motives galore. Let's say that Cat felt jilted and wanted revenge—she might have murdered Dennis and then arranged the accidents to throw suspicion around in a false direction."

"I can't believe Cat is capable of murder, dear. We've known her most of her life."

"Yes, but do we *really* know her, Jayne? Anyway, you can see my point—the more I investigate this case, the more complicated everything seems. Just a few hours ago, I was certain that Peter McDavis with an accomplice or two was the killer. Now I'm not sure of anything!"

"You shouldn't become discouraged, darling. I think you're an absolutely *wonderful* detective."

"Sometimes I think even Morgenfield and Marcotti could do a better job!" I complained.

At that moment the door to the suite swung open. It was Morgenfield and Marcotti, and their faces were not happy.

The best defense, as they say, is a good offense. I let go of Jayne, reluctantly, and turned to the two detectives.

"So *there* you are!" I cried angrily. "I've been looking for you everywhere!"

"You've been looking for *us?*" Detective Morgenfield asked, taken aback.

"Are you kidding? I've been running around the entire neighborhood trying to find you! But never mind—you're here at last. I want to report a murder, gentlemen."

Chapter 39

There are three things I remember about the Thursday broadcast of "Good Morning, U.S.A." The first was that I was exhausted. The basic problem, as I have mentioned in earlier reports, is that my sleep requirements run to the order of ten or eleven hours of unconsciousness during each twenty-four. This has nothing whatever to do with laziness. In fact, I ordinarily work seven days a week, and far more than the traditional eight-hours-per-day at that. My condition is not as serious as that of the out-and-out narcoleptics, who are given to nodding off at all hours of the day and who therefore are advised not to drive automobiles or operate heavy machinery. To see if anything could be done about my sleep-cycle problem I put myself, a year or so ago, into the Cedars-Mount Sinai Sleep Disorders Clinic in Los Angeles. But, other than finding that I'm sometimes a bit disorderly while sleeping, they told me that nothing could be done to change sleep-cycles. How I envy those rare individuals such as Thomas Edison or China's Choen Lai, who are reported to have required only two or three hours of sleep per night. Further complicating the problem in this instance was the fact that Morgenfield and Marcotti kept Jayne and me occupied until after midnight. When my alarm clock rang at four in the morning I was in no mood to say good morning to anyone at all—let alone the entire country. I was so tired that a yawn escaped on-camera, despite a heroic attempt to wrestle it into submission. Cat was forced to make a joke about how the sophisticated nightlife of Manhattan was catching up with me.

The second thing I remember about the show is that Bob Hutchinson predicted a new winter storm would hit the city Friday night—a blizzard that would make the storm earlier in the week seem like nothing in comparison. What was so memorable about this weather prediction was that it turned out to be accurate. Unfortunately, since it came from Bob Hutchinson, some New Yorkers prepared for a weekend of balmy sunshine.

The third point of interest was that I identified the tall man built like a football player I had seen last night in the ballroom of the Plaza Hotel—the same man, I believed, that Edward the horse taxi driver had noticed in the shadows of Central Park with a rifle in the lining of his overcoat.

I made the identification halfway through the show during a commercial break when Danny Ferraro, one of the stagehands, rolled the Steinway grand from the wings onto the set for me to play in the next segment. Danny had someone new helping him this morning move the piano, a young African-American with a bright smiling face.

"Where's Lucky this morning?" I asked pleasantly. Lucky Mendoza, Danny's usual helper, was a guy built like a football player. Gongs went off in my head. *Lucky Mendoza!* The biggest, heftiest stagehand on the set of "Good Morning, U.S.A." I had been slow not to recognize him last night in the ballroom. I can only say in my own defense that I did not know Lucky well, I had not been expecting to see him at the Plaza, and the change of costume, from beige overalls to a tuxedo, had thrown me off the track. Some people look very different in formal clothing and in an unexpected situation. Such are my excuses, weak though they might be.

"Lucky called in sick this morning," Danny told me.

"I bet he did! Do you know him well?"

"Not particularly. We've never gotten together outside of work, if that's what you mean. To tell you the truth, the guy scares me a little."

"That's understandable. Do you know where he lives?"

"Haven't a clue," Danny said.

Time is a luxury on live television—a luxury we did not have at the moment. Danny moved away to allow Carlos, the new audioman, and Emily, his assistant, to check my microphone and get a quick sound level on the piano. I found myself back on the air before I knew it. Somehow I muddled through a tune. Fortunately it was a song the lyrics to which I had written myself years ago—George Duning's theme from the film *Picnic*. Even so, I was so distracted that I forgot a line of the bridge and was forced to do an ad-lib replacement. The moment we were off the air, I found Danny again.

"This could be very important," I told him. "How long has Lucky Mendoza been working here?"

"About six weeks, Mr. Allen. He's a new guy."

"Do you know who hired him?"

"Don Shipley—the floor manager. He has the final word, at least, about the crew."

"Who does Lucky hang out with from the show? I'm curious to know his friends?"

"I don't think he *has* any. I wish I could be more helpful, but Lucky always keeps to himself. A very standoffish guy. I've never seen him talk with anyone—at least beyond the few minimum phrases necessary to get the job done."

During the next break I approached Don Shipley, the floor manager, an overworked young man with thinning hair and an anxious expression in his eyes, perhaps from running a stage where everything had been going wrong.

"Just a moment, Don," I said, stopping him in the midst of a dozen tasks. "I'm trying to get some information on Lucky Mendoza, the stagehand."

"He didn't show up this morning. *Sick,* I'm told! Last thing in the world I need to worry about!"

"I bet. You hired him, didn't you?"

"No. I just okayed him—but if he gets sick too many times without warning like he did today, out he goes."

"You okayed him? You mean he was sent to you by the personnel department?"

"That's usually the way it works. But not in this case. He was recommended by one of the brass—I hate it when the bosses interfere with stuff they shouldn't concern themselves with. Maybe he's someone's nephew or cousin, or something. You look at a guy like Lucky Mendoza, you wouldn't think he had friends in high places."

I was ready for the big question.

"So who told you to hire Lucky?"

"Our producer. Zeke Roth."

Chapter 40

As soon as we were off the air, I stormed down the maze of twisty corridors to Roth's office. There was no one in the outer office, though the computer on the secretary's desk was on, softly humming with whatever cyberdreams computers have when they are left unattended. The phone rang and then rang again five more times before the caller gave up. All my senses became alert to a sense of danger. I didn't like the abandoned, empty feeling of Zeke's outer office.

The door to his inner office was closed. I stepped toward it cautiously and put my ear against the door. There was no sound from inside. I put my hand on the doorknob, and took a deep breath to still my beating heart. Then I flung open the door with a quick motion.

I'm not sure what I expected to find inside. A dead body, perhaps. A ransacked office. Blood and mayhem. But what I saw was different from anything I could have imagined. Zeke Roth was sitting in his swivel chair behind his desk, and his blond secretary, Candy, was cuddled on his lap. They were kissing when I flung open the door. They broke away and stared at me with understandable annoyance and embarrassment.

"What are you, a Peeping Tom?" Zeke exploded. "Don't you believe in knocking?"

"Sorry," I said lamely. "There was nobody in the outer office. I was worried about you, actually."

Candy, jumping up from her employer's lap, managed to knock over the framed photograph of Zeke's wife and small children that was on his desk. Zeke lovingly restored the photograph to an upright position.

"I feel like a schmuck," he said with a heavy sigh, staring unhappily at the photograph. "I'm racked with guilt."

"That's because you're so sensitive, Zeke," Candy assured him.

"Yes, I *am* sensitive," he agreed. "No one understands me but you. For my wife and kids, I'm just a money machine."

"Better go back to work, Candy. Mr. Allen and I have got some things to discuss," he told her.

"I'll be right there in the outer office," she promised.

As soon as Candy had closed the door behind her, Zeke gestured for me to sit in the armchair opposite his desk.

"I should have broken off with Candy months ago, but I just couldn't find the words to do it," he said wearily. "Oh, well, it doesn't matter now."

"Why not?"

"Do you know what some son of a bitch from this damn show did to me? Sent an anonymous letter to my wife with a photograph of me kissing Candy! Actually it was a peck on the cheek, but it looked bad. This show is destroying me, I tell you! My wife was furious—says she's going to split. I'm finished, man. Even my health is going. I don't like to advertise the fact, but I had a heart attack three years ago. My doctor said I should take it easy. Avoid stress, he says! *He* should be the producer of a show like this! Sometimes I have this weird feeling there's someone out there trying to kill me. Just one more incident—another light falling from the ceiling, *anything* at all . . . with my blood pressure, I could drop dead in an instant!''

''Tell me more about the letter your wife received,'' I said.

''It arrived yesterday, a computer printout. Unsigned. YOUR HUSBAND IS UNFAITHFUL was all it said. And then the picture. Let me tell you, the last thing I need is another divorce, another ex-wife—more alimony to pay. The problem is, I have no self-control around pretty broads.''

''You've been hurting financially, haven't you, Zeke?''

''You bet. There's Diana in California with our first son, Billy. I pay her $750 a month, which isn't too bad—I got off lightly in that divorce because I was young and not too successful yet. But then came Andrea and the little girl we had together, Kirsten—when *that* divorce happened eight years later, I really got the shaft. I pay two grand a month for alimony and child support. God knows what Rachel is going to hit me up for!— Rachel's my present wife. They might as well put me in debtor's prison! Anyway, it's all over now. That scene you saw just now as you walked into my office, between Candy and me. I was just really trying to say goodbye.''

''It's then that those louses go back to their spouses,'' I said, quoting the famous lyric from the film ''Gentlemen Prefer Blondes.''

''I'm a cooked goose, man. It's not just my domestic problems either. Or my bum heart. Carol told me that she told you about . . . well, you know. . . .''

''That you embezzled money from the show?''

''Yeah. Only I hate that word, embezzle. I only meant it as a loan. Hell, what's a measly fifty grand to a network like this? I was planning to repay it, of course . . . but things just haven't worked out as I planned.''

''Zeke, I can't understand how a smart guy like you got in such a financial hole. It can't all be alimony.''

He shook his head, disgusted with himself. ''No, the ex-wives were only part of it. I got carried away with my own success. I was a big TV producer, you see—I had to have a nice condo in Manhattan, and a house in Connecticut, and a couple of matching BMW convertibles for me and the wife to get back and forth. Add all that to the private schools for the children, summer trips to Europe, restaurants and plays in New York, a ski condo we keep in Aspen . . . and you start to get the picture. I make twenty times more money than my parents ever dreamed of making, and still I'm always broke. *More* than broke. To be perfectly honest, I'm nearly two hundred thousand dollars in debt and it's all about to unravel. American Express canceled my Platinum Card last week, and I'm starting to get some fairly unpleasant phone calls from creditors. So there you have my tragic tale, Steve. If you want to go to Mr. Kinley and tell him that I've been embezzling money, go ahead—be my guest. I'm beyond caring.''

He looked beyond caring. His necktie was askew, his hair tousled, even his glasses were crooked on his nose. At first I had put his appearance down to the compromising position with Candy in which I had found him as I came into the office. But looking at him more closer, I could see it was more than that. He was a man over the edge. He grinned at me as I studied him.

''I'm a mess, aren't I?'' he asked almost proudly.

''Well, you're *in* a mess,'' I said cautiously. There were a number of questions I wanted to ask Zeke. I was considering how to play him when he reached in his top drawer and pulled out the pistol I had found there earlier. It was the huge Colt .45 with a long barrel that looked like something Wyatt Earp might have used. Still grinning, he pointed it at me.

''Now, Zeke, trying to scare me isn't going to solve any of your problems,'' I warned.

''No, I guess not,'' he agreed cheerfully. He put the gun down on his desk with the barrel still facing my direction. It was within easy reach though, and it added a harsh element to our conversation.

"Look, let's talk this over," I said in a calm voice. "Maybe your situation isn't as bad as you think."

"Oh, it's bad!" he assured me. "I'm two hundred grand in debt, my wife is about to leave me, I might drop dead any moment from the stress, and Mr. Kinley's going to give me the old heave-ho the moment he finds out I've been stealing his money. You think anyone in this business is ever going to hire me again once word gets out what I've done? Even Candy—she's a sweet girl, but do you think she's going to want to hold the hand of a broken, unemployed middle-aged man?"

"Maybe her love for you is real?"

"Naw. She *thinks* it's real, but that's only because she doesn't know my world is crumbling. It's a lot easier to love a rich sugar daddy who takes you fancy places than a has-been failure without a cent."

"Aren't you forgetting some of your assets, Zeke?"

"Like what?"

"Like your half interest in the restaurant you own with Bob Hutchinson. Surely that's worth something. And who knows—the restaurant could still be a big success."

Zeke laughed unpleasantly. "Unless your partner is Wolfgang Puck, don't ever buy a restaurant, pal. Eighty percent of them go under the first year. It's a real money pit—endless expenses and few rewards."

"Then why did you go into it with Bob? I've never understood that partnership. You seem to hate each other's guts."

"Oh, we were bosom buddies at one time. *Before* the restaurant, that is. Bob's a real wheeler-dealer—maybe you didn't know that. He owns a car dealership on Long Island, part of a shopping mall in Scarsdale, even a chain of health clubs upstate. He convinced me that there was a fortune to be made in a little English restaurant-pub on Third Avenue. I was still in my big-shot producer phase, you see, and it appealed to my ego. I thought we were going to make so much money I could afford to take on a few more ex-wives! But it didn't work out that way. Bob fooled me, the bastard. Frankly, I suspect he was looking for one of his investments to lose money so he could take a tax loss.''

"He won't buy you out?''

"No way! I can't even get a free meal there anymore! The son of a bitch is ruthless. And now, if you'll excuse me, I believe it is time to take the big exit.''

To my horror, Zeke picked up the huge pistol and pointed the barrel to his right temple.

"Hold it!'' I said in a steady voice. "Killing yourself is not the answer. Think about your children.''

"It will be easier for them if I'm dead rather than in prison as an embezzler.''

"Look, Zeke—I personally don't feel any compulsion to tell Stephen Kinley about the missing money. Perhaps you can still pay it back. . . .''

"I've *tried* to pay it back. I borrowed money from Carol Ardman—but I spent it on other things. I had to, there were just too many debts. And as for Kinley, he's going to discover the theft soon enough even if you don't tell him—the semiannual audit of the show's accounts takes place in two weeks. So it's time say adios . . . you might want to look away. This could be kind of messy.''

"Wait!'' I cried. "Let me just ask you one more question.''

"Shoot,'' he said. "I have all eternity ahead of me—I guess I can give you another minute.''

"Tell me about Lucky Mendoza, the stagehand you asked Don Shipley to hire.''

He stared at me in amazement. "I'm about to kill myself, and you're asking me about a stagehand?''

"He's important, Zeke. I'm virtually certain he killed Gene Ptak last night. You remember Gene, don't you?''

"Sure. I hired the guy to try to get some dirt on Carol and then later Bob Hutchinson. But it was hopeless. I was squirming in my death throes trying to figure a way out of my problems—but there was no way. Why the hell would Lucky murder a harmless putz like Ptak?"

"That's what I'm trying to figure out. My guess is that Lucky is someone's accomplice—he's not doing this on his own. That's why I'm asking how you happened to recommend him to the floor manager."

"It wasn't my idea. Bob asked me to hire Lucky Mendoza."

"Bob *Hutchinson?* I don't understand—you hate Bob's guts. Why would you do him a favor?"

Zeke shrugged. "It was a deal we made. Bob gave me ten thousand dollars of my money back—a small part of my investment from the restaurant. It wasn't much, but it came in handy."

"He gave you the money in exchange for recommending Lucky to Don Shipley?"

"That's it. It seemed like no sweat on my part, so I figured why not?"

"Weren't you curious why Lucky Mendoza was worth ten grand to Bob Hutchinson?"

"To tell the truth, no. I needed the money too badly to worry about the whys and wherefores."

"I understand. But before you kill yourself, I want Lucky's home address."

Zeke sighed and shook his head. But he put the huge pistol down on his desk for a moment and picked up the phone to talk to Candy in the outer office.

"Sweetheart, call personnel and get a phone number and home address for Lucky Mendoza to give to Mr. Allen. You can give it to him on his way out. He's just leaving."

While Zeke was on the phone, I reached for the gun on the desk and managed to grab it before he did.

"I'll just jump out the window," he assured me dramatically after he put the phone down. "You can't stop me from dying."

"You're right about that," I told him.

"God, I think I'm feeling a chest pain!" he cried suddenly, rubbing the area over his heart with his hand. "Tell Candy to call my doctor, okay?"

One moment he was talking about shooting himself and jumping out a window, and the next he was in a cold sweat imagining chest pains. I sensed his urge to live was quite a bit stronger than his talk of suicide.

I kept the Colt .45 anyway. Where I was going, I figured I had a lot more need of a gun than he did.

Chapter 41

I wouldn't want to give the impression that small matters such as death, arson, and intrigue might deter my wife from her favorite New York activity: shopping. On Thursday morning, Jayne made the rounds of Bonwit Teller, Saks, and Bloomingdale's, and then met me at Harry's Bar, on the Fifth Avenue side of the Sherry Netherland Hotel, where we had agreed to have a late lunch.

"Cass phoned early this morning from New Mexico," Jayne mentioned over our appetizers—fresh figs and prosciutto.

"He was in Santa Fe?"

"He called from the road, somewhere between Santa Fe and Taos. He's got a line on Peter's ski cabin in the mountains. He said to tell you that if Peter McDavis is in New Mexico, he'll find him."

"Good old Cass!" I said, studying the menu for the next course. I was torn between a shamefully rich pasta and a low-cal, low-fat alternative of grilled swordfish with lemon. I opted for the pasta. One does not have lunch at Harry's Bar every day; I could go back to my diet tomorrow.

"Darling, I've been hesitant to mention this, but there seems to be a huge lump in your jacket," Jayne said.

"It's a revolver," I whispered. "An old Colt .45, just like they used to pack in the West. I bought a swell shoulder holster for it at an army surplus store on my way here from the studio. It makes me feel very Raymond Chandler, and all that. I would take it out and show it to you but I don't think Harry would approve."

"Jayne might not approve either," said Jayne. "Isn't it illegal to carry a concealed weapon?"

"Not in Texas," I assured her.

"We're in New York."

"I'd like to survive my encounter with Lucky Mendoza. He's the big guy built like a football player who likes to go around shooting people through windows. I thought I would drop by his place later in the afternoon."

"I'll go with you."

"No, you won't. Surely there must be another dress to. . ."

"Sweetheart, shopping can wait. If there's any danger, I want to be there."

"Jayne, I'm not kidding. This guy is a bad cat. This is man's work."

We argued this question back and forth over the pasta and chocolate torte we had for dessert. Lunch was only a zillion calories, nothing to worry about. But it was probably responsible for the moral torpor I felt afterward, in which I gave in to Jayne.

"All right, you can come along," I told her. "But I'm the boss, okay? And you have to do everything I say."

"Don't I always?" Jayne argued, lying through her teeth.

After lunch I got rid of the network limo that Jayne had been using all morning on her shopping spree. A limo is helpful, but I wasn't in a mood to trust anything connected to the show. We grabbed a cab instead. I gave the driver the address I had for Lucky Mendoza on Sutton Place.

Jayne cocked an eyebrow at me. "Sutton Place? That's an awfully expensive address. Didn't you say Mr. Mendoza was a stagehand?"

"He may have a few fingers in a few different pies. And probably being a hit man is a lot more profitable than moving my piano back and forth on Studio B."

"And how do you plan to approach this charming individual?"

"I thought I'd charm the doorman and see where that led. If all else fails, I figure I can take out the Colt and start blasting."

"It's a good thing I've come along," Jayne said. "I can see that this project needs a woman's touch . . . Driver, would you mind stopping at that bar for a moment? I need to make a phone call—I won't be but a minute."

The taxi swerved to the curb in front of McCaulley's Saloon on First Avenue, which appeared to be a dark place intended for serious drinking. Jayne took the piece of paper I had with Lucky Mendoza's phone number and address.

"You're just going to call him?" I asked.

"Why not? He won't be frightened by a damsel in distress. I'll suggest a rendezvous."

"Not bad," I agreed. "But I'm not letting you go into McCaulley's Saloon on your own."

"Nonsense, Steve. You'd better keep the taxi. If any drunk gives me trouble, I'll slap him silly with my handbag."

Jayne's handbag when fully loaded is heavy enough to knock cold a rampaging gorilla, so I relaxed while she went into the bar to use the telephone. She emerged a few minutes later humming "Melancholy Baby." There was a smile of success on her lips.

"Well?"

"He was there. I fluttered and flirted, and did all the things a poor damsel might do. I said I was in desperate trouble and I needed a man who wasn't afraid to take on a dangerous assignment. I said money was no object."

"He responded?"

"Cautiously. He pretended not to understand my meaning but he was willing to meet. Not at his apartment, however. He gave me the address of a sushi bar on First Avenue and Ninety-second Street. He said to be there in fifteen minutes. Alone."

"Did you say who you were?"

"Naturally. I had to. I introduced myself as Mrs. Steve Allen, wife of the TV personality. Frankly I hinted—just *hinted,* mind you—that despite your talent, I was looking for a hit man to rough you up."

"Charming!"

"Don't worry. The entire time I talked on the phone with him, I had my fingers crossed."

Chapter 42

The restaurant, called Mr. Sushi, was brightly lit and cheerful, with green plants in the windows. A sign on the door said that all their sushi was made with organic brown rice and no sugar. It was encouraging to know that our hit man was into natural foods.

We told the taxi to let us out a block past the bar. The plan was for Jayne to go into the restaurant by herself. Meanwhile I would lurk in a doorway across the street, and when I saw Lucky enter the place, I would come in after him. Then Jayne and I would hold him down with chopsticks—or whatever means we found at hand—and get him to talk about all the dark deeds he had done.

That was the plan. I insisted that Jayne take the Colt .45 since she would be alone with the killer for a moment or two. The pistol joined all the other dangerous items in her handbag and she went off down First Avenue by herself, looking as lovely as any Mata Hari. I waited three minutes by my watch, then I crossed the avenue and found a convenient doorway opposite the sushi bar. The doorway belonged to a restaurant that was closed during the day, a nice German place, and I spent the next ten minutes pretending to read the menu that was posted on the door. It seemed to me that some method acting was required for a professional stakeout. Should I have the *schnitzel* or the *sauerbraten* with red cabbage? I wondered. Neither, I decided. But of course I had eaten so much Italian food at lunch, I thought I might never want to eat again.

All the time, naturally, I was keeping an eye peeled across the street for any sign of an assassin built like a football player. He did not come. Two young people, a man and a woman, entered the sushi bar, and then an elderly priest with a cane. But it was nearly three o'clock and lunch was mostly over; most of the customers I saw were leaving rather than coming.

Lurking in a doorway, I soon discovered, is not an easy thing to do, particularly in January in New York. A cold wind was blowing down First Avenue and after five minutes my cheeks were burning with the icy blast, and my hands and feet were numb. I shifted from one foot to another. I read the menu yet again. Time passed tediously slowly. And still no Lucky Mendoza. When half an hour elapsed I knew I must either move or turn into a pillar of ice. I decided I would cross the street and gaze at the menu in the window of Mr. Sushi—and hopefully get a glimpse of Jayne.

I crossed First Avenue with the light and ambled casually toward the sushi bar. It is not easy to amble casually when the temperature outside is twenty-five degrees with a windchill factor of a scintillating zero. I did my best. I glanced in the window of Mr. Sushi as though I were debating between the Japanese or the German restaurant across the street to provide for dinner tonight.

I couldn't see Jayne through the window, but finally I said the hell with it and simply walked into the sushi bar. Two young Japanese men were behind the bar working with knives and pieces of raw fish on a counter. Both men wore headbands and white kung fu outfits and looked like extras in a Bruce Lee movie. I spotted Jayne at a back table, and to my surprise, she was not alone.

Across from her at a plain wooden table sat the elderly priest I had seen enter the restaurant at the beginning of my vigil. I smiled foolishly when I realized my mistake. There was platter of raw fish and seaweed and other icky things on the table. The old priest was eating with a pair of chopsticks and a very hefty appetite. Jayne simply had a cup of tea in front of her.

"Mr. Mendoza," I said with all smiles, "how *lucky* running into you like this!" I said as I approached the table. The priest had his back to me. When he turned and looked up into my face, I saw that this was no old cleric at all, of course. It was a truly masterful disguise, but despite the clever makeup and a silver wig, I recognized Lucky Mendoza—if that indeed was his real name. The massive shoulders were gone and the ex-stagehand did not appear even slightly like a football player this afternoon—but I realized with a shock that *that* had been a disguise as well.

"I hope you're here for confession," I said with sarcasm, sitting down next to Jayne. "It will do your soul some good. Actually, for a man with as many sins on his conscience as you must have, you've picked a most inappropriate costume."

The priest smiled. "Your wife has been doing an admirable job trying to deceive me, Mr. Allen. But of course I wasn't fooled. I saw you across the street in that doorway looking very cold and silly. I suggest you stick to television in the future and avoid espionage. You're not very good at it."

"No? We'll have to see who comes out ahead in this game," I said with more bluster than I felt.

"Very well. Meanwhile you might as well enjoy the best health food sushi in Manhattan," he offered with a genial smile.

"No thank you. I prefer my fish cooked," I replied.

"Suit yourself. As it happens, the Japanese diet is extremely low-fat. They enjoy the lowest instance of heart disease among any industrialized country."

"Mr. Mendoza, we did not get you here to discuss international cuisine. What I want to know is who hired you to murder Dennis Lovelace and Gene Ptak? I know that Bob Hutchinson helped to get you the job at the network, but I suspect there's more to it than that."

"Really? And who *do* you suspect?" he asked. Despite his ridiculous outfit, his eyes were twinkling, and he was much too self-confident for my taste.

"Peter McDavis, naturally. Look, we're going to get him. We know the motive, everything. There are just a few details left to uncover, and then you're going down, Lucky, along with the creep who hired you. So you might as well cooperate and save yourself a lot of trouble."

He did something then that I really hated. He laughed in my face. It truly is disagreeable to have a hired killer dressed up like a priest laugh in your face at a sushi bar. But I suppose I had it coming. Not only was I bluffing, but I was doing a bad job of it as well.

Jayne tried another approach. Flattery. "You are obviously a professional," she said. "I'm sure that you're going to leave this sushi bar and disappear into the crowd and we'll never see you again. So won't you tell us who hired you? What difference does it make to you now?"

"That would be most unprofessional, Mrs. Allen," he replied courteously. "I have to think of my reputation. Besides, you two have caused me some trouble. Now I either have to kill you both or abandon my Sutton Place apartment and take up a new residence. It's really most inconvenient. I was getting very fond of my view of the East River."

While he was talking, I reached underneath the table to Jayne's gargantuan handbag.

"You're not going to get away, Mr. Mendoza—or whatever your real name is," I said loudly, to conceal the sounds I made opening the bag.

"Oh? Why not?"

"Because I am pointing a gun at you under the table. It's a real monster too, a Colt .45, big enough to shoot a buffalo. So keep your hands in sight and do exactly as I tell you."

His smile only seemed to broaden.

"You've never shot anyone, Mr. Allen. And I don't believe you are capable of doing so."

"There's always a first time," I said. "You're right in that I haven't shot anyone yet, but I was trained to do so at good old Camp Roberts during the big war so I'm—"

"Were you really?" he said. "That's odd; so was my father. What kind of a company were you in?"

"Heavy weapons," I said.

"Well, I imagine your Colt .45 must seem a little heavy to you at the moment," he said with an insufferable smile. "And now," he added, "I'll be running along."

He simply wasn't frightened of me, damn it! It was infuriating. I put on my toughest voice. I sneered. I scowled. Then I did my best George Raft imitation.

"All right, buster. I warned you. Make one move and you're going straight to the worm farm!"

He laughed and stood up. I brought the gun out from under the table and pointed it at him. Two customers nearby screamed. A waitress dropped a plate of sushi that she was carrying. I suppose it wasn't very good for my image, pointing a huge pistol at what appeared to be a man of the cloth. But I was beyond caring.

"This is your last warning!" I urged. "I mean it!"

He shook his head, amused. "No, you're just not the killer type. I've always been a fan of yours, so I'm going to give you one hint about who hired me. Here it is: What is sweet as honey, yet the most bitter herb of all? . . . Now goodbye, Mr. Allen. I believe I will let you pay my bill for lunch."

"Wait a minute! What kind of hint is that?"

He turned to go. I cocked the hammer of the pistol and tried to tell myself that the world would be a lot better off minus one professional hit man. But he was right—except in self-defense—I was incapable of shooting someone in the back. Particularly when that someone had the improbable appearance of an old priest who was walking calmly out the door of a sushi bar.

I pointed the barrel at the ceiling—stupidly, I admit—closed my eyes and pulled the trigger. There was a deafening explosion in the room. Plaster rained down from the ceiling. All around me people were screaming and ducking under tables. At least I got Lucky Mendoza's attention. He turned just as he was leaving the restaurant.

"Bad move, Pops," he said. "You're in for an awful afternoon with the NYPD. I don't believe Detective Sergeant Morgenfield is particularly fond of TV celebrities who shoot up restaurants."

The priest turned and left. I ran to the open doorway, gun in hand, but the assassin had already melted into the New York afternoon.

Chapter 43

Alas, Jayne and I spent nearly four hours in jail, and then another three hours being interrogated by detectives Morgenfield and Marcotti. We might be in jail still except I decided it was time to cooperate with the police. I told the detectives everything, the complete, unexpurgated story of what we had done and seen in New York. Or nearly everything, for there was just one teensy-weensy tidbit I held back. It hurt to give away so much information and realize that now the police would probably solve the case before I could do so myself.

By the time Jayne and I had convinced Morgenfield and Marcotti that we had actually sat across a table from the killer, Lucky Mendoza had time to be on a plane to Paris or Rio de Janeiro. I heard later that the cops searched the Sutton Place apartment, but they didn't find a clue as to the man's real identity, not even a fingerprint. Somehow it didn't surprise me.

It was nearly ten o'clock in the evening when Morgenfield let us go, and Jayne and I were actually hungry again.

"What would you say to bangers and mash?" I asked Jayne in the taxi as we rode from the police station.

"Oh, are you in an English mood?"

"Or a nice steak and kidney pie? Perhaps a pint of bitter and a game of darts?"

"I think I'm getting your drift, Steve. But wouldn't you prefer I scramble up some eggs at home? You must be exhausted. And you have to get up at four in the morning tomorrow to do that nasty show again."

"I don't need sleep, my dear, nearly as much as I need to figure out who hired Mendoza." Suddenly I laughed.

"What's funny?"

"I just remembered," I said, "I used that name in a song I wrote based on one of Fat Jack Leonard's crazy lines. Remember how he used to mutter obscure song titles at odd moments? One of the things he used to say was, 'Now Rufus Mendoza—was a colored composah.' "

"Oh, yes," Jayne said, "now I remember. I've heard you do the number. But what's that got to do with the price of eggs?"

"Or egg-beaters," I added. "You're quite right, I am guilty, once again, of digression. Sometimes it seems to me that I first digressed at birth and have yet to get back on the track, whatever it might have been. But I would like to go to the English pub even though I don't think Bob's likely to be there at the moment. I just want to get the feel of the place. And if Bob *is* there, I'd like to ask him why he was willing to give Zeke ten thousand dollars of his investment money back in return for hiring Lucky Mendoza."

"You don't believe Bob is the person behind the murders?"

"I can't see that he has a motive particularly. My guess is that he was doing a favor for someone else—and that someone else is the author of all this unpleasantness. But who knows?"

"You know, darling, I couldn't help but notice that there was *one* thing you didn't tell Morgenfield and Marcotti."

"Well, I wouldn't want to do *all* their work for them."

I hadn't passed on the hint the hit man had been so kind to mention as he was leaving the sushi bar.

" 'What is sweet as honey, yet the most bitter herb of all?' " Jayne repeated. "What do you think it means?"

"Haven't a clue. It may be nonsense, of course. Something to confuse things even more—if that is possible! And yet somehow I doubt it. Mendoza strikes me as a guy with a huge ego who enjoys playing games and matching his wits against the world. He's the sort of killer who *might* give you a clue. And the funny thing is, I *almost* have it. I have this annoying sense that I should know what's sweet as honey, yet the most bitter herb of all—but I just can't quite dredge the answer from my brain. It's like not being able to remember a name. Frustrating."

"You're tired, sweetheart. Forget about it, and the answer will come to you."

"I suppose so," I agreed. But it's hard to forget about something you're trying to remember. Jayne and I arrived at As You Like It, the English pub on Third Avenue and Fifty-fifth Street, each deep in our own thoughts, trying to solve the riddle. The pub, we saw from the start, was probably one of the last remaining New York singles bars in the age of AIDS. A good deal of money had been spent on the decor—dark wood, low beams, and such—to make it seem as if one had stepped from Third Avenue back into Elizabethan England. The bartenders and waitresses were all good-looking and seemed very much at their ease—most likely actresses and actors, dancers and musicians, waiting for their big break. The customers were mostly young professionals. The bar was fairly crowded with men and women smiling and talking and playing out the age-old mating rituals. A TV set above the bar was turned on to a basketball game, but the sound was muted, covered up by generic pop music on the stereo. I would have preferred the basketball game. Jayne and I sat at a heavy dark wood table whose surface had been pounded with hammers to make it look old and atmospheric.

A pretty waitress with dark hair came our way with menus. The fare at As You Like It was simple but hearty. Besides the bangers and mash, there were fish and chips and a dozen kinds of burgers with inventive names such as the Princess Di (1/3 lb. of ground beef served with low-fat cottage cheese, tomato, and green salad) to the Falstaff Deluxe (1/2 lb. of ground beef, cheddar cheese, bacon, avocado, and grilled onion served on French bread with thick-cut fries). It was food that you needed to be young and hungry in order to eat, and all the prices were below ten dollars. The menu also listed about fifty different kinds of beer, mostly imported. Jayne and I decided to try the Queen Anne Salad, dressing on the side, as the least harmful item we might consume here. We also each ordered a half pint of Guinness stout, doing our best to get into the mood.

"I'm sure a place like this must be a lot of fun," Jayne said, "if you happen to be twenty-nine years old, unmarried, with a stomach of steel."

"Well, it appears successful, at least," I told her. "I'm going to find a pay phone and see if Cass left a message on our answering machine."

I wound my way through the flirting young—who paid no attention to me, since I happen to be well over fifty. The phone was near the dartboard and I was nervous lest someone take me for the bull's-eye. I waited for the phone five minutes while a young man did his best to apologize to a woman named Melissa about some romantic problem that remained undefined. When I got the phone, the receiver smelled of beer and stale cigarettes.

How did we ever exist before answering machines? I pressed a code when the machine answered, and in a moment my messages were played back to me. A Broadway actress—a very grand dame, one of Jayne's friends—invited us to lunch on Sunday. Edith Kinley called for me and asked me to call back. Her husband, Stephen the Second, also called, separately, and wished for me to call back, leaving the same telephone number as his wife—their residence, I presumed. And last of all came Cass. His voice was like a cool mountain stream in the midst of all the Manhattan sophistication.

"Hey, Steve!" he cried. "Hope you and Jayne are doing okay in the big city without me to look after you! New Mexico is a swell place. Lots of desert and sky and mountains that go on forever—I think you would like it out here. Santa Fe's a little rich for my blood, so many movie people you'd think you were in Beverly Hills. But I stopped off at this really neat Indian pueblo on the way to Taos . . ."

Cass went on in maddening detail about the Indian pueblo he had visited, giving me his full tourist treatment of his adventures in New Mexico. Cass is one of those people who seemingly can't distinguish between big and small—all things are equally delightful to him and he is apt to ramble if you aren't there in person to keep him on track. Finally he got to what I was waiting to hear.

"Anyway, I *did* manage to get directions to Peter McDavis's cabin, though I haven't been there yet. It's in the mountains just a few miles from Taos, close to the Colorado border. I tracked him down through some of the locals. The word is, he's been here in northern New Mexico all week, but I haven't been able to confirm that for a fact. One guy, his handyman, said he spoke to McDavis on the phone but didn't actually see him. Same thing with a young gal who does some cleaning for him once a week. I wasn't sure whether I should go to the cabin and approach him yet—I wanted to wait to hear from you first, to see what you want me to do. This afternoon I thought I'd go up to the ski resort, rent some equipment, and ask around about him some more. Supposedly the guy's a real maniac for skiing, and if he *was* here this week, that's where he would have been—on the slopes."

I could tell Cass was excited about getting on the slopes

himself, though he tried to pretend that skiing this afternoon was strictly business. Before he hung up, he left the number of a motel in Taos where I could call him back later that night.

After listening to Cass's message, I tried to get Edith and Stephen Kinley at the number they had left, but I only reached their answering machine. In this modern age you can have lengthy conversations one answering machine to another, never speaking directly to a human being. I left a message to say I was returning their call, and though I was not anyplace they could reach me at the moment, they could certainly have a good long chat with *my* machine anytime night or day. This accomplished, I returned to Jayne at the table.

I saw that our salads had arrived, two huge things in wooden bowls. Along with our salads, another huge thing had come to our table as well: Bob Hutchinson.

Chapter 44

"Hey, Steverino!" he called out when he saw me. "So glad to see you and the wife at my humble establishment! Only I'm not going to let you get away with eating only a couple a' *salads*. I gotta put some weight on you guys! ... Honey!" he shouted to a passing waitress, "bring my friends a couple a' Henry the Eighth Burgers! Bring me one, too, why don'cha?"

"Bob, we're still digesting lunch," I objected.

"Nonsense! Eat hearty and party hearty, that's my motto. If you don't finish 'em, you can take 'em home. A Henry the Eighth Burger can feed an average family for about a week!"

Bob was in a good mood. Seated at his side was a small brunette woman, quite pretty, who was half his age and size.

"Steve, this is my *very* favorite waitress, Bimba . . . Bimba, meet Jayne's better half, Steve Allen."

"Charmed, I'm sure," she said. Only she said it in the broadest New Yorkese that is beyond my power to reproduce accurately in English script.

"Bim*ba?*" I repeated, to make certain I had it right.

She giggled at me.

"So, my dear, how long have you been a waitress?" Jayne asked pleasantly.

"Two weeks!" she replied breathily. "But I'm such a klutz, you know. I dropped a Princess Di Burger on a customer the other day!"

"She has other talents," Bob assured us with a wink.

"Well Bob, I wasn't sure we would find you here tonight," I said, eager to change the subject.

"Oh, I drop by one or two evenings a week to see how things are going. I'm a pretty busy guy, you know. Besides all the scientific stuff I gotta do to predict the weather accurately, I have a few little sticks in the fire—a shopping mall. A car dealership on Long Island . . . hey, you guys ever want a good deal on a new Cadillac, you come to me!"

Jayne rolled her eyes.

"We're okay for wheels at the moment," I assured Bob. "But thanks for the offer. Whatever made you decide to get into the restaurant business?"

"Diversification," he said, still in his confidential whisper mode. "I figure if the economy goes to hell, no one will be able to afford a Cadillac. But people still gotta eat, right? A good meal for under ten bucks, I says to myself, how can I go wrong? I hardly make any profit on the food, but I figure if I pack 'em in here, I can really sock it to 'em on the booze. A pint of ale is five bucks—these young kids start playing darts and drinking, they don't realize how much money they're spending."

"So you're doing well?"

"Man, it's a killing!" he grinned. Which struck me as an unfortunate choice of words, given the circumstances.

"Glad to hear that," I said agreeably. "For you and Zeke Roth both . . . I understand Zeke is your partner in this venture?"

Bob's expression changed from friendly to wary.

"I like to keep Zeke a very *silent* partner," he admitted. "I did the guy a favor by letting him in the ground floor of a very good deal, but he doesn't know diddly about running a business. Frankly, I've been regretting the association.''

"But you two were great friends?''

"*Were* great friends. It's a whole different ball game now, Steve, starting a business together. You know the score—we used to go out drinking sometimes. One year we went on a fishing trip to Colorado. We started fantasizing running a restaurant together and all the waitresses we'd—excuse me, Bimba—and it was lots of fun to talk about in the abstract. My mistake was thinking he was for real. But hell, you live and learn.''

"You're equal partners?''

"We started out that way. Fifty-fifty. But then he started whining about how he needed money so badly. Whining— that's all I ever got from the guy. So I let him have ten grand of his investment back, and now I'm the majority shareholder and I get to call the shots.'' Bob flashed a very cunning smile. "Zeke didn't consider that part of it when I gave him the dough. As I said, he has no head for business.''

"Why don't you buy him out completely?'' Jayne asked.

"Well, maybe I will. One day. But at the moment, Jayne, it's a statistical fact that most new restaurants go under within a year or two, and I find it pleasant to share the risks. Particularly now that I'm the boss and old Zeke-boy can't do a thing about it.''

"It sounds like you got the better of him,'' I mentioned.

"You bet!'' Bob laughed. "But he was desperate. Hell, you can always make money off a guy that's desperate!''

"Now, Bob,'' I said, "I heard this story about the ten grand from Zeke Roth, but he tells it a little differently.''

"I guess he would!'' Bob gloated.

"Have you ever heard the name Lucky Mendoza?'' I asked.

"Lucky who?''

"Mendoza.''

"Doesn't ring a bell. But of course I meet a lot of people."

"Maybe you should remember a little harder, Bob. Lucky Mendoza is the guy you wanted Zeke to hire as a stagehand."

Bob shook his head, baffled. "I do a lot of favors for people, Steve. Help people get jobs. I don't really remember this particular instance. . . ."

"No?" I decided to do some creative fibbing. "Zeke mentioned he has written records about this. I believe he said he recorded a phone conversation with you—"

"Oh, *that* Lucky Mendoza!" Bob cried, suddenly remembering. "Sure. I got it now. Lucky was a friend of a friend. The kid was trying to get into television, so I passed on the word to Zeke. No biggie. I'm always glad to help a kid get a foothold in the business."

I shook my head. "That won't do, Bob. What happened is this: Zeke had been begging for his money back for weeks. Finally you told him that if he managed to get Lucky Mendoza on the payroll, you'd give him ten grand—his own money, not such a generous deal. But as you said, he was desperate. Now what I want to know, is what was it about Lucky Mendoza that made it worth your while to cut such a deal?"

"You got this all wrong," Bob pleaded. But he was suddenly red-faced, and I knew I was on the right track.

"As you know perfectly well, Lucky Mendoza—or whatever his real name might be—is a hired killer. He's the guy who murdered Dennis Lovelace and the private detective, Gene Ptak, and nearly killed Cat as well. He probably fooled with the lights to cause those near-accidents too. The point is, Bob, the police are very interested in this individual, and they're going to be even *more* fascinated to discover why you had a ten-thousand-dollar stake in seeing him get a job on the show."

Bob turned to his girlfriend. "Sweetheart, go powder your nose. We got a few things to discuss here." Bimba disappeared without a protest, and Bob turned back to me.

"You got this all wrong," he said for the second time. "First of all, I already explained to you how giving Zeke back the ten grand was to *my* advantage, not his. Frankly, I used this Lucky Mendoza character as an excuse. I *pretended* it was worth a lot of money to me to hire the dude, so Zeke wouldn't tumble to the fact that I was pushing some investment money back his way so I would become the majority shareholder. You get the picture?''

"The picture's coming in bright and clear, Bob. But I don't believe a word of it, and neither will the police." I told him earnestly. "You have to tell me why you wanted Lucky to have a job."

"I already told you! I was doing a favor for a friend."

"What friend?"

"I can't tell you. This friend . . . well, he has a Sicilian last name, if you see what I mean."

"There are lots of very fine Americans with Sicilian last names," I said.

"Hey, don't act dumb all of the sudden. You know what I mean. It was a favor I couldn't refuse."

"You're telling me you're in with the mob, Bob?"

"Jesus! I'm not *in* with the mob! But a guy who runs a car dealership meets a lot of diverse people. So okay, there's this one guy with a Sicilian last name who did me a little favor once. No big deal. But I owe him a little. We're not talking dead bodies here, or nothing. But I figured, why not help his friend get a job in television?"

"And screw Zeke Roth at the same time!"

"Sure. Why not? I figure I might as well advance my own agenda while I do a favor for a friend. You have trouble with that, Steve? It's how America was built!"

"What's your Sicilian friend's name?" I insisted.

"Look, Steve, I'm going to do you a favor now. You *don't* want to know my friend's name, believe me . . . Jayne, talk some sense into this guy or he's going to end up in the East River!"

"Oh, we've had trouble with those gentlemen before."

Bob sighed. "Anyway, I didn't even deal with my Sicilian friend directly. It was a messenger, someone who came to me with a letter of introduction. Okay? Will you be satisfied if I give you him?"

"It will be a start," I agreed.

"All right. He was an Indian guy. But I don't know his name."

Jayne and I exchanged glances. Then I looked back at the frightened weatherman.

"This isn't very helpful, Bob. Did he wear a white turban?"

"What do you mean, a white turban? Indians don't wear white turbans."

"Of course they do!"

"Steve, I think you're making the same mistake Christopher Columbus did," Jayne interrupted.

I got it.

"Oh, an *Indian!*" I cried. "Like a bow and arrow sort of Indian?"

"That's what I said," Bob told me. "Don't you understand English?"

But my mind was buzzing with sudden insights and connections. "Imagine that," I said to Jayne. "An Indian. . . ."

Chapter 45

Friday morning, too early, I sat in Nadia Wolfe's makeup chair while she dabbed and dusted my face for the merciless glass eye of the camera.

"You look awfully good, Steve . . . considering," she said, examining me. Over the past week, Nadia had taken a motherly interest in me. I gazed up into her round glasses, her wrinkled, warm old face. The relationship between a makeup artist and a person like me about to face a coast-to-coast audience is an intimate one. She shook her head.

I was not in the mood for mixed compliments at six o'clock in the morning. I wanted someone to tell me that I looked gorgeous, and twenty-five years old, and still young enough to live on three or four hours of sleep and sheer excitement—and not show it.

"What do you mean, 'considering'?" I asked.

"Oh, nothing. I probably shouldn't say anything."

"Nadia! I'm going to strangle you if you don't tell me what's on your mind."

"Well, it's just the stories I've been hearing about you,

Steve! Running around New York at all hours. One night you're
at an arson fire in the East Village, two nights later you *happen*
to be sitting next to someone who's murdered at the Plaza
Hotel! Goodness, I've seen some fast-living celebrities in my
profession, but you take the cake!''

''I am *not* some fast-living celebrity,'' I insisted, sourly. ''I
am a calm, witty, intellectual, mature individual. It's just that
fast living is sometimes thrust upon me.''

''Well, I'm just saying that *considering* the hours and company you've been keeping, you look pretty good this morning.''

''Thank you! I'll take that as a compliment.''

At that moment there was a knock on the dressing-room
door.

''Come in!'' I called.

The door opened but no one was there. A ghost, it seemed.
But I was leaning back in Nadia's chair, looking up when I
should have been looking down. I adjusted my gaze to the
proper level and saw a small person. It was Sherry Gold's nine-
year-old son with the strange eyes and rock generation name—
Crystal Rainbow. He stood mutely in the doorway studying me
in the makeup chair with his nearly violet eyes. I sat up and
studied him back just as hard. He was dressed up like an Indian,
wearing a buckskin shirt, brown pants, and a headband with a
feather sticking up at the back of his head. Kids used to dress
like Indians a lot at one time of course, but I hadn't seen one
do so in many years. It took me by surprise. There was no
denying a bizarre Indian current, East and West, to recent
events. Was it a coincidence? I really couldn't say.

''Hey, how you doing Chris?'' I said. ''That's quite an outfit
you're wearing. Come in, son.''

For a child, he had the most serious expression I have ever
seen. He came into the dressing room, closed the door behind
him, and then stood a few inches from the makeup chair and
continued to stare at me.

"That's a nice feather you're wearing," I told him.

"It's an eagle feather," he said proudly. "A golden eagle."

"That so? Where did you get it."

"A friend."

I looked at it more closely. The feather was huge, a beautiful mixture of black, dark brown, and white spots at the base. I had never seen anything quite like it. It *could* have come from a golden eagle, for all I knew—though it would be strictly against the law to possess such a feather from a protected species.

"Is your friend an Indian?" I asked.

"Yes."

"Really? How interesting." I was hoping to get him talking about his Native American friend, but he only continued to stare at me. Frankly, the boy struck me as a little spooky. I've been putting people at ease on various television shows for forty years—but I couldn't get anywhere with Crystal Rainbow. Finally he pushed out a fist in my direction and I saw there was a piece of paper in his hand.

"My mother said to give you this."

I took the paper and read.

Steve,

Whatever you do this weekend, *don't* travel anywhere, please. I read your Tarot cards last night because I had an anxious feeling in my spirit. You had the Death card over the Chariot in the Major Arcana—well, it's a lot to explain, and I know you don't believe in the spirit world as I do, so I won't bother you with the details. *But stay put.* Believe me. No trains, planes, taxis, or buses until Monday morning. Take the subway if you absolutely *must* leave your apartment, but take only the lines that travel *underground!!!*

By the way, I've guessed your astrological sign. You're a Capricorn—right?

I'll be praying for you this weekend.

                                                                    Sherry

I was not certain whether to laugh or cry. As a matter of fact, Sherry *had* gotten my astrological sign right—my birthday is December twenty-sixth and I am a Capricorn but the date has been widely publicized. The letter, with its many underlined words and exclamation points, was hysterical and strange. But since little Crystal Rainbow was studying my face for a reaction, I only nodded sagely.

"Please thank your mother for me," I told him. "And say I'll take her advice very seriously."

I felt as if we were ambassadors from different planets. He nodded gravely and left the makeup room.

"Odd child!" I said to Nadia when he was gone.

"Sherry's not exactly Miss Normal herself," Nadia remarked.

"What do you mean?"

"Well, all that astrology and Tarot card business! It gives me the creeps! She frightened poor Nancy Vandenberg to death with her predictions. Read her cards one morning here in the makeup room—Sherry said that Nancy was going to die at the age of fifty-three in a car wreck."

"That wouldn't be too pleasant to hear, particularly early in the morning."

"Well, it was the *details* that were so gruesome. Sherry went into a kind of trance for a few minutes and then told Nancy that the car was going to run off a bridge into a body of water— either a lake or an ocean—and that Nancy would be trapped underwater and suffocate to death slowly."

"I thought psychics kept those sort of details to themselves."

"They should, certainly. Poor Nancy had a dreadful morning.

Flubbed her TelePrompTer cues something terrible that day. It was only three weeks later that Mr. Kinley gave her the ax. . . .''

So much had been going on recently that I hadn't given much thought to Nancy Vandenberg, the co-anchor who had the job before Cat Lawrence took over.

"If I recall, on Monday you were about to tell me something about why Nancy was fired, Nadia."

"Oh, you probably think I'm an old gossip, Steve!"

"Not a bit," I lied.

"Well . . ."

There was another knock on the door. I wouldn't have been surprised by anything—spacey children, Indians, Mafia assassins—but it was only Debbie Driscoll, the cheerful production assistant.

"Mr. Allen, Mr. Kinley asked if you would drop by his office after the show."

"I think that would be a good idea," I said.

"It's upstairs on the top floor."

"I'll be there."

"Great. Five minutes to show time, by the way."

Debbie disappeared with her clipboard, and I got out of the makeup chair.

"I bet everyone tells you everything, don't they, Nadia?"

She smiled and did not tell me I was wrong.

"So what was it about Nancy Vandenberg," I asked. "I always assumed it was the ratings. She was too young and sexy for the morning show."

"She *was* too young and sexy. But not just for the morning show, Steve. For Peter McDavis. *That's* why she had to go."

"Peter and Nancy . . ."

"She was Peter's New York honey. They were almost living together."

"And Peter's wife, Angela, in New Mexico—did she know?"

"She found out. Someone wrote her an anonymous letter.

Angela's in a wheelchair, as you may know. Peter put her there—a car accident when he was drunk. It's a sad situation, of course. He feels guilty, responsible for his wife's condition. But at the same time, a pretty young woman comes along . . . he's in New York by himself . . . well, it's hard to resist.''

''I'm sure it is. And Nancy . . .''

''Angela told Peter he had to decide between them. She threatened to divorce Peter if he kept working as co-anchor with Nancy every morning. So Peter went to Stephen Kinley and said it was either him or Nancy—one of them had to go. Peter, of course, is the big name, so it wasn't really open to question.''

There was no more time for talk since I needed to hurry to get onto the set. I wondered who wrote this new anonymous letter—the second anonymous letter that I had heard about in two days? A nasty piece of business that had ended with Nancy Vandenberg getting shoved off the show.

Chapter 46

Friday's show went as smoothly as though we were all the best of friends. I interviewed a U.S. senator with presidential aspirations who had just written a mystery novel—everybody's getting into the act—and in the next half-hour a famous white football player who was raising money to help inner-city children.

Cat was charming and sophisticated. Bob Hutchinson, smiling like everybody's favorite uncle, told the weather around the nation and kept to his prediction that a blizzard would move into New York late Friday evening. On the half hour, Dan De Vries and Carol Ardman read the news, and late in the show, Sherry Gold did her daily astrology report. She told Aquarians that it was a good day to make a financial investment, and Pisces to postpone all major decisions until Monday. When she got to my sign, Capricorn, she seemed to peer more intensely into the camera, as though she were looking only at me: "Mercury is in a regressive phase against Saturn and Mars, Cap. This means possible danger on the road and in the air, so don't travel this weekend unless you absolutely must. Why don't you stay at home this weekend in front of a roaring fire with a good book?''

Did I take her prediction seriously? Of course not! Yet I was relieved I had no travel plans, and the idea of a roaring fire and a good book had an appeal. By the time nine o'clock came and we were off the air, I was feeling like a veteran of morning television.

"Congratulations Steve on finishing your first week!" Cat said, giving me a big kiss on the cheek. "You're doing a fabulous job. I wouldn't be surprised if Stephen Kinley offers you a permanent slot on the show."

"Whoa!" I cried. "The way this week has gone, Cat, believe me—I'll be glad to get home safe and sound to California! Two weeks of this show will be quite sufficient, thank you."

I left Studio B, changed clothes in my dressing room, and then made my way up the elevator to the top floor, where all the executive offices were located. The decor at these executive heights was different from the lower regions where the actual broadcasting took place. I left the elevator and floated on a soft cream-colored carpet toward a muted reception area. An elegant, gray-haired woman sat behind a huge oak desk and asked me to take a seat on a leather sofa while she told Mr. Kinley that I had arrived. I noticed a Picasso sketch on the wall above the receptionist's head. There was a tangible aura of money everywhere I looked.

"Let me take you back Mr. Allen," said the receptionist in a melodious voice. She led the way down a corridor to a double door and I was ushered into an office that was larger than many people's homes. Stephen Kinley the Second sat behind a mighty desk at the far end of the room, across an entire football field of thick carpeting.

He stood up. "Steve, thank you for coming."

He seemed to me older than the last time I saw him—a small figure dwarfed by the magnificence of his office. Part of this may have been the effect of the grand view behind him. Mr.

Kinley had a corner suite, and the two walls of floor-to-ceiling windows met behind his desk and revealed a panoramic view of the Hudson River. I could see a huge ocean liner pulling into dock, guided by two tugboats. An enormous yacht was moving the other direction, toward the open sea. In the sky, a jet plane was streaming toward Newark Airport in the distance, and a police helicopter was racing downriver toward the Statue of Liberty. With all this activity outside the window, it was hard to focus on the small, worried-looking man behind the desk.

"Incredible view!" I said.

"I suppose it is," he sighed. "Funny, I hardly even see it anymore."

I didn't notice Edith Kinley at first. She was sitting in a huge armchair to one side of her husband's enormous desk. The gargantuan proportions of everything in the office—the desk, the chairs, the view in the background—worked to make the human figures insignificant by comparison.

"Nice to see you, Edith," I said, taking a seat in one of the huge armchairs.

"Steve, my husband has something to say to you. Don't you, Stephen?"

The chairman cleared his throat unhappily.

"I understand Edith has told you about our son, Stephen Kinley the Third," he began. "I realize that from your point of view I probably behaved badly, getting that girl thrown out of school ... but I thought I had my son's best interest in mind. . . ."

"Stephen! I think we've all had quite enough of your justifications," Edith chided. "What you did was wrong, and you know it."

"Yes, yes," he admitted. "It was wrong. That poor girl ... she was very nice, actually. I dream about her sometimes. I've tried to forget her, but I can't. I blame myself for her suicide.

The reason we've called you here this morning, Steve, is that
Edith insists I tell you everything.''

"There's more to the story than what I heard?"

The old man sighed. "I kept just one thing back from Edith,"
he admitted. "Until yesterday. I couldn't live with myself keeping it secret anymore.''

"You see, my son contacted me three years ago. He was in
trouble, and he wanted help."

"How did he contact you?"

"By telephone. He . . . well, he was running from the law.
He had done something very foolish—he said he had tried to
rob a bank. It was a bungled job, apparently, and he didn't get
away with any money, but the police and the FBI were looking
for him. He asked me for some cash so he could buy a fake
passport and flee the country. He said there was a net closing
around him and he wouldn't have called me, but he was desperate, and this was his last chance. I . . . I'm afraid I responded
badly.''

"What did you do?"

"I gave him nothing. Only a lecture about how I was not
going to have any dealings with a bank robber. I told him if
he tried to call me again, I would turn him over to the police.
Then I hung up the phone.''

"*You* drove him to these desperate acts, Stephen, by killing
that girl!'' Edith said accusingly.

"Edith, please. I ruined my son's life, and I should have
been more supportive when he called. But I decided to wash
my hands of him—I didn't even tell Edith about the call until
yesterday. We haven't seen our little Stevie for nearly twenty
years, you understand. I thought it best for Edith just to forget
about him. Why get upset all over again?''

"You're certain it was your son on the line?"

"Yes, entirely certain.''

"Did you tell him that his grandfather had made him a very
rich man in his will?''

Stephen Kinley shook his head slowly. "How could I hand the network over to a bank robber? I thought it best for him not to know about the will."

"Stephen!" cried his wife once again.

"Yes, I know—it was wrong. My son was begging me for money, and I didn't even let him know that he was in fact a very rich man—*I* was the one who would be poor, if he ever claimed his inheritance."

"Did you hear from him again?"

"No. I don't know if he got out of the country, or if he's in prison now, or still on the run. He never tried to reach me again."

"And you made no attempt to try to find him—even though you had a legal and moral responsibility to let him know the terms of his grandfather's will?"

Again, the chairman shook his head slowly.

"Where was your son calling from three years ago?" I asked. Strangely enough, I almost knew the answer in advance.

"Somewhere in New Mexico. He told me he was hiding out on an Indian reservation."

Chapter 47

Despite Sherry Gold's warning not to travel this weekend, we were strapped into our seats in the network's Lear jet that was set to take off from La Guardia into a sky heavy with the promise of snow. It was late Friday afternoon. Stephen Kinley had put the jet at our disposal for the weekend, and we were headed to Santa Fe and the Land of Enchantment, where so many trails seemed to converge. Neither Jayne nor I was eager to fly again in the Lear after our last experience, but commercial jets, I discovered, did not fly into Santa Fe, only Albuquerque. Since I needed to be back in Manhattan for the show early Monday morning, my time was very limited. I had little alternative but to accept Mr. Kinley's offer.

Edith had given us a photograph of her son and once we were in the air, Jayne took it from her handbag to study more closely. The picture showed Stevie the Third at the age of seventeen—a handsome boy with shaggy, brown-blond hair and a wide-open smile. Edith told us the picture had been taken several months before the tragedy of his girlfriend's suicide.

In the photographs, the young man seemed untouched by sorrow, full of eager life and promise.

"What an attractive boy!" Jayne remarked. "It's terrible what his father did to him."

"Yes. But a kid has to grow up eventually and accept responsibility for his actions. No matter what kind of lousy childhood you had, it's still no excuse to rob a bank."

Jayne agreed, but she could not help but look at the photograph with a motherly eye. "I wonder what ever happened to him?"

"Perhaps we'll find out," I told her. The odds were against us. Of course little Stevie Kinley would not look anything today like the innocent boy in the photograph. He would have a new name and a face altered by age and tragedy. And, of course, he might be long gone from New Mexico. Nevertheless, I was hopeful we would learn something of his fate.

The plane's microwave was working today and Brittany, the attractive young stewardess, served us what she described as "a small supper"—smoked Scotch salmon for an appetizer, followed by Caesar salad, sautéed duck with wild mushrooms and rice pilaf, and finally chocolate torte with fresh raspberries on top. Afterward we put our seats back and managed to sleep for a few hours.

The trip took slightly more than four hours. We raced the sun westward and came down in Santa Fe just in time to catch a dramatic sunset over the mountains. Cass was at the airport to meet us, and it was wonderful to see his friendly face with the sneaky cowboy eyes, like those of the film actor Ben Johnson. In the short time he had been in New Mexico, he had already gone native. He wore a cowboy hat and a bolo tie that had a turquoise clip. Of course, Cass was from Wyoming originally—a neighbor, as space went in this huge part of the world. Looking at him with his hat and bolo tie, you'd think his watery blue eyes had been gazing out upon desert and mountains for the last twenty years, rather than the urban sprawl of Los Angeles.

"Hey, amigo!" he said giving me a hug. "How do, Jayne."

"I do fine, Cass. New Mexico appears to be agreeing with you."

"I can't kick."

Actually, Santa Fe is not exactly my idea of the wide-open spaces. Imagine Rodeo Drive with Southwestern architecture—cute adobe buildings and narrow streets. Movie stars who have traded in their Jaguar convertibles for Land Cruisers. Chichi restaurants that cost an arm and a leg. New Mexico has become Hollywood's refuge of choice in recent years. Jane Fonda and Ted Turner have a huge ranch here, people like Ted Danson and Ali McGraw and Lauren Hutton keep houses in Santa Fe, while Julia Roberts lives in the northern town of Taos.

"I've booked us into the Eldorado Hotel," Cass said. "Nice place two blocks from the main plaza—looks like an old Indian pueblo with a swimming pool on the roof."

"I didn't know Indians *had* swimming pools on their roofs," I remarked caustically.

"In Santa Fe, they do. Do you want to go to the hotel first to freshen up, or straight to Angela McDavis's house? I called her as you told me, and she's expecting us for dinner tonight."

"Dinner!"

"I bet you guys are hungry after that long flight. Don't worry, Mrs. McDavis said she was going to treat you to a real New Mexican feast—blue corn enchiladas, sopadillas with honey, posole, the works."

"Let's go see Mrs. McDavis first," I told Cass. "*You* can eat."

I tend to think of New Mexico as desert, forgetting that Santa Fe sits at an altitude of seven thousand feet, nestled against the side of the Sangre de Cristo Mountain range. The air was sharp and cold, and there was an inch of snow on the ground—and much more snow, I could see in the fading light, on the nearby mountains. Cass had rented a four-wheel drive Jeep Cherokee, and he drove us to an area of expensive houses on large tracts of land at the north edge of the city off the Old Santa Fe Trail. The McDavis house was a sprawling, two-story adobe sitting on several acres of piñon forest.

An aging Spanish butler with a dignified face answered the doorbell and showed us into the living room. The room was very traditional, with a beehive-shaped kiva fireplace at one end, and a ceiling made out of twigs in a herringbone pattern, held in place by *vigas*—entire trees stripped of their bark running from wall to wall. We could have been in a museum. There were beautiful Navajo rugs on the walls, and Indian bowls and kachina dolls in glass cases. We were admiring the artwork when Angela McDavis came into the room, propelling herself forward in her wheelchair.

"Steve, it's been years!" she said, offering her hand. "Jayne, I don't believe we ever met in Los Angeles . . . and you must be Cass."

Angela McDavis had changed a great deal in the years since she had been a singer. It wasn't only the wheelchair. Her face had become thin and sharp, her eyes as watchful and unsmiling as a hawk's. She had a new poise that came with money and marriage to a famous television personality. But there was a bitter downturn at the edges of her mouth that had not been there as a young woman. She did not look happy, though she was very gracious. The butler brought drinks and appetizers while she politely explained the history of many of the Indian art objects in the room. I found the kachina dolls fascinating, but Jayne and I had not flown all this way to talk about Southwestern art.

"Angela, I'm sure you know that there have been two murders this week of people connected with 'Good Morning, U.S.A.' A young woman's house was set on fire, an entire light bar broke loose above my head while I was on-camera . . . in short, sitting in for Peter has not been much fun. I need to speak to him as soon as possible."

"Well, you're in luck. The great man actually condescended

to phone me from Taos an hour ago. When I told him you were coming, he suggested you drive up to his cabin tomorrow—he's planning to take you skiing.''

"Skiing!" I cried. "Look, I don't think Peter appreciates the seriousness of the situation. Is there some way I can reach him by phone?''

Angela shook her head. "He doesn't have a telephone there. Very stubborn of him, of course. And convenient, too.''

"Convenient for what?''

She smiled unpleasantly. "So I can't reach him and find out if he's playing nookie with some little ski bunny he's picked up on the slopes. *I* used to enjoy skiing. Did you know that, Steve? Of course, I'm not going to be anyone's ski bunny anymore.''

"I'm awfully sorry about your accident, Angela.''

"*Accident!*" she scoffed.

"Wasn't it one?''

"Only if you consider driving home after a party on an icy road with five martinis in your belly an accident. Peter had been flirting with a young girl that night, and we were fighting about it in the car. He was angry with me for spotting the obvious, and he was driving too fast.''

"It sounds dreadful, my dear,'' Jayne sympathized. "But what I can't understand is why you stay with him? Pardon me for saying so, but you don't seem to be in love with Peter anymore.''

"In *love* with him!'' she shrieked. A malevolent light came into her eyes. "No, it's not exactly love, Jayne. But do you think I'm going to let him go scot-free after what he did to me? No, thank you! I plan to stick around so he doesn't ever forget that little drive on the icy road! Probably you're wondering why he doesn't leave *me?* . . . He'd never dare ask for a divorce. He's tied to me by guilt, you see. And besides, he knows if he tries to divorce me, I'll take him for every cent he has. . . . Have some chips and salsa, Jayne.''

"Angela," I asked, "is it possible that Peter was not actually in Taos this past week? Could he have gone secretly to New York?"

She shrugged. "With Peter, anything's possible. He phoned once in the middle of week, but of course he could have done that from anywhere." Her eyes narrowed into hard slits. "Damn! If he saw that Nancy Vandenberg creature, I'll kill him! I don't mind the ski bunnies, but I won't tolerate an affair that half of New York knows about."

"I don't think he went to New York to see Nancy. If he *was* there—and I'm not entirely sure he was—it was to break his contract with Stephen Kinley."

"What?"

"You haven't heard? Peter's received an offer to do the evening news at another network. I don't know what the figures are, but it's clearly a huge step up in his career—*if* he can get free of Stephen Kinley. And that's a big *if,* I understand."

"That son of a bitch! He didn't tell me!" Angela said. "But he's been acting very sneaky lately. I *knew* there was something going on!"

"You see what I'm hinting at, don't you?" I asked cautiously.

She met my eyes. "I see *exactly* what you're implying, Steve. How does a person like Peter McDavis get out of a binding contract to accept a much better job? He arranges a few accidents and murders to show how unsafe it is to work for Stephen Kinley. Any court in the country would let him off the hook!"

"I want you to tell me something, Angela. You know Peter probably better than anyone. Do you think he's capable of murder to advance his career? Is he ruthless enough?"

Knowing how Angela hated her husband, I was prepared for a character assassination. But she surprised me. She shook her head and said, "To tell the truth, I don't know. Frankly, I would have thought he was too much of a wimp to kill anybody. But maybe I've been making his life too miserable, pushing him too hard. A new job and a lot more money—perhaps he could afford to divorce me after all.''

''You can see why I need to know exactly where he's been the past week. A remote Taos ski cabin without a telephone is a tad too convenient for him.''

''I'll check it out for you. I have a friend up there who's been my spy from time to time. I'll call her later tonight. Meanwhile, if you go up to the Taos Ski Valley and ask around, they might be able to tell you if he's actually been there or not. If he was in New Mexico this past week rather than New York, I guarantee, that's where he would have been—on the steepest chutes and expert runs. He skis like a madman.''

''I appreciate your help, Angela. Meanwhile, I have a photograph I want you to look at. Probably it's crazy—New Mexico is a large place, and it's a very remote chance you'll recognize the person in the picture. But I'm curious if you've seen him here.''

Jayne took the photograph of Stevie Kinley the Third from her bag and handed it to Angela McDavis. To my surprise, Angela recognized the face immediately.

''Goodness! It's Stevie Bad Hand—a lot younger than when I knew him, but there's no mistaking that grin.''

''Bad Hand?'' I repeated. ''Is that an Indian name?''

''Yes. He gave the name to himself—I suppose he didn't like his real name. He's an Anglo, of course, one of those white kids who came to New Mexico wanting to live off the land. Stevie lived on a hippie commune near Taos for a few years, then he went to India for a while. Poor kid, he was always trying to find himself, and I'm not sure he ever did—at least during the time I knew him. For all I know, he's a stockbroker now.''

''How did you know him?'' Jayne asked.

''We studied Transcendental Meditation from the same teacher in Santa Fe.

''This was about seven years ago, shortly after Peter put me in a wheelchair. I thought perhaps meditation was the answer, a way to forget my crippled body and find peace of mind. But I was wrong, and I gave it up after a few months.''

"So that was the only time you saw him? During the meditation class?'' I asked.

"No, he came to see me afterward, here at my home. He was worried about me. He said he knew exactly what it was like to have someone do you a terrible harm. He was very sympathetic really—a sweet kid. He had no money, so I gave him work around the house for about a year. He worked on the garden, did some painting, hauled my trash—that sort of thing. Then one day he just stopped coming, and I never saw him again.''

"How long ago was that?''

"Five years ago, maybe. I've wondered about him sometimes, what ever became of him. Something was torturing him, but I never knew what it was.''

"He never talked about his problems?''

"Not once. And I felt it would be intruding to ask. But I had a feeling that something very profoundly bad had happened in his life. I hoped one day he would feel comfortable enough with me to open up. But he never did.''

"And you never knew his true last name?''

"No, never. Tell me, Steve—now you have my curiosity aroused. Who *is* he?''

"The person you knew as Stevie Bad Hand is in fact Stephen Kinley the Third.''

Angela McDavis's mouth opened in almost a comical manner. She gaped before she found her voice.

"You mean he's the son of *Mr.* Kinley, the head of the network? I never suspected. What a small world! And I always felt sorry for him that he never had any money. I found ways to slip him an extra twenty dollars here and there.''

I did not tell Angela what an extraordinarily rich young man Stevie Bad Hand actually was—if he could ever be found.

"Do you have any idea, Angela, where he might be if he's still in New Mexico?"

"I really don't know," she said. "The only place I can think of is a long shot. He had an Indian friend, Howard Mirabel. They were close. Howard is from the Santa Anita Pueblo which is up in the northern part of the state between Taos and Abiqui—not far from where Georgia O'Keeffe used to live. I've always thought that if anyone would know what happened to Stevie, Howard would. If *he's* still in New Mexico, of course. As I said, it's a long shot."

"It's worth a try. Thanks for your help, Angela."

The Spanish butler came in to announce that dinner was served.

For the sake of politeness, and hot on the trail of a murder, Jayne and I forced ourselves to take a few bites of yet another four-course dinner.

Chapter 48

About the only good thing I can say for indigestion is that occasionally you have some fairly brilliant thoughts at three in the morning when you can't sleep. Lying on my back with my eyes wide-open, staring at the ceiling of our room at the Eldorado Hotel, I solved the riddle that Lucky Mendoza, the professional hit man, had condescended to toss my way before making his exit from Mr. Sushi.

I was so excited, I woke Jayne.

"'What is sweet as honey, yet the most bitter herb of all?' I got it! It was right in front of me all the time!"

I told Jayne the answer of the riddle.

"Of course, Steve," she said grumpily, not enthusiastic that I had woken her. "I knew the answer all the time."

"Ha!" I challenged. "I'll bet! If you knew, why didn't you tell me?"

"Because it was so obvious, that's why. A child could have figured it out. Now go back to sleep, darling."

She was right, of course. The answer was obvious. A child could have figured it out. Nevertheless it had eluded me until this moment. I felt pretty silly, but I suppose better late than never at all.

In the morning, I phoned the front desk of the hotel to rent a second car. With time at a premium, and many deeds to accomplish, it seemed best to separate for the day. Jayne planned to go to the Santa Anita Pueblo, and I would go to Taos. Over breakfast we divided our resources—Cass, that is, on the one hand, and the Colt .45 revolver on the other. As a chivalrous husband, I wanted Jayne to take both Cass *and* the gun, in case she ran into trouble. "Nonsense," said Jayne. Women were the stronger sex and she would survive quite well on her wits, thank you. *I* was the one who needed the help of a weapon and a friend. We argued the point over egg-beater Spanish omelettes served in our room. I insisted that if Cass went with me, she take the gun at least.

"A deal," she agreed at last. "At least it will keep you from shooting any more ceilings."

So that's how we left it. After breakfast, Jayne dropped the huge six-shooter into her handbag and headed northwest in the Jeep Cherokee, while Cass and I headed northeast to Taos in a Toyota Land Cruiser. Chivalry compels me to recount my wife's adventures first:

Jayne told me later that she fell in love with New Mexico that day. The sky was a deep and perfect blue, a color one does not ordinarily see in California or New York. She drove on a two-lane highway which snaked its way through a land of red mesa tops and piñon, with snowcapped mountains always visible on the horizon. The view was spectacular, and Jayne found herself singing happily by herself in the car. After a week in Manhattan, she was struck by how gloriously open and empty was this land of northern New Mexico. You could look for a hundred miles in any direction and not see a house or a telephone pole, nor any sign of human activity. Hawks were floating in the sky, and at one point Jayne was certain she saw an eagle. The country was wild and untamed, and to tell the truth, she was not entirely sorry she had the Colt .45 in her handbag.

Jayne drove for nearly two hours. She rose up out of a valley into a mountain pass that was deep with snow, and then down the other side onto a high desert plateau. When the pavement ended and she found herself on a narrow dirt road which followed a small but swiftly moving river. Around a bend she came upon a flock of sheep that were blocking the road. An old Indian man on horseback was herding the sheep.

Jayne rolled down her window. "Excuse me!" she called. "Is this the way to the Santa Anita Pueblo?"

The old man's face was as red and wrinkled as the land itself. Without a word he raised an arm and pointed toward the western horizon.

"The pueblo's over there?" Jayne asked dubiously. "I don't see anything but sagebrush and hills."

"Twenty miles," said the old man.

It seemed to Jayne that she had dropped off the face of the known earth into some forgotten pocket where time had stopped. She drove in second gear, bouncing over ruts and gullies. At one point she forded a small stream. The journey seemed to take forever. Then, after so much driving, she came upon the Indian village unexpectedly. The adobe, mud-colored houses were so indistinguishable from the earth that they were not visible until you were right up on them. Jayne parked in a main plaza next to an ancient pickup truck. A few Indian children were kicking a soccer ball in the plaza, and two old men with blankets wrapped around their heads sat on a bench watching her. It was hard to believe that she was still in twentieth-century America.

At the far side of the plaza, she saw an ancient sign on the front of one of the adobe houses that said, "RED BUFFALO INDIAN CURIOS. SODA POP & CIGARETTES. CREDIT CARDS GLADLY ACCEPTED." She crossed the plaza and went inside. The store was crowded with kachina dolls,

T-shirts, rugs, postcards, and Indian jewelry of silver and turquoise—much of it quite exquisite. A young woman with a
baby in her arms sat in a rocking chair before a small kiva
fireplace.

"Hello. What a delightful village this is!" Jayne said. "And
such a beautiful spot!"

The young Indian woman smiled. "Everything is fifty percent off today. It's our midwinter sale."

"Actually, I'm not here to shop. I'm hoping for some information."

The young woman's smile became vague. "We have several
books on the area, if you are interested."

"I'm trying to find a person named Howard Mirabel. I know
he lived here a few years ago."

"At the Santa Anita Pueblo? Are you sure?"

"I think so, yes."

"Howard . . . ?"

"Mirabel," Jayne repeated.

The young woman shook her head. "No, I don't know him.
I'm sorry."

There was something indefinite about the young woman that
caused Jayne to hesitate. She began to browse through the store,
stopping at the glass jewelry case. There was a silver bracelet
set with a beautifully polished turquoise stone that particularly
caught her eye.

"What a lovely bracelet! It looks quite old."

The young woman stood up from the rocking chair. She set
the baby down in a crib and came around to the glass case.

"Yes, it is perhaps a hundred years old. An antique. Wonderful workmanship, don't you think?"

"Well, perhaps I can try it on. . . ."

Jayne, of course, feels a day is hardly well spent unless she
is spending some of our money. The jewelry in the case was
irresistible. Can I blame her for interrupting detective-work-
in-progress for a little shopping? Of course not! I only wish

she had stopped with the bracelet, however, and had never seen the concha belt of beaten silver, or the earrings that were shaped like small eagles.

"Julia Roberts bought a pair of earrings just like those," the young woman purred.

"Julia Roberts? My goodness . . . well, perhaps I should try them on."

"And have you seen this belt? Bob Redford picked up one that was almost identical last summer."

"*Bob* Redford?" Jayne inquired. This outpost far from civilization was seeming less remote by the minute.

"Bob often drops by from Utah," the girl said. "I think the Sundance Film Festival is really a marvelous idea, don't you? My cousin is trying to raise money to make an independent film about life on the reservation. Bob has been awfully helpful. . . ."

Hollywood, you understand, is no longer a geographical entity located in Southern California; it is a state of mind that has spread across the planet for better *and* worse. Jayne was slightly disappointed she had not arrived in some pure and mythical adobe village where no one had ever heard the names Robert Redford or Julia Roberts, but her disappointment did not keep her from adding the concha belt or the earrings to her purchase. The concha belt, naturally, was a present for me. A guilt offering, so I could not object to the earrings and bracelet.

As Jayne was putting her credit cards away, she noticed the photograph of young Stevie Kinley in her bag and remembered that she had not come all this way to shop.

"This is the person I'm actually hoping to find," Jayne said, handing the photo to the girl. "I was told that Howard Mirabel is his friend. His name is Stevie Kinley, but I believe he calls himself Stevie Bad Hand. . . ."

Jayne stopped speaking. The young woman was staring at the photograph with a look of surprise in her eyes. Her hand was trembling.

"You know him, don't you?"

"No!" she cried with vehemence.

"My dear, I wish you would help me. I'm a friend of this young man's parents in New York . . . well, perhaps friend is the wrong word. But I very much want to find Stevie, for his own good. Among other things, he has inherited a great deal of money from his grandfather."

"I don't know Stevie Bad Hand," she insisted.

"I think you do," Jayne said softly. "Now look at me, dear. Do I look like the sort of person who would do him any harm? Won't you at least let me speak to him?"

"No," she said. She shook her head violently. "I can not help you. But you can ask my father."

"Your father?"

She looked up into Jayne's eyes. "I am Krishna Mirabel. My father is Howard Mirabel."

"Krishna! What a curious name for a Native American!" Jayne said, hoping for more information. But the girl was not forthcoming.

"Ask my father," she repeated. "Do you know the Golden Mesa?"

"No, I'm afraid not."

"I'll draw you a map. It's a short distance—only forty miles."

Chapter 49

A forty-mile drive on the freeway is nothing—if you chance to live in Montana, where there are no speed limits, a mere ten minutes or so. But the road that Jayne took went up and down through steep ravines and arroyos, through snow in the higher elevations, and mud down below. Some parts of the road were hardly wider than a goat track; in other places the road was so wide and washed-out that Jayne was no longer certain she was *on* a road. Often she had to stop to open a gate, drive through, stop again, and close the gate behind her.

The land was strange and remote. Occasionally Jayne passed the ruins of an adobe hut. Once, on a distant meadow, she spotted a trailer with smoke coming out the chimney; she wondered what sort of person could live in such a lonely place. Up and down she rode for several hours. She passed many mesas of different shades of brown and red. The mesas came in all sorts of shapes and sizes. But none of them was golden.

Jayne was not certain exactly what she was looking for. "You'll know you're there when you see it," the Indian girl, Krishna Mirabel, had told her. The light was starting to fade from the short winter day when Jayne drove over the top of a hill and saw a strange sight below her: a glow of golden light coming from a spot in the desert a few miles away. Jayne kept driving. As she approached the exotic glow, she saw that it was made up of different colors—reds, oranges, blues, and greens shooting flames of colors into the twilight sky. Closer still and the lights began to flash and beckon. Finally the lights spelled out letters and words. THE GOLDEN MESA, Jayne read, quite to her surprise. And then a final word dispelled the mystery of the place: CASINO.

"Ah!" she said. Driving such a long time by herself in the desert, she had begun to talk to herself. "But what in the world is a casino doing in the middle of nowhere?"

In a moment this mystery too was solved. Passing around a final curve she saw a busy four-lane highway in front of her. Jayne pulled into the crowded parking lot and gazed at the building in astonishment. It was a huge translucent bubble, built out of some plastic material, glowing from inside. On the outside giant neon lights wrote and erased themselves. "THE BEST INDIAN GAMING IN NEW MEXICO," one sign proclaimed. "SLOTS. VIDEO POKER. $1,000,000 JACKPOT!" There was all the hype and glitter of Las Vegas, though everything had an Indian twist. A billboard facing the highway announced the appearance of "Tommy and the Tomahawks" this evening, as well as a ninety-nine-cent breakfast that was served twenty-four hours a day.

Jayne felt a bit like Dorothy approaching Oz. But when she entered the casino, she saw that it was pretty much like a large casino anywhere. The lights of slot machines flashed and glittered. There was the jingle of money and an occasional buzzer as someone won big. Even the same bored faces of the people pumping quarters into the machines reminded her of Vegas. Beyond the rows of slot machines and video poker machines, she glimpsed the green velvet tables and roulette wheels that attracted the more serious gamblers. There was no alcohol since the casino was on Native American land, and to Jayne this at least seemed an improvement.

She went up to a cashier's kiosk at one side of the room. "Excuse me, I'm looking for Howard Mirabel. Do you know where I might find him?"

"Let me call and see if he's here." The cashier was a large woman. She picked up a phone in her kiosk and spoke in a Native American language—Tiwa, Jayne later discovered—to someone on the other end. Then she put down the phone and told Jayne that Mr. Mirabel had been expecting her. Someone would come in a moment to take Jayne to Mr. Mirabel's office.

The someone was a huge Native American security guard, a young man who must have weighed three hundred pounds. Jayne followed him through the casino, through a door marked "Employees Only," and into a wing of modern offices. The security guard knocked on a door upon which was written, "Howard Mirabel, General Manager."

"Come in!"

Jayne entered a large office and found Howard Mirabel seated behind a desk. He was an extremely distinguished-looking Native American in his early forties, dressed in a white dinner jacket. He regarded Jayne warily, but rose to his feet in a show of friendliness.

"I'm happy to meet you, Mrs. Allen," he said. "My daughter phoned from the pueblo to let me know that you were on your way."

"After seeing the pueblo, I didn't quite expect all this . . . glitz," Jayne said, searching for the right word.

Howard smiled slightly. "This is the new 'Indian' reality. Gambling may be the red man's revenge for all the broken treaties we've endured from white people. We may have the last laugh after all, Mrs. Allen. My daughter prefers the old ways—she's looking for her roots, you see. Which is why she stays in that old shop. Personally, I'm more inclined to move with the times. I understand you're looking for Stevie Bad Hand?''

''Yes. I was told you are his friend.''

''And who told you that, if I may ask?''

''Angela McDavis in Santa Fe.''

''Ah, yes. Well, she is perfectly right. Stevie and I go way back. We were at Choate together.''

''Really?''

''You look surprised. I was a scholarship student, of course. In the seventies, Indians were quite the hip minority you know, and some of the expensive prep schools and colleges went out of their way to give a few of us an education. Choate was a very snobbish place of course, lots of old money and old families—I was terrifically lonely. The only person who made an effort to be my friend was Stevie Kinley, as I knew him then. And so a few years later when our positions were reversed, and he was the one who needed help, I did what I could for him. He wanted to be an Indian for a while, change his name, be part of the tribe—anything to forget his *real* tribe. So I arranged it.''

''How long did he live on the reservation?''

''On and off for nearly ten years. Of course Stevie was always restless, always looking for some great answer in the sky. He came and went. He lived on a commune near Taos for a while, and then he got involved in yoga and meditation and all that—he was in India for a time. He got me into Hindu philosophy for a while as well, which is how I ended up calling my daughter Krishna. But with Stevie, none of it lasted very long. Generally he came back here whenever he was broke and in big trouble. His life tended toward high drama, Mrs. Allen.''

''Please, you must call me Jayne.''

''Well, Jayne, if you want to know the truth, there have been times I've regretted my friendship with Stevie Kinley Bad Hand. An unhappy, screwed-up kid. Self-destructive. Stevie Bad Trouble is what some of the people around here call him.

My daughter told me you have a photograph of him—may I
see it, please?''

Jayne handed him the picture of Stevie. Howard studied it
for quite a long time before handing it back.

"A handsome kid, wasn't he?" Howard asked. "So much
wasted promise! There are times I would gladly strangle that
father of his for what he did to Stevie. After Ann committed
suicide, Stevie just seemed to go crazy. He didn't care anymore
whether he lived or died."

Jayne asked the big question: "Do you know where he is
now, Howard."

"Certainly. But I'm not sure I should take you to him."

"I hope you will, Howard. Among other things, I need to
tell Stevie that his grandfather left him a great deal of money."

"Did he now? A great deal of money! Well, well—we had
better go see him then."

Howard led the way out a back door to his car, a BMW
convertible, that was sitting in a small private lot behind the
casino. Night had fallen and a moon that was nearly full gave
an unearthly glow to the New Mexico landscape.

"Where are we going?" Jayne asked.

"You'll see."

Howard refused to answer any of Jayne's questions as they
rode in the car. He drove for less than ten minutes on a dirt
road into the desert, and then stopped abruptly in the middle
of nowhere. There was not a house, nor a light, nor any other
human in sight.

Howard got out of the BMW. "Come on," he said.

"Here?"

"You'll see," he said again.

There was nothing for Jayne to do but follow the Indian
down a path into a ravine. Jayne was glad the moonlight lit
the way, but still she was anxious to be in such a strange place
at night with someone she really did not know. Howard walked
a few feet ahead of her, and she struggled to keep up.

Jayne expected they would turn a bend and come to a cabin. But after walking for a few minutes, Howard simply stopped by a large and quite beautiful piñon tree.

"Here we are," he said.

"Here?" Then she saw a small wooden cross at the foot of the tree. "Oh!" she exclaimed.

"Yes. Stevie is dead. His grandfather's money won't do him a bit of good now."

"But when did he die? And how?"

"As I told you, he used to come back to the reservation when he was in trouble. The last time was three years ago—he was heavily into drugs by then, and he had tried to rob a bank in Albuquerque. But he was a failure even at that. Unfortunately the video cameras in the bank got a good look at his face, so he needed someplace to hide. He set up a tepee right here in this ravine, and I would bring him supplies. No one would have found him out here—he could have lived here forever."

"Then what happened?"

"He had a small .22 rifle for hunting rabbits. One afternoon I came with his weekly supplies and I found he had shot himself. He left a note for me—I have it at home in case you're curious. It was a very short note. It said, 'Sorry, old buddy, and thanks for all your help over the years. I guess when I was friendly to you that freshman year at Choate, you didn't know what you were getting in for. Nothing's ever worked out for me since Ann died, so I thought I might as well join her. Maybe she's waiting for me at the far side of the great divide ... Stevie.' "

Jayne wept during the ride from the grave back to the casino. She had never known Stevie Kinley, but it seemed awfully tragic for such a good-looking boy, the heir to a great television empire, to end up so terribly alone in an obscure ravine in New Mexico.

"Why don't you come in and have a drink?" Howard offered

when they were back at the casino. "I keep a bottle of old cognac in my desk."

"No thank you," Jayne said, dabbing the tears from her cheeks with a handkerchief. "I'd better get back to Santa Fe."

"Well, stop by again if ever you feel like it," Howard told her. He waved and began to head back inside the casino, while Jayne walked toward her rented Jeep.

Howard took a few steps, then turned and called to her. "Hey, Jayne, I was just thinking about all that money you said Stevie was supposed to inherit. You think some of it might go now to his son?"

Jayne stopped in her tracks. "His son?" she asked. "Stevie had a *son?*"

Jayne forgot about going to Santa Fe. She followed Howard Mirabel instead back into the casino for that glass of cognac.

Chapter 50

"Come on, take off your clothes and jump in, boys! Don't be shy!" Peter McDavis said grandly to Cass and me. "You guys are going to freeze out there."

"Thank you," Cass replied with cowboy humor. "But I've already had my bath for the week."

"How about you, Steve? I never took you for a square or a prude."

"I'm not," I agreed. "Nevertheless, I'll keep my clothes on."

"Well, suit yourselves—no pun intended," Peter said merrily. "Nancy, darling, I'll take another glass of the bubbly, if you will be so kind."

Cass and I averted our eyes as Nancy Vandenberg stepped stark naked from Peter's hot tub. Fingers of steam rose into the winter sky, encircling her like some mythological nymph. She was a beautiful woman, I couldn't help but notice out of a rebellious corner of my eye. After all, I might be called one day to testify about this afternoon in a court of law; a detective must force himself to be ever observant. Nancy took a dark green bottle of Dom Pérignon from where it was sticking up out of the snow and returned with it into the hot tub. Cass's face was the color of a steamed carrot.

"Help yourselves to some glasses from the kitchen," Peter offered. "We'll have a party."

"Peter," I said, "we did not come here to party. We came to get answers to some questions."

"A pity," he said with a shake of his head. "Personally, after working ten years on a morning news program, I'm ready to bust out and have some fun. My philosophy is if you see something you want—grab it!"

Peter lurched forward and indeed grabbed his ex-co-anchor underwater. Nancy let out a happy little scream and spilled half a glass of champagne into the swirling, steaming water.

I need to back up. Cass and I had arrived in Taos in the late morning, and from town we had made our way into the mountains to Peter McDavis's ski chalet, secluded in a dense forest of Douglas fir. The air up here was noticeably thin, and Cass assured me that we had arrived at an elevation of over nine thousand feet. From a recent snowfall, several inches of powdery snow weighing down the branches of every tree, but now the clouds had cleared and the sky was a brilliant blue. It was a picture-perfect day. A winter wonderland. Besides the fluffy new powder, there was a base of five or six feet of snow already on the ground. Without any doubt, snow in the high mountains of New Mexico was a lot prettier to look at than its white cousin in New York City.

Peter's "cabin," as he liked to call it, was a two-story redwood A-frame with an eminently practical steep roof. When Cass and I rang the doorbell, Peter shouted at us to come around the side of the house to the patio at the back. And this is where we found Peter and Nancy *au naturel* in a steaming hot tub surrounded by deep drifts of snow. Peter McDavis, as television viewers know, is a good-looking man in his late forties. He has a classic matinee idol profile, wavy brown hair, penetrating eyes, and a good speaking voice—qualities which have made him such a success on "Good Morning, U.S.A." As I studied him, I tried to decide whether with a turban on his head and a little makeup, he might be transformed into Mr. Abawashi, late guest of the Plaza Hotel. It was possible, I suppose, but frankly, I was unsure. The problem was I had only had a very brief glimpse of Mr. Abawashi when he had walked from the Oak Room through the bar to the lobby of the hotel.

Nancy Vandenberg—if you did not catch her on the show before she was dismissed—is in her late twenties, a blond, blue-eyed beauty. There is a pertness about her that is positively electric—perhaps too electric for an early morning audience that is not yet completely awake. Today in the hot tub, without the dignity of clothes, both Peter and Nancy looked somewhat older and less attractive than they did on the tube—particularly Peter, whose face was haggard with exhaustion. A person has to be very young indeed to parade about naked with impunity.

For no reason of which I was conscious, my mind flashed back to a story told to me by a musician who worked on one of my TV comedy shows when—I believe the year was 1958—we originated a program from Havana, shortly before Castro's takeover. Around the gambling casino and hotel at which we did our live telecast there were the usual complement of attractive young women. Indeed there were even more than usual because dancers and models had been imported as part of the production. One of the fellows in the band told me that since he was going to be in town for only three days, and had been immediately smitten by a particularly attractive chorus-girl, he thought it might enhance his chances of sleeping with her if he invited her to that famous or infamous Cuban spectacle known as The Circus, a presentation of blatantly sexual entertainment in which, at least at certain climactic moments, very little was left to the imagination. The young woman accepted his invitation, let us hope in the ignorance of what she was about to witness, and during the early portions of the evening's entertainment, my associate's joy knew no bounds, given the nature of his hopes. But as the evening progressed and the sexual activity on stage became more blunt and explicit— well, I'll quote the gentleman: "What the two of us saw—and remember I'd just met the girl—what the two of us saw was so disgusting that when we left the joint, I took her right back to her hotel room and said 'goodnight' and lost all interest in sex itself for quite sometime."

"Here's to 'Good Morning, U.S.A.!' " Peter declared, raising his glass in a toast.

"Good *night,* U.S.A.!" Nancy echoed, clinking her glass with his.

They both thought this was hilarious.

"Stick it in your ear, U.S.A.!" Nancy cried happily. And they laughed even more.

"It sounds like you're saying goodbye to the show forever, Peter," I said.

"Forever?" he giggled. "No more getting up at four o'clock in the morning? *Never* having to smile at Bob Hutchinson again? How ever would I cope with such a loss?"

"I'm not sure," I told him. "Particularly since you have an unbreakable contract with Stephen Kinley."

"All things are breakable, my boy," Peter said with a smile of satisfaction. "Ours is a fragile world. Steve, our glasses seem to be unfortunately empty. Would you mind?"

I was glad to save Nancy the trouble of emerging for the bottle. Peter and Nancy held their glasses upward as I poured into their steaming caldron.

"Come on! Join the celebration!" Peter urged.

"But I don't even know what we're celebrating," I said.

"Why, life and love and downhill skiing!" he declared.

"And freedom from your contract?"

He grinned mysteriously.

"Steve, without getting into specifics, how would you like to have a permanent berth on early morning television?"

"No thank you. Two weeks of 'Good Morning, U.S.A.' is more than enough. Now let's stop playing games. I know all about *your* big chance—to be the anchor for the evening news on another network. *If* you can break your present contract."

"So what?" he said airily, taking a sip of champagne. "We all have the right to better our situation, if we can."

"By legal means, yes. But unfortunately, Stephen Kinley has you so tied up that legal means are not available to you. I can prove that you are behind the sabotage that's been happening in Studio B," I said bravely—possessing no such evidence at all. "Your only hope is to show an unsafe work environment so a judge will let you out of your contract. I also know that you've been in New York this past week rather than here in Taos. The only question in my mind is whether you were behind the murders of Dennis Lovelace and Gene Ptak."

Both Peter and Nancy regarded me cautiously from the steam.

"Bull!" Nancy said after a moment. "You can't prove anything. And I'll gladly testify that Peter's been here with me for the entire past week."

"I don't think so, Nancy. I think you both arrived here yesterday morning. I also believe it's highly likely that you are Peter's accomplice in crime and that you may be in for a very long vacation courtesy of the taxpayer."

Nancy's face became ugly. Peter put a hand on her shoulder and laughed. "Don't let Steverino rile you, sweets! He's just playing amateur detective and having a bit of fun. Look, Steve, my man—I'm sorry you've had a bad week in New York," he said reasonably. "I've always had great respect for you as a professional and a colleague, you know, and it wasn't *my* idea to get you involved in that horror show of a television broadcast. Believe me, I would have gladly spared you, if I could."

"You *were* in New York this past week, weren't you?" I pressed.

"Well, yes—you're right on that score. There was some

business I needed to conduct, and I didn't want anyone to know I was in town.''

"So you left your apartment and stayed at the Plaza in disguise? The turban was very cute, Mr. Abawashi!''

"Pete, don't tell him!'' Nancy cautioned.

"Now, sweets, the man is too clever for us,'' Peter insisted. "I think it's best to tell him everything and throw ourselves upon his mercy. When he knows all the facts, I'm certain he will be on our side—won't you, pardner?''

"I suggest you tell me the facts, Peter, and then I'll decide whose side I'm on.''

He smiled. "It's a deal. But not now, I'm afraid. It was rather sad to be stuck in New York this week rather than on the slopes—I have a lot of skiing to make up for. Nancy and I are heading up the mountain this afternoon, so I suggest we talk on the chairlift. There will be plenty of time for conversation between runs. What do you say?''

"Let's finish this conversation now, Peter. It's been thirty years since I skied and I was no good at it then.''

"Sorry. I just don't have time to dawdle. Nancy, my sweets, I think we've just got time for a dip in the creek. . . .''

To Cass's embarrassment—and my dismay—Peter and Nancy hopped out of the hot tub and ran naked through the snow toward a swiftly moving creek at the edge of the woods. With howls of delight, they sat down in the icy water, submerged themselves briefly, and then ran back toward the house.

"Peter!'' I called. "This is ridiculous! If you truly refuse to talk now, I'll catch you this evening after skiing.''

"No way! Nancy and I have a romantic agenda tonight, and the two of you would definitely be a crowd,'' he shouted en route from the creek to a sliding glass door.

"But I don't even have skis!'' I objected.

"You can rent everything there. Tell you what—there's a small clearing near the top of the front side of the mountain that the locals call Doobie Rock—I'll let you figure out the

reason for the name. It's not marked on the trail map but a fine
detective such as yourself should have no trouble finding it.
I'll meet you there at two o'clock pronto.''

"Peter! . . .''

But it was too late. Peter and Nancy had disappeared inside
the house, closing the sliding glass door behind them.

"Can I look now?'' Cass asked.

"You can look.'' I banged on the glass door. "Peter, I am
not skiing!'' I shouted. I would have barged in on them, since
they had abdicated their right to modesty, but the door was
locked.

"No ski, no talk!'' Peter shouted back at me from inside.
"Anyway, it'll do you a world of good. Frankly after a week
of morning television, you seem a little stressed-out, yourself!''

I did not give up easily. Cass and I did not budge. We waited
fifteen minutes in the cold until Peter and Nancy emerged in
ski clothes, moving quickly from the house toward their four-
wheel drive Land Cruiser. I insisted that Peter stop this foolish-
ness.

I told him he'd better sit down with me immediately to
discuss serious matters. But he only laughed at me. He got in
his car and drove away.

"See you at two o'clock!'' he shouted out the window.
"Doobie Rock! You'll know you're there by the aroma!''

Chapter 51

"This," I told Cass emphatically, "is crazy!"

"Steve, relax—you're going to have a ball," he replied.

We were riding side by side on a chairlift up the steepest mountain I had ever seen. I was dressed in an orange powdersuit with goggles, gloves, and a blue hat with a tassel on top. Worse still—as if it were not bad enough to make a sartorial fool of myself—I had skis on my feet, and poles in my hand. Cass was dressed in a garish yellow powdersuit that had red lightning bolts down the side. All of our equipment was rented from a sadistic young man who probably sold coffins on the side. I had detected a glint in his eye as he took an imprint of my credit card and had me sign the blank form—in case I never returned alive. Below us on the chairlift, fiendishly agile young men and women were sliding down the mountain at tremendous speeds with plumes of snow shooting up behind them. To my astonishment, they actually seemed to be having fun.

"I hope you'll put in a good word for me at my funeral, Cass. Tell the world I was foolish but brave."

"Hey, man, you're getting all psyched-up for nothing, Steve.

You don't have to go straight down the fall-line like those kids. We'll get you zigzagging side to side in a nice, safe snowplow. Nothing to it.''

I tried to believe him, but my stomach was doing acrobatics just looking at the mountain below me. We passed over ski trails and treetops and sheer granite cliffs where even a wise eagle might fear to go. Up and up we went for nearly ten minutes until I saw a small building at the top of the lift and a level platform of snow upon which we were to unload.

"All you gotta do is stand up when I tell you, and gravity will do the rest," Cass said.

I was not reassured. "Gravity bears an odd similarity to the word 'grave,' " I muttered.

"Merely a coincidence . . . now upsy-daisy. Stand . . . now!"

My skis touched the snow and I found myself gliding down a gentle decline toward a flat area where a number of people were adjusting their boots and poles. I was still on my feet, but the sensation of motion was alarming.

"Let's stop by that tree and check the trail map," Cass suggested.

"Stop," I repeated, "Great idea, but *how?*"

"Do the snowplow, Steve. Nice little wedge . . ."

I would have been more than happy to do a nice little wedge, as he put it. But I was moving quickly upon a group of ski instructors in yellow jackets, and my legs refused to obey my brain. One of the instructors, a woman, was bending forward to tighten her boots.

"Look out!" I shouted. "I'm out of control!"

The woman had her back to me and did not see me until it was too late. I knocked her over like a bowling ball hitting a pin. As for myself, I ended up facefirst in the snow.

"I'm so sorry!" I told her, coming up for air. "Are you all right?"

"I'm fine," she said with a smile—a rather nice smile, I thought, under the circumstances, She rose to her feet and offered me a hand up. "Let me guess—this is your first time on skis."

"First time in thirty years," I told her. "Snow didn't seem quite so slippery back them."

"Take a lesson," she advised.

"He's going to do fine—he's with me," Cass assured her, gliding our way. "Listen, do you know a place on the mountain the locals call Doobie Rock?"

The ski instructor gave Cass a very dubious look, and then glanced even more skeptically at me. She was a pretty young woman, athletic in appearance, deeply tanned. I'm sure Cass and I were quite a sight to her, two old codgers in outrageously bright powdersuits.

"Gentlemen, I believe Doobie Rock would be wasted on you," she decided. Then she skied briskly and gracefully away.

"Great!" I fumed. "We're off to a splendid start! Cass, that was stupid to ask an instructor about Doobie Rock. You might as well have asked the ski patrol—or a cop."

"I don't get you. What's wrong with asking directions from a nice lady?"

"Don't you know what a doobie is?"

"It's a kind of bird, isn't it?"

Sometimes I don't know about Cass. He's awfully innocent for a grown man.

"A doobie," I told him patiently, "is a joint."

"I see! Like a saloon or a place to go dancing! That sounds kind of fun, Steve, to have a place like that on the mountain."

I sighed. "Not *that* kind of joint, man! Where have you been living the past thirty years? A joint is a marijuana cigarette—Doobie Rock must be a place where the kids light up."

Cass opened his mouth and appeared seriously shocked. "Why would they want to do a thing like that here?"

"I can't tell you," I replied grumpily. "Skiing looks to me plenty dangerous even without drugs!"

Cass and I stood to the side of the trail, watching skiers

disembark from the chairlift. At last we found a young fellow
with long hair and a Grateful Dead emblem on his ski outfit
who seemed a likely candidate for the kind of information we
were seeking. He said to ski down the short trail to the next
lift, take that lift to the very top of the mountain, and then go
about two hundred yards down a trail called Bambi. We would
see a narrow path through the trees to our right.

"Hey, got an extra bud, man?" asked the Deadhead hopefully.

"No!" I barked.

I was not a happy skier. The thought of taking a lift to the
top of the mountain was terrifying. The only solace I could
find was in the name Bambi—it sounded, at least, like a slope
fit for beginners. I won't detail my many falls and close encoun-
ters with death on the way to Doobie Rock. Cass spent ten
minutes teaching me the snowplow—how to force my skis into
a wedge, press on one ski or the other to turn, and traverse the
trail from side to side to avoid plummeting straight down the
mountain like a falling rock. I got the technique, more or less,
though there was always a terrifying moment in the middle of
each turn when my skis faced directly downhill and I was
tempted to give up, sit down, and wait for a friendly Saint
Bernard. Meanwhile there were bumps in the snow, trees to
contend with, and skiers whizzing by at reckless speeds. Not
to mention my rented ski boots, which were medieval torture
chambers.

"Fun, isn't it?" Cass cried.

"Oh, loads," I agreed.

As for Cass, he streaked down the trail with his poles flying,
his feet wide apart, his butt in the air, letting out an occasional
cowboy whoop of delight. Alberto Tomba he was not; but he
was as fearless as a ten-year-old, and he was having the time
of his life. He even managed to stay perpendicular most of the
time, which is more than I can claim for myself. We took the
lift to the top of the mountain, and I would have enjoyed the

magnificent view—a line of snowcapped mountains, one after the other, clear into Colorado—except for the thought that what goes up, must come down. Including yours truly.

Bambi, thank God, lived up to its name—a trail that was almost easy. A few hundred yards down the slope we found the short footpath through the trees to Doobie Rock—a small clearing with a stomach-churning view to a valley far below. There were several smokers leaning on their ski poles while admiring the grandeur of nature.

"Wow! Far out, man!" said smoker number one, a young man with a ponytail.

"Yeah," said smoker number two, a young woman also with a ponytail—though her ponytail was not nearly as magnificent as the one belonging to the man.

"Nothing like a little weed to get you in tune with the Zen of skiing," said smoker number three who closeup was none other than Peter McDavis, celebrated TV personality. With his goggles and cap pulled low on his forehead, I doubt if the other smokers recognized him. He grinned when he saw me.

"I knew you were a cool guy, Steve! I had not the slightest doubt you would make it!"

"Where's Nancy?" I asked.

"I left her down on the bunny slopes. A great chick, but skiing is not one of her many talents. Have a toke, man."

"I can't," I explained "and morality has nothing to do with it. I've never even smoked a straight cigarette."

"Why the hell not?"

"Because the smell of burning tobacco strikes me as disgusting. The fact that my mother was a heavy smoker has something to do with it."

"Well," he said, "I guess on the whole you're lucky."

"All right, Peter. You told me to meet you here, so here I am. Now either you start talking or I'm going to the cops. There's a certain Detective Sergeant Morgenfield of the NYPD who's going to be fascinated to learn that you were secretly in New York last week."

The word *cops* made the two young smokers decidedly uneasy. Only Peter continued to smile.

"If you want to talk, that's no problem. Come on, I know a nice spot off-*piste* where we can have some privacy."

"Off-*piste*?"

"Off trail, man. Into the forest in the deep powder where the *real* skiers go."

"*Peter!*"

But he was already skiing away.

"You'll love it!" he called back to Cass and me. "Anyway, only sissies stay on the marked trails!"

When it came to skiing that was me, I'm afraid—a sissy of the first degree. Nevertheless, I had no choice. If I wanted to hear what McDavis had to say, there was nothing for me to do but follow him into the steep, deep reaches of the snowy forest.

Chapter 52

Peter passed beneath an orange ribbon strung among the trees that bordered the edge of the trail. If there was any question what the orange ribbon meant, the small sign in front solved the ambiguity: AREA CLOSED.

"Peter! The area beyond the orange ribbon is closed!" I called to him ahead.

"That's only for beginners," he called back.

"I *am* a beginner!"

"Nonsense. You got the snowplow down perfect, man. That's all you need here."

"That's not *all* I need," I grouched. "I need my head examined for agreeing to this!"

Peter led the way into the forest depths. Cass followed in Peter's fresh tracks, and there was not much for me to do but follow after Cass. Frankly I suspected Cass of enjoying the situation—to follow in the tracks of a good skier into authentic off-*piste* terrain. If Cass had only waited, I would have let Peter ski under the orange ribbon without us. But as it was, my only choice was to turn back and make my way down the entire mountain alone. So I stayed with the others.

I was glad when Peter skied across the slant of the mountain at a very gentle angle, instead of straight down. Still the closeness of the trees was unnerving, and I took a few falls from sheer panic when I believed I was about to collide with one of these immovable natural objects. The deep snow made for a soft landing, but it was like quicksand to get out of once you were down. I fell in ridiculous ways, crossing my skis and getting as tied up as a pretzel.

"Hey, you got so much snow on you, you look like a snowman!" Cass laughed, turning to see how I was making out.

"Thanks!" I growled. "But I am not a snowman, I am your employer—you might remember that. And this is work, not fun."

We skied through the forest for some time. A bird sat on a snowy branch and called down at me angrily for invading his terrain. "Shut up!" I told him. You can see what sort of mood I was in.

At last we came out of the trees and arrived at quite a fantastic place. Above us a mountain peak rose several thousand feet at a steep angle, forming a majestic bowl of snow. Below us the world seemed to stretch out forever—valleys and mountains on end, with a hint of the brown desert to the west. It was the sort of horizon the early explorers like Kit Carson must have seen, hundreds of miles without a hint of a house or a telephone pole.

"This is my favorite view," Peter declared grandly.

"I'm not *into* views at the moment. I'm sure it's a very fine view at another time, but right now I demand some answers, Peter. And I want them now. Why the hell have you brought us here?"

He smiled. "No reason. I was having some fun, I suppose.

I thought you could use some mountain air and a change of pace. Now go ahead—ask your questions.''

"Let's start with the biggie, shall we? Did you arrange to kill Dennis the audioman and the private eye?"

"No, I did not. But it's, well, a somewhat ambiguous situation. . . .''

"There's no ambiguity about it. Either you did it, or you did not.''

"Well, let me give you a hypothetical situation. Let's say I *knew* who the killer was, but for reasons of my own, I did nothing to stop it.''

"I would say that makes you an accessory.''

"You think so? But let's say—this is still hypothetical, mind you—let's say I never lifted a finger to help the killer. The killer doesn't even know that *I* know, if you see what I mean. What do you think a court would make of that? I simply let nature do its work, as it were.''

I was about to answer that the issue was very clear—someone who knew a murder was about to happen but did nothing to stop it was guilty, guilty, guilty. But I bit my tongue—literally, alas, when I slipped and fell in the snow. (I am such a bad skier I can't even *stand* on the damnable boards without an accident!)

"Probably it would depend on the precise scenario," I told him when I was able. "Why don't you tell me what happened?"

"Okay. It's like this—''

But then a rifle shot shattered the snowy quiet. I heard the thud of a bullet hit a nearby fir tree. We all looked around frantically for the source of the shot. To my astonishment I saw the stagehand I once knew as Lucky Mendoza, whom I had last seen making his exit from Mr. Sushi. At that moment, *I* had been the one with the gun, you will remember, making a rather bad mess of the ceiling. But now the hit man was thirty or forty feet above us in the bowl of the glacier-like snowfield, and he had a rifle with a telescopic sight in his arms.

He waved hello at me. I really hated that. The guy had nerve.

"Just a warning shot across the bow, Mr. Allen," he called down. "But don't be alarmed. You are not my prey. Adios, Mr. McDavis."

Peter understood his danger too late. He began to pole frantically toward the cover of the forest as the ex-stagehand raised the rifle and took careful aim. The shot rang out and echoed from one mountaintop to another. Peter cried out and fell a few feet downhill before coming to a stop, gasping in the snow. I was still absorbing this when I heard a new sound, a crack which seemed to split the air. It was like a rifle shot only louder and longer lasting, like thunder. I looked up the hill to see what new deadly surprise the hired killer had devised for us. But his rifle was lowered and he was peering about with a wild expression.

"Steve, we've got to get out of here," Cass said urgently.

"We can't just leave Peter here—what if he's still alive?"

Cass and I skied down to where Peter was lying in the snow. Or rather I should say Cass skied; I slid part of the way, and fell the rest until I was by Peter's side. All this happened very quickly, I should say. The man with the rifle was still thirty or forty feet above us with a bewildered expression on his face. For some reason he seemed terrified to move.

"Avalanche coming," Peter whispered. There was blood at the corner of his mouth. "Get in the trees!"

"Cass, let's drag him out of here."

"No time," Peter managed, looking at us with glazed eyes. "What a way to go, huh?"

There was another peal of strange thunder, louder than before. I looked up and saw a terrible sight. Above us on the snowy bowl—forty or fifty feet above where the hit man was standing—a huge yawning crack had appeared in the snow. The mountain was moving, ripping apart in slow motion.

I knew it was time to get out of there, if it wasn't too late already. And what, you may well ask, was I thinking about at this penultimate moment? My curiosity wouldn't leave me alone.

"Peter, you must tell me—who is it? Who's behind these killings?"

He was losing strength fast. He opened his mouth and whispered a name, but I wasn't certain I had heard him right. "Say it again," I urged, bending forward and putting my ear to his mouth.

He said the name again, and this time I heard him. Cass told me later that a very profound frown came upon my face. I simply could not believe the name he had said.

"But why?" I pleaded. "What was the motive?"

But Peter McDavis was not answering any more questions. His eyes stared emptily toward the sky.

"Steve, let's get out of here!" Cass shouted.

I stood to my feet. There was less than ten feet between us and the trees. I heard a scream and looked up the mountain to see the hit man just as he was engulfed in a wave of moving snow. The avalanche had begun in seeming slow motion, but now it was gathering speed, cascading down the mountain to where Cass and I were struggling. Cass was ahead of me. "Hurry up!" he cried. I used my poles and all my body to propel myself toward the line of trees. But it was like one of those dreams where you run and run but you never get anywhere. I could hear the avalanche close by, a terrifying roar.

I might have made it to safety—the comparative safety that is—of the forest—but I did a stupid thing. I lost my balance and fell. The moment I was down, an overwhelming ocean of cold whiteness crashed down upon me. I put my arms above my head for protection and I was tossed and rolled like a leaf in a storm. I don't know how long I fell. It seemed to be forever. Then all motion ceased and I found myself in a sightless cocoon of solid snow. Fortunately there was a small amount of air in my cocoon, but I knew it would not last long. I had to face the fact that I was buried alive.

"Damn!" I huffed, wasting some air.

I can't adequately describe how frustrating it was to finally know the identity of the killer, but not be able to do a thing about it!

Chapter 53

It snowed all that weekend in New York. Millions of fluffy white snowflakes floating down, one of the biggest winter storms to hit the East Coast in years. I like to think the weather was acting out in sympathetic response to my snowy tomb in the far-off mountains of northern New Mexico.

The viewers of "Good Morning, U.S.A." were disappointed, I am certain, when your obedient servant did not appear on their screens Monday morning to wish them a cheery start to the week. Cat did the show alone that morning, and I'm told an actual tear glistened in her eye as she interviewed a movie star who was pushing his latest project—normally my job. At the half hour news headlines, Carol Ardman sadly announced the death of Peter McDavis as well as the disappearance of Steve Allen and his faithful friend and employee, Jimmy Cassidy, who had been lost in an avalanche over the weekend in the Sangre de Cristo Mountains near Taos, New Mexico. The body of Peter McDavis, along with an unidentified skier, had been found by specially trained dogs, but Steve Allen and Jimmy Cassidy were still missing. Carol neglected to mention the fact that

Peter's body contained the slug of a high-powered rifle, but this was because the police withheld information rather than Carol's lack of skill as a television reporter. For the moment, the authorities were just as happy to let Mother Nature take the rap while they sorted out the various and confusing facts.

Dan De Vries interviewed an avalanche expert, who spoke of the number of people who have been lost in recent years, particularly in Colorado. Skiers should always stay on marked trails, he said, and use great caution during years of heavy snowfall. I wish he had told that to Peter. The expert had some other advice as well about what a person should do if he or she happened to be caught in an avalanche. "Whatever you do, don't panic," he suggested. Ha! That's easy to say, of course, from the safety of a television studio! My own advice to avoid the danger of an avalanche is simply to stay home in your snug living room in California. Then you only have to worry about earthquakes—all in all, a much friendlier sort of natural catastrophe than finding yourself buried alive in snow.

Bob Hutchinson managed to work my avalanche into his weather report. Sherry Gold, I am told, also spoke with a new sense of self-importance, for one of her predictions had finally been right as well—it had definitely been a bad weekend for a Capricorn to travel.

On Tuesday morning Steve Allen had still not reappeared on the show, nor on Wednesday morning. The cast and crew of "Good Morning, U.S.A." feared that Mr. Allen was lost forever. Two stagehands went so far as to roll the Steinway grand piano from Studio B to a storage area down the hall.

And then Wednesday afternoon something odd happened. People began to receive invitations to a special dinner party that was to be held Thursday evening at the very chic restaurant, 21. All sorts of people received these invitations—not only the VIPs like Cat Lawrence and Dan De Vries, but also Nadia Wolfe, the makeup lady, and Debbie Driscoll, the young production assistant. Most strangely of all, the invitations were issued by Detective Sergeant Howard Morgenfield of the NYPD—a man not renowned for his social graces. There was no question about R.S.V.P.'ing. "Be there!" he growled, whether he was speaking to Stephen Kinley the Second, head of the network, or to Don Shipley, the floor manager. Naturally there were a good many whispered conversations concerning this strange dinner party among those who worked at the network. What could it be about?

On Thursday evening, the special guests arrived at the restaurant, each with an expression of curiosity etched upon their faces—an entire range of expressions I should add, that covered the gamut from bemused curiosity to downright fear. As the guests showed their invitations, the headwaiter led them up a wide staircase to a private dining room on the second floor. Inside the dining room a splendid long table was covered with white linen and good silver, set for thirty guests. Waiters hovered nearby filling water glasses and putting baskets of bread and small pots of butter at strategic locations on the long table. This was to be expected. But, rather oddly, four uniformed policemen took positions, one in each corner of the room.

Nearly everyone knew each other well, though there were exceptions, and a few had not seen one another in years. There was a New Mexico contingent—Nancy Vandenberg, Peter's girlfriend, had arrived from Taos, and Angela, Peter's wife, came from Santa Fe—which made for an awkward situation. Angela was in her wheelchair of course, and arrived at the second floor of the restaurant in a small elevator. When she spotted Nancy, she made a point of sitting as far away as the long table would permit.

Friends greeted one another somewhat awkwardly, not quite certain what this was all about. A few like Bob Hutchinson affected a loud bluster of unconcern. The seating was open, so various cliques were free to gather together. The technical crew took up one corner—Don Shipley, Danny Ferraro (the stagehand who had worked with Lucky Mendoza)—and a few other assorted grips and electricians. Ken Byrnes, the director, sat next to Zeke Roth. Nadia Wolfe gathered with Cat Lawrence, Carol Ardman, Dan De Vries, and Bob Hutchinson. There were several pairs—Sherry Gold and her nine-year-old son, Crystal Rainbow. Stephen and Edith Kinley sat side by side, looking very grim and uncomfortable. And next to them, detectives Morgenfield and Marcotti, equally grim, perhaps even more uncomfortable to be at such an elegant though bizarre dinner party.

Among the group there were also a few loners, such as Heather Dorn—Dennis Lovelace's girlfriend, who had recently moved out of our Fifth Avenue duplex into a new studio in SoHo. And Howard Mirabel, the elegant Native American who ran the Golden Mesa Casino and had once been the friend of Stevie Kinley the Third. Howard sat without saying a word, glancing occasionally with vast disapproval at Stephen and Edith across from him.

The dinner party had been set for seven o'clock and by seven-twenty nearly everyone who had been invited had arrived. There were only three empty places. At seven twenty-five one of these empty places, so to speak, walked magnificently into the room, her red hair high on her head, wearing a lovely white dress that she had somehow managed to buy in Santa Fe despite her limited time there. It was, of course, my own sweet Jayne.

"Ah-*ha!* So *you're* the one behind this mysterious party!" Cat said with a laugh. "I should have known it!"

"No dear, I'm only partly responsible," Jayne admitted. Nevertheless she took the opportunity to call for quiet around the table. "Thank you so much for coming, everyone," she said when the table had settled down. "Since we're such a large group, I took it upon myself to do the ordering. You have only to make a choice between soup or salad, and then tournedos Rossini for you meat eaters, or a rather nice grilled swordfish for everybody else."

"But what is this all about, Jayne?" asked Heather Dorn.

"We'll come to that presently, of course. I think we'll save it as a surprise, along with dessert."

"I love surprises," said Bob Hutchinson.

Jayne smiled, while thinking to herself that Bob might not love this particular surprise very much at all. Dinner was fabulous, as it always is at 21, and many of the guests became so relaxed they soon forgot this was no ordinary party.

Dessert was a non-Pritikin *crème brûlée*. When everyone had coffee, Jayne stood up once again. She struck her wineglass with a fork to get everyone's attention and faced the long table of well-fed faces—altogether a happier group than the one that had entered the restaurant an hour or so before.

"And now that we have dined so well, I would like to present my husband Steve . . . and our good friend, Jimmy Cassidy."

Cass and I walked to the long table and the room was suddenly so quiet you could hear a pin—or a cliché—drop.

"You're alive!" Zeke gasped.

"Yes. And I know how happy all of you at this table must be—except one of you—to find me in such good health."

Chapter 54

"I've gathered you together tonight to solve a murder mystery," I began. "Or to be precise, three murders and some serious sabotage that might easily have resulted in murder.

"Let's begin with what we know. Peter McDavis and Gene Ptak—a private eye some of you know—were both killed by a hired gunman who worked briefly on Studio B as a stagehand—"

"Hold on!" objected Dan De Vries. As an experienced newsman, he wasn't about to let what he believed to be a wrong statement go by unchallenged. "According to the New Mexico police, Peter was killed in the avalanche, *not* by some hired gunman."

I turned to Detective Morgenfield, who was in the process of eating an extra dessert—a *crême brûlée* which Nadia Wolfe had not managed to consume herself.

"Detective Morgenfield, perhaps you can clear up this one point before we proceed further."

The detective rose from his chair, leaving the custard with reluctance.

"Peter McDavis was shot," he said, and then sat down again.

"The New Mexico police cooperated with the NYPD to leave the shooting out of the media for a few days in order to make the investigation easier," I added. "The marksman, by the way, was the 'unidentified skier' who was mentioned in the news reports—in fact our ex-stagehand, Lucky Mendoza. The FBI only managed to establish his real identity this morning. His name is Alan Margolies, from Denver, Colorado, and he has no criminal record—the police were only able to discover who he was by matching dental records since his fingerprints are not on file anywhere. Nevertheless, they believe he was a top assassin who went by the professional name of Soldier X and worked on a freelance basis for whoever had the money to pay—the Mafia, private individuals with a grudge, young women who wanted to rid themselves of rich older husbands, you name it.

"So we have murder by proxy, a hired killer who was definitely a slick customer, though perhaps overly confident. What we need to discover, of course, is who employed him in this instance. And did he, in fact, kill all three victims? Cass and I can testify that he shot Peter, and there is a driver of a horse taxi who saw him shoot Gene Ptak from across the street from the Plaza. But did Alan Margolies murder Dennis Lovelace, the audioman, with a sharp pointed object into the heart, or did the *real* killer do that piece of nasty work—the faceless person who is behind all this mayhem?

"Now I told you that our Mr. Margolies was confident. He was *so* confident of his abilities that when I spoke to him at a sushi bar last week, he even condescended to give me a clue as to his employer's identity. This is the riddle he told me: 'What is sweet as honey, yet the most bitter herb of all?' My brain was working slowly last week and it took me nearly twenty-four hours to come up with the answer. Probably most of you have figured it out already. Revenge is the thing that is sweet as honey, some might say, yet very bitter indeed.

"Revenge! What a terrible, consuming passion! Yet it has certainly been at the heart of many a murder. Once I figured out the riddle, it should have been easy, I thought, to decipher the crime. Yet it wasn't such an easy clue after all. Unfortunately among this querulous group, each of you connected in some way with 'Good Morning, U.S.A.,' there is such bad blood and so many old scores to settle that *many* of you might desire revenge of some sort. Let's start with . . . well, Zeke Roth, for instance."

Zeke turned pale and rose from his seat. "Mr. Kinley, I have a confession to make," he said quickly. "I sort of *borrowed* a little money from the production budget. Nothing *major,* you understand—a mere fifty thousand dollars which I've been trying like crazy to pay back. I've been meaning to tell you this for a few months actually, but I thought I'd better get it out in the open before Steve goes any further."

Stephen Kinley opened his mouth in outrage. "Fifty thousand dollars!" he cried. Edith took his hand, and I saw him make a visible effort to calm down. "Well, it's only money, I suppose. We'll have to talk about how you're going to pay this back, Zeke."

"Yes, sir! Thank you, sir!"

"With interest!" Mr. Kinley pressed.

"Oh, yes, absolutely!"

"Zeke took the money because he was in desperate financial straits," I added.

"That's right!" he agreed quickly. "I was desperate."

"In fact, this has been a terrible few months for you, hasn't it, Zeke?"

"You bet it has!" he admitted. "Producing this show has been one nightmare after another. Frankly I'm not sure I can stand the stress much longer."

"You have a bad heart, Zeke. Don't you?"

The producer stared at me. "How did you find out about that? I've been trying to keep my heart condition secret—I was afraid Mr. Kinley might not renew my contract when it comes up in the spring, and that would *really* put me in hole, financially speaking!''

"I talked to your doctor, Zeke. But let's put your health aside for the moment and get back to your desperate financial situation. Much of your money problems are due to Bob Hutchinson,'' I said, taking charge once more of my after-dinner denouement. I explained to the rest of the table: ''Bob convinced Zeke to go in with him as a partner in a business venture—a restaurant on Third Avenue. Now Zeke may be one competent television producer, but when it came to running a restaurant, no dice. Zeke wanted a quick return on his money, not understanding that a restaurant is the sort of venture which can gobble up huge outlays of money, and *if* it is successful, the profits can take years to materialize. Bob, I think it is fair to add, did his best to keep Zeke unenlightened.''

"That's a lie!'' Bob interrupted angrily. ''Besides, Zeke's a grown-up—if he wants to invest his money, it's up to him to do some research. It's not *my* fault that Zeke believed he could bang all the waitresses and at the end of the night grab hundred-dollar bills from the register!''

"You're the one banging the waitresses, you son of a bitch!'' Zeke shouted. ''And I never took any money from that cash register, not once!''

"Gentlemen, please sit down,'' I cautioned. Then I addressed the rest of the table. ''Remember, we're talking about revenge here. Zeke needed his money back from the restaurant, but Bob was unsympathetic. He worked out a slippery deal to give Zeke ten thousand dollars of his investment back, but that was in fact merely a clever way for Bob to get majority control of the business so he could call the shots. So Zeke found himself in a worse position than ever, and he was angry as a hornet. The question is—was Zeke so desirous of revenge that he might resort to murder? And if so, why would he kill the three people who died rather than Bob Hutchinson? We'll let this question dangle unanswered for the time being.

"I'd like to mention just one more point about Zeke Roth's problems that has some bearing on the case. Desperate to figure out some way to get his money out of the restaurant, Zeke hired a second-rate and not entirely honest private eye named Gene Ptak to investigate Bob Hutchinson. To be frank, Zeke was hoping to get some dirt on Bob that he could use as leverage in getting his money back. Blackmail may be too strong a word for what Zeke had in mind, but it's close. Gene also became Zeke's messenger boy, delivering a monthly payment to Carol Ardman to repay a personal loan. As it happened, this was not Gene's first involvement with 'Good Morning, U.S.A.'— a number of years ago, Stephen Kinley had hired him on a delicate personal mission. As a result, the private detective knew a great deal about the undercurrents of the show—knowledge which was eventually to cost him his life. We'll get back to Gene Ptak in a bit—he became a rogue element in all the shenanigans, trying to fiddle some deal for himself, but the main theme here, remember, is revenge.

"So who else might have a motive? Well, there's Nancy Vandenberg, ex-co-anchor, who lost her job. Nancy was Peter's girlfriend as well, which did not make Angela McDavis very happy. It is interesting to note that Angela discovered her husband's infidelity from an anonymous letter. Who sent that note, I wonder? The result was unfortunate—Angela threatened her husband with divorce unless he used his great prestige and influence at the network to get Nancy thrown off the show. So Nancy has a possible motive to seek revenge—she has certainly been wronged. And Angela, as a wife confined to a wheelchair, might feel badly used herself.

"In fact, the possibilities for revenge go on and on. Dan De Vries felt himself jilted by Carol Ardman. Cat Lawrence—I'm sorry to be indiscreet here—was having an affair with Dennis

Lovelace, which could not have pleased Dennis's girlfriend Heather Dorn. Nor was Cat happy when Dennis broke it off.

"Well, I could go on for hours, but time is running short," I told the gathering. "So we'll pass now from small angers to the huge burning passions that kill."

Chapter 55

I could sense the tension in the faces up and down the table as the cast and crew, lovers and family members connected to the ill-fated show, "Good Morning, U.S.A.," waited for me to continue. Detective Sergeant Morgenfield was eating his third dessert, and the room was so quiet that the sound of his spoon scraping against the glass dish rang out loudly. The detective looked up from his *crème brûlée,* saw every eye at the table upon him, and pushed the half-finished dessert away with a self-conscious grunt.

"All right. I'm afraid I must recount a very unpleasant story at this point. As all of you surely know, the UBS network was started in 1933 by Stephen Kinley the First, a brilliant and ruthless pioneer of broadcasting. He began with a single radio station in Omaha, Nebraska, and by the time he died in 1979, his empire included hundreds of radio and television stations throughout the country and controlled a major market share of what America heard and watched on the airwaves. The company went public in 1941, selling stock in order to expand, but Stephen Kinley always remained the majority shareholder as well as keeping his position as chairman of the board. As some of you in this room will surely agree, the man was a tyrant.

"Now, like a lot of brilliant pioneers, Stephen Kinley put a good deal more thought and energy into his career than into his own family. He had a son to whom he gave his own name, Stephen Kinley, Jr.—our present chairman of the board—but I'm afraid his son was a disappointment to him."

Halfway down the table, Stephen the Second pursed his mouth tightly, clasped his hands in front of his empty place, and lowered his eyes. Edith, sitting by his side, looked bravely at me, unwavering. I do not enjoy delivering blunt personal criticism, but there were certain things that needed to be said if the sad, tangled events concerning "Good Morning, U.S.A." were ever to be understood.

"Unlike his father, Stephen the Second grew up in a mansion with maids and butlers. He went to the best private schools, and eventually graduated from Yale. I don't want to suggest that our present Mr. Kinley grew up to be a truly bad man, but he was narrow-minded, a social snob, and he entirely lacked his father's energy or drive. This left the old man in a dilemma. The pioneer had a huge ego, and he wanted to be the founder of a lasting media empire that would bear his name—he had hoped to leave what he had built to his son, but he was shrewd enough to see that his son was not his equal."

There was naturally a good deal of surprise around the table to hear me say such terrible things about our employer—and more surprising still, that he continued to sit there with his eyes lowered. I noticed Cat give him a curious glance and then quickly look away.

"In time, the old tyrant's son married and had a child himself, whom he named Stephen Kinley the Third, hoping to please his father. And in fact the old man was very pleased indeed. Little Stevie was the apple of his grandfather's eye—bright and mischievous, full of life and energy. Like a lot of other young people who grew up in the late sixties and early seventies, Stevie had some radical notions—but this did not bother the grandfather who had always been an extremely unconventional figure himself. But it *did* bother the father—Stephen the Second,—who even as a young man had been stuffy and extremely proper as a way to compensate perhaps for his lack of originality. I wouldn't be surprised if Stephen the Second was jealous of his son, and of the attention his father was lavishing on the boy—attention that his father had certainly never lavished on *him.*

"And then in his senior year at prep school, little Stevie's rebellious and adventurous nature took a new direction—he fell in love with a girl, a very nice girl named Ann, and like a lot of seventeen-year-old boys, he believed this would be the one enduring love of his life. Love sublime, love forever! The girl, however, happened to be an African-American, and while this did not bother Stevie in the least—nor, I should add, the old grandfather—it *did* most certainly bother the father, Stephen the Second. In his defense, I'd like to say that I don't believe Stephen the Second is particularly a racist—I know, for example, that during his tenure as chairman of the board he has been very fair in promoting minorities to high positions. But he believed his son was descending the social ladder to have such a romance. Little Stevie, who was always the sort of boy to be carried away by his enthusiasms, was saying wild things—that he wanted to marry the girl. A wiser father would have let the romance run its course, but our Mr. Kinley was a fool. He decided to interfere and separate the young lovers. As it happened, Ann was a scholarship student at a fancy girls' school where the Kinley family had some influence—Stephen the Second went to the headmistress and managed to have Ann expelled. Ann was seventeen, smart and pretty and ambitious to make her way in the world, and for her this expulsion seemed the end of all her dreams. She went home to Alabama and committed suicide.

"Imagine what it must be like to be in love with a girl and have your father drive her to her death! Stevie was more than furious—his entire life was changed and ultimately destroyed. He dropped out of school, left home; he got into drugs and the various counterculture movements of the time, and he refused to see his mother or father ever again—though for a time he wrote his mother a brief Christmas letter once a year.

"Ann committed suicide in 1975. The old tyrant, Stephen the First, lived another four years but he never recovered from losing his beloved grandson. His heart was broken, and he was furious at his son for acting so foolishly as to have had the girl expelled. The irony is that Stephen the First probably *was* a racist—under *his* tenure as chairman, the network had an abysmal record in promoting minorities beyond the most menial positions. Nevertheless, the old man was immensely practical, and he would never have done anything to hurt his grandson. Not only was the old man furious at his son for driving his grandson away, but to witness such bad judgment made him realize that his son was not worthy to run the broadcasting empire he had built.

"In 1979, the old man's health was fading and he knew he would not live much longer. He was in a difficult dilemma— as I said, he had a huge ego, and he wished to leave behind a broadcasting dynasty bearing his name. At this point, Stevie had been gone four years. The grandfather received yearly updates about the boy's life from Edith Kinley, who let him read the yearly Christmas letters. Stevie had become quite a hippie by now, living in communes in New Mexico and India, and I doubt if the old man was very pleased with the news. Still, he loved his grandson and he believed the boy would eventually grow out of his rebellious phase. He was a shrewd old man, whatever else you may say about him, and his final will and testament, prepared only a few weeks before his death, was a very shrewd and unusual document.''

I stopped speaking for a moment to take a drink of water. Even the waiters had stopped to listen intently to this tragic family tale.

"I spent some time this morning at the offices of Hubert, Donaldson, Pfieffer, Smith, and Knudson—the Kinley family lawyers—and I had a chance to read the old man's will. He left his entire estate—the majority shares in the network, a Park Avenue triplex, a mansion in Greenwich, Connecticut, and all his money—in trust to his grandson, with his son as the trustee. *But* there were several conditions. First, the terms of the will were to remain secret. The old man was afraid his son would be a lame duck chairman and find himself in an intolerably weak position if word got out that he was merely a caretaker, in charge of the network only until the day that little Stevie might return to take his rightful place. The way it was set up, this could happen at any moment—the day after the old man's death, or twenty years in the future. The terms of the will state that Stevie Kinley only had to present himself at the offices of Hubert, Donaldson, Pfieffer, Smith, and Knudson with his hair cut short and wearing a clean business suit—this attire was specifically mentioned in the will—and the entire empire would be turned over to him. However, it was also specified that this information was not to be given freely to Stevie Kinley—he had to discover it for himself in order to prove himself worthy of such tremendous wealth. The old man loved his grandson, as I said, but he wanted to make certain the boy showed some gumption before he actually was given the reins of the network. It was the sort of test a prince might be given to do in a fairy tale.

"There were two codicils to the will that need concern us—first, in the event of Stevie Kinley's death, the entire estate would go to Stevie's eldest child, if such a child did in fact exist. And second, if Stevie died without a child, and without ever claiming his kingdom, the estate—reluctantly—would go in its entirety to Stephen the Second, his son."

"Good God, what a story!" Nadia Wolfe, the makeup lady, exclaimed. "Don't keep us in suspense—where *is* Stevie Kinley now?"

I smiled sadly. "In a very simple grave in New Mexico, I'm sorry to say Stevie never really got over his father's part in Ann's suicide—he drifted, he did self-destructive things, he became dependent on drugs, and finally four years ago he even turned to crime. He tried to rob a bank in Albuquerque, but things had become so bad for him that he was a failure even at that. He was so desperate he actually contacted his father after the failed bank robbery asking for enough money to buy a fake passport and leave the country. But his father refused him. Of course, according to the will, he was not *legally* compelled to tell his son that he was a rich man, but the moral obligation is another matter."

"I was not prepared to help a bank robber buy a false passport!" Stephen Kinley spoke for the first time, but he was a shadow of his old self.

"Certainly you did not need to help him escape the country, but you could have gotten him a good lawyer and some help with his drug problems. However then, one day, he might have appeared in the offices of Hubert, Donaldson, Pfieffer, Smith, and Knudson wearing a clean business suit with his hair cut short. Wasn't that what you were really afraid of Mr. Kinley?"

Stephen Kinley did not answer. He merely lowered his eyes once more to the table, a defeated man.

"So if the son's dead, *he's* still our boss, huh?" asked Don Shipley, the floor manager, in a voice filled with disgust.

"Well, not really," I told the gathering. Eyes were moving quickly around the table, and I think there were a few people in the room who made the logical leap before I put it into words.

I walked around the table and stopped by Sherry Gold and

her nine-year-old son with the strange name and exotic eyes. I put a hand gently on the boy's shoulder.

''I would like you to meet Crystal Rainbow Kinley, rightful heir to the Kinley fortune and your future chairman of the board.''

Chapter 56

There was quite an uproar in the dining room. Stephen Kinley buried his head in his hands and wept. Edith Kinley rose to her feet and stared at the nine-year-old boy, Crystal Rainbow, with a combination of shock and adoration. I think she might have fainted had not Debbie Driscoll, the P.A., held on to her elbow.

Everyone stared at the child in astonishment.

The boy stared back at the gathering with grave composure and his eyes came to rest finally upon his grandmother. He was a born prince—so much attention was upon the boy that no one took much immediate notice of the woman by his side, Sherry Gold, whose face had turned pale.

"I warned you that we were going to have a tale of grand passions," I said, "leading to some equally Olympian revenge. I have introduced you to the heir, and now I want you to meet the mother of the heir—our show's astrologer, the woman who loved Stevie Kinley in his long exile, Sherry Gold. However, that was not her name twelve years ago when she was living on a New Age commune in northern New Mexico, a place called Shining Star Ranch.''

"Steve, I wish you would stop this," Sherry objected. "What I did twelve years ago, and what name I used, is no one's business but my own."

"I'm afraid that is not true, Sherry. There are still a few knots here that need to be untangled, as well as motives to be examined. Sherry then called herself Dawn Diamond, and she was looking for inner peace and the meaning of life just like Stevie. There's nothing to be embarrassed about, Sherry. I've been doing some investigating the past few days and I know you came from an abusive family in New Jersey. Your father left when you were young, your mother was an alcoholic— I'm sure you could have done a lot worse for yourself than end up in a New Mexico commune for four years."

"It was quite a lovely place actually, Shining Star."

"I'm sure it was. Jayne actually went there and told me what a beautiful location it is. You grew your own food, made your own clothes, played guitars, sang, and meditated on the meaning of life. There are stressed-out people on the fast track in this city who might be envious. You met an intense and interesting young man in the commune who called himself by an Indian name—Stevie Bad Hand—and it was many years before you had an inkling that he was Stephen Kinley the Third, heir to a great fortune."

"I loved him," Sherry said simply.

"Yes, and I can understand why. A prince in exile is always an attractive figure, even when he obviously has problems— but then, what prince in exile *doesn't* have problems? I imagine you mothered him a bit, didn't you, Sherry?"

Her eyes glistened and she seemed far away on the wide-open spaces of New Mexico.

"He took a lot of drugs," she said. "Not just marijuana— we were all smoking pot in those days. But heroin, speed, LSD, anything he could get his hands on. He was such a beautiful person, I couldn't bear it that he seemed so intent on destroying himself. He told me that his parents ran a hardware store in Los Angeles, but I never believed it. There was something very fine and sad and gentle about him—a mystery I couldn't quite figure out. We were lovers for three years . . . we never married.''

"Why did it end?"

"I got pregnant, and I wouldn't have an abortion. Stevie refused to be a father. He said that fathers were terrible creatures who ate their children alive, and he never would be like that. I didn't understand then why he should think such a thing—I told him he would be a wonderful father. But maybe he wasn't ready for the responsibility. But it went deeper than that. I caught him with another woman one night. It was just a way to get out of his relationship with me. He said he felt trapped, that he didn't want to do the whole family thing. So one day he simply packed his backpack and left the commune. I only saw him once again after that.''

"When was that?"

Sherry looked across the table at Howard Mirabel.

"Howard came to me a little over three years ago. I was in Los Angeles then, studying astrology, but I knew Howard from when I had been with Stevie, and we had stayed in touch—he knew where to find me. He said Stevie was living in a tepee on the reservation and was in bad shape. He thought perhaps I could help, and it might do Stevie some good to know that he had a son. So I went to him and took Crystal, but it was no use. Stevie was so far gone on drugs he was barely coherent. He cried when I told him that Crystal was his son, and then he screamed that if I didn't leave, he would kill us both. He actually threatened us with his .22. He said he had bad blood—that's why he called himself Bad Hand—and that we should go away and never try to find him again. Two months after that Howard phoned me to say Stevie had killed himself. Then he told me about Ann, and Steve's real name, and all about what his father had done to him. I had never known the true story before.''

"You were angry, weren't you?''

"I was more than angry. I was overwhelmed! I couldn't accept that a father could be so cruel to his only son. I still can't accept it. . . . You destroyed Stevie's life, you horrible man!'' Sherry shouted across the table at the unhappy Stephen Kinley. "You monster! I hope you're reborn as a worm for the next five thousand lives to come!''

Stephen Kinley only continued to bury his head in his hands. It was hard not to feel a little sorry for him. He had been dethroned, publicly humiliated. He had lost everything, including his pride.

I turned my attention back to Sherry. "So you were extremely angry when you discovered that the man you loved, the father of your child, had been destroyed by *his* father,'' I continued. "The question is *how* angry were you? And why did you seek a job on this network that was run by a man you hated? What kind of revenge did you have in mind, Sherry?''

"I don't know,'' she whispered. "Something . . . anything. I wasn't sure what I wanted to do, frankly. After all, the man *was* Crystal's grandfather. I didn't know at the time anything about the first Stephen Kinley's will, but even so, I wasn't certain what sort of reception Crystal would get. It seemed best to come to New York quietly and keep our identity to ourselves for a while. I had been doing an astrology segment for a local L.A. station and I was able to convince Zeke Roth that it would help the ratings if he gave me a job on 'Good Morning, U.S.A.' So I got myself in the palace, so to speak, and I was looking things over, trying to decide our best option.''

"The private eye, Gene Ptak, guessed who you were, didn't he? And more importantly, he knew who Crystal was?''

"Yes,'' she said. "He came to me two weeks ago and told me that my son was rich—the true owner of the network. I didn't believe him at first, but he showed me a photocopy of the first Stephen Kinley's will.''

"Did he explain how he got this important document?''

"No. I gathered he had been snooping around for some time. He wanted a deal—a ten percent cut of the estate in return for establishing proof that Crystal Rainbow was the legitimate heir. He said that without his help, everyone would say Crystal was a phony, and that I was nothing but a fortune hunter.''

"And what did you tell him?''

"I told him to go straight to hell!''

"Did you hire the man who called himself Soldier X to kill Gene Ptak?''

"No, I did not.''

"Did you have anything to do with the deaths of Dennis Lovelace or Peter McDavis?''

"No! Why would I want to harm either of them?''

"How about Stephen Kinley? Did you plan to murder him?''

Sherry lowered her eyes. "I thought of it,'' she admitted. "But I couldn't do it. I hate him—but when it comes right down to it, I believe that all life is sacred, even his. I'm not a murderer.''

I smiled grimly. "I know you're not, Sherry. Thank you for being so candid. The real killer,'' I said, looking about the table. "The real killer, I'm sorry to say, is my old friend . . . Cat Lawrence.''

Chapter 57

Cat was sitting halfway down the table looking very green-eyed lovely this evening in a chic, tight-fitting, black dress. I had caught her entirely by surprise, which had been my intention. Her mouth fell open, and her eyes went wide with shock.

"Yes, Cat is the killer," I said unhappily, for I could still visualize the bright, mischievous little girl I had known as a child, the tomboy who used to wave at me from across the street.

Cat took a deep breath and did her best to recover her poise. She even made a brave attempt to laugh. "You're joking! Very funny, Steve!"

"No, I'm not—and this is going to be a little harder for you to get out of than when you stole that petty cash from my office so many years ago."

"You're serious aren't you? My God, Steve! Why in the world would I hire an assassin to kill Dennis and Peter . . . and what's his name—a private eye I never even met?"

"You killed Dennis yourself—that wasn't the doing of Soldier X. And, unfortunately, you knew Gene Ptak better than you wished.''

"But this is absurd! What motive would I have to kill anyone?''

"Revenge, of course. Remember our riddle: 'What is sweet as honey, yet the most bitter herb of all?' ''

She tried to look baffled, but little Cathy Lawrence was not a good actress.

"Revenge? For *what?*'' she cried.

"For the death of your father,'' I replied.

I have to hand it to Cat—she knew the game was up when I mentioned her father, and from that moment she no longer bothered to argue. She only sat as if frozen in her chair, her eyes strangely far away, her arms folded across her breast as if she were hugging herself to keep warm.

"Cat's father was the TV producer, Ed Lawrence,'' I explained to the table. "He rode high for a number of years with the hit cop show, 'Chicago PD.' But he became a drunk when his career failed, and he eventually committed suicide back in the seventies. A depressing story. Some of you in this room may remember Ed Lawrence—you do, Mr. Kinley, because you were the executive in charge of production. Your father was still alive then of course, and he gave you the job because he wanted you to get some experience in the business. And Zeke, you knew Ed Lawrence also—you were Ed's assistant back then, a young guy hoping to rise in the world and be a big shot producer yourself one day. I should have remembered all this—Ed was my friend for a while and he used to talk about the show sometimes. When Peter whispered with his dying breath that Cat was the killer, I had to go back and figure out why she did it. It was only then that I remembered you two had been involved with that old show.''

"This is really quite extraordinary!'' Ken Byrnes, the young director, remarked. "You said revenge was her motive. But revenge for what?''

"Cat loved her father," I explained. "She was Daddy's girl. And she loved the nice house where she grew up across the street from my own. But her happy childhood came tumbling down when she was eleven years old—an impressionable age. Ed lost his job through a very nasty bit of intrigue and slander, and nothing was the same in the Lawrence household after that. As I already mentioned, Ed started drinking when he couldn't find another job, his wife left him, the lovely house was sold— and Cat had to grow up fast. She never really got over her interrupted childhood—did you, Cat?"

When she heard her name, she seemed to come back from some great distance. Her eyes slowly focused, and she looked at me. "When those bastards ruined my father, they destroyed my life, too. They didn't care, Steve—it was just business to them. My revenge was only just getting started."

"I know, Cat. Why don't you tell us what Zeke Roth and Stephen Kinley, Jr. did to your father?"

She took a deep breath then pressed her lips together so tightly the blood seemed to go out of them. I thought I had lost her. But after a moment she began to speak.

"Zeke was my father's assistant, as you said—his title was 'associate producer.' Stephen Kinley here was the so-called 'executive producer,' an empty title, really—it was just a cushy job his father gave to him. *My* father used to make fun of Stephen as a spoiled rich kid who didn't know anything about television production. I guess Dad wasn't very discreet about his opinions. He certainly didn't treat Stephen with respect. He figured he had a hit show—'Chicago PD' was in its fifth season—and there was no reason to kowtow to the boss's son. But Stephen was just as full of stuffy pride as he is today, and he didn't take very kindly to being treated as a sort of useless appendage.

"Zeke was ambitious—he wanted my father's job, to be the producer of 'Chicago PD' rather than just the associate producer. Naturally, he had been kissing up to Stephen the whole time, telling that useless rich kid what a marvelous executive he was, and how my father wasn't treating him with any respect. Stephen, of course, wanted to do well as executive producer to impress *his* father back in New York. So Zeke played this all very well until he and Stephen were thick as thieves. They both had their reasons for wanting to get rid of my dad, but Stephen couldn't just come out and fire Dad for no reason— after all, 'Chicago PD' was a big hit. So what they did is they manufactured a reason. Ten years earlier they would probably have accused him of being a communist—that was a good way to get rid of the competition in the blacklisting era. But by the seventies, that tactic no longer worked. So they got him on a trumped-up morals charge.''

Cat was silent briefly. I could see all the old anger flooding into her face as she remembered.

"Go on," I said gently.

"You have to remember, the morals of the early seventies were fairly loose—even respectable people were smoking dope, and there wasn't much going on in Hollywood that had the power to shock. So Zeke and Stephen had to come up with something pretty good. They . . . they used me, the bastards! They said my Dad was molesting me. They even had photographs, but none of it was true!''

"What kind of photographs, Cat?"

"It was so unfair! My mom and dad used to skinny-dip in our backyard pool—and I used to join them, you see. It was no big thing back then. It wasn't sexual! You have to remember to remember the whole sixties message—liberate yourself, be unconventional, do your thing—it all became fairly mainstream by the early seventies. Remember the play *Hair?* The entire cast took off their clothes every evening at one point in the play and just stood there being . . . well, *free.* So that's what we were doing in our backyard. It was very innocent. Unfortunately, Dad mentioned it one time to Zeke, and Zeke hired a photographer to climb over our backyard fence with a camera.

He got a bunch of pictures of me naked on my father's shoulders in the pool. We were splashing around, playing. I'm sure the photos looked very sinister to dirty minds. Zeke took them to the show's sponsor, a very conservative manufacturer from the Midwest, pretending a tabloid photographer had shot them and that they were about to appear in a magazine. The sponsor made a big fuss—he didn't want his toothpaste connected with child molesting! Stephen Kinley the First—the old man, that is, in New York—had no choice but to let my father go, using the morals clause in his contract. Zeke Roth was given the job as producer . . . and my father's life, and my life, and my mother's life as well all went down the drain. The story was kept from the public, but it leaked around Hollywood and my dad couldn't get a job anywhere. Two years later he killed himself—so chalk up one more suicide for Stephen Kinley the Second!''

Stephen sat at the table looking like a victim of shell shock. He had already lost so much tonight that I'm not certain he was capable of absorbing anything more. Zeke now found himself the object of hard stares from around the table, and he made a feeble attempt to justify himself.

"She's lying!'' he said. "Well, all right—I *did* hire a photographer to get those pictures, but I was doing it for her sake. To protect her from her father.''

"Liar!'' Cat snarled at him. "You know perfectly well that everything that happened in our backyard was absolutely innocent.''

"You just don't remember what really happened,'' he said weakly.

Cat only glared at him with such venom in her eyes that Zeke's words trailed off.

"And now a few closing words,'' I said, "and then we can all go home. As a young woman, Cat harbored her hopes for revenge, and when Stephen Kinley, Jr., hired her for 'Good Morning, U.S.A.' she saw her chance to get even. Did Stephen realize he had hired the daughter of a man he had helped to ruin? Frankly, I think he did—and that some lingering guilt about what he had done was part of the reason he gave Cat the chance. Isn't that right, Mr. Kinley?''

The ruined shell of Mr. Stephen Kinley nodded very faintly. ''Yes,'' he whispered. ''Guilt.''

''Once Cat was on the show,'' I continued, ''she began to make her plans. She needed help, of course, to wreak the sort of havoc she intended—and I want to emphasize that what we've seen so far, a bit of sabotage and a few deaths, was only the start of what Cat hoped to do. Cat had some underground contacts, I imagine, from her seamy days in California, when she was walking on the wild side. Through these contacts she was able to find Alan Margolies—the infamous Soldier X— and get him hired onto the show as the stagehand we knew as Lucky Mendoza. This hiring was done indirectly so it wouldn't appear as if she had any connection with Lucky—she had a mobster she knows put pressure on Bob Hutchinson, who in turn asked Zeke to hire the man. Just to confuse the trail a little more, in case anyone should be interested, an American Indian—or probably someone dressed up like an Indian—was the one who actually put the pressure on Bob. Cat was aware of the New Mexico angle to this affair, and she knew a Native American would point any detective, like me, on the wrong path.

''With Lucky as her ally, Cat began to sabotage large and small matters upon the set, creating a number of dangerous incidents—klieg lights falling from the ceiling, upholstery tacks spilled in the hallways, et cetera. She was careful to make it appear as though she herself might have been a victim of these accidents. Actually, there was not much danger that she would be hurt. I talked with a police forensic expert yesterday who told me that in a closed studio with no breeze, a loose light would fall straight down in a predictable manner. As long as Cat knew where the light would fall, she could easily avoid that spot. The purpose of these accidents was to gradually erode Zeke's authority as producer and make it seem that things were out of control. This was supposed to be slow torture you understand. Everything was designed to make Zeke pull his hair in frustration, for matters to get worse and worse with him . . . until the final coup de grâce. I imagine you knew that Zeke had a bad heart—didn't you, Cat?''

She nodded slowly, her eyes far away. "I did my research. I knew all there was to know about Zeke—his money problems, his health, everything. But I didn't want him to die of a heart attack—a natural death would have been too good for him. I wanted him to suffer, to drive him nearly to the point of suicide . . . and then I was going to come for him and kill him.''

"You sent the anonymous note to Zeke's wife saying he was having an affair with his secretary, didn't you?''

"You bet. I thought it would be fun to break up his marriage. I knew he couldn't afford another divorce, the bastard!''

"And you also sent the anonymous letter to Angela McDavis, saying that Peter was having an affair with Nancy Vandenberg. Your motive for that, of course, was to make a spot for yourself on the show. You had done your research with extraordinary care. So it was a nasty surprise when Dennis overheard a whispered conversation you had one morning with Alan Margolies—your paid accomplice. That's what really broke up your affair with Dennis, wasn't it?''

"Yes,'' she answered. "It was after the show. I was talking to Alan about sabotaging the lights, and I forgot I was still hooked up with a microphone. Dennis was fooling around with his tape recorder, running some tests—it was just an accident that he actually recorded our conversation. It put him off me— he actually had the nerve to say I was a dangerous bitch! Of course, at this point none of the sabotage had been very serious. But on the Friday morning when the klieg light fell, he came to me and said I'd better stop what I was doing or he would tell what he knew. That's when I decided I had to kill him. If a falling light bothered him, he certainly wasn't going to sit still for what else I had in mind!''

"What did you kill him with?"

"Why should I tell you anything more? *You* figure out the murder weapon, Steve!''

"Well, it doesn't really matter. An ice pick, a hatpin—whatever it was, I'm sure the police will find it when they search your apartment. And if not, we have your confession.''

I turned to the rest of the table: "Cat killed Dennis, and then she had to get rid of the tape. Unfortunately she didn't know at first exactly where Dennis had put the tape, but she believed it was somewhere at his house on East Fourth Street that he shared with Heather Dorn. It seemed simplest to set the whole building on fire—a sure way to get rid of any evidence against her.''

"But I don't understand," Sherry objected. "Cat was attacked herself.''

"That was only to throw us off the track, and she wasn't actually hurt. Cat realized that if bad things were happening on the set, something bad had to happen to her, or she would find herself under suspicion. Remember—Cat refused to stay in the hospital or allow more than a cursory examination in the emergency room. She knew that a doctor would have a hard time finding anything really wrong with her. As for the light which fell on the desk that Friday, it served a double function. Part of it was seriously to undermine Zeke's authority as producer, to throw one more wrench into the works and create an atmosphere on the set that would make Zeke pull his hair in frustration. And, of course, if Cat made herself appear a near-victim, she hoped the police wouldn't believe she was the perpetrator. I've studied the videotape of that Friday's show, and it's obvious that Cat was sitting well back from the desk that morning and wasn't in any actual danger.

"You see, Cat's hope was to draw this whole thing out in order to cause Zeke maximum unhappiness. But the scenario became complicated by two rogue elements—Gene Ptak and Peter McDavis, each of whom had his own agenda and who eventually came to realize that Cat was the person behind all the mischief on the set.

"Let's talk about the private eye first. As we've heard, Gene Ptak had an old involvement with the network—a decade ago, Stephen Kinley had hired the P.I. to find his son. Ptak was unsuccessful at the time, but he kept at it over the years, hoping to get his hands on some of the huge amounts of money that were at stake. Gene knew about the terms of the will, of course, and he saw this as his golden chance to get rich. All he needed to do was find the heir. Naturally he was delighted when Zeke hired him to find some dirt on Bob Hutchinson and Carol Ardman—this gave him the excuse to hang around the network and dig for information. So Gene set about investigating Bob and Carol, always keeping an eye out to discover the fate of Stevie Kinley—when quite by chance he discovered a new piece of potentially profitable information—that Cat Lawrence had set about to systematically wreck 'Good Morning, U.S.A.' Remember, Gene Ptak was a foolish and greedy private eye," I reminded the group. Then I turned directly to Cat. "He tried to hit you up for blackmail, didn't he, Cat?"

Cat did not answer. After being briefly forthcoming, now she seemed in a sort of trance, staring straight in front of her with a strange half-smile on her lips.

"But how did the private eye find out about Cat?" Ken Byrnes asked.

"Simple," I replied. "He had the tape Dennis had made earlier of the conversation he had overheard between Cat and her Soldier X—Lucky Mendoza, as we knew him. The police found the cassette in Gene Ptak's file cabinet in his Sheridan Square apartment. It's quite a damning piece of evidence, by the way, in which Cat can be heard discussing how to set up the supposed accident. The tape came to be in Gene's possession in a roundabout manner. Dennis, you see, didn't quite know what to do with it. After a good deal of thought, he decided to give it to Peter.''

"To *Peter?*" Ken asked, puzzled. "Then how in the world did it end up in Ptak's filing cabinet?"

I turned to Nancy Vandenberg. "Perhaps you can explain this odd twist of events, Nancy."

Nancy was silent for a moment. "I'm not sure I should," she said at last.

"I think you had better, my dear. Anyway, Peter is dead now, and the truth can't hurt him anymore."

Nancy scowled thoughtfully and then began. "Peter and Dennis had been friendly over the years. When Dennis discovered that Cat was the one doing all the sabotage he thought it was his duty to tell someone, but he didn't want to go all the way to the top—to Zeke Roth or Stephen Kinley—and risk getting Cat fired. Dennis gave the tape to Peter, hoping that Peter would talk to Cat and convince her to stop what she was doing."

"But Peter didn't try to stop her, did he?"

"No," Nancy admitted. "Peter wanted the sabotage to continue. He was trying to break his contract with the network, and it was very useful to him for all these accidents to happen— as long as he didn't get hurt himself, of course. That's why he decided to leave the show for a few weeks. He told everyone he was going to New Mexico."

"But he didn't actually go to New Mexico?"

"No. He stayed secretly at the Plaza in order to meet with his lawyers and prepare for his new job. We flew to New Mexico together last Thursday."

"But Gene Ptak found him at the Plaza, I imagine?"

"Yes. And it was very annoying for Peter."

"Why did Peter give him the cassette tape then?"

"After Dennis was killed last Monday, Peter became frightened he might be next. He wasn't certain if Cat knew Dennis had given him the tape, but he didn't want to take any chances. So he gave Ptak some money to hold the tape for him.''

"He chose Gene Ptak because he knew the private eye was dishonest,'' I explained to the rest of the table. ''Peter knew he was in a compromising position—knowing about the sabotage but not doing anything to stop it. He thought it best to seek help from an individual he knew was not overly scrupulous. I imagine the next thing he did was to let Cat know the tape was no longer in his keeping, and that if any harm should befall him, it would be delivered to the police.''

"That's right,'' Nancy agreed. ''He telephoned Cat on Tuesday afternoon. I was with him when he made the call—he said he didn't care what Cat did to anybody else, as long as she left him alone.''

"Unfortunately, Peter made a fatal mistake by assuming that Dennis had told her what he had done with the tape—as a matter of fact, he had *not* told her,'' I said. ''On Monday night, as I've already mentioned, Cat set fire to the old church on East Fourth Street, believing the tape was there. Now on Tuesday she learned that Peter had it, at least briefly, and she guessed that it must have passed to Gene Ptak. Cat of course was utterly ruthless. Not only was she was determined to ruin Zeke Roth, and ultimately Stephen Kinley by destroying 'Good Morning, U.S.A.,' but she planned to get away with it as well. She could not afford to have two people know the truth, so she arranged with her hit man to get rid of Peter and Gene both.''

I turned at last to Cat, who was still in a trancelike stupor. I wasn't certain she was even following our conversation.

"All this, of course, was only a prologue to what you planned to do to Zeke. Tell me, Cat—when were you planning to murder him? How long were you going to play your nasty game of psychological torture?''

She slowly turned her head in my direction. ''As long as I could stretch it out. I was piling on the stress a little more day by day. You shouldn't have stopped me, Steve.''

"I had to, Cat. Your idea of revenge was not so sweet after all."

She smiled strangely. "Oh, but it's been sweet for me!" she whispered.

Without warning, Cat reached for a steak knife and leaped across the table at Zeke Roth. She moved fast, but not fast enough. With a crash of plates and glasses, both detectives Morgenfield and Marcotti leaped onto the table and restrained her just in time, holding on to her legs. Cat flayed wildly with the steak knife only inches from Zeke's neck, but she could not quite reach him. She cried out in rage and frustration.

"You bastard! I'll kill you yet!" she shrieked.

Zeke had stood up from his chair when Cat leaped at him. There was a look of terror and disbelief on his face as he watched Cat slash at him with the steak knife. I'm not certain he understood the two cops had a good hold on her, and that he was safe. From Zeke's point of view, it must have seemed that some wild creature had set upon him, screaming for his blood.

It was one shock too many for Zeke Roth. As we watched, the overwrought producer clutched his chest, and his face seemed to drain of blood. He stood for a moment, gasping for breath, and then slowly collapsed upon the floor. The paramedics arrived within minutes, but it was too late. At the hospital, a doctor judged the cause of death to be cardiac arrest. But personally I would say Zeke died of accumulated stress, victim to his own youthful ambitions and the chain of events he had set in motion years earlier when he had so unfairly destroyed Ed Lawrence.

Cat's campaign of terror had paid off at last.

Chapter 58

The Kinley mansion in Greenwich, Connecticut was a stately two-story redbrick house on several acres of well-manicured grounds, surrounded by a high stone wall that had not managed to keep trouble from the family. A majestic sweep of front lawn led directly to Long Island Sound, a private beach, and a dock. On Sunday the front lawn was covered with a sparkling cover of snow. But the sky was blue, and there was a hint of warmth in the air, a harbinger of spring.

Jayne and I had come to the Kinley estate at the request of Sherry Gold, who was nervous about making her first official family visit with Crystal Rainbow and was in need of moral support. The inside of the house was formal, elegant, and not particularly comfortable. We sat through an old-fashioned mid-day Sunday dinner that was served by a butler at a long table beneath a huge crystal chandelier, eating roast turkey and potatoes and green beans with slivered almonds, struggling awkwardly for conversation. Stephen Kinley, Jr., sat at the head of the table. His hair seemed whiter, and he had become an old man overnight. Edith Kinley sat at the opposite end of the table, her eyes glued upon her grandson—as though, if she looked away for an instant, he might disappear forever. The boy ate with a serious expression on his face, accepting the seconds and thirds that were piled on his plate.

"Well, Crystal—what is your very favorite food?" Edith asked. "You have to tell me so I can make certain we have it for your next visit."

"Tofu," he answered.

Edith was puzzled. "Goodness! I believe I've *heard* of tofu, but I don't entirely know what it is."

"Bean curd," Sherry told her.

"Bean, *curd?*" Edith repeated in a bewildered voice.

"Well, *I've* heard of tofu," Stephen said graciously. He, too, was trying very hard. "It's supposed to be terrifically healthy. I'd like to try it sometime."

"I'll tell you what. Why don't you two come to dinner at my apartment sometime this week?" Sherry suggested. "I'll cook up my favorite tofu recipe for you—a Thai dish with curry and coconut milk and shiitake mushrooms."

I have to hand it to Edith and Stephen Kinley. I could tell from their faces that the prospect of eating tofu and coconut milk and strange mushrooms was not appealing. But they made gracious noises and accepted the invitation as though nothing might please them more. Jayne and I made an effort to stay fairly quiet during the meal, not wishing to interfere with the Kinleys' opportunity to become acquainted with Sherry and their grandson. It was an odd meeting to witness. Several times I was afraid an argument might break out—particularly when Stephen asked the boy which television shows he liked, and Crystal Rainbow replied gravely that he didn't like television much at all, but greatly preferred to read a good book. For a moment, Stephen Kinley's face took on the same look of stuffy petulance I had seen at the Four Seasons when Heather insisted that television sucked a person's brain out of their head. But then Edith said quickly, "I think it's wonderful that you like to read!" And Stephen quickly agreed.

After dinner, Stephen took the boy on a tour of the boathouse and the dock while Edith led Sherry, Jayne, and me to a rigidly elegant sitting room for coffee and tea. The butler added a log to the fire, and we sat looking out the window as Stephen and Crystal Rainbow made their way together across the snow-covered lawn to the water's edge.

"I can't tell you how much this means to us—your bringing Crystal here," Edith said to Sherry.

"I'm not going to pretend it's easy to be here," Sherry admitted. "I've been bitter all these years about what you did. But you know, watching how Cat let herself become consumed with hatred and a desire for revenge has cured me of my own bad feelings about the past. I think it's best to let the past be—don't you think? And all of us can hope for a better future."

"That's very wise of you, my dear," Jayne put in. "There is really no sweetness to revenge."

Edith smiled bravely. "Well, Sherry, this is all yours now—the house, the network, everything. I understand from our attorney that you'll be acting as Crystal's guardian until he's eighteen. Personally, I'm looking forward to the change. This house—our lives, in fact—have become a sort of prison. But would it be all right, do you think, if we stay on here until the end of the month? It's going to take a few weeks to pack up."

Sherry appeared shocked. "Oh, Edith! How could you imagine that Crystal and I would put you out? I want you to know that this house is yours for the rest of your lives—the apartment in town as well. And, of course, Stephen must keep his position at the network for another few years, if I can persuade him to stay. I want to run the network myself eventually, of course—that is, until Crystal's old enough to do it himself. But I have so very much to learn and I'm rather desperately hoping your husband will stay and be my guide."

Edith's eyes had filled with tears. "Sherry! How very won-

derful of you! I can certainly see why my son loved you.
Perhaps then—if it's all right—Stephen and I will keep on
here in Greenwich, at least for the time being. But you must
certainly take the Manhattan town house. It's *much* too big for
the two of us. Perhaps we'll rent something quite small in town,
if you really want Stephen to stay on for a while at the network.''

"Oh, I do, Edith! Crystal and I would be lost without him.
You must convince him of that if he has any doubts about it.
Or if he feels, well . . . awkward.''

Jayne and I looked at each other and smiled. A warm glow
had settled into each of our hearts at witnessing the reconcilia-
tion. Stephen and his grandson returned to the house after a
few minutes. The boy was talking excitedly about the sailboat
he had seen in the boathouse, and how his grandfather was
going to teach him how to sail this summer.

"I want to be a sailor when I grow up!" Crystal said dreamily. "Maybe one day I'll sail around the world all by myself!"

"Of course, sailing's fine in the summer,'' the old man said
sternly, wagging a finger at his grandson. "But when you grow
up, you're going to be the head of a great television empire.
You need to study hard, my boy—we'll get you into Choate
where your father went. And then I think Yale for your undergraduate work, and then Harvard Business School. . . .''

Old ways of thinking die hard. Stephen Kinley spoke so
enthusiastically to imagine his grandson's future that he did
not notice at first that the sitting room had become stone silent.
He looked about and saw his wife giving him a disapproving
look. Then he laughed and shook his head, and finally sighed.

"But if you would rather be a sailor,'' he said, "that's all
right, too.''

"Oh, I would!" said the boy. "We'll sail together, Grandpa,
you and I—across the ocean to someplace where there are palm
trees and lovely beaches.''

Old Stephen Kinley took his grandson's hand and they shook

on it. He didn't look so stodgy and conventional now. His face filled with a kind of rapture.

Jayne smiled at me again and I later learned she had read my mind at the moment. She was recalling that a few weeks earlier, at a comedy concert, someone in the audience had asked of all the things I had done—the comedy, Broadway, Las Vegas, films, jazz, television—which was my favorite activity. And I had responded that without any question, my favorite role was that of "grandpa," and I do love the time spent with my darling grandchildren. It was good to know that such pleasures lay ahead for Stephen Kinley.

"Yes," he said. "The two of us sailing together. To a lovely beach with palm trees . . . some warm and dreamy place where there is never any snow!"

THE MYSTERIES OF MARY ROBERTS RINEHART

THE AFTER HOUSE   (0-8217-4246-6, $3.99/$4.99)

THE CIRCULAR STAIRCASE   (0-8217-3528-4, $3.95/$4.95)

THE DOOR   (0-8217-3526-8, $3.95/$4.95)

THE FRIGHTENED WIFE   (0-8217-3494-6, $3.95/$4.95)

A LIGHT IN THE WINDOW   (0-8217-4021-0, $3.99/$4.99)

THE STATE VS.   (0-8217-2412-6, $3.50/$4.50)
ELINOR NORTON

THE SWIMMING POOL   (0-8217-3679-5, $3.95/$4.95)

THE WALL   (0-8217-4017-2, $3.99/$4.99)

THE WINDOW AT THE WHITE CAT
                       (0-8217-4246-9, $3.99/$4.99)

THREE COMPLETE NOVELS: THE BAT, THE HAUNTED
LADY, THE YELLOW ROOM
                       (0-8217-114-4, $13.00/$16.00)